Praise for the Works of Dave Duncan

"Dave Duncan has long been one of the great unsung figures of Canadian fantasy and science fiction, graced with a fertile imagination, a prolific output, and keen writerly skills. With this new novel, Duncan again forges a bold new world, populated with varied and complex characters, distinctive cultures, and a complex system of mythology and science." — Quill and Quire

"That supreme trickster Dave Duncan . . . is an expert at producing page-turning adventure, and Future Indefinite fully lives up to the suspense promised in its title. It's all throughly entertaining, while it leaves us wondering, right down to the final pages, whether the end will fall into the classical category of comedy or tragedy. Quite a performance, Mr. Duncan!" — Locus

"Duncan writes with unusual flair, drawing upon folklore, myth, and his gift for creating ingenious plots." — Year's Best Fantasy and Horror

Dave Duncan writes rollicking adventure novels filled with subtle characterization and made bitter-sweet by an underlying darkness. Without striving for grand effects or momentous meetings between genres, he has produced one excellent book after another. — Locus

"Duncan writes with unusual flair, drawing upon folklore, myth, and his gift for creating ingenious plots." — Year's Best Fantasy and Horror

Books by
Dave Duncan

Pock's World

DAVE DUNCAN

EDGE SCIENCE FICTION AND FANTASY PUBLISHING
AN IMPRINT OF HADES PUBLICATIONS, INC.
CALGARY

Edge Science Fiction and Fantasy Publishing
An Imprint of Hades Publications Inc.
P.O. Box 1714, Calgary, Alberta, T2P 2L7, Canada

In house editing by Dave Gross
Interior design by Brian Hades
Cover Painting by Doug Levitt
Photographer: Kevin Stenhouse

ISBN: 978-1-894063-47-0

EDGE Science Fiction and Fantasy Publishing and Hades Publications, Inc.
acknowledges the ongoing support of the Canada Council for the Arts and the
Alberta Foundation for the Arts for our publishing programme.

Library and Archives Canada Cataloguing in Publication

Duncan, Dave, 1933-
Pock's world / Dave Duncan.

ISBN 978-1-894063-47-0

I. Title.

PS8557.U5373P63 2010   C813'.54   C2010-904497-5

FIRST EDITION
(g-20100824)
Printed in Canada
www.edgewebsite.com

POCK'S WORLD

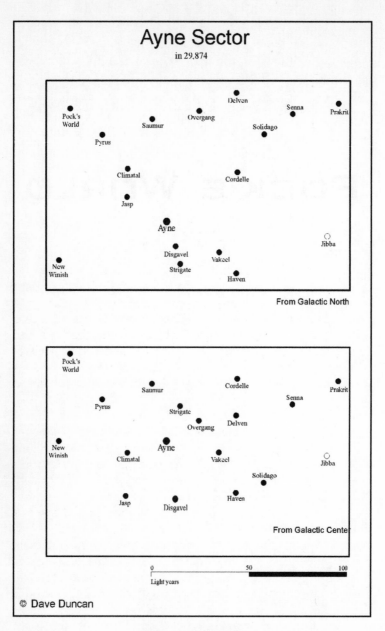

Star Map

Wundy

The heavens thundered and the suborbital from Annatto dropped out of the dawn sky like an angel of fire. Braked by a repeller beam from Shadoof Landing, it slowed almost to a stop and then sank while its heat shield blazed white, then red, and finally orange. Stillness and blessed silence returned. Seemingly reassured, the craft nudged in close to a blockhouse and set down on three delicate legs with the grace of a bird settling on her nest. Umbilicals snaked out from the blockhouse and locked on.

Having no baggage, Brother Andre was the first passenger to emerge on the blockhouse roof. Wrinkles and silver hair proclaimed his age now, but he strode along as determinedly as ever—tall, spare, straight-backed, and barefoot, with the hem of his brown habit swirling around his ankles.

He felt a great sense of escape. All his life he had enjoyed anonymity, but within the last week his jagged features had become famous on all of the seventeen worlds. He had been recognized in the suborbital's cabin, even questioned, and at the end some of his fellow travelers had knelt to ask his blessing. Fame was an unwelcome burden, but what he had so narrowly escaped two days ago would have been much worse. He hoped that whatever new prospect lay ahead of him now would not be too terrible. *Non mea voluntas sed tua fiat*—not my will but Thine be done.

No one had come to meet him, which was both a relief and a reminder not to let fame go to his head. He inspected the line of air cars with distaste. Capuchin friars were required to travel on foot whenever possible, but that was hardly practical when the first few steps included a thirty-meter drop. Also, the pope had been insistent that he come as fast and unobtrusively as possible. Sighing, Andre went to the far end of the line, where the small cars were, and sat on the wickedly comfortable bench of a two-seater. The canopy closed.

—*Destination?* The inquiry came via his Broca implant.

The Vatican.

—*Confirm identity.*

Brother Andre, Order of Friars Minor Capuchin.

—*Brother Andre, your credit currently stands at zero.*

Priority code Gomorrah.

—*Temporary credit valid.*

The car rose with a quiet hum and headed north.

Andre had been granted the special credit when he flatly informed the Holy Father that Annatto Mission could not afford to finance jaunts halfway around the world. Thirty thousand years ago, St. Francis had forbidden his followers to use money. Electronic credit would appall him.

Leaving Shadoof, the car climbed over fertile plains where energy fences marked off circular grain fields amid undisturbed woodlands, then leveled and cruised high above Straint Gulf and its innumerable islands—blue-green water, beaches rimmed with white surf, aloof mansions owned by prosperous citizens. Andre did not envy the rich their good fortune, but he did wonder why they could not share the planet's abundance a little more equitably. The mission back in Annatto was swamped by hungry, indigent people. At times he had no food to offer them, nor beds for the sick and unwanted dying. He did not understand, but he was not surprised. Thirty millennia ago, the Lord had given fair warning when he said, *The poor are always with you.*

As the car crossed the northern shore he saw his destination far ahead, and his mood brightened. St. Peter in the Clouds was unquestionably the most beautiful cathedral on Ayne, probably the most beautiful church on any of the seventeen worlds of the Ayne sector. It might even be the finest place of worship in the entire Galaxy, although no mortal could ever know what God had wrought outside the limits of the sector. Sixteen centuries ago, it had been carved from the living rock of Vatican Mountain, a tough, micaceous schist that shone like silver in the low light. In the early-morning chill, the scummy swamps surrounding the hill were blanketed by roiling white fog from the warm springs that fed them, so the cathedral's name was entirely appropriate, a sculpted rock floating above the clouds.

For the last two small-months, the eyes of the faithful all over the sector had been fixed on the Vatican—first for the death watch on old Pope Margaret III, then for her grandiose funeral, and finally for the conclave of cardinals assembled from all over the sector to elect her successor. Even non-Catholics had enjoyed watching that spectacle, and not a few of the faithful had joined them in laying bets on the clerical horse race. Away in Annatto, Brother Andre had been far too busy with the work of his mission to pay any heed. Their Eminences had no need of his advice or approval. Whomever God had chosen would be fine by him. So he had assumed.

He had discovered his error right after the first ballot, when Brother Matthew had burst in shouting that more votes had been cast for Brother Andre, OFM Capuchin, than for anyone else. Not in twelve hundred years had a conclave elected anyone other than a cardinal to the throne of St. Peter on Ayne, but there was nothing in the rules to forbid it. Brother Andre had turned on his implant and started paying attention.

With exactly ninety cardinals in attendance, sixty-one votes were needed for election. To his horror, by the third ballot his tally had crept up to fifty-five, and an obscure friar, scarcely known outside the Church hierarchy, was suddenly an interstellar celebrity. His face was everywhere, as was the late pope's quip that it resembled a mountain peak with frostbite. Whatever were the reverend ladies and gentlemen thinking? To Andre's intense relief, his support dropped to fifty-two on the next ballot, showing that he could not reach the necessary two-thirds plus one. The pre-conclave favorite, Cardinal Paul Favela, had slowly emerged from the pack, and on the thirteenth ballot had been elected 503rd pontiff of the Ayne Sector Catholic Church. He had taken the name Cyril-Pius XXII.

Brother Andre had given thanks to God that the papal cup had been taken from him, and he rejoiced that his sudden fame would make fund-raising for the mission easier—donors were already calling from all over the sector. Although he could barely admit it, even to himself, he was uneasy about the eminent cardinals' choice. He and Favela had first met as adolescents in St. Jude's seminary more than sixty years ago and had never agreed on anything, then or since. Like brooms, new popes swept clean, and doubtless this one would make changes that Brother Andre would dislike.

Andre was prepared for that. He had not expected that virtually the first act of the new pontiff would be to summon his old opponent from the far side of the globe, for reasons unstated. The pope must have called him in the middle of the night, Vatican time. Well, Andre would soon learn why. Already the air car was close enough for him to make out the houses of Vatican City on the slopes, and other cars like flitting insects, coming and going from the landing ground in front of the cathedral's great west door.

Car, priority Gomorrah. Take me to the east landing.

—Privilege acknowledged, Brother Andre.

The car banked. Andre sat back again to watch the great pillared dome turn before him. In the half century since he had first set eyes on it, it had never ceased to impress him. As the car settled to the courtyard, he was relieved to see how empty it was. Neither honor guard nor gawking cognition witnesses stood shivering in the nippy dawn. Even the pope had trouble keeping secrets, but apparently he had succeeded this time.

There were always guards there, of course. They wore bright motley and were armed with swords or pikes, but those weapons were much more than the tourist fodder they seemed, and numerous specialized brain implants must lurk under the archaic metal helmets. The pope himself might be watching his visitor's arrival through those youthful eyes.

A black-robed priest met Andre at the door. He had the face of a teenager framed between an old man's ears. He was likely into his seventies, not far short of medical interdict. "You are expected, Brother."

"I am pleased to hear it, Father. Lead on."

Whatever the problem, it was urgent. There was no delay, no cooling of heels in antechambers. He went past a few curious, resentful glances, but no one else spoke to him. In a minor reception room he had not seen in years, Andre knelt to kiss the Fisherman's ring. The soundproof door closed quietly on the private audience.

Favela had always been small, scrawny, and restless, and the papal robes hung on him as if he had already shrunk under the weight of his office. He was past interdict now, and the years were catching up with him, just as they were with Andre—wrinkles, silvered hair, a loss of youthful tone. Sadly, Andre felt again that sensation of dealing with a man who always had too many agendas, who never doubted that ends justified means. Nevertheless, whatever Cyril-Pius's faults, and they were few,

gloating was not one of them. Although he could have left his
visitor on his knees, he bade Andre be seated as if nothing had
changed between them. His own chair was a throne, but the one
offered was comfortable enough.

Favela's eyes always reminded Andre of a bird's, and now
perhaps a worried bird's. His smile was bloodless. "Your congratulations were welcome. No hard feelings, I hope?"

"None at all, Holy Father. I assure you that all my prayers
now include thanks that I was not chosen."

The pope nodded. "I will admit to you, old friend—because
we know each other so well—that I did harbor hopes of being
elevated. I thought I was prepared, and yet, when the result was
announced and old Marius came to kneel before me and ask if
I would serve, I was appalled." He sighed under the weight of
the sins of seventeen worlds. "I thought I would recover soon
enough, but suddenly the prospect grows even grimmer." The
perfunctory small talk ended abruptly. "Andre, you are familiar with Pock's World."

"I served about five hundred days there, yes—fifty years
ago."

"Tell me about it."

Why? Andre had been very young, very eager, and in the
end very indiscreet. He had been recalled and reprimanded, but
those sins were long since confessed, repented, and forgiven.
Surely a newly elected pope could not be so spiteful as to rum-
mage through the Vatican Brain hunting for a scandal to pin on
the man who had nearly preempted him? If Paul Favela were
as petty as that, he wouldn't be so dangerous.

"A peculiar world, Holiness, only marginally habitable.
Thinly settled. The first settlers called it Cain's World. Not a
true planet..." If the pope needed mere facts, he could access the
Brain, which knew everything. He wanted a personal opinion.
"It's classed as low-tech, but that's a matter of choice. They keep
the scenery rural and use high tech where it matters, in hospitals
and so on.

"The Church is poorly represented on Pock's. A very heretical world. Pagan, really. It has some Buddhists, Moslems, and
Calvinists, but most people follow the local mother-goddess
cult. They seemed happy enough when I was there. The state
of their souls is more worrisome, of course."

If Cyril-Pius was planning some grandiose mission to convert Pock's World, then he must be tactfully advised to consult
the Brain's history files. A dozen such attempts had been made

over the millennia, and none had made any impression on the Mother cult.

"The state of their souls just became extremely urgent," the pope said harshly. "Yesterday STARS Inc. quarantined Pock's World."

Ah! Suddenly everything made sense. If a pandemic was raging on Pock's and the Holy Father wished to organize a relief fund or a medical mission, then the newly famous Brother Andre would be the logical person to put in charge. It would be both a staggering responsibility and a noble cause.

"I suppose that should not surprise us, Holy Father. The environment there is loaded with free radicals and other carcinogens that act as mutagens on unicellular life. Or is it a virus? What sort of mortality rate?"

Cyril-Pius raised a thin-veined hand. "I am not talking of a disease. I am talking about a Diallelon abomination."

"Sweet Jesus!" Andre fell back in his chair. *Hail Mary, full of grace, the Lord is with thee... strength to bear this burden... mercy on millions of innocents.* Pock's was the least populous world of the sector, but even so... He opened his eyes and stared bleakly at his old rival. No wonder Favela looked haggard—after fewer than three days on the throne he faced a disaster worse than any the sector had known in five centuries, a planetary death sentence.

"Cuckoos? How sure are they?"

The pope shrugged. "When has STARS ever admitted to doubts?"

"They don't just mean parthenogenesis, do they? I mean, the priestesses of the Mother have always—"

"No, Andre. I do know enough to ask that. They say it's undoubtedly Diallelon chimerazation-cuckoos, synthetic hominins, Frankensteins, androids, devil spawn, GM supermen, call them what you will. Satanic creations that look like men and think they are better than men."

The very idea of supermen, genetically modified or otherwise, was an insult to God. He made man in his own image; man made by man in an "improved" image was the work of the devil. In a hundred thousand years, mankind had faced no real rivals except those it had made itself. So far it seemed that no world, and perhaps no galaxy, was big enough for two sentient species.

"Quarantine I can understand," said Andre. "There is no rush to resort to more drastic measures, surely?"

The pope sighed. "I pray not. Night and day, I pray not. But I fear what STARS may be planni ng. It has agreed to admit a fact-finding mission."

"Then there must be some room for discussion."

The Church drew a strict line between permissible and forbidden genetic tampering. Eve's children had been designed by evolution for one specific planet. They needed the right gravity, the right partial pressure of oxygen, trace elements like copper. They sickened unless even trivia like the length of day suited their metabolism. Some common elements like arsenic or beryllium destroyed them. They could develop fatal allergies to almost anything. The list was endless.

To terraform a world would take centuries and unimaginable amounts of money; it would inevitably throw the existing ecosystem into chaos or destroy it. Far easier to modify DNA in test tubes, when less than one cc of fertilized ova would suffice to populate a planet. Every colonized world, therefore, received a new variety of colonist. The Church had long ago bowed to the inevitable and recognized the resulting hominins as human. Ayne boasted that it was a dead ringer for original Earth, but its inhabitants had been modified back from whatever their ancestors had become on a journey through a dozen stepping-stone worlds.

But Diallelon chimerazation went beyond modifications to the creation of new species. Such invention was anathema, the threat to replace *Homo sapiens* with something different. Pock's was an extreme world, and it required extreme people. Had STARS genuinely discovered something new and forbidden on Pock's, or had it merely decided to reclassify the Pocosins as non-human? If the latter, there ought to be room for argument somewhere, or at least delay, and Andre clutched at that straw of hope.

"I cannot see a need for sterilization," he said. "When I was there, Pock's had nothing approaching independent space capability..."

That had been a lifetime ago. Values were eternal, but technology changed.

Why me, Lord? Like Job, a believer must never ask that question. "Holy Father, I will do whatever I can."

"I do not doubt this. We have not always agreed, Andre, but I have never doubted your honesty and intelligence. It will be matter of only a few days. You and a few others will be shown the evidence, then you will return to submit your report. Reports, plural, if you do not all reach the same conclusion."

"A few days to decide the fate of a world?"

"Better than nothing. I'm appointing you my legate." His Holiness did not ask whether Andre accepted the appointment. Three knots tied a Franciscan's girdle as reminders of the three oaths: poverty, celibacy, and obedience.

"To do what, exactly? To confirm that there these abominations exist? To discover what means are available to control them? Surely the local authorities can be trusted to uncover and destroy the means of production and transmission? Surely the rest of the sector will rush in to help? We all know how STARS will react to a Diallelon."

STARS never admitted a mistake in a matter of this magnitude. If it decided that Pock's World should be sterilized, then it would go ahead no matter what anyone said.

The Holy Father leaned back in his throne and sighed. "This is a weighty burden I have been given, Andre, and I feel a sense of relief because I know I can lay it on your shoulders for a brief time. I need two things of you."

"I am at your command."

Favela studied him thoughtfully. "First, a promise. I am insulting you by asking, but I want your word that you will not let our old friendship sway your decision. If you conclude that sterilization is required, you will tell me so without consideration for my feelings. The Lord has called me to the papacy, and I will perform my duties as He would want."

Andre was aghast. "You will not oppose geocide?" World murder.

The avian eyes glittered. "Not if it is required. That will depend on your report, of course, but many good Catholics work for STARS and would need our reassurance in performing a distasteful task. If a new chimerazation abomination has arisen, then we shall have no option but to declare a Crusade." *We* meant *I*, Andre realized. The old zeal was showing. Popes who proclaimed crusades were remembered—but would Favela let hundreds of millions die just to carve himself a place in history? Would he want to be reviled like Benedict LII?

"Your Holiness can count on me to serve according to my oath."

Cyril-Pius smiled. "I knew it. And my other request is your forgiveness, old friend. The Lord works in mysterious ways. You would always have been my first choice for this terrible task, but I could never have appointed you if you had remained the obscure friar you were a small-month ago. If a crusade becomes necessary—if Pock's World must burn—then the Church must show that the decision is justified. The people will take your word. They will weep with the Saint of Annatto."

Had anyone else called him by that name, Andre would have barked. *The Saint of Annatto* had been the vulgar cog-doc broadcast that had launched him into fame. "Of course you have it, Holy Father, and my prayers as well. Who else goes on this mission? When does it leave?"

"I do not know who else. I was informed by a certain Sulcus Immit, Director of Security in STARS. He wanted to lift you directly to orbit and only reluctantly agreed to wait until I could instruct you in person. He said the rest of the team would be ready by the time you arrived. A public announcement will be made after your liftoff. Kneel and receive our blessing on your mission."

→••◦◄ ◄▤ ── ▤► ►◦••←

A dozen pairs of eyes scrutinized the old friar emerging from the reception room. A curia already in turmoil as it sought to adjust to a new pope must wonder what to make of a long-term associate so soon summoned to the steps of the throne. Was the now-celebrated Brother Andre to be promoted to the summit of the curia, ordered to accept the red hat he had so often begged Pope Margaret not to bestow on him? Brother Andre did not even notice their appraisal. He crossed the antechamber, and, as he emerged into the corridor, he sensed cognition.

—Priority call from Sulcus Immit.

Andre thoroughly disapproved of implants, believing that God's was the only voice he should hear inside his head, but the Church insisted that every priest have one so that he or she could be summoned in an emergency. He had accepted only the bare minimum implant, voice contact. Before leaving Annatto, he had diverted all incoming calls to Brother Matthew, but he was not surprised that STARS had ways of bypassing his ban.

Accept.

—We have a shuttle standing by, Brother. A car will pick you up at the main door in ten minutes.

Make it thirty, Friend Sulcis.

—Time is running out.

Thirty.

—You are inconveniencing a lot of people.

Thirty.

As you wish. Cognition ended.

Evidently that was one STARS employee who was not a good Catholic. Andre rode the gravity shaft up to the cathedral. The terrible news had left him numb. He needed time to pray: *Heavenly Father, do not forsake Thy children on Pock's World, even those who have forsaken Thee.*

Chapter 2

Ratty Turnsole had spent an indeterminate time cognizing, sleeping, and cursing Brother Andre when he was awakened by a hot sexual dream turning into an incoming call. He had not known his system could be overridden like that. The caller wore a businessman's tunic and looked as if he might enjoy wrestling bears.

Without opening his eyes, Ratty said, *Who're you and what the hell are you doing in my head?*

—*Sulcus Immit, Vice-President, STARS, Inc. 'Morning, Friend Turnsole. Am I interrupting anything important?*

I don't know you. How long had he been in orgy mode? He was ravenous and light-headed.

—*You know me as much as you need to. I have a hot tip for you.*

Fully awake now, Ratty diverted the optical implant in his left lateral geniculate nucleus to scan his oeuvre file and confirm that he had never based a story on a STARS lead. STARS, Inc.'s releases were the dullest in the universe, all about entanglement links broken or restored, or about probes due to reach their objective in a few centuries. STARS *leaks* were nonexistent. This must be a hoax. One of Ratty's pack was having a little fun with the boss. He directed both mind's eyes on the caller again.

I'll call you back.

—*Sulcus. S-U-L-C-U-S.*

It's on your tunic. I can read. Ratty broke the connection and sat up with a groan. Fortunately the simulation that callers saw was based on Brain archives; only facial expressions were current.

Use public channel. Call Vice-President Sulcus at STARS.

If Sulcus was willing to be called back, he must be genuine. Amazingly, the call was accepted at once, and there was Superman again, looking meaner than ever. He was real.

—Ready now?

Ready.

—Not for attribution, two-hour embargo?

Agreed, as long as this is exclusive.

—It is. Ayne Sector STARS, Inc. has quarantined Pock's World and is considering sterilization.

Not since the afternoon eleven years back when the loveliest girl he knew had introduced a precocious adolescent to openmouth kissing had Ratty Turnsole been so at a loss for words. After a moment he whispered, "Jesus!" He never bothered with foreign planets, because the Ayne public knew nothing about them except what they saw on stupid cog-dramas, so nobody cared what happened there, only here at home. But Pock's World was no isolated mining asteroid. It had a culture, didn't it? Cities? What was its population? This could be the biggest story to break in his lifetime.

He queried, *Cuckoos?*

—What else? GM freaks. We're allowing a fact-finding mission in, to view the evidence and publish. Do you want to be included?

Stupid question, Sulcus.

—It may be dangerous. There could be riots.

Ratty sent an image of a male STARS employee engaged in a perversion.

—We'll have a car pick you up in fifteen minutes.

You know where I am?

—Stupid question, Turnsole.

Wait!

Too late. The face had gone, leaving only the sneer behind. Ratty hurtled off the bed.

⤐⭇⭜ — ⭝⭞⤏

Ratty Turnsole was a professional reporter, the world's best brain-to-brain communicator. No matter what the news—an election, a gory crime, a natural disaster—citizens accessing the Brain to find out what it meant usually began by cognizing RATTY. Smiling, confident, Ratty would present eyewitness memories of the event, spliced in with world authorities explaining it and himself interpreting the tricky bits without ever talking down to his audience. Reassured by his explanation and the sense of being well informed, billions of Ayne folk would go back to beach or bed or aromatherapy, or whatever else held their current fancy. Direct cognition was the most efficient communication ever devised.

He employed a dozen human assistants and the best equipment money could buy. His head held a dozen implants, which was twice the safe limit, and several of his were too experimental even to be banned yet. All his waking perceptions were routinely stored in the Ayne Brain, and his ability to collect a week's jumbled images cognized by a team of observers and turn them into a coherent narrative was positively eerie, even if he said so himself, which he did. But the real secret of his success was skill with people. None of his helpers could come close to Ratty at seeing through a lie, debunking a phony, or breaking a hostile witness. He also had an infallible nose for news. No one could turn cute into sordid or vice versa better than he could.

Although Catholics were a minority of the Ayne population, for many days the world story had been the death of Pope Maggie and the ensuing conclave. Ratty and his pack had come close to scoring a stunning triumph, because the unexpected stampede to elect Brother Andre had been a direct result of his cog-doc, *The Saint of Annatto*. Ratty had been holding it in the can for release as soon as the old crone croaked. He had come within six votes of electing a pope! Indeed, he had almost won the consolation prize of bringing Cardinal Favela's candidacy crashing down in heaps of exposed hypocrisy. He would have done so had the cardinals dithered for just one more ballot. A very close near-miss! *Weep me an ocean.* He was young and resilient; there would be other scoops.

He had been working nonstop for days, using his K47G8 implant to suppress the diurnal rhythm of his suprachiasmatic nucleus. He would have preferred to retire to one of his coastal villas to party with a close friend, but the sad truth was that the celebrated Ratty Turnsole had no close friend at the moment. Success brought more work, more work more helpers, more helpers a higher payroll to meet.... Over the last couple of years the ebullient Ratty had become a workaholic. Only temporarily, of course, but at the moment he had no time to enjoy the good things he owned, and he had even less time to make friends. Rose had withered; Robyn had flown; Patience had tired of waiting. All that remained of his sex life these days was playback in seven senses—sight, sound, smell, touch, taste, motion, and excitement. The experience was completely convincing and could even be customized by amplifying selected brain areas, but it lacked the spontaneity of the real thing.

So, why not a jaunt off-world? At worst he had earned a vacation and a chance to mix it up with some girls.

First stop was the house medic. It grumbled about dehydration, low blood sugar and drug residues, but then it dispensed a liter of purple liquid and instructions to report back in an hour. Ratty drank the former and ignored the latter. While he was showering, he called the pack and told Jake to break the story in 110 minutes and carry it in his absence. Clean again, clad in a smart lemon-and-scarlet tunic and gold sandals, he was on his roof with three minutes to spare. STARS would appreciate punctuality.

Ratty owned six—or was it seven?—cars, but none as large and comfortable as the fancy military-style vehicle that swooped out of the sky to blow dust in his eyes. It had room for ten or more on its circular bench and it was more than—*whoosh!*—nippy in takeoff. He watched his hideaway vanish into the forest as the car hurtled upward and headed out over the strait.

The inside of the door bore STARS's insignia of a human hand clutching a five-pointed star, and the name, *S.T.A.R.S.* That was odd. He queried the Brain.

Explain origin of the acronym, STARS, as in STARS, Inc.

—Stellar Transport and Research Section.

Section of what, fergawdsake?

—That information not on file. Earliest reference in archives is dated standard 17,747.

Ratty made a note to check out STARS's origin for a possible story. The portable recorder he had brought was the best that credit could buy, a coin-sized disk on a ribbon, boasting a two-petabyte capacity, which should easily hold all his perceptions for a long-month. Leaving it turned off, he hung it around his neck and tucked in inside his tunic. He must do some research before he lost contact with the Brain.

Report on Jibba.

Audio only: *—Jacob Jibba the poet, or Jibba the planet, or Jibba—*

The planet.

Optic: a plumpish woman behind a desk. Her hair style and prim costume suggested she had been memorized at least three hundred years ago. Her accent was bizarre and her appearance so vague that he could not even tell whether she was smiling.

—Jibba received its first settlers in 19,556, from New Flote, an outlying world of the Avens sector. It quickly established an industrial base and in 20,345 dispatched the first linking probes to other promising worlds, including Solidago and Haven. Technically Jibba was not the first planet of the Ayne sector to be settled, an honor that belongs to Pock's World, but Pock's was not regarded as part of the Ayne sector until after the loss of contact with Malacostraca. Jibba ranked 8.4 on the Motmot Terrestrial Scale, with its principal—

Cut! He must refine his question. He was starving. *Car?*

No answer. Surprise twisted through anger to worry. He had never known a car to refuse a query before. That would be all right if this junket were just his pack playing tricks on him, but STARS was answerable to no one, and Ratty Turnsole had made a galaxy of enemies during his career. Was he about to be vanished? The lake country going by beneath him suggested he was not heading to Shadoof Landing.

He went back to his research.

Report on sterilization of Jibba.

The same woman, still wearing the flowery gown, still vague

—In 29,174 a colony of synthetic hominins was detected on the smaller continent. STARS immediately clamped a quarantine on the planet, and local authorities hastened to wipe out the infection, whose members became known as the "Soldier Ants." Although the nest was small, later that year it became evident that some juveniles had escaped. Determined to block any chance of the pseudo-species spreading off-world, STARS sterilized the planet by asteroid diversion. Subsequent surveys have confirmed the absence of eukaryotic life forms.

Ratty whispered, "Christ!" *How many poor bastards died, then?*

—Population at sterilization was estimated at 3,350,452,778 Homo sapiens *and between twenty-four and forty-three Soldier Ants.*

Report on origin of term Diallelon Abomination.

This time the authority was, unsurprisingly, a Catholic priest, elderly, smugly infallible, and probably thousands of years dead. He sat at a desk and lectured.

—Jules, or Julius, Diallelon was a philosopher of probably the third millennium. Nothing is known of his personal life. He is remembered only for his suggestion that science should be used to improve the human germline to produce supermen. The Church declared this teaching heretical. Efforts have been made from time to time to put his idea into practice. The results are known as Diallelon abominations and are widely regarded as non-human. Most secular jurisdictions deny such abominations rights of citizenship, and the Church—

Cut!

Before he could ask any more questions, he realized that the car was landing and that bulging eyesore was the dome of St. Peter's. That made sense. Obviously STARS would like to have clerical authority for an act of geocide, and the Catholic Church was the largest denomination in the sector, with a hierarchal structure that most sects lacked. A rabbi or mullah picked at random would carry no weight, but a cardinal might. And hadn't the Church supported geocide before?

Report Catholic Church's attitude to the sterilization of Jibba.

The ghost appeared again. —*Pope Benedict LII declared the Soldier Ants an abomination and proclaimed a crusade against them. When Jibba was sterilized, he expressed regret but issued a plenary indulgence to all who had participated.*

Yuck!

The car settled gently in St. Peter's Square and spoke.

—*There will be a fifteen-minute delay here.*

I need something to eat.

—*There are vendors.*

The voice sounded like the one that had wakened him. Ratty cognized the Brain and confirmed the match. Predictably, the Brain claimed it lacked files on STARS personnel and thus could not confirm the speaker's identity.

He told the car to open the canopy and summon the nearest snack cart. Plastic cups of beer and roasted reis roe in a bun were the sort of diet he thought he had left behind years ago, but he ordered three of each, and they tasted better than his normal five-star cuisine.

With the door closed again, he could enjoy watching the tourists without having to endure his usual celebrity stares. On Ayne it took a sharp eye to distinguish twenties from forties and even sixties, but interdiction was down to seventy-two years and a few days now, and natural decay came rapidly after that. An unusual percentage of the crowd in the square were decrepits—boning up for their finals, no doubt. Even the youngest women were too modestly garbed or his taste, but he admired the bright-colored lads with the pikes and their ability to wear such absurd garments without showing embarrassment. He had no desire to visit St. Peter's itself. He had been there before, and all the carved rock, gilt, and colored glass in the world did not impress him. Its great age merely showed that mankind never learned anything.

The canopy lifted, and he blinked out at his second surprise of the day, a gangling, pole-thin old man in a brown robe and hood—the villain himself, Brother Andre! Although Ratty had never personally set eyes on the man before, he had set Jake's eyes and Mako's eyes on him. Barefoot, the future saint stepped into the car and sat opposite Ratty. The canopy closed, and the car rushed upward at a speed that gave Ratty pangs of jealousy.

Andre's face was a brown ruin, wrinkled and weathered, although the famous eyes were as blue and piercing as the legends said. He reached across, pulling his lips back to reveal an incomplete set of teeth. "I am Brother Andre. I assume we are to journey together?"

He did not know Ratty! Before Ratty could recover from shock number three, he had accepted the hand, rough as coral. He spoke his name and at last saw recognition.

"The muckraker?"

"I prefer 'reporter.' You never access cog-news?"

The friar shook his head. "The days are far too short already. I hear you reported a deal of nonsense about me recently."

"I damned nearly made you pope!"

"Well, I forgive you."

"Forgive me for failing?"

"Forgive you for trying."

And that was the famous smile? Yes, it was a good one.

Oh! "I would have succeeded if only you had accepted my calls or granted Mako an interview."

"I was busy that day."

"Scrubbing floors, Mako said."

Wrinkles deepened in a smile. "Also cleaning bed pans."

The cardinals had dithered through a dozen ballots before holding their noses and electing Favela. By the time Ratty had decided to go ahead without Brother Andre's testimony, he had been too late to deflate that nasty little hypocrite.

The car banked.

"Of course," Brother Andre added benevolently, "while your efforts were misguided, they brought the mission much publicity, and for that I am grateful."

His smile displayed amusement and confidence. Would anything ever rattle Brother Andre? This was the man the old pope had reputedly called, "A silken hand in a titanium glove." A cardinal had explained, "If you need help, he will give you everything he has. If you don't, then he expects you to give him everything you have."

"I have a religious question for you, Brother."

"Ask, and I will do the best I can." His pose of humility hid galactic arrogance.

"My views on religion were set when I was nine. We were on a family picnic—my parents, baby sister, me. A sudden rain squall sent us all running for shelter. I reached the car first. I turned around just in time to see a lightning bolt strike them. I ran back, of course. My father was obviously dead. My mother was still twitching, but they had been holding hands and were welded together. My sister had been fried. The Brain detected the deaths, but the aid it sent arrived too late. I was inherited by grandparents, who saw me as an undeserved burden. They leased a nanbot and more or less told it to keep me out of sight until I was adult and knew how to behave. How can I be expected to worship a god who does such things?"

"By faith, Brother. If you believe in a god, you must trust Him." The friar raised a callused hand to block comment. "I know that is not an adequate answer. If you truly wish private religious instruction, I shall happily spare you as much time as possible on our journey. We can study the Book of Job together, but I admit that you may not understand the Lord's motives until He explains them to you himself, as I am sure He will."

About to ask when that would be, Ratty guessed the answer and switched to a safer and more useful topic.

"Who else will be traveling with us to Pock's?"

"I would prefer not to discuss our journey until we lift off, if you don't mind."

Even if Ratty did mind, obviously. Meaning the friar knew no more than he did. The old man would never admit that, because the Church must not confess to ignorance or accept that STARS was pulling its strings just as it pulled every string in the galaxy.

"Since we have time on our hands at the moment," Brother Andre conceded, "I shall be happy to answer your questions on other matters."

"Very kind of you, Brother." It was too late to prevent Cardinal Favela becoming pope, but confirmation might be useful some other time. This was all being recorded for the pack. "Do you go to Guacharo often?"

"No."

"It's close to Annatto, I understand."

Andre shrugged. Emaciated though he was, his shoulders were broad. "About a two-day walk over the hills."

Oh yes, there was that. Conspicuous humility was an especially odious sort of pride. "You are not walking now."

"Papal orders overrule the rule of my order." Eyes twinkling, Andre waited with insufferable patience for the next question.

"I understand that the hospital at Guacharo is run by your mission."

"No. It is staffed by Capuchins but remains independent of Annatto." Why did he not ask why Ratty was asking about Guacharo?

"You visited Guacharo last year, around midsummer?"

"No."

Ratty's most expensive and experimental implant, the VERIT45, integrated visual and auditory input to determine if a speaker was lying. So far Brother Andre had not raised a twitch from it. Balked, Ratty tried another tack.

"The new pope is the same age as you?"

"Within a few days." Still no sign of curiosity or any indication that the old man wondered where the questions were leading.

"Your Church supports the population limitation laws?"

"Some of them, including the interdict law." Andre's eyes were bright. "I had hoped you wanted to discuss the work of the mission, Friend Turnsole, not just dabble in gossip."

Ah! Age had not dulled the old man's wits after all. Good. Ratty enjoyed a tussle.

"What gossip did you have in mind, Brother?"

"I do not repeat slander. If you care to dirty your mouth with it, then I will refute any statements I know to be false. Where possible, I will confirm what I know to be true."

You cannot like him, one archbishop had said, *but you must admire his honesty and fear his example.*

"Several witnesses told me," Ratty said, "that Cardinal Favela underwent heart surgery in Guacharo hospital last year, and that you spoke with him there. He was past interdict age then, of course. It is no secret that the rich and powerful can find ways around the interdict laws, but for a senior cleric to do so would be a major hypocrisy as well as a crime." That was the news that would have sunk Favela's candidacy.

Andre seemed unconcerned. "My information is that he underwent no surgery and received no medication. He experienced a dizzy spell brought on by overwork and was granted some bed rest and nursing care. Those are not forbidden, Ratty.

Nor are painkillers, but so far as I know he did not need any. I spoke with him, but only by cognition, from Annatto. I offered my best wishes and my prayers. Your informants may be conflating a brief trip I made to Guacharo in the spring. I toured the wards on that occasion." The eyes glittered. "You were thinking, perhaps, that the untruths you mentioned would have thrown the conclave into disarray? Not so. The rumor was already going around. Several cardinals cognized me to ask whether there was anything to the tale, and I gave them the truth as I knew it. Besides, surgery leaves traces—records in the Brain and scars on the patient. The calumny could easily have been discredited by unbuttoning a shirt."

"And did Cardinal Favela bare his breast for the cardinals?"

"I cannot say, because I was not there."

Still not a tweet from the GBA4445. Ratty reluctantly concluded that he had found a witness who would never lie.

Ratty did, though. "I am grateful to you for correcting me."

Judging by Andre's grim expression, he was undeceived. "You worry, I suppose, that our new pope seeks to bury his guilty secret by silencing those who knew of it?—me, who doubtless helped stitch up his incision, and you, who threaten to unmask his perfidy. Obviously he has called in some favor from STARS and arranged for us both to die in an unfortunate interstellar accident."

Ratty had not gotten quite that far yet. With a twinge of alarm, he said, "If you think that, then why are you going?"

"I don't think that." The friar smiled pityingly. "I am going because the Holy Father told me to. You must have made many more enemies than he in your career, Brother Ratty. Does STARS have cause to hate you?"

"Yes."

"Then you have even less chance of returning than I do. Besides, in the line of work you have attributed to me, Friend Turnsole, martyrdom is usually regarded as an upward career move. Not in yours, though. Are you still determined to accompany us?"

"Try and stop me!"

"I should not dream of it," Andre said, and a wonderfully warm smile spread over his age-wracked features. "I look forward to your company. Let us agree to be good foes and fence with the buttons on our rapiers. I am sure your counsel will be valuable."

Feeling strangely out-maneuvered by that smile, Ratty wondered what Jake and the pack were making of all this. "Do you suppose the team will produce a unanimous report?"

"On, no." The friar sighed. "I do not even know what it is expected to produce. I am afraid it is not expected to produce anything. I see we have arrived at the landing."

◦═◄ ◅ — ▻ ►═◦

Ayne was a beautiful world, said to be the most earthlike planet ever discovered, and the one thing on which almost every one of its inhabitants agreed was that it must be cherished and well husbanded, not desecrated by the sort of "terra-deforming" that some long-settled planets had suffered. So people hid their houses from sight and designed all buildings to make the smallest possible demands on the environment. They kept their population to a number the world should be able to support forever, according to the wise.

Landings were a necessary exception to such rules. Shadoof was a repellent expanse of permcrete, a sterile plain supporting a dozen isolated block houses like giant warts. Both they and the aprons around them were calcined red and black by the hellish energies that bathed them so often. Two were playing host to shuttles like larger versions of suborbitals, and it was to one of those that the car headed.

Ratty was trying to ignore a childish excitement at the prospect of his first trip off-world. Who else would be chosen for the star-studded jury? He walked in silence beside the friar across the roof to the down shaft. The moment he set foot in it, his sensory implants went dead. He had known that would happen eventually, but he had expected it after liftoff, and it was a startling experience, as if his clothes and skin had disappeared. Angry, he activated the portable recorder.

He thought he heard voices, but there was only one person in the lounge, a woman in severe clothes and stark haircut, perched primly on the edge of a chair. She recognized him, and her eyes widened. They were rather wide eyes at the best of times, protuberant.

"Ratty Turnsole! This is a surprise, Friend Ratty!"

He had never seen her before, and his normal reaction would have been to use the implant in the facial recognition area of his mid-fusiform gyrus to access the Brain and provide her name. As it was, he mumbled, "A happy one, but I confess I don't know—"

"Doctor Mildred Backet, Director of Health and Population Studies for the Sector Council. Call me Millie." She simpered.

He oiled. "And obviously an expert enlisted to aid our investigation. You recognize Brother Andre, of course?"

"Oh, yes, I know him from your wonderful *Saint of Annatto!*" She regarded Andre with some doubt. "An honor, er, Brother."

"The Lord be with you," Andre said.

"You are traveling to Pock's World?" Ratty asked.

"Oh, yes. The secretary general said I should go myself. On such an important matter, you know, she needs firsthand advice."

The sector secretary general was much too shrewd a politico to let herself be associated with anything as messy as geocide, or even genocide.

The lounge held seats for fifty or more people. The wall screens showed no person or machine working around the shuttle, but there was an air car approaching from the west.

"Brother Andre," said a syrupy mechanical voice overhead, "confirm your identity and your destination as Pock's World."

"Confirmed."

"Please connect with the medic in the corner. Visitors to Pock's World require extensive tonic."

As Andre crossed the lounge, Backet said, "You won't like it. Traveler tonic for Pock's tastes worse than any I have had, and this will be the eighth world I have visited."

Ratty said, "That is a remarkable record, Millie. Which one impressed you most?"

"Oh, none of them can compare with Ayne, Ratty. I had better not express preferences, though. Not in my position."

He eyed a compact but bulging portmanteau beside her. "You bring luggage?"

"Diplomatic privilege." Her expression could only be described as a smirk, but interstellar baggage fees were hundreds of times the value of anything she could have packed. No doubt the taxpayers of Ayne Sector would foot the bill.

Andre had placed his wrist in the medic's stirrup, setting lights a-flicker. "You are slightly malnourished," the machine announced, "and suffering from sleep deprivation. Leg and foot joints show signs of overuse, but otherwise functional deterioration consequent upon discontinuance of medical maintenance is in the lowest quartile for your age. You must remove your abrasive undergarment before reaching Pock's World or you will incur severe dermatitis from the pollutants. Personalized tonic will now be provided; drink it right away. Further medication will be required during your journey and while you are resident on Pock's World. Confirm that your stay will last at least three Ayne days and not more than seven."

"That is my understanding."

The beaker in the dispenser began to fill with a purple fluid.

"Ratty Turnsole, confirm your identity and your destination as Pock's World."

"Confirmed." He headed for the medic.

The friar tasted his brew and said, "Ugh! I had forgotten just how bad it was."

"I warned you!" Backet said with a harsh laugh. "Are you allowed to count that against your next penance?"

The old man drained the beaker and shuddered. "It should be the equal of two hours' flagellation."

She pouted at him, not sure whether he was joking.

The medic said, "Confirm that you have not brought any non-standard medications or recreational chemicals with you and do not intend to continue their use during your visit to Pock's World."

Ratty disliked being scolded, especially in public. "I have brought none. I'll party with the locals if they ask me."

"How much can you tell us about the evidence we shall be inspecting on Pock's, Director?" Andre asked.

Busily eavesdropping on the medic, Backet did not reply.

"Be warned," the machine said, "that many local drugs are unsafe for visitors. Your use of supplementary, nonstandard medication may result in unusually rapid deterioration when you reach interdict age. In the short term, expect some loss of sexual function during withdrawal."

Backet coughed. "Evidence? I expect it to be convincing. STARS would not take such drastic steps without good reason."

Turnsole took a sip of the tonic and blasphemed.

At that moment a woman sauntered into the lounge and scanned the room with an arrogant glance, as if she owned the world. In a sense she almost did, for Athena Fimble was Minority Leader of the Ayne Senate, the third most powerful politician on the planet.

Ratty blasphemed again. Star-studded indeed!

Chapter 3

In a sense, Athena's journey had begun a week earlier, on a moonlit night at Portolan. The daylong party had ended when the air cars hummed away into the warm dark. Alone with her problem and her ghosts, she sat on the terrace steps and watched ripples lap the beach. The small moon was rising. The air was scented velvet, the waves' song a lullaby. She had the world to herself except for a few small sail boats in the distance, where avid fishers hunted night eels.

Inevitably, she thought of her lost child, Chyle, who had died doing that on a night like this. Slysharks had never been reported in the Buttonwood Islands before that evening and only once in all the years since. Fortunately she had not been there to see the monster surface, smash the boat, and eat the occupants—eat half of each of them, a gruesome detail that somehow made the tragedy seem much worse. Sudden death had taken both Chyle and his father, but Athena's partnership with Sprunt had been long over by then, so his death had not smitten her as hard.

She had drowned her grief in politics, and she was still splashing around in the kettle. Today she had played hostess for all her senior advisers and their families. There had been feasting and games, children sporting on sand and sea, adolescents frolicking in the shrubbery, and serious policy discussions behind closed doors. It was the children, especially, who had brought back the memories, and it was the thought of another that complicated the decision she would make that night.

Closeted with the politicos in the great hall, overlooking the sea and silvery beaches, she had asked for frank advice. Her present office had grown wearisome and frustrating. She did not feel ready to retire, and there were only two ambitions left to her—secretary general of the Sector Council or president of Ayne, and only the second of those titles was worth having. She had known what most of her listeners would say, for they that had been nagging her for a year to declare. Of course she must seek the party's nomination, they insisted, for the Carabin administration was corrupt, tired, and stained with sleaze. She had earned the privilege with decades of eating tasteless banquet food and listening to mind-destroying blather. The public was ready for the more humane social policies she had advocated for years, and no other candidate came close to her in experience.

As for finance... That was when the fizz had flown. No doubt the party's usual supporters would finance the presidential campaign, but how many would back Athena Fimble in the nomination free-for-all beforehand?

Two bare, muscular arms wrapped around her. She turned her head; Proser kissed her with carnal intent. She broke it off.

"Come to bed," he said. "It's been a long day."

"I need to think."

"You'll think better in the morning. I can drive your cares away." Proser was her chief of staff and sleeping partner. The best aide and finest lover she had ever known, he was not much older than Chyle would be if he had lived...

"Not yet, love. I am going to decide tonight, here and now." That had always been her way.

"What is there to decide? The planet needs you. Carabin has been a disaster. And what have you got to lose, anyway?"

"Portolan," she said.

"Ah!"

Portolan had been the Fimble family home for a dozen generations, kennel for a celebrated line of artists, judges, soldiers, politicians, and even clergy. It was antiquated and located inconveniently far from the capital, but it reeked of aristocracy and old money, and it never failed to impress. With Chyle gone, Athena was the last of the Fimbles. Most of the old money had gone also, but Portolan she had preserved, and it trumpeted to all comers that here was a politician too rich to be dishonest. In truth she was too honest to be rich. She had squandered her inheritance financing her career. It had let her rise to the highest ranks without becoming overly beholden to anyone, which was rare indeed, but to progress farther she would need other support, and a lot of it. Hence today's conference.

"If I try for the nomination, love, I'll have to gamble everything. I may lose everything, even Portolan." It was the dread of defeat in the primaries that haunted her, of seeing the great Fimble line die out in a humiliating footnote and personal poverty.

"That's a worst case," Proser said, "but only you can make the decision."

"The alternative is to give you that child you want."

His embrace tightened. "You're serious?"

"Of course I'm serious!"

Although she had used up her birthright bearing Chyle, she knew Proser was anxious to use his. She was well past natural bearing age, but that was a legal problem, not a medical one. Ayne had a blue-stocking attitude to lab-assisted reproduction. Many planets with looser standards welcomed tourists with the avowed purpose of "adopting" babies. "Star children," they were called, and they usually grew up to look astonishingly like the rest of the family. Nevertheless, off-world bottle babies were a shady evasion of the law, and the moment it was suspected that Athena Fimble had followed that course, her political career would end. She must choose one or the other.

"You really intend to decide tonight?" Proser could spend ten minutes deciding what color tunic to wear. "Finally? Irrevocably?"

"Absolutely! You know me. I will decide on pure, unadulterated logic, and if it feels wrong, I'll switch right away."

He chuckled admiringly. "I will be gloriously happy either way. Be quick. I'll be waiting with some soft music and hard flesh."

"I promise." She kissed him. He sprang up and strode into to the house.

Athena went back to analyzing her problem. To run or not to run? She was not old, politically. She did not feel old, look old, or behave old. Her picture now was indistinguishable from any taken when she was eighteen, and Proser never had cause to complain of his love life. Next year was her last chance, though. If she did not challenge and topple Carabin next year, she never would.

Her alternative was to retire with honor now. And that raised the question of her duty to Proser and the Fimble ghosts, including Chyle. It was not impossible to combine motherhood and career, although she had never seen how it would be possible to do justice to either without short changing the other. A child raised by a nanbot was usually half a machine itself, sadly lacking in humanity. Athena Fimble could never compromise her standards; that was her trouble.

—Priority call.

She started. She had diverted all calls. Who, other than the president himself, could overrule her priority? Annoyed yet intrigued, she accepted.

Audio only: *—Do you recognize my thought pattern, Athena?*

Good God! *Linn? What do you want at this time of night?*

The unseen caller chuckled. *—Ask rather what you want. The problem is finance, isn't it? I'm sure they all cheered and whooped until you got down to talking about money. How much are you going to need?*

Linn Lazuline might have bugged her conference, but more likely he had simply had it analyzed beforehand. If he was not the world's richest person, the difference did not matter, and his machines would have been able to predict the course of the meeting almost down to individual speeches.

She thought, *Twenty million libras for the nomination. Eight more for the campaign.*

—Let's talk about that twenty.

Now?

—Now, while you're alone. Such arrogance was typical of Linn, but even the minority leader did not tell the world's richest man to go screw himself and call her office in the morning.

Where are you?

—On the water.

She looked up and saw that the nearest boat was anchored, even if its purely ornamental sail was still raised. Only the swell moving past it gave it the appearance of moving. She laughed. *Welcome to Portolan, then.*

She saw a faint splash as he dived, then his arms flailed silver as he swam to shore along the ribbon of moonlight. Linn had always swum like a torpedo snake. She cognized Proser. His image wore a formal knee-length business tunic, whereas the real man would almost certainly not be wearing anything by now, but his surprised expression was genuine.

Listen, love, I'm about to have a visitor.
—At this hour? Who?
Linn Lazuline.
—Good God!
That's what I said. I'll leave you in play, she added, and spliced him in.

Linn ran up the beach. She had known him since they were children, for his family owned the next island—a family even older than the Fimbles, although it ran to leaders of industry, not public servants. The years had changed him no more than her. He looked as good now in trunks as he had when they were at college. Sparkling silver in the moonlight, he sat down on the step beside her and grinned, puffing from the swim.

"Fine evening, Friend Fimble."

"Yes it is, Friend Lazuline. Can I offer you refreshment?"

He shook his head then ran his hands over it to squeeze water out of his honey-colored curls, which he had always worn long, in a mop. "This will only take a couple of minutes, yea or nay. I know to the ninety-ninth percentile why you called that meeting and why you called it here and who was invited and what they said. It's your last ambition."

She was beginning to see where he was heading and why he had chosen this time and place. After all these years? "Carry on."

"And you're mine, Athena."

"Your what?"

"My last ambition."

The moonlight was bright enough that he would notice if she blushed, but years ago she had undergone thoracoscopic sympathectomy; now she never blushed. Never in her life had she lost her temper.

"I am happily and legally partnered with a man I love a lot."

He shrugged. "I was thinking informal and brief."

"I ought to order you to leave and never darken my doorstep again."

"Go ahead."

She laughed. "Linn, you haven't changed a bit! You always were a cold-blooded bastard."

Teeth flashed. "Thank you. But I've been tidying up some of life's loose ends. You're one of them. You were the only girl I couldn't make. You want to hear my offer?"

"Out with it."

"Twenty million libras."

She caught her breath. "For what?"

"Two nights in your bed, plus reasonable cooperation."

"That's an insulting and degrading suggestion."

He chuckled. "I'd say it was pretty flattering. I've hungered for you since I was fourteen, Athena, and you know it. I've managed to buy or steal anything else I ever coveted. Now, at last, you need something I can provide and no one else can. You do not find me displeasing, do you?"

He was very far from displeasing. His genes were stupendous, blazing signals like a quasar; his muscles were as fascinating as his pheromones. He had money like most men had follicles. He was all a woman could ask for on a tropic beach by moonlight.

"You're the fanciest stud genetics can engineer, Linn. I don't deny it."

"So why have you always refused me? Mm? I wish you'd tell me. My life logger tells me this is the seventeenth time I've propositioned you. I was always willing to share you with the pack. You used to play a pretty wild field in those days."

"Those were the days," she agreed. "But it was narrower than you think. Boys brag."

"But why not me? Just to keep me humble?" His grin had lost none of its charm.

"You don't know what humble means. Because I was the only one you couldn't buy, I think. It amused me to see you frustrated."

"Not buy with even twenty million?"

Could any woman refuse that kind of bribe? This was rapidly becoming one of those stop-me-before-I-do-something-stupid experiences. Because she had never liked his politics. Because he had always wanted to control everything and own everything. "I would feel like a trophy in a glass case."

"You will be! Top shelf, front row. Private collection, though. I never brag, Athena, you know that. I never tell. I can make you president and ever after have the satisfaction of knowing I have made the president, but only you and I will ever know how."

He was smart enough to stop there and let her think about it. She did think about it, even to wishing she had not let Proser eavesdrop. Ripples splashed on the sand, trees danced in the trade winds under the moons. The offer was extraordinarily tempting. She had no doubt Linn would be good in bed, because anything less than perfection there would diminish his self-image. Finance on the scale he was promising would make her campaign a cakewalk. She would be free of financial worries. God, it was tempting!

So why hesitate?

"Linn, your politics and mine are about as far apart as you'll find outside a nut factory."

"The money's a free gift," he said seriously. "Spend it as you like. It's your body I'm buying, not your soul. You need me. The regulars won't back you, because they don't trust you. You're too honest to stay bought and give value for money."

That was unpleasantly true. "But if it ever got around that you—"

"It won't. No one will ever know."

Easy for him to say. She sighed. "Linn, there are a dozen people who plan my life to the minute and shepherd me around. Even here at Portolan, I'm never alone. There are eight—"

"Trust me. I can arrange our liaison so no one will know, and I can arrange that the funds come to you openly and legitimately through other people." The great Linn Lazuline sounded very close to begging. "Big money can do anything, Athena. I bypassed your cognition protocols, didn't I? Even Homeworld Security can't do that. I did. It cost me, but just for tonight I thought it was worth it."

To impress her? Like a hunter savage with a string of carnivore teeth around his neck.

"I'll have to think about it," she muttered.

"What's to think about? Ask the kid what he thinks."

"What kid?"

"Your bed boy. He cognizing this, isn't he?"

"Damn you!" *Proser?*

—*Can you trust him to pay up?* Proser was grinning. As usual, he had gone straight to the heart of the matter.

She looked at the glint of moonlight in Lin's eyes and the flash of his teeth and knew that he had heard the query. Eavesdropping on a private cognition was totally impossible, but he was doing it. Big money could do anything, he had said. Even the Brain was ultimately run by humans, and humans could be bribed or intimidated.

Yes, I can.

—*And trust him not to blackmail you later?*

She hesitated.

"I swear," Linn said softly.

Yes.

—Then go for it. Ball him blue and tell me all about it afterward.

Athena gasped and Linn bellowed with laughter in the night.

"You are a despicable brute, Linn Lazuline!"

"And proud of it. You agree?"

"Suppose I said forty million?"

"So now we're haggling? No, twenty million and two nights, all I can eat."

Omigod! Had even her grandfather ever had that much money? She patted Lin's thick shoulder, snatching her hand back before he could grab it. "I'm sorry, Linn. Maybe one day, just for old times' sake, but I do have to live with myself, and I couldn't, not after that. I've decided not to run."

"Take a day or two to think about it."

"No. I decided." She should be grateful, for he had shown her what she really did want, and it was a child, not a presidential seal. "Goodnight, Linn."

She rose and went into the house without a backward glance, back to Proser, who couldn't keep two libras to jingle but was a dream of a lover and could legally father a child.

※⟨⟨ — ⟩⟩※

Proser's second most important function was to vet her incoming calls, those that junior staff had already passed. A few days later he called her in the middle of a vital finance committee meeting.

—I think you have to take this one, darling.

In five years, he had never interrupted anything really important. She muttered an apology to the others around the table, let her eyes lose focus.

Accept.

The face she saw was not one she recognized. He wore a black tunic with stars on the lapels.

—Sulcus Immit, Director of Security, STARS, Inc. My apologies if I am intruding, Senator. I am calling on a matter of extreme urgency.

She had never spoken to anyone in STARS higher than a link technician. When senate committees subpoenaed STARS officers, they would refuse, claiming STARS was not subject to planetary jurisdiction.

Please be brief.

—*We need your help. The matter is highly sensitive. If this news leaves out before we are ready, there might be widespread panic. Will you promise to treat what I tell you as confidential?*

Subject to the oath I swore when I took office.

His expression was grave, unvarying. —*There will be no conflict with that. Is this call being monitored?*

Only by a human who keeps his mouth shut.

A nod. —*Very briefly, then, a Diallelon Abomination has been identified on Pock's World. Quarantine is in place but will not be announced until tomorrow. Meanwhile we are organizing a small but high-profile commission to go to Pock's World, inspect the evidence, and return to report to the public. If sterilization proves necessary, the rest of the sector should know that STARS, Inc had good reason for its actions. We have already arranged for representatives from the Church, the Sector Council, and industry. We hope to include a judge or ex-judge, a media person, and an elected official. You are an obvious choice for that. Will you please help us?*

Her mind had locked wheels at the word "Diallelon" and needed a moment to track to the end of the speech. *You mean you want me to decide the fate of an entire planet?*

Or was this an elaborate politic trap, to smear her with geocide? No matter what happened to Pock's, whether she was seen as guilty of destroying a world or of protecting monsters, any involvement would end her political career. But she had already given that up, hadn't she? She had told Proser to start arranging meetings with fertility experts, as a first step, because she would rather bear his child the traditional way—and she had also told him to do his damnedest in the meantime, for which he needed no encouragement. So political ambition could not interfere with her decision.

Sulcus was shaking his head. —*The decision will be STARS's. You will just inspect the evidence, interview some witnesses, form an opinion. STARS will do its duty as it sees it, but we are not monsters, Senator. We detest the thought as much as you do—more, in fact, because the blood will be on our hands. There are six hundred million human lives at stake; we need only four or five days of your time.*

Ask President Carabin to name a special envoy.

—*No. If we let one planetary government do that, then all the rest will want to meddle also. The point is that you are highly respected and universally known, but you do not speak for a government.*

Her mind shied away from the implications. This could not possibly be genuine. Far more likely, it was political hoax intended to expose her to ridicule. Such an elaborate attack might be flattering, but was also annoying. Had she still had presidential ambitions, her answer must be an unequivocal *No!* because this venture would compromise her fatally, no matter which way the story ended. Her political future was no longer an issue, although only Proser knew that so far. And if there was the slightest shadow of a possibility that it was genuine, then she could never stand aside and let six hundred million... She felt insects crawl on her skin.

Before I agree, I must confirm your identity.

For the first time he smiled. *—Will you take the pope's word for it?*

Certainly. Ask His Holiness to expect a call from my chief of staff, Proser Ryepeck. He's a good Catholic lad. She ended cognition and returned to discussing the planetary budget for fiscal 29,875.

She was waiting on the roof when the air car came for her next morning.

Chapter 4

Athena Fimble scanned the lounge with eyes as dark and brilliant as jet. Her thick black hair was coiled and pinned high with silver combs; the hem of her pleated white tunic floated well above her knees, the neckline dipped low over her breasts.

Suppressing a reflex to drool, Ratty glanced at his companions to see their reaction. Millie Backet had flushed red with annoyance. Brother Andre had withdrawn inside his brown hood, ignoring a woman who displayed so much of herself. Athena's costume would not have been decent around the mission in Annatto, but it was standard wear for the Beautiful People, of which she was most certainly one. Her parents might have spent a fortune tinkering with her genes both before and after she was born, although more likely she had been perfect since the moment her father's perfect sperm was introduced to her mother's perfect ovum and their union was placed in the perfect nest prepared for it—regardless of whether that nest had been perfected by generations of germ-plasm improvement and medical care or built by skilled bottling plant engineers. She was as well adapted to the planet as if her ancestors had lived on Ayne for a million years. Even interdict held few terrors for the elite; barring accidents, they could stay healthy well into their second century, and they could afford trips to other worlds that were more liberal with medical care.

Athena floated across the room on long, brown legs that would neither burn in summer nor fade in winter. Her smile was glorious.

"Brother Andre! This is a joyful honor. I spoke to your superiors as you suggested, and they will be happy to let you testify before our medical provision committee."

The friar looked up in shock. "*You* are Senator, er...?"

"Fimble, Athena Fimble, yes. And Director Backet!" Her hesitation had been barely perceptible, so either her memory for faces was extraordinary or her implants had not been deactivated like Ratty's. "My, it has been a long time since those infertility hearings, Millie, hasn't it? I see this group is going to wield a lot of heft; you and Brother Andre and..." She laughed. "And Terrible Turnsole! Ratty, yours will be the only voice the worlds will heed."

Flattery for all! Ratty liked Athena. She fed him snippets once in a while, and sometimes he would reciprocate by slanting a story her way. The worst he had ever managed to dig up on her was that she had once been slow to abandon one lover after acquiring another, and that story had no legs. Although a clever woman, she was depressingly honest and much too independent; her party would never trust her with a presidential nomination.

"Will all the planets be sending representatives?" Backet demanded, nose firmly out of joint.

"I was told not," Athena said smoothly. "You are the only government representative, I think, Millie. I'm here on my own, just a generic political hack. There may be other people rendezvousing with us at Pock's, of course. I don't know if that's the case, but it sounded like a small team. Church, government, industry, the law, and media, Sulcus said. Still waiting for law and industry?"

"No one from STARS itself?" Ratty asked. "No helpful helpers along to guide our thinking?"

The ramp door closed. The umbilical door opened.

"The journey to Ayne 3," said Control's synthetic voice, "will take approximately twenty-seven minutes. You will proceed from there by entanglement links to Pock's Station via Climatal 2 and Pyrus 1. Senator Fimble, please confirm your identity and come to the medic. The rest of you may board the shuttle now."

"But don't ask impertinent questions," Ratty muttered.

He felt blind and deaf without his implants' constant babble, and furious that he might be recording the greatest story of his career while handicapped by their absence. The portable's limited sensitivity would not convey the dramatic immediacy his fans expected.

The door clumped shut. Although he had not traveled in space before, Ratty knew what to expect—a circle of padded bench under a transparent dome, an oversized air car. He found himself seated across from the Backet woman, who was a lame-brain but an experienced traveler, so he did what she did, leaning back, relaxing, taking slow breaths. Her tunic was calf-length and dowdy, her legs pudgy and veined. He should have sat where he could feast his eyes on Athena. She was wasted on Brother Andre.

"Prepare for liftoff," Control said. "Liftoff."

Roar! The bench shuddered and pushed hard against him as the shuttle rushed up through the atmosphere into space. Then the noise died away to a low internal rumble. One pane of roof phased out to mask the sun, and the rest of the sky turned black and starry.

Athena's presence was surprising. Why should she care a spit for a horrible wasteland planet? There were no votes there for her. Why not ask?

"Senator Fimble, as a politician, are you not taking a risk in being associated with this crisis?"

The sultry eyes inspected him as if he were the most fascinating object in the galaxy. "Yes, Ratty, very much so. If STARS decides to burn Pock's, I will be known ever after as one of the killers. If it doesn't, there will be lunatics screaming that we've endangered the human species. That goes for all of us."

"Then why are you here?"

"Because there are an estimated 607,603,523 people on Pock's World. If I can do anything to save them, I will."

She was a wonderful subject, leading the next question every time. "So you will vote to acquit, no matter what evidence is put before the court?"

"I may find the accused guilty, but I can never vote for a death sentence on innocent bystanders. After so many thousands of years, there must be better ways of containing a Diallelon abomination."

"And your career?"

"Is much less important than so many lives."

Noticing everyone staring past him, Ratty turned his head. The shuttle had tilted, and Ayne was spread out behind him like a fuzzy-edged blue tablecloth. It made him feel dizzy, so he looked away.

"Who's in charge here?" he asked. "Did STARS nominate a chair for this committee?"

The silence grew awkward.

"Brother Andre is senior," Athena Fimble observed.

For the first time since Ratty had met him, the old man laughed. "You certainly do not want me presiding over our debates, because my rulings would be based on logic that you would find peculiar. Besides, my duty is to report my own conclusions directly to the Holy Father, in confidence, so I must refuse to be bound by any vote. Who, then?" He smiled ominously around the group.

Ratty said, "I pass. I'm a reporter, not a decider."

"That is an honest answer," said Andre. "Senator, by experience and public standing, you are the logical choice, but whatever our group eventually concludes, you will be accused of playing politics." He smiled to rid the words of offense.

"That leaves me," Millie Backet said quickly. "The distinguished senator represents only one of the seventeen worlds, and the other sixteen will undoubtedly ask why Ayne should be so favored. If anyone is to lead our deliberations and activities, then surely it must be the one delegate whose constituency is sector-wide!"

"The Church is galaxy-wide," Andre said reprovingly, "although I grant you our flock is thin on some worlds. But whoever the rest of you care to choose, I will cooperate as best I can."

Ratty watched as Millie waited for her two companions to nominate and second her so she could cast the deciding vote. She might be efficient enough in her job of shuffling statistics, filing reports, and bullying aides, but she was sadly outclassed in this group. Her tunic was cheap; her overall flabbiness suggested that she could not even afford decent tonic. The secretary general probably sent her flitting around the seventeen worlds just to keep her out from underfoot.

Athena said, "This discussion is premature. STARS has not yet confirmed that we are the complete team. We may find other members joining us at Ayne 3, or delegates from other planets waiting for us when we reach Pock's. I suggest we postpone a decision on chairing."

"I agree." Smirking again, Backet produced a small box. "But we can pass the time preparing for our labors. Our implants are specific to Ayne, of course. Before visiting other worlds, I always have my staff download relevant material into a portable. I find it wonderfully helpful."

In Ratty's experience, people who spoke of "my staff" were usually too incompetent to velk their own tunics. Obviously her staff could control her thinking by choosing the material they gave her. Given time, he would have downloaded relevant files from the Brain into his portable, but he would have made his own selection. He stared in disbelief at the device she now held on her lap—a *voice* recorder? What epoch did she live in? Why not bring a wagonload of inscribed stone tablets?

Mercifully, Athena objected. "Is that a good idea, Millie? We are a jury. We should wait and let the prosecution present its case, not prejudge the sort of evidence we expect to see."

Backet looked aghast, as if the thought of thinking for herself was unthinkable.

Ratty said, "Why don't we discuss a totally irrelevant matter? Politics, perhaps? Something like the Mongo Bill?"

Athena flashed him an appreciative glance and said nothing.

Brother Andre smiled. "I am ignorant. Tell us about the Mongo Bill, then."

"The senator is more knowledgeable than I am."

"But not as skilled at manipulating a conversation," Athena said, smiling. "It may be a serious problem, and odiously relevant." Her voice was low and compelling. "There is a bill before the Senate that would assert planetary ownership and control of all space facilities and equipment on Ayne or in its stellar system. If this should pass, expect to see the other worlds follow—as goes Ayne, so goes the sector. Such measures have been proposed and defeated innumerable times in the past, but this one seems to be gaining significant support." She glanced at each of her companions in turn. "After all, why should STARS have a monopoly on space travel? If such monolithic control is necessary, why is it not run by the Sector Council, instead of by some faceless self-perpetrating clique, a secret elite accountable to no one?"

Backet nodded vigorously. "A good question! The sector speaks for everyone."

"To keep the galaxy safe for humankind," Ratty suggested. "That's the historical excuse. We have never discovered another intelligent species, only cuckoos, who are us transformed. But STARS has always argued that interplanetary warfare would be too terrible to be entrusted to governments, that only a disinterested impersonal authority, namely STARS, can hold the power of life and death over worlds. Being answerable to no one, it cannot be bribed or corrupted, so it says."

"That is the standard explanation," Athena agreed. "So it may be that this entire operation is a hoax. Or perhaps I should say a murderous conspiracy. You have a comment, Brother?"

"Nothing," the friar said, his weathered face grim. "I was just thinking that I belong to another age-old self-perpetuating organization. The difference is that we welcome recruits and we are answerable to God, but I see your point, and it is terrifying. You really think STARS plans to make an example of Pock's World just to bring the rest of the sector to heel? That it will try to hoodwink us? That is a serious allegation, Senator. Have you any evidence?"

Athena shrugged. "Only timing. The Mongo Bill starts to gather support and suddenly, after seven hundred years, monsters pop up again. Not since Jibba burned have we heard a word about synthetic hominins."

Ratty could have disagreed, but didn't. Pock's had originally been part of the Canaster sector, settled from Malacostraca long before anyone had set foot on Ayne, but its link to Malacostracan had been broken about five hundred years ago, two hundred years *after* the cauterization of Jibba. An entanglement link needed a clear line of sight, and Ayne history records stated that an interstellar dust cloud intervened between Pock's and Malacostraca. Conspiracy lovers claimed that the Canaster STARS had blasted Malacostraca, ostensibly because it had been infected by a Diallelon abomination. It was certainly curious that the Ayne Sector's links to its neighbors, Canaster and Avens Sectors, had been severed within a mere two centuries. Ratty knew as well as anyone how evidence could be suppressed or distorted.

Millie protested. "Surely you cannot believe that STARS would deliberately wipe out a whole world just to preserve its monopoly?"

"Monopolies are worth a lot of money," Ratty said. "But I won't discuss that topic in a STARS vehicle."

Brother Andre's wrinkles deepened to form a smile. "Like me, he believes that we mortals are capable of almost any evil. On an older, safer, matter then... Friend Ratty, you said that we have never encountered another intelligent species."

"Then of course I was wrong, Brother. There are several smart species even in Ayne sector, like the hieroglyph spiders of Cordelle, but we have never found another 'handy' species, one that uses fire and other tools and may someday acquire space technology."

"We found traces of one," the old man said. "The chief tourist attractions of Pock's World are the Querent ruins. They have been dated as at least a million years old and look it. They were certainly built with tools. There are fireplaces at Quassia itself—hearths and kilns. I fully believe there are other sentient races to be discovered elsewhere in the Galaxy. The Church has never claimed that creation was limited to humankind."

"I shall be surprised if any living Querent have turned up after all this time," Athena said. "That can't be what STARS's worried about."

Millie bounced back into the conversation. "I do hope we get a chance to see the ruins, though! This will be the eighth world I have visited, and I always try to get in a little sightseeing between all the meetings and conferences and so on."

On Sector Council expense account, no doubt. "Tell us about Pock's World, Brother," Ratty said. "You spent some time there."

"An age ago, I did." The friar shook his head. "Pock's has no climate, only weather, and that's usually horrible. When people call Pock's 'barely habitable' they mean more 'barely' than 'habitable.' Carbon dioxide often reaches two percent. You could not survive in that for more than a few days without special tonic. During major eruptions, even the natives wear gas masks." He smiled reassurance. "I survived more than an Ayne year there, so it is possible. The problems get worse if you stay longer. You lose bone mass in the lower gravity. Heavy metal toxicity builds up—lead, cadmium, mercury—so you require gene therapy and eventually chelation treatment. There's arsenic everywhere, and that's a major cause of cancer. The natives die much younger than inhabitants of other planets."

Again his face made that strange transition from stern to serene, as if sunlight warmed it.

"But it is beautiful. Pock's is all scenery, as the tourist industry says. You know it's not a planet, but a satellite of Javel, a gas giant orbiting a star, which the locals call the sun and astronomers just number-so-and-so. Satellites are supposed to orbit their primary in the equatorial plane and keep one face constantly turned toward it. Pock's doesn't. It was originally a planet in its own right and was captured by Javel."

"Tidal stress," Athena Fimble said.

"Enormous tidal stress. The world is constantly being flexed—by its own rotation, by the tilt and eccentricity of its orbit, and even by Javel's equatorial bulge. Tidal stress generates the heat that drives the volcanoes. There's always an eruption or two going on. Sounds terrible, doesn't it? But when one starts to blow, everyone just moves out of the way."

"It has good government?" Backet asked. "The Pocosin Ambassador to the Sector Council often brags how peaceful it is."

"It has petty wars from time to time," the friar said. "We mortals cannot live without fighting, it seems. The Pocosins have no unified planetary government, like most planets, but they are reasonably civilized in the way they settle their quarrels."

"Is that because they do have a unified planetary religion?" Ratty asked innocently.

The old man's craggy jaw clicked shut. "The Church of the Mother is the largest religion on Pock's, but it is by no means universal. It worships the planet Javel."

Millie chuckled. "Oh, you'll never get everyone to agree on religion, Brother! But as long as their morals and ethics are reasonable, I can't see that the details matter. The Church of the Mother is benevolent, I understand."

Andre glared at her. "Only if you regard human sacrifice as benevolent. They don't admit it to outsiders, but I know for a fact that human sacrifice is not merely condoned but a central part of their ritual."

"There's Ayne 3 ahead," Athena said.

"It always reminds me of melted cheese," said Millie.

Chapter 5

Until that mention of the abomination of planet-worship, Andre had been savoring a bitter-sweet nostalgia. The shuttle was identical to the one he had ridden up to Ayne 3 fifty years ago, although much less crowded, and the station now in sight had not changed at all. "It looks as if it melted," was what he had said then. He had not been a friar in those days, just newly ordained Father Jame Mangold, much younger than he thought he was, heading out on his first mission with his mentor, wonderful old Cardinal Trinal.

Trinal had known that he would never return from Pock's. The carcinogens would strike him down again, and even Ayne medicine would not cure him a third time. The doctors had told him so plainly, but he had insisted on going back to Pock's to resume his duties. Yes, he had been a true saint, a sharp-eyed bishop who had plucked more than one orphan boy out of poverty and seen him educated. Andre had failed him. Andre had been recalled from Pock's in disgrace. It was still incredible to him that he was on his way back there now. Yesterday, at Compline, he had remembered the good cardinal in his prayers, as he always did. He would never have believed that he would soon be on his way back to Pock's World and might even be able to visit his dear friend's grave. The Lord moved in mysterious ways.

"It *was* melted," Trinal had said of Ayne 3, "at least on the outside. Space is not quite empty, you know, and I'm not talking about heavenly spirits this time. Gas, dust, very hard radiation.

Push something through the galactic medium at a good fraction of the speed of light and its leading surface is bound to heat up. If STARS used metal boxes instead of captured asteroids, the entanglement mechanism would be fried before the probe ever arrived at its destination. The wonder is that even this lump did not turn into a shower of nickel-iron rain."

A gray potato shape against the stars, a rock as old as the stars.

"You mean that lump came from Pock's?" one of the others had asked—Father Thomas, probably.

"Not Pock's. Ayne 3 is linked to Jasp, Vakeel, and Climatal, so this lump as you call it must have brought one end of an entanglement link from one of those worlds in a voyage that would have taken several human lifetimes."

Andre smiled at the memory of those companions. Trinal had been a martyr, and yet in all his suffering he had never lost his wonderful sense of humor. He ranked close to St. Francis himself as a worthy role model.

Theo Phare was the current cardinal-archbishop of Pock's. He was a native and ought to live longer than an off-worlder. Andre knew nothing about him. Fifty-three years ago... Probably no one he had known on Pock's would be alive now.

What of his present company? In appointing Andre, the pope had made it clear that he retained the authority to make the final decision, but Director Backet was obviously terrified of the responsibility that had been thrust upon her. The secretary general—whatever her name was—could hide behind the Council or her helpers. Backet was far more likely to reap blame than credit from this mission, and massive guilt as well.

Ratty Turnsole was certainly a personable young man whose cherubic appearance hid a quick and deadly mind, plus a total lack of scruples. His impatience with Backet was probably just youthful arrogance, not a conscious desire to hurt, but it was a great pity he could not see the potential for evil in his professional activities.

The senator? Now there was an impressive woman who would make a clear-headed and unemotional judgment. A woman of her station should set a better example in dress.

All eyes were on Ayne 3 as it drew closer. Now details were becoming visible, pimples of human meddling on a mini-world several kilometers across. Antennae and docked shuttles emphasized the size of the enormous main body.

"I'm so glad it's Ayne 3 we're going to," Mildred Backet said. "Ayne 2 is so shabby! It seems so old. Ayne 1 is even worse, I understand."

Athena said, "All three stations are old, Director, older than any building still standing. Ayne 1 is needed to hold secondary backups for some of the busier links."

The station loomed above them, filling the sky.

"Maybe now we'll get some answers," Ratty Turnsole said grumpily.

⋯⋯⋯

No, they got no answers. An impersonal voice welcomed them to Ayne 3. It warned them to be careful in the corridors and to ignore any sensation of falling.

"Don't you just hate it when a machine bids you welcome?" Millie grumbled.

In fact Andre detested all talking machinery, but he had forgotten how much fun the energized corridors were, even if one took them with proper clerical decorum, standing upright as one was wafted along. They were circular in cross section, like gigantic wormholes drilled through the nickel-iron, their walls lined with some furry beige substance. With no effort on their part, visitors were swept along with their feet floating just above the surface. The two women went first, followed by Ratty, with Andre bringing up the rear. He recalled Cardinal Trinal jesting that this form of travel made him feel like a corpuscle in an artery and that he should have worn his red robes. Children would always try somersaults or handstands, of course, but the repeller field would keep them from hurting themselves. Now Turnsole tried to touch the surface, probably wondering if it was as soft as it looked. He yelped as he was set to spinning like a top.

"Just relax and it will stabilize you!" Andre said.

It stabilized him the wrong way around, so Ratty completed the journey facing backward, looking sheepish but not daring to try to right himself.

The journey was a long one. The corridor passed unlit side tunnels and several times turned at right angles—then it was important to resist an illusion of falling vertically downward. Eventually the travelers floated into a lounge and were gently set down, held in place by local pseudo-gravity. There was no one present to answer questions, just seating for about thirty people and of course no windows deep in the heart of the probe.

A wall screen showed a view of the world floating by underneath. In one corner stood a group of food dispensers and a small podium; in another a heavy metal door blocked the way to the entangler.

"Where is everybody?" Millie demanded. "Why is there nobody here, answering questions, passing out snacks?"

"This is hardly appropriate treatment for a blue-ribbon committee," the senator agreed.

"You want the scary answer?" Ratty asked.

"What scary answer?"

He was trying to hide his nervousness, but his confident air did not deceive Andre. "We've been forgotten. Pock's World has been quarantined, the link is shut down, and nobody knows we're here."

All eyes went to the way they had entered, which was now closed off by a door having no visible handle. They were deep in the heart of a nickel-iron asteroid.

"Hardly!" Andre floated down on a seat and folded his hands in his sleeves. "We travel by way of Climatal and Pyrus, remember? The quarantine guard will be at Pyrus. What seems like discourtesy may just be an attempt at secrecy. News of our mission has not been made public yet."

Yet the absence of attendants did seem foreboding. Even the drab beige decor and the dim lighting were repellent. Andre had not noticed that on his previous visit, but then he had been too young, too excited, too starry-eyed to care. Also, there had been a lot of chattering people in the lounge—and STARS attendants, also, he recalled.

"Tell us more about Pock's, Brother," Athena said. "I know that volcanic soil is very fertile. Pock's and Prakrit are said to be the only habitable worlds without plate tectonics, but I don't know why that matters."

"I'm sure the natives will be happy to explain if you ask them," Andre said. "Their language is unintelligible, but STARS will surely hand out translators."

Mildred Backet sniffed. "I'm sure it can't be worse than what they speak on Haven or New Winish."

It was, of course. Those tongues belonged to the same language family as Ayne Standard, but Pock's had been settled from Malacostraca and its various dialects bore no relation to any language spoken elsewhere in the sector. The two roads that Adam's children had followed to Ayne sector had diverged at least twelve thousand years ago.

"What are the good points of Pock's World, Brother?" the senator asked. "It must have some."

"Oh, many!" he said. "Its people are a happy, helpful folk. Adversity brings out the best in us, you know. When the clouds part, the scenery is stupendous. Active volcanoes are landscape extraordinaire. Also, the local fauna is so alien to us—or we are so alien to them—that they tend to ignore us. Bugs buzz in your ears at night, but they don't bite you. There are places where the rain never stops and everything in sight is covered with mold and fungus, except the people, fortunately. Clothes and houses rot because they're made of Pock's local materials, but human skin doesn't. It just gets dirty. Of course any world develops its own diseases in time. You will be immunized against those."

Andre decided he must warn them about time keeping. "Pock's is, of course, a satellite of the gas giant Javel. Javel's orbital period around the sun is approximately six hundred and fifty days, or almost twice an Ayne year. The translators will interpret this as a year, so an eight-year-old is pubescent. You keep track of years by watching the stars, but there is so little seasonal change that nobody bothers.

"Pock's turns on its axis roughly once every fourteen of our days. The interpreters call this a fortnight, or sometimes a half-month. You get bright week followed by dark week."

"You *don't* mean," Millie said, "that it has seven-day nights?"

Andre was amused by her woebegone expression. "And seven-night days! Yes, I do. But it's not so bad, because the world goes around Javel in close to one of our days. During bright week the sun is in the sky all the time and during dark week it isn't, but Javel rises in the west every day and sets in the east. Javel is huge! It subtends an angle of thirty degrees. If its lower edge is on the horizon, the upper edge is a third of the way to the zenith. Javel gives plenty of light, believe me. You don't miss the sun." The Devil would not have found it hard to deceive pagans into worshiping the great planet.

"So the interpreters refer to one rise and set of Javel as a day. The day officially begins when the world enters the planet's shadow, and eclipse lasts about two hours. " He looked around at their faces and laughed. "You won't be on Pock's long, so I suggest you don't worry about it."

"Which will we have—day or night?" Athena asked, frowning.

"That depends where we are on the world. And Pock's is small enough that a moderate air trip can put you in a different longitude."

Director Backet and he had their backs to the door. Ratty and Athena were facing it. When Andre saw them register shock, he twisted around to see who had arrived—one man, large and imposing, with a bush of curly blond hair. His tunic was as blatantly close to indecent as the senator's and probably as absurdly expensive. He was grinning.

"I'm happy to that see you accepted, Athena."

Fimble looked furious. "Linn! Is this all your doing? Is this nothing but a cruel hoax?"

The newcomer's amusement vanished as he noted Ratty. "Hoax? Rather call it conspiracy to geocide, but it was none of my doing." He walked around to take the seat next to Athena. "STARS invited me, and I suggested your name, that's all. I didn't know they would be stupid enough to include a sleazy muckraker like Ratty Turnsole."

Ratty wore the grin now. He looked delighted. "I couldn't sink much lower than being in the company of Linn Lazuline, now, could I? Do you know this person, Brother Andre? Do you, Director? Friend Lazuline is the richest man in the sector. He has fingers in every shady deal on seventeen worlds."

"You keep your lips welded shut, Turnsole," the newcomer said, "or I'll see you spend the next hundred years in jail."

The reporter was blissfully undeterred. "He also owns more lawyers than all the judicial systems put together. He rarely follows through, though. I showed his paw marks on the psychobed factory they uncovered in Tugrik. He blustered and threatened, but he didn't dare file suit."

Ignoring him, Lazuline looked to Andre. "I know who you are, Brother. A brilliant choice for delegate."

"Hit him up for a donation!" Ratty's tones conjured visions of snakes slithering. "A billion's a nice round sum."

"Friend Lazuline," Andre said, "has contributed to the Annatto Mission for many years through the Lazuline Foundation." He saw no need to mention that the Foundation had tripled its donation after the *Saint of Annatto* nonsense. "Do you know Friend Backet, Director of Health and Population Studies for the Sector Council?"

Mildred said, "Do call me Millie!"

"I hope you will call me Linn."

Athena Fimble broke in angrily. "Let's see if we can actually discover some facts about this fact-finding mission. Why did you not come up on the same shuttle as the rest of us?"

Andre wondered why she was so suspicious. Was she hinting that she would have refused to travel with Lazuline?

Linn studied her for a moment. "Because I was in Lagan when they called me, working on a hundred-million-libra takeover. It probably cost me fifteen million to close the deal soon enough to come. I flew up directly, just got here."

"You didn't start this story of a Diallelon cuckoo just to help STARS in its political troubles?"

"Me?" he scoffed. "Even Mudslinger Turnsole has never accused me of being a STARS racketeer. I am no friend of STARS. Its tariffs are obscene. No, I told you. Sulcus asked me to serve on the team he was raising. I said I would if you would."

"Why me?"

"Because your reputation is that you can't be bought and STARS is capable of buying almost anyone else." Lazuline glanced around the group. "They certainly won't buy Brother Andre there, and they can't buy me."

"Don't you feel all cozy when he endears himself like that?" Ratty asked Backet, who had flushed at the implication.

"I was about to add, Friend Ratty, that they won't *fool* you, which is something. As for—"

Athena interrupted. "You believe the Diallelon report is a fabrication?"

The financier laughed aloud. "I'm certain of it. They're fighting the Mongo Bill, trying to scare people. Any evidence they show us will be faked. It's a monstrous, age-old fraud."

The others exchanged glances. Ratty said, "Why do you think that?" just as Andre began to ask, "Do you really—"

Andre began again, louder. "You truly believe that STARS intends to wipe out Pock's World just to further its own political ends?"

Linn turned a carefully sincere regard on him. "Believe? Yes, I believe exactly that. STARS has committed that same atrocity many times and gotten away with it. The funniest thing about belief, Brother, is that the more absurd the story people are required to believe in, the more strongly they will hold to their belief. No offense intended, but to an unbeliever your own faith seems like a perfect example. No doubt my tenets seem equally illogical to you. If you look at it rationally, the whole Diallelon scam is utter rubbish. Cuckoos, we are told, are artificial hominin species created out of our own—for reasons unknown, by persons unknown, at places unknown, starting at least twenty-five thousand years ago. They have an irresistible instinct to invade human-inhabited worlds, take them over, and destroy the *Homo sapiens* residents. That last bit I can accept, because there is evidence that our *sapiens* ancestors disposed of earlier hominin competitors with the same single-minded fanaticism. We deal with rivals within our own species in much the same way. But the cuckoos themselves are a mirage."

Director Backet broke the silence. "You cannot prove those allegations! You expect us to believe that you are right and everyone else is wrong?"

Linn's smile was brighter than a billion suns. "Not everyone else, Millie, just a lot of people, those who have swallowed the STARS propaganda without questioning it. It cannot be true! Where do they keep coming from, mm? The original cuckoo men, and all the more recent variations—the Soldier Ants, the Zombies, the Ghouls. They're bogeymen, all of them! Whenever STARS's monopoly is threatened, it invents monsters and burns another planet. Jibba, Malacostraca, Sweven, and a line of cin-. der worlds all the way back to Earth itself. We know of six sterilizations for certain and likely at least another four. That's a world every three thousand years, and God knows—begging your pardon Brother—what else has been going on in other parts of human-occupied space, outside the tiny corner of it that we know."

Andre could not let this blasphemy go unchallenged. "In several cases the Church supported the sterilization. Are you suggesting that Pope Benedict was deluded into calling for a crusade against the Soldier Ants?"

Lazuline glanced at the others as if measuring his support. "People who believe in one superstition are easily convinced of another, Brother. Only believers in God are frightened of devils, or witchcraft. Rational minds scoff at them all. Yes, I think he was hoodwinked. Either that or bribed."

"You believe that popes cauterize worlds without checking their facts?"

"Albigensians? Hussites? Huguenots?"

"Let's stay with cuckoos. Benedict saw the evidence for Jibba. You will forgive me if I believe him before you?"

"He saw something, Brother," Linn said patiently, "or his representatives did. But STARS always insists that any world infected by cuckoos inevitably goes dark, and once the mutants have seized control they set out to infest more worlds, so *an infected world must be destroyed as soon as possible!* Whatever evidence was reported to your esteemed Benedict was incinerated with the alleged cuckoos. We have to take it on faith now."

Andre shivered as he sensed the overpowering presence of evil. "What I take on faith, Linn Lazuline, is that Diallelon abominations are the work of Satan and that anyone who defends them is doing the devil's work."

The lights dimmed and brightened again. Control said, "Your attention, please. Entanglement is the safest form of transportation in the galaxy. You may now proceed to Climatal 2 Station, en route to Pock's World. The door presently illuminated leads to the link cubicle, which will transmit you directly to your destination. Your journey will take no time at all, because the BERM in this station is maintained in a state of entanglement with an identical BERM in Climatal 2 station. Any change in one is instantaneously recorded in the other. Please enter the door one at a time and follow instructions."

"What's a BERM?" Athena asked.

"That's the Bose-Einstein Reference Mass," Millie said.

Everyone rose. Linn moved toward the door, which had slid open, but Millie cut him off, scurrying ahead of him with unseemly haste. She stepped through, and the door shut behind her.

"What's her hurry?" the financier said.

"She's leading," Ratty said cheerfully. "She is our leader. She just can't talk as loud as you can."

The door slid open again, revealing an empty corridor.

"Why don't you go and keep her company?" Linn said with distaste. "With luck the entangler will malfunction."

When the reporter had complied, Linn gestured for Brother Andre to go next. He was unsubtly trying to gain a private word with Athena Fimble.

When Andre's turn came, the hem of his robe caught in the door. It opened again a fraction so he could pull it free.

He heard the woman say, "...and I meant no!"

"Think about it, darling. Where else could we be so—"

The door closed.

Chapter 6

The door hissed shut behind Ratty, stranding him in another of the beige tubes. As before, he was lifted and swept along by some ghostly electronic wind. The journey this time was shorter but included three sharp bends. It was no comfort to know that those were designed to block any leakage of hard radiation from the entangler back to the waiting room. Too much knowledge was a dangerous thing. Most people knew that entanglement was the safest form of transportation in the galaxy. Ratty knew that the statistics came from STARS, Inc.

In moments he saw a doorway straight ahead. In sudden panic, he made a wild grab for the doorframe, but the system seemed to anticipate the move. It swung him around so that his hands touched nothing, then set him down within a metal box no larger than a cheap shower cubicle. The door closed.

"Your heartbeat is elevated," Control said. "There is no cause for alarm. Entanglement is the safest form of transportation in the galaxy. Please breathe deeply and slowly... in... out..."

He told the machine to do some inning and outing of its own.

"Take a deep breath and hold it..."

Ratty also knew that entanglement's fatality rate was one hundred percent. His body would now be scanned by a high energy beam that would record the atomic number, location, and energy state of every atom, but in the process it would blast those atoms away from the molecules they constituted and reduce him to nothing. The data would be transmitted to the BERM and thus to the other BERM at the receiving end, which would pass the information to a 3D printer that would create an exact replica of him, using atoms salvaged from other travelers going the other way. The replica would have all his memories and emotions, but it would not be the original Ratty. He was about to die. The fact that no one ever complained of having being turned into feedstock was no comfort.

"You may breathe normally," said a different voice. "Welcome to Climatal 2 Station. We are about to adjust air pressure. If you feel discomfort in your ears, please hold your nose and swallow."

Hiss. The door opened.

He stepped out into a lounge almost exactly like the one he had just left, except that the decor was red and green, the lights a little brighter. It smelled funny, and a circular wall screen displayed a sunlit, cloud-streaked planetscape, mostly ocean. He felt like himself, not a doppelgänger.

Backet was at a snack dispenser. "I am puzzled," she said sourly, "by the absence of attendants. You'd think we were the ones under quarantine, not the Pocosins! I have never known these lounges not to be staffed by humans."

"The lowly may not have been told the news yet." Ratty joined her. He fancied a hot drink, but his hands were still shaking too much to take out of his pockets.

"You must try these," she chirruped. "Gosan pods, a Climatal specialty." She bit into whatever it was. "A sort of fishy chocolate taste."

Ratty had heard of Gosan pods. They were insect pupae, with the larva inside. He declined politely.

Brother Andre entered.

Then Athena Fimble, eyes flashing warnings.

And Linn Lazuline wearing an expression of extreme smugness.

Ratty's nose for a story twitched. Why were those two striking sparks? Had a certain politician been hitting up a certain trillionair for a donation? Or had Lazuline been trying to buy her vote on something? If so, then why had STARS, which knew everything, included them both on this little jaunt?

When everyone had collected a snack and found a seat, he set to work in his demon reporter role. "*Dear* Friend Linn, if you believe that STARS is spinning us moonbeams, then why are you here at all? Your time is worth several thousand libras a minute. Why waste days chasing rainbows?"

He received the usual stare of intense dislike. Very few people ever dared to cross Linn Lazuline, but Ratty got away with it because his research was faultless. The financier's empire was so huge that it contained dozens of smelly little corners where good stories could root.

"Because, sonny, those moonbeams are going to scare the bowels out of the stock market. Pock's is the smallest and least industrialized of the seventeen, so the direct loss of trade would be relatively slight, but the loss of confidence would be huge, and the sectoral economy would not recover for years."

"How much will it cost you personally?"

"Billions."

"So you think that if the great Linn Lazuline proclaims that there is nothing to the story, then people will necessarily believe you?"

Linn sneered. "If my word did not carry weight, STARS would not have invited me to be a witness, would it?"

"Your word *in favor* of sterilization would impress," Ratty said, "just because the result would hurt you. Your word *against* it will seem like the sort of special pleading tycoons always spout, equating the public interest with their own profit." He saw where his own arguments led. "That suggests that STARS must be very sure of its ability to convince you." Interesting!

Lazuline laughed and hurled his empty cup across the lounge. It veered strangely in the artificial gravity and missed the bucket. "Does it? You think I confuse the public's interests with my own, and STARS doesn't? You're always accusing me of being a robber baron, Turnsole, but STARS set up the entanglement links thousands of years ago, and ever since then it's been extracting enormous tariffs for doing no more than maintaining its equipment. Yes, I know it claims to be financing a program of exploration and settlement, but if has added one world to Ayne sector since Prakrit, nineteen centuries ago, it hasn't told any of us peons. It has always defended its monopoly by any means it can find, and bogeymen are its favorite. Sonny, I know for a fact that there never has been an artificial hominin and almost certainly never will be."

"Your evidence for that sweeping statement?" the friar said coldly.

"It is a matter of scientific limits, Brother." Lazuline's tone was barely more respectful than the one he had been using on Ratty. "I own several companies that turn out genetic materials and perform genetic miracles, and I know the billions of libras of research that have to go into changing even one tiny factor in the human genome. To imagine that anyone could redesign us into a new species in less than a hundred thousand years or so is just plain lunacy. The first cuckoos supposedly sprang up less than five thousand years after the start of the Diaspora. We can't create new species now, and scientists of twenty-five millennia ago certainly could not."

"But we modify the basic human genome every time we settle a new world," Backet protested. "I have visited seven worlds, and every time I get doped up with all sorts of horrible chemicals that the natives don't need."

Linn nodded with excessive respect, as if amazed that she could make a pertinent comment. "This is true, Director. We cannot terraform the worlds, so we adapt people. Ayne is said to be the most Earth-like world ever found, but if a traditional earthling—say Brother Andre's St. Francis—had been miraculously transported to Ayne, he would not have survived a month, perhaps not a day.

"We are especially maladapted for Pock's World. In a sense, we all suffer from genetic diseases so far as Pock's is concerned. Our bones and muscles do not fit the gravity, our skins cannot resist the damp and the carcinogens. For short stays, we can get by with drugs and vaccines. To survive longer, we should need extensive gene therapy."

Millie's brow was crumpled in bewilderment. "Aren't you just contradicting what you just said?"

"No," Linn said. "It is a matter of degree."

He turned away to talk to Athena.

Unusually, from Ratty's point of view, he had been speaking the truth. While most people thought that the genetic code was a string of beads that could be cut and spliced at will, it was infinitely more complicated. Every one of the terrestrial species humankind had brought with it on its diaspora—dogs, cats, parrots, even mushrooms—was constructed by a virtually identical set of genes. But genes make up only about two percent of human DNA. The other ninety-eight did not code for proteins, but were equally vital.

One of the ninety-eight's most important functions was to switch genes on and off. It was those 'enhancers' that made the genes produce a Linn Lazuline or a cobra, or something completely different. Much more laboratory tinkering was done with enhancers than with genes. The double helix of DNA was wound around a framework of histone proteins, which were even more complex than the DNA itself. The physical position of the gene in the nucleus at a given stage in development was important in determining how it acted. A single change could produce a cascade of unexpected consequences.

"Well, I believe in cuckoos, Friend Millie," Andre said. "For every world settled we must produce a new subspecies, but they are definitely sub-species. A Pocosin, for example, can mate with a Vakelian and produce viable, if sickly, offspring. Pocosins are very tall; Prakrit people are small; Overgang's are enormous, but all are still human. The Soldier Ants on Jibba, we were told, were an entirely new species, incapable of cross-breeding with us. This made them an abomination in the eyes of the Church and a threat in STARS's, even if they had been well-behaved, which they were not. It only takes one cuckoo in a nest to destroy the legitimate brood."

Millie nodded agreement.

Linn returned to the argument. "But these 'cuckoo men' have been around almost since the beginning? Who had the knowledge then that we lack now? Who—government, person, party, or cult—could ever fund such an effort and keep it secret? Why would anyone be so stupid? For what reason? To create something that would steal away their own children's inheritance and take over the Galaxy? Forget it."

His speech was answered with glum silence. He was articulate, but he was still arguing in his own interests. As Ratty had foreseen, that fact made him less convincing. Was STARS subtle enough to count on that contrarian effect? Would Lazuline's telling the truth persuade people of the lies?

Millie said, "I can never understand why a new species would be such a danger anyway. Surely intelligent races could get along? Isn't the galaxy big enough for all of us?"

No, it wouldn't be. A synthetic hominin would be utterly deadly, because one of the most basic premises of biology was that two species could not occupy the same ecological niche. One must always drive out the other. A sentient competitor would automatically be a mortal foe to humanity, and vice versa. *They* could never be *us*.

"We were created by God in His image," Brother Andre said. "Real threat or not, a man or woman created by mankind must be an abomination in the sight of the Lord. It would have no soul."

"Bully for the Lord," Ratty said. "What evidence do you expect STARS to offer us? A stuffed hand with two opposable thumbs?"

Lazuline shrugged. "Notice that they did not invite any scientists."

"Except me," Backet said.

"No offense intended, Director. You are known as an administrator, not an academic or experimentalist."

The light dimmed and brightened again. Control informed them that it was time to move on.

⊷⊷⊷ ⊷ ⊷ ⊷ ⊷⊷⊷

The lounge in Pyrus 1 was decorated in green, but the air was chilly and stank of chlorine. The wall screen showed a nighttime world, with few lights except a flickering electrical storm and some auroras. No host or hostess stood on the podium to welcome the visitors. They huddled down on the benches to wait.

"I feel like a cookie in a digestive tract," Ratty said, wishing he had brought a warm overcoat. "STARS needs a laxative."

Ignoring him, Backet said, "Why are there no *people?*"

"Because," Athena said, "we will speak more readily without attendants present, and our hosts want to eavesdrop on our talk."

"Oh."

"But I don't care. Friend Linn?"

"Yes, Senator?"

"You tell us that you do not believe in synthetic hominins. I said that I would never vote for sterilization. Let's put those together and find out where we all stand. You first: Will any evidence convince you that Pock's World is a real threat to the sector, and will you then vote to sterilize it?"

"And why should I be first in the hot seat?"

"Because you've done all the talking so far."

He chuckled. "All right. I have strong opinions, but I never close my mind. If STARS shows me a nest of living, breathing, obviously non-human people, then I will believe. And you can bet your bellybutton I will vote to sterilize!"

"Thank you. Brother Andre?"

The old friar sighed. "My duty is merely to report my observations to the Holy Father. I do believe the historical evidence, so I can be convinced in this case, yes. If His Holiness then asks my opinion, I may well say I believe the abomination must be cauterized."

"Director?"

"Well..." Millie seemed to flutter without actually moving. "I suppose I am in the same position as Brother Andre. I will pass on my conclusions to the secretary general, and she can quote it verbatim to the Sector Council or reject it, as she pleases."

Ratty could imagine her report already—fiercely ambivalent. She was a bureaucrat and made a career out of equivocation. Ratty wasted much of his life trying to prize straight answers out of Millie Backets.

Athena showed no annoyance. "Please try to answer the question. Can you be convinced, and will you then advocate sterilization?"

"Yes. And, er... no. Only the Sector Council can decide to take action against a world that threatens the security of the others." Backet smiled at having thus weaseled herself out of danger.

Athena gave up and turned her lustrous gaze on Ratty. He squirmed, for he was accustomed to being a spectator, not a player. His only decision, normally, was how to slant the story, and even now his first reaction was to wonder which would play best. *Alien Monsters Poised to Attack* won easily over *STARS Tries to Hoodwink Public*. Even without that, though...

"Yes, and... probably. I'd much rather vote for an extended quarantine. Pock's World has only one orbital station, connected to only one other world. If you'll pardon some black humor, sterilization is quite literally overkill. It is far more extreme than the situation requires."

"That remains my position," Athena said. "You can easily check the DNA of everyone wanting to leave Pock's World and pick out any that aren't human."

"STARS will reject that argument!" Linn said stubbornly. "You cannot vet a whole world for illicit technology. Sooner or later the monsters would emerge into space. They would establish their own entanglement link to the next habitable star."

"But that would take centuries!" Backet protested. "First they have to capture a couple of nickel-iron asteroids, because nothing else makes a platform stable enough for long-lasted entanglement and sufficiently tough and radiation-proof to survive interstellar travel. They must hollow them, equip them, and maneuver them into a suitable orbit, which alone takes years. Then establish the entanglement link. Then they have to send one of them across twenty or thirty light years."

Full marks to Millie! Ratty couldn't have put it better himself, so far as it went. In fact he suspected that Pock's, although it was reputedly mostly a low-tech world, would have a couple of big advantages if it ever wanted to develop space technology: its initial escape velocity must be low, and Javel's enormous gravity well would provide powerful slingshot boosts.

Lazuline growled impatiently. "But that is precisely STARS's argument—that only STARS can act on the necessary timescale and politicians never see past the next election. STARS is immortal. Like your church, Brother Andre?"

"Let's stay away from controversy," Athena said, "for the Pocosins' sake, if not our own. Who do you fancy in the Spaceball Classic, Ratty?"

Of course nothing ignited controversy faster than sports. Linn was soon rooting for the Comets, which one of his cousins owned, Athena for the Shooting Stars, and Millie, surprisingly, turned out to be an avid fan of the Black Holers. The argument waxed furious until suddenly the lights dimmed again.

A hologram of a young woman in a STARS tunic flickered into view at the podium, obviously a recording. "Your attention, please. Entanglement is the safest form of transportation in the galaxy. You may now proceed to Pock's Station."

Chapter 7

Musing that technology could whisk her across the light years faster than it could brush her hair, Athena was first into the entangler. It was this very ease of interstellar travel that made the Diallelon threat so potent. She stepped out into muggy heat and dimness, plus an overpowering sulfurous stench. By the time all the others had joined her, she had almost stopped coughing, but her eyes still streamed tears. In the twilight she registered only a large room with some furniture; the brightest thing in sight was the customary wall screen displaying the world below the station.

"Gawdamity!" Ratty exclaimed between splutters. "Who put the skunks in the sauna?"

"Welcome to Pock's World," said a singsong voice.

The visitors turned as one.

"I greet you on behalf of the Pocosin STARS. Live and die happy, as we are saying here. My name is Braata, and I will be your host during your stay on Pock's Station."

The speaker on the podium had the extra height found in natives of low gravity worlds, exaggerated by the sinewy build of youth. He wore black shorts supported by suspender straps crossed over his chest in an X, black sandals, and a narrow black headband. There were STARS insignia on the straps and the word 'Steward' on his headband. His hair hung in dark ringlets almost to his shoulders. Surprisingly for what Athena had heard about Pocosins, a fine gold chain around his neck carried a small gold crucifix.

"This is Pock's normal atmosphere?" Linn demanded.

The boy laughed. "I regret to inform that this is diluted. Worldside is more so. Some people find it much unpleasant and decide to terminate their journey here, returning home most imminently. Most tour companies rebate part of fare."

For a moment Athena was tempted to accept that offer—not because of Linn's insistence that this junket was a STARS hoax, but because of her own suspicion that it was a Lazuline hoax. The timing had been much too convenient! But no, she had never been a quitter. Besides, she had promised Proser that she was giving up politics in favor of motherhood.

"We are not tourists!" Backet said. "We are—"

"Indeed I am aware of your honored status," the boy proclaimed cheerfully. "No one else is arriving or departing anymore. You will need a further dose of tonic before descending, and a fungicidal shower. Most Pocosin flora and fauns will not bother you, but Ayne infections may prosper if not removed. Also it is custom here to offer arriving visitors suitable clothing at obscenely inflated prices, but I am authorized to provide same without charge. Downworld your own will fall apart in a day or two. Translators I am also directed to distribute without fee."

Athena had met Pocosins a few times and, as her eyes adjusted to the lighting, she recognized his strange red coloration, as if he had taken a scorching sunburn all over. That explanation would hardly accord with his beaming smile. If he was not as young and eager to please as he was implying, he was a very good actor. She postponed judgment, suspecting he was smarter than he was pretending.

"We just get wet and stay wet?" she asked. "Won't we peel?"

"Not if you take your tonic. Our skins are augmented, you may see. We secrete vernix to repel the water, this being what babies do to keep from wrinkling in the uterus, where high humidity is likewise the norm. Our rad-resistant pigments are modified carotenes, making us this pretty color." His smile was close to a flirt.

"We should have been greeted by an official delegation!" Backet huffed.

"I agree, honored friend, but I am only one choice left on station. High ranks draw lines at purveying haberdashery. I have no shame to extol to you the excellent toughness of our garments, made of seeming amphibian hide, but actually a fungoid fabric grown in vats and almost indestructible. I have had these since I was just nine—Pocosin years." That would be about sixteen Ayne years.

"Then lead us to the tailor," Linn growled.

Ratty muttered, "Take me to your lederhosen."

The store was better lit and well stocked with bright-colored shorts and sandals, which Braata insisted were standard wear. There were also scanty tops for women—but very few bothered with them, he added encouragingly. He offered visors, needed to keep rain out of eyes.

"Do your superiors approve of the way you are wearing yours?" Athena asked, for his was presently perched on the back of his head.

"Is correct this way indoors." He peered around the store. "We have hats somewhere, but only tourists wear them."

"It doesn't rain all the time," Brother Andre said cheerfully. "And, as Friend Braata says, this leathery stuff never gets wet."

The visitors were assigned thumbprint lockers to hold their off-world clothes. Athena had no compunction about going topless; she was not surprised that Millie did. Brother Andre retained his brown robe, accepting only sandals.

When they had showered and changed, young Braata reappeared, towering over all of them, even Linn. He produced a box of earplugs. "Translators," he announced. "Your implants inoperate on Pock's, but ours will convert your speech for us, and these will serve same for you."

"Oh, we know all that," Millie said. "Off-world implants can't communicate with local Brains because they process cognition differently."

Athena put a plug in her ear, and said, "How do I sound?"

Braata replied in Pocosin. Inside her ear a thin voice said, "Very good. Nonetheless I shall not sing to you. The speakers are shrill."

When he led them back to the lounge, he reverted to speaking his personal version of Ayne. "And now I impart bad news. A solar flare has arrived at Javel, and in this wise at Pock's. Javel's prodigious magnetosphere gets most excited at these times. You are completely safe here inside Pock's Station, but the shuttle is not so well shielded against radiation flux. Is needed to wait."

"How long?" several voices demanded.

He shrugged bony shoulders. "Latest estimate was four hours, so expect eight. Is unfortunate, because my superiors were most anxious to show you something and were urgent that you be brought downworld as soon as possible, but is now likely will be too late."

"Do you know what they were to show us?" Linn barked. "Or where it is? Or why we are now too late?" He nodded when the youngster shook his head. "I thought not."

Athena said, "We wish to speak with your supervisor."

To no one's surprise, Braata continued to stonewall, insisting he was the only person left on the station, admitting only that he had been ordered to greet a fact-finding panel of exactly five persons and had no knowledge of a planned sixth. He named no names, either. With the quarantine now official, he would be going downworld with them, evacuating Ayne Station completely.

Director Backet was miffed. "It is very odd that STARS would invite this commission and then not have high-ranking executives here to greet us! But come to think of it, in traveling to eight worlds I have never met anyone in STARS of higher rank than yours!"

Braata nodded solemnly. "That is most curious, Director."

"Why do STARS's senior personnel never reveal their identities? Why are you all so secretive?"

"I have no leave to tell you that, even if I knew."

Ratty laughed. "That's a nice clear answer, for once. How about a hot meal?"

"Expecting there will still be food, but to eat my cooking will indeed be a test of manhood, honored friend."

"You don't have *machines* to do that?"

"I am not sure. I have never been in the kitchens."

"Oh, you're doing great, General! You will go far. Come and give us some geography lessons." Ratty stalked across to inspect the wall screen and the others followed. "Pock's World is very spotty, isn't it?"

Now Braata talked freely. They were viewing dayside, and the white patches were storms, but none were the big Coriolis swirls found on planets with faster rotation. Pock's he said, in what was evidently a standard joke, had no climate, only weather. The little blue patches were seas. There were no oceans. That pinkish circle was a dried-out sea, a salt bed—probably a caldera, but maybe an impact crater. Blacks and some whites were mountains. Red and yellow were active ones. That one was Volcano Bubinga, very active just then. The honored guests would see more actives on the night side shortly. Very few cities.

"We have massive contamination with heavy metals, but no ore deposits of any size. Here and there a little is all. Everything gets so mixed up that you can find lead in your well water one day and arsenic the next. Vegetation gets cooked into coal and that's another source of contamination. We have few metals, so most of our machine parts are grown in vats."

There was a lot of green, but a lot of everything else, too. Athena decided she was not surprised that the air stank if all that yellow was sulfur.

"That is Draff Water," their guide said. "Our largest sea. It extends under that steam. It is most irregular shape, as you can see, because it is subsiding. The bottom is falling out! Then lava rises and you get steam. Ready-cooked fish!"

"Can you eat the fish?" Ratty asked.

"Yes. There are no native fish, because our seas do not last long enough to evolve the same, only amphibians, able to cross country. Off-world fish introduced and so edible. Crops also. Earth rice does well, also Ayne water grass, most tasty."

After a few minutes the station's orbit brought it over the terminator, and Braata pointed out the red glow of erupting volcanoes and the flicker of thunderstorms.

"If nothing is going to happen for a while," Ratty announced, "I am going to unpeel my eyes." He stretched out on a bench and in moments was snoring.

"It's not even lunchtime!" Backet said. "He must have taken taluqdar training."

"More likely a sleep implant in his hypothalamus," Linn said. "They're expensive and dangerous."

Backet drifted away by herself to listen to her recorded briefing. Braata and Brother Andre disappeared into the gloom without saying where they were going. Athena remained, staring at the screen. Not realizing that Linn was still there, she jumped when he spoke right behind her.

"You believe me now when I say STARS's playing games with us?"

She turned. "I thought that before. Now I think it's you playing games. That night at Portolan you hinted at something exactly like this—a few days with no aides around, somewhere we would not be recognized."

"Athena, I told you!" He looked and sounded exasperated. "It was coincidence, I swear! If I had contrived a sex-orgy getaway, do you think I would have invited that bottom-feeding gossip-shitting Turnsole along? And I would certainly have found a more salubrious planet than Pock's. You flatter me if you think I can manipulate STARS. I did suggest you, yes. When Sulcus called, I tried to think of people who couldn't be bought or bamboozled, and yours was the first and last name that came to mind. Will you forget what was said at Portolan? I offered, you declined. Why don't we go back to being old friends?"

She smiled. "All right. Pock's certainly doesn't sound like a honeymoon heaven. Or smell like it."

"They produce some intriguing wines, I'm told," Linn said. "And several very kinky recreational drugs. If you do change your mind, just let me know." Chuckling, he walked away.

Athena stood and stared at a world she might have to condemn to death.

Toody

Ratty was awakened by Linn Lazuline's shouting at him—there was a break in the rad storm, the boat was leaving *right* now, and Lazuline would like nothing better than to leave him behind. Still groggy, Ratty tumbled off the bench and ran after him.

Braata was waiting by a small circular hatch. "This is the lifeboat," he explained, flashing his habitual grin. "Storm is lulled but not stopped, and this gets us out of hot zone faster. Very much faster!"

The interior was barely large enough for six people in three rows of two. Ratty was the last of the off-worlders to board, and the STARS man squeezed in beside him at the back. The two women had the front seats, but even they had no window. At least Pocosin designers provided ample leg room.

"We will be making a fast descent," Control announced. "Please lean back and place your hands at your sides."

"These craft are peppy," Braata warned.

Somewhat! The launch felt like an explosion, flattening the occupants against their chair backs. Braata muttered, "Wow!" and Ratty wondered how the kid could manage to say even that with several tons of rock piled on his chest.

The noise and pressure increased.

"They aren't messing around," the Pocosin mumbled.

Ratty wanted to ask whether it was it better to be pureed than fried, but he couldn't move his tongue, and his mouth felt stretched out to his ears.

After a brief lifetime the awful weight eased briefly. Then it came back, as great as ever. Braking, no doubt. Ratty wondered how old Brother Andre was taking this.

A deep rumble, vibration. "Atmosphere!" Braata said.

At last came silence and a great sense of relief.

"Welcome to Elaterin Landing," Control said. "None of you received radiation dosage in excess of 2.5 rems, so no treatment will be required."

Linn said, "Nice of them to tell us that."

Braata laughed uneasily. "That was probably a record descent, honored friends. Any faster than that and they award certificates posthumously. I have never heard of Elaterin Landing, so welcome to Pock's World."

Andre twisted around to frown at him. "You charge extra for heart attacks, my son? If so, I owe for four."

The boy chuckled. "Normally we administer extreme unction before takeoff, Brother."

Something bumped against the hull. The door opened, admitting a blast of choking, sulfurous steam. Ratty puzzled over the deep roaring sound and realized that it was raining enthusiastically. Coughing and choking, he followed Braata out and staggered under the impact of the deluge. Handheld lights glimmered through a silver mist, but otherwise the night was pitch black and hot as a shower; it was also swarming with lofty half-naked people, all trying to help. With needles hammering into his back and drops drumming on his visor, he was hurried across what seemed to be a wooden bridge to a doorway cut through a wall of cut stone blocks, shining glassily in the rain.

In spite of Pock's low gravity, heavy rain could hurt just as much as it could on Ayne; the drops must reach about the same terminal velocity.

Then he was standing in a stark, bare room, no longer being rained upon but having trouble breathing air so wet. Apparently total saturation was normal on Pock's, for no one mentioned towels. Four other drenched emissaries joined him, with Brother Andre coming last.

Across from the visitors stood a score or so equally soaked men and women in shorts and visors. None of the women wore tops; low gravity was wonderfully supportive.

Between the two groups stood three armed men with their backs to the visitors. Guards? In a flash of alarm, Ratty registered danger. These strangers had come to help decide whether this world should be destroyed. It made sense that the inhabitants must resent that prospect and might try to take out their anger on the commissioners. Braata had vanished. The three muscle-bound red men were not STARS, but they might as well have had *cop* tattooed all over them.

Smiling welcome, a wrinkled man limped forward with a bunch of trumpet-shaped blossoms that glowed fluorescent silver. He shouted something over the waterfall boom of the rain on the roof. Ratty had removed his earplug and had to hunt for it. He was handed a blossom anyway.

When that ceremony had been completed, the visitors were escorted down a long stone staircase—no moving ramps here—and out once more into the pounding, needling downpour. A strong hand emerged from the darkness to grip his arm and help, almost lift, him up a couple of steps into a wagon. A *wagon!* What sort of historical pageant had he fallen into? But at least it had a thatched roof to keep the rain off, and the bench was comfortably padded. He could see almost nothing outside through the sheets of water streaming off the top. The others were boarding, and so were the cops.

A sodden Brother Andre squelched down beside him.

"Did I miss the briefing on time warps, Brother?"

The old friar laughed as if he were enjoying himself hugely. "I forgot to give it, I'm afraid." He raised his voice to include the others. "Pock's World is chronically short of metals, which makes powered machinery expensive, but it will grow a forest in an afternoon, so they use a lot of wood. They have some aircraft, but whenever possible they prefer the slow life. They seem to find the best of both high and low tech. It's only a short ride to the inn, they said."

"Elaterin is an emergency landing," said one of the cops. "We are not on main commercial routes."

Glad to hear it. The wagon began to move—rocking slightly, but not bumping much. Not going very fast, either. The rain dropped to a drizzle and stopped. Everything was still dark, still hot. Ratty could not see what was pulling the wagon, except that they were big, there were two of them, and they had antlers.

⊷⊷⋖⊰ — ⊱⋗⊶⊷

The inn was a collection of sheds with thatched roofs and wicker walls, all of them shining a bright welcome in the dark. They were lit by globes hung on ropes from the rafters, and those were certainly not candles. Human servants, mostly children, were running back and forth between buildings, fetching covered dishes, and making Ratty realize that he was starving. His companions seemed to feel the same way, for they all quickly found seats around a table, overly high seats for off-worlders.

"I suggest you try a little of everything first," Brother Andre said. "That's pickled sparge, a carnivorous plant. Most dishes are spicy, but that looks like scrob, which is bland. And I suspect that's talion. If you would pass it..." He tried it. "Mm, yes! Talion is an acquired taste."

"Where does talion come from, Brother?" Linn inquired suspiciously.

"Ask me after you've tried it."

"I want to know before I try it."

"Rotted tree octopus."

"I shall never know what it tastes like."

Ratty declined the talion, but he did try half a dozen other dishes, found two he liked, and heaped his plate with more of those. The pitchers held a green liquid that tasted like a dry wine and was actually *cold*. This world was starting to show a more hospitable face.

The cops still stood guard, most of the servants departed. Rain was falling again, although not so hard, and a faint light under the eaves heralded dawn. The elderly man of the blossoms reappeared, this time accompanied by a younger man whose standard garb of shorts and visor was augmented by an elbow-length green-and-blue cape, a gauzy cloth pinned at his neck and draped over his left shoulder. Since it served no purpose, it must be important.

"Live and die happy!" he said. "Please continue eating. I welcome you to our world. I am Treddle, gownsman for Gule County. I see our reeve has made you as comfortable as possible on such short notice."

"Very comfortable, thank you," Millie said quickly. "I am Director Backet, of the Sector Council, pleased to meet you, Gownsman, and now I should introduce my fellow commissioners—"

Intercepting a surprised glance from Treddle, Ratty realized that he had been grinning. If this circus did not quickly become known as the Backet Commission, it would be over Millie's dead body. She introduced Athena and Linn, and the Pocosin responded warmly, but when she named Brother Andre, Treddle's reaction was coldly polite.

"You want your co-religionists informed of your arrival, honored friend?"

"If you would be so kind," the friar said. "Cardinal Phare. Pray inform him I am sent by the pope."

Treddle closed his eyes for a moment, cognizing. Then he nodded to Andre. "He greets you in Christ's name and will hasten to meet you. And last but, I am sure, not least?"

"Friend Turnsole," Backet said apologetically.

"A mere reporter," Ratty explained.

The Pocosin smiled again. "Not mere! Even on Pock's we follow your work and admire it, although much subtlety is lost in translation. You are most welcome. I wish your visit could have been for a happier cause."

He was smooth: Ratty thanked him.

"Please excuse my ignorance, gownsmen Treddle, but will you explain what a gownsman is and does?"

"Happily." Treddle chose a seat with a good view of Athena. He was older than Braata, but not much bulkier. His neck was extraordinarily thin. "Governments on Pock's World are mostly democratic, although we have a few kingdoms, one small empire, and some other oddities. All recognize Monody's overall authority. She appoints the priestesses, who tend our spiritual needs, and gownsman, who are her representatives in worldly matters. That's what I *am*. What I *do* is a little less clear. Most of the time I'm a father, a lover, and an agrologist, in about that order, but as a gownsman I'm a general wiper of noses. If Reeve Votal starts oppressing the people of Elaterin or a judge gives bad rulings, then people complain to me. I investigate and try to mediate. If my advice is not accepted, I report the matter to Her Holiness. Your visit is a planetary matter, so I have assumed jurisdiction from the reeve. I will see the village is reimbursed for the costs of sheltering you." He flashed his winning smile. "That sort of thing. I have already reported your presence to Her Holiness. Your arrival here at Elaterin took us by surprise, but her officials are on their way. If you wish to take a few hours' rest, they should be ready to meet with you when you awake."

Backet opened her mouth, but Linn was faster. "How about STARS? Will it be sending someone? It invited us! Do we get to see the evidence that has upset it so much?"

"STARS is far above and beyond my jurisdiction," Treddle said sadly. "I suspect it does not even take orders from Monody. As for the evidence, I am told that it will be shown to you."

"Then it exists?"

The gownsman looked startled. "Oh, yes! Why would you have come so far if..." He peered at their faces. "We do not deny that there are cuckoos loose on Pock's World, honored friends! We just ask for time to hunt them down before you put us all to death."

Chapter 2

The day was hazy and even stuffier than the night had been, with a colorless sky and a flat light from what he assumed was east. It felt like rain. It always felt like rain on Pock's, Brother Andre said. Ratty remarked that the air seemed less stinky that it had earlier. Partial paralysis of the nasal membranes, explained the friar. The visitors were assigned cabins and the others went off to rest for a while, but Ratty was a reporter with a need to record; besides, his implant-initiated sleep on Pock's Station had reset his circadian rhythm to morning. He set off to explore; no one stopped or questioned him.

The inn stood at the edge of a wide clearing, perhaps a kilometer across, and this was clearly an ancient lava bed, a plain of black rock, sharp and ropy. So now he knew why his sandals had such thick soles. He could see no reason for the lava to be there, no volcanic vent or cone, although there was a snow-capped peak in the distance. An expanse of bare rock like that was a ready-made landing ground, and the ugly shuttle still stood in the center, beside the lonely blockhouse. The inn itself comprised a dozen or so wooden buildings, all of them on skids as if they had been brought from elsewhere. Or was that in case they might have to be moved out in a hurry? He inspected the wagon and a paddock containing four of the antlered things, massive slabs of muscle with short legs. He had seen similar brutes before, so their species had been imported from some other world. Edible, likely.

Now what? All around the landing stood dark green jungle, dense, menacing, and impenetrable, but a cleared trail led off from the inn and disappeared around a bend. He set off at a leisurely stroll, which was as fast as he wanted to move in the muggy heat, despite his strange new buoyancy.

The roadway was natural and sloped slightly uphill, the original flow that had flooded the area where the inn now stood; it was ancient, though, being colonized by weeds. Things hiding in them scuttled away from his feet. He wondered if he was being foolhardy in wandering around without a guide. Were tree octopuses dangerous? He decided he would go as far as the bend and then turn back, but when he reached it he saw the view opened up to a wide green meadow. He carried on to inspect that.

There he found a steaming natural pool with a diving board. To swim or not to swim? No one would set up a diving board where man-eating scaly things lurked, would there? He couldn't be any wetter than he was already. A cluster of roofs in the distance must be a town or small village, probably Elaterin itself. There were benches beside the pool, and he sat down gratefully. What the picture needed were some children splashing and laughing: *A World About to Die,* by Ratty Turnsole.

He didn't want to think about that. Reporters must stay objective. He sat and pondered a problem that had been growing on him: Why was STARS so bloody-minded about cuckoos? Granted that they might be dangerous, obviously quarantine would be a workable solution, at least for a few years. Why the frantic haste to destroy an entire world?

Something buzzed high overhead, two somethings. They wheeled around, changed their note to a deeper hum, circled lower. After a couple of circuits they sank down vertically, landing alongside the pool. Intrigued, he rose and walked over to see.

At first glance they looked—and had certainly sounded—like giant insects, but he soon saw that they were non-metallic machines of whimsically insectile design. Each had four transparent wings and six thin legs sprouting from its central thorax, which was furry and doubled as a seat for the rider. The head sported two thin antennae curled backward to serve as handlebars, and two shiny, globular things resembling insect eyes. Behind the thorax, the black, chitinous abdomen was longer than the head and thorax together.

The two riders wore one-shoulder capes, like Treddle's, which suggested that Pock's society was hierarchal, with low-tech wagons for the poor and hi-tech gizmos for the rich.

The drivers had dismounted. They wore the usual leathery shorts, but goggles instead of visors. The gownsman had declared that his cape was a symbol of office, but these two aeronauts were too young to be government officials. Children of the ruling elite? The girl was slender and juvenile, unashamedly displaying conical breasts. The boy was a year or two older and hefty, regarding Ratty with a suspicious scowl and keeping one hand on a nasty-looking device at his waist that was certainly a weapon. His cape was a rusty red; hers was white.

"You're one of the off-worlders," the girl announced. She had pushed her goggles up on her forehead. Her skin was nearer an Ayne folk brown color than a Pocosin red.

Ratty offered a half bow, trying not to stare at her delicious rosy nipples. "I am Ratty Turnsole from Ayne, at your service."

"Of course!" She grinned. "I'm Joy." She did not introduce her pouting companion.

"And a joy to look at."

The boy snarled, "Mind your manners!" He was a full-blooded redskin, in the large economy size. All Pocosin men were tall; add breadth and you got life-threatening beef.

Ratty had made the pun without thinking, but evidently her name translated. It meant what it said. "Are you an off-worlder, too, Friend Joy?"

"*Me?*" Joy laughed. "No, I'm a throwback." She gave him a solemn little-girl pout. "Are you going to let STARS burn Pock's World?"

"Not if I can help it. We haven't seen any evidence yet. We haven't even heard what the evidence is, but Gownsman Treddle told us there is some."

"Yes, there is. We caught one of them at Hederal!" She turned to her companion. "This is as good a place for me to wait as any. Go and fill up the tanks."

The boy turned his pout into a glower. "I won't leave you with *him*."

"Yes, you will! I've had quite enough of you and your fast mouth, Scrob, and if I get one more word of backtalk out of you, I'll send you back to the farm and you'll never see me again. Now go and do as you're told!" If that wasn't high dudgeon, it was getting up there.

She shoved him. She could probably have pummeled him with her dainty fists for an hour without producing any effect at all, but he yielded without argument. Glaring over his shoulder at Ratty, he went back to the two bug-like flying machines and threw a meaty leg over one of them.

"You behave yourself, off-worlder!" he shouted. "Or I'll come after you and kill you!"

Joy yelled, "Grow up, Scrob!"

Scrob manipulated something on the insectile head. Both machines sprang into life, their wings a sudden blur of motion, blowing the grass flat. Then both lifted and flew off, low over the meadow, heading for the village.

Joy took Ratty's hand and pulled him to the nearest bench. "Come and sit over here and tell me about Ayne, Ratty. That's right, isn't it? I call you Ratty, not whatever the other bit was? We get by with one name at a time."

"Yes, call me Ratty. I thought scrob was something one ate."

Joy plumped down on the bench and pulled him down beside her. She sniggered. "A scrob is a tasteless dumpling. I named him that." She pulled off her goggles and shook her springy mop of curls, half of them bleached white and the rest a sort of reddish brown to match her cape. The result should have been absurd and was spectacular. "Do you think he's beautiful?"

"I can't judge boys. I know a beautiful girl when I see one." And the temptation to put an arm around this one was sorely testing his self-control. It had been a very long time since Rose, Robyn, or Patience.

Joy pulled a face of exasperation. "Mother thinks he is. Once—just once!—I told her I liked boys with muscles and she's been throwing them at me ever since. He does have nice shoulders, I suppose."

"And his calves go up and down when he walks," Ratty said helpfully.

She nodded. "And his buns go in and out. But he's a bit short of head jelly, don't you think?"

This was a wonderful conversation and Ratty was recording it all. By Ayne standards she was certainly overdoing the ingénue, but here on Pock's it might be genuine.

"That can be important. Head jelly, I mean."

She shrugged. "Not really. I mean I don't want anything permanent yet."

"Does he? Do you know what Scrob wants?"

"Oh, yes, he wants to make me have a baby."

A magnificent, classic, prize-winning conversation! "Then he doesn't sound very stupid to me."

She sighed. "I don't want all that work quite yet. And I'm worried about getting addicted. Mother's always so bitchy when Bedel is away more than one night. Scrob might be all right, I suppose. If I don't take him, she'll probably just find me someone even worse."

"Your Mother will? Is Scrob your bodyguard? Or is your mother trying to, er, match-make?"

"Both," Joy said. "No one would hurt me, but sometimes a mirbane will attack a flyer, so Scrob carries a zapper to stun it. Stun the mirbane, I mean. He can't hit a blockhouse at arm's length."

Ratty needed a moment to analyze all that, and he was interrupted by a sudden vibration and a strange noise. The pool lapped at its banks. "Earthquake!"

Joy looked at him oddly. "Don't you have those on Ayne?" She had to shout over the noise. The trees were flailing wildly. It stopped.

"Not very often."

She shrugged. "We get one or two a day."

That would explain why the inn buildings looked so portable. Better to bounce than collapse or be overrun by lava. Low-tech might have some advantages.

"We don't have anything like those flyers! I bet they're marvelous fun."

"You don't?" Her eyes went out of focus for a moment. "Ah, lower gravity! And a denser atmosphere, it says. Here comes Scrob now, see. Would you like a ride, just to try one?"

Ratty distrusted Joy's innocently raised eyebrow, but he wasn't going to spoil the Elysian mood by saying so. He would love to take a flyer on a flyer, he said.

The boy set the machines down on the sward nearby and scowled at Ratty when he and Joy arrived. Scrob looked more barroom-brawlish than saintly, but Joy's mother must have chosen him because he had a Brother-Andre-type conscience. At his age Ratty would have bedded this addle-witted young miss on the first attempt. Even now he was tempted, although it would be far too easy to be sporting.

"Get off!" Joy said. "I'm going to let Ratty try."

"And leave me here?"

"Of course not, dummy. You just sit on that one, Ratty darling, and I'll drive them both."

The unfortunate Scrob yielded his seat to Joy and his goggles to Ratty. Ratty straddled the flyer. The seat was surprisingly comfortable, and the faceted eyes were obviously control panels, displaying indicators and buttons labeled in an unfamiliar script. The veined transparent wings howled into life. He just had time to grab the antennae before the ground rushed away beneath him.

"Isn't this fun?" Joy yelled, barely audible over the almighty buzz. "Put your feet on the pedals!"

The pedals were the flyer's two front legs, conveniently placed for resting sandals on. Yes, it was fun, tremendous fun. There was the inn, and the landing field, and the hamlet of a dozen or so houses. Joy increased the power and conversation became totally impossible.

The flyers rose steadily, heading for a sinister-looking thunderhead on the horizon. The world spread out below him, the wind blew scrumptiously cool on his chest and face, and Joy's white cape streamed out behind her. Why was she not turning? How far were they going? Ratty twisted around to look back and could just make out poor Scrob racing across the meadow to the village.

Running in that heat! Why? What was alarming the big lad?

Then Ratty registered the triumphant grin under Joy's goggles and remembered that it was only Ayne implants that did not work on Pock's World. Joy and Scrob could chatter as much as they liked.

He was not going back. Joy had other plans.

Chapter 3

"Did he leave no clue at all where he was going?"

Athena looked around the table, and the others all shook their heads. Gownsman Treddle was back, the commissioners had assembled in the dining room, but Ratty was missing. His bed had not been slept in. To Athena that felt like a bad omen. The foul air was making her nauseated and headachy; she had been unable to rest for worrying about the task ahead of her. Treddle's ready admission that there were Diallelon monsters loose had shocked her to the marrow. She had been in denial all along, convinced that STARS was promoting a giant political scam. Now cruel reality had stripped away her blinkers—the locals believed.

"The only place he could have gone is the village," the gownsman said for the third or fourth time. "Elaterin. The reeve has not seen him, but he'll ask around."

"Are there dangers in the jungle?" Backet asked.

"Oh, yes. Nothing that would deliberately harm him, but if he stepped on a snake or a tenfoot it would attack. I am sure he will turn up safe and sound. It is to nobody's advantage to hamper your work or injure any of you. He may have just twisted an ankle."

"Let's hope he's broken his neck," Linn Lazuline said cheerfully. "If you find out who did it, I'll be happy to pay his legal bills. Meanwhile I suggest we get down to business. What do you have for us, Gownsman?"

Treddle closed his eyes for a moment. "The ship is just tying up. It has brought Gownsmen Oxindole and Skerry. Gownsman

Oxindole is consort and chief advisor to Her Holiness. Gownsman Skerry is her senior advisor on technical matters. In your terms, they are roughly Monody's prime minister and minister of science. You cannot go higher on Pock's World than them, honored friends, except to Her Holiness herself, and I am sure she will grant you an audience."

"No one from STARS?" Linn scowled.

Treddle shrugged. "STARS informed Gownsman Oxindole where you landed and told him to show you the evidence. STARS is beholden to no man, or woman. I urge you to proceed with your inquiry, honored friends, and leave the problem of your missing commissioner to us. We will find him for you, I promise, and send him on."

Athena said, "We shall not be conferring with the gownsmen here?"

"Oh, no, Senator. They have come to escort you to view the evidence." Treddle smiled faintly. "I do not know where it is kept, or even exactly what it is, because obviously such matters must be closely guarded. If you are ready, you may board now. They will answer your questions on the journey."

Athena felt foolish, but obviously the others had misunderstood the program as much as she had. No translation could ever be perfect. She left the room with Millie Backet. They climbed into the waiting wagon.

"Airships are favored by the low gravity, I assume," Athena said.

"No, Senator, although that is an easy misconception." Evidently Millie had been listening to more of her briefing files. "The lifting capability of helium or hydrogen is not affected by gravity, because the air also loses weight in the same proportion. Nor is it affected by pressure, which is quite high because Pock's formed far enough from its sun to capture a lot of volatiles and so has a thick atmosphere. Airships do have a slight advantage here only because average wind velocity is less. The world's slow rotation does not produce cyclonic storms."

Athena wished she had not asked.

The wagon rocked and rattled across the landing ground to where the airship was moored above the blockhouse, shiny, greenish, and enormous, filling the sky. The moment the wagon stopped, Millie scrambled down and practically ran to the staircase. Athena let Treddle disembark next and accepted his helping hand.

He said, "It has been an honor to meet you, Senator."

"And we are grateful for your help. You did say 'consort'? Gownsman Oxindole—you called him 'consort' to the High Priestess?"

"Is that remarkable?" Treddle asked blandly, although there was a twinkle in his eye.

"Your religion is not one of those that require priestesses to remain virginal?"

He laughed aloud. "Of course not! How could she incarnate the Mother for us then?" He touched one knee to the ground. "Live and die happy."

"And you also, Gownsman. Believe me, we shall do everything we can to save your world." She started up the stairs, with Linn and Brother Andre following.

⋯⋯◄ ◄ ◄ ⋅ ⋅⋅ ⋅ ▸ ▸►⋯⋯

The front of the gondola was a small flight deck, occupied by a crew of two gangly young men. The center portion held the motors, a tiny galley, and a toilet. A passenger cabin made up the rear third, but its horseshoe of padded bench was hard put to hold seven people. The walls were all window, offering a soaring panoramic view that was hard to ignore, even when the topic being discussed was the fate of a world. A screen beside the door showed a forward view. Athena's feet only just reached the floor, on this planet of giants.

Gownsman Oxindole was impressive—big and slow-spoken, with silver patches at his temples and more body fat than would be regarded as decent on Ayne; his breasts and neck were flabby. He was courteous to Millie, while seeming unimpressed by her hints that she was in charge of the mission. He queried each of them carefully about their qualifications, pronouncing deliberate, penetrating questions, and his steady stare implied that his impressions were being recorded. That was only to be expected. It was possible, even likely, that the effective ruler of this theocratic world was currently watching the proceedings through her consort's eyes.

The science minister, Gownsman Skerry, was small and scrawny, with every rib showing. He tried to keep his hands clasped on his lap, but when he was talking he would forget and start gesturing, and then they trembled. He was certainly not a well man. Even when silent he tended to move his mouth all the time, and Athena suspected he was in pain. His mini-cape of office was green with fine white stripes, whereas Oxindole's was a rusty red, not far off the color of his skin. She wondered how many varieties there were.

The seventh person present was a boy of nine or ten, introduced as Skerry's son, Solan. He sat beside his father and watched him anxiously, not even paying much attention to the scenery, although at least three volcanoes were visible over the curve of the world and one of them was vomiting red lava. Most Ayne boys would have been staring at that.

When Oxindole came to Brother Andre, his manner cooled. He established that the friar was a papal legate and what that meant.

"And what is your church's attitude to this world of heretics, priest?"

It was never possible to rattle Andre. "If you mean to ask how we feel about your present troubles, the answer is that we are appalled. All human beings are God's children, and we will do anything in our power to help you in your time of need."

"And if Pock's World is harboring an abomination?"

"Then that abomination must be cauterized. Do you plan to defend it?"

"Cauterized? At any cost, you mean? Leaving the Mother with no worshipers? Leaving one less church in the sector to contend with yours?"

The friar kept his voice gentle. "The current problem is not the state of your souls, Gownsman, but of your lives. If you want a character reference for me, ask Emeritus Wisdom for one."

"Your mockery is unseemly!"

"I do not mock. I knew her when I was here many years ago. My name then was Jame Mangold."

Oxindole stared glassily at him for a long minute and then nodded. "Your pardon, Brother. Her Highness sends her greetings." He turned to his companion. "Skerry, please explain the situation to the honored emissaries and tell them what we will show them at Hederal. Answer all their questions fully and volunteer all relevant information."

The thin man nodded several times, like a bird. "As you know, honored friends, any planet tends to vacuum up passing space debris, and the resulting impacts can be deadly. Pock's is especially at risk because we live deep within Javel's enormous gravity well. The energy released in an impact varies as the square of the missile's velocity, so even a tiny asteroid becomes a planet-killer when accelerated by the Mother of Worlds."

The giant planet almost filled the sky behind him, and Athena had to fight hard not to gape at that marvel instead of listening to him. It might officially subtend an angle of thirty degrees, but it looked much bigger, and it was all striped with bands and whorls of red and white cloud. Only at the base was a sliver of it left in shadow, but even that was visible as a faint blue ghost in the sky.

Below that surreal vision, Pock's landscape seemed so conventional as to be almost banal. There were no cities or great rivers, just soft green fields, wooded hummocks, and a scattering of hamlets and whitewashed cottages, each conveniently provided with a little stream or pond. Animals drawing wagons along unpaved lanes! As art it would make her gorge rise; as reality it had an appealing ancestral innocence. Only when she looked for them could she signs of Pock's strangeness: dead lava fields or metallic blue pools that steamed in the sunshine.

"One of STARS's duties," Skerry said, speaking as if he had rehearsed his speech or given it several times before, "in any inhabited system, is to inventory all bodies representing potential impact threats, and to change their orbits if necessary. Seventeen days ago, STARS informed me that its monitoring equipment on Pock's Station had detected a previously unrecorded body in an unstable retrograde orbit around Javel. Detailed observations confirmed that it was of iron-nickel composition, approximately five kilometers in maximum dimension, and had a relatively high temperature, very unevenly distributed. That was proof that it had been used as an interstellar probe. Later that day, high resolution imagery detected artifacts on its surface."

"A probe from where?" Linn barked.

"That was not an easy question to answer. Its present orbit is an elongated ellipse, extending from far outside Pock's orbit, down almost into Javel's atmosphere. We believe that it had been using cloud-skimming as a brake, a dangerous but not impossible tactic. Alternatively, it had been set on a suicide orbit where close encounters with Javel would break it up and eventually absorb it. A third, less likely, possibility is that a slight course deflection will cause it to be hurled out of the system by Javel's gravity, in the direction of New Winish.

"Without knowing when it entered the system or what maneuvers were used to brake it, we could not tell where the pirate came from, or when. Not only did STARS have no record of such a vessel, but the implication was that this one had deliberately come in at high speed, without using the power braking that would have revealed it to STARS monitoring. In other words, it arrived in the Pock's system clandestinely. We cannot be certain, but most likely it came from the neighboring Canaster sector, and almost certainly from the nearest inhabited world, Malacostraca. All others are much farther away, beyond safe entanglement limit."

Brother Andre said, "I thought Malacostraca was sterilized centuries ago."

Skerry glanced around his listeners, almost as if worried he might be boring them. "We do not know that. The link was broken and contact was lost. Even STARS says it does not know why. So it says now."

"Interesting. Please continue, and excuse my interruption."

"We had a lucky break when we reexamined old records and discovered images of a dim, blue-shifted star that appeared more than a hundred years ago, several degrees off the direct Malacostracan line of sight, against a background of a globular cluster containing millions of stars. It had been overlooked, as had its subsequent disappearance, which of course would have been when powered braking was discontinued. By analyses of Doppler shifts in the earlier radiation, we established the most probable trajectory, and then examined recent records that should have caught sight of it. By elimination, we concluded that the pirate could have left the Malacostracan system about three centuries ago and arrived in the Pock's system within the last two or three fortnights. This is our best guess."

Athena said, "And STARS insists that it does not know whether Malacostraca is still inhabited? Or by whom?"

Skerry smiled mirthlessly. "STARS has put out several stories about Malacostraca. This year's version is that it does not know what happened. It is popular belief that the Canaster Sector STARS took out the world to destroy a synthetic hominin strain known as the Zombies, but that has never been confirmed."

"I don't see why it should be a mystery," Millie complained. "Can't you detect radio signals from Malacostraca?"

"Not really, Director," Skerry kept his smile courteous, although his son was pulling faces as if even he knew the answer.

Even Athena did. Technically a radio message could be beamed to another inhabited world. In practice the senders would have to wait several lifetimes for a reply and nobody at the other end would be listening, so they would never get one. Mere eavesdropping was not practical at stellar distances. For secrecy and economy and several technical reasons, modern electromagnetic signals were transmitted in short bursts on varying frequencies and the lowest possible power. If they could even be detected, they could not be separated or read without the appropriate protocol, and the chatter of an entire planet would appear as white noise.

"Malacostraca might be inhabited, but we can't tell," Skerry said. "If there were ever Zombies there, they may have won. We don't know."

"And now they want to kill us!" said the boy.

He had tears in his eyes. Solan was about the age Chyle had been when he drowned. If a child like him must be aboard this ship at all, he ought to be forward with the crew, pretending to fly it, not listening to horror stories.

His father's nod was both agreement and a gentle indication that he should not interrupt. "STARS has limited space-faring capability within this system, and the pirate's retrograde, eccentric orbit made it difficult to intercept. At apoapsis it is out of range, at periapsis it is hurtling over Javel's cloud tops a third of a million kilometers per hour. But a vessel was found and a mission sent to investigate. Logistics limited it to a crew of five and restricted their stay to a few hours."

"You mean a STARS expedition, of course?" Linn said skeptically.

Skerry started to shake his head and was taken with a sudden coughing fit. Gownsman Oxindole had been watching his sick friend with obvious concern and now intervened.

"No, a joint expedition. STARS has been extremely cooperative in this venture. It is definitely as worried as we are. It provided two men to run the ship. The other three were experts provided by three of the larger planetary governments, at Monody's request."

"And what did this joint expedition discover?"

"They forced an entry and found living quarters that had been recently used. We had thought to include a police forensic expert, and she recovered fingerprints of at least twelve persons; fresh prints, not years old. Also, I regret to report, traces of DNA, which has been identified as hominin but not human."

So there it was—the case against Pock's. Athena felt ill. STARS had not been bluffing. She glanced at the faces: Millie horrified, Brother Andre black as thunder, Linn perhaps still skeptical.

"They analyzed bits of the asteroid," young Solan said hesitantly. Receiving a smile and a nod from Oxindole, he went on. "And the isotopes were right for the Malacostraca system. The stuff on the outside was mostly burned away, but they found a Wong-Hui projector and an entangler inside."

Skerry had recovered. He chuckled and patted his son's knee. "You have big ears! As my assistant says, honored friends, the isotope ratios were compatible with an origin in the Malacostracan system, as defined by ancient records. The exterior equipment had been damaged by one or more passages through the Javel's exosphere but did include identifiable remains of two shuttle cradles, both empty. The entanglement equipment had been reset so we could not establish what the linkage parameters had been."

"Very neat," Linn murmured. "The dreaded cuckoos launched the probe centuries ago, sending it by a devious route. When it neared this system, the remote descendants of the original cuckoos dispatched a force of at least twelve through the entangler—"

Skerry said, "We estimate from the layout of the quarters and the size of the shuttle cradles that the force probably comprised about fifty persons. We have not finished analyzing DNA residue, but it represents at least a score of individuals, and we suspect both men and women, as you would expect in a colonizing mission."

"Really?" Athena said. "I was imagining a cuckoo invading force as an army of identical clones." Why did she think that? Had she been cognizing too many space operas?

"Would that they were, Senator! Then it would be child's play for us to tailor a virus that killed them all dead and merely made us sneeze. Cloning is a sort of parthenogenesis, asexual reproduction. Many plants and some animal species reproduce asexually. It works well in the short term, but the result is a monoculture that is highly susceptible to disease. In asexual species, whenever a new bug comes along that can kill a mother and her daughters, then their whole line is likely to get wiped out. One of the main benefits of sex is that the father may introduce genes to provide some immunity to some of the offspring. I dearly wish that the cuckoos were clones."

Linn said, "So this suicide squad rode the hellfire around Javel a time or two until the mother ship had dropped enough velocity to let the shuttles make safe landings on Pock's World. That's it? Mission accomplished?"

Oxindole broke in angrily. "Do you disbelieve us, Lazuline? You imagine we are making all this up just to give STARS an excuse to burn our world to cinders and destroy us all?"

Undeterred, Linn stared back coldly. "No. I just suspect that STARS could have faked it all to deceive us by deceiving you. You may not be aware of this, but STARS is politically threatened elsewhere in the sector and may be preparing to cut your throats and then shout that there are killers loose. Have you found the shuttles yet?"

Skerry was leaning back, exhausted by his long lecture, clasping his son's hand. Oxindole answered.

"We found one. Thirteen volcanoes are currently active. It would be easy to put a shuttle on remote and run it into a lava lake, so we looked there first. We saw what we believe to be the remains of a shuttle, half melted and completely out of reach. STARS hoped to be able to show it to you, but you were delayed by the solar flare. The last of the wreckage disappeared yesterday."

"Very convenient! Everything is always just out of reach."

"Not quite all!" Oxindole frowned and closed his eyes. Then his frown became a scowl, and after a moment he opened them again and glared across at Brother Andre.

"Are you familiar with a man named Braata?"

"I have met him, yes."

"He is extraordinarily anxious to speak with you. He has bullied his way up through the hierarchy of your church to Cardinal Phare, and now Phare has talked his way through my defenses also, although I threatened to behead people if I was interrupted."

The friar smiled faintly. "Braata is impressive! A STARS trainee, he met us on Pock's Station. He is a member of my church."

"You spoke with him privately when we landed," Linn said. "You were the last to come into the blockhouse. He never did."

"He asked my blessing. We shared a moment of prayer in the rain. But I do not know why he should be so anxious to speak with me now."

The airship was already turning.

"It seems we have to find out," the gownsman said crossly. "However urgent our business, it has to wait for Friend Braata. We are well out over Draff Water now, and so is he, chasing us on a flyer. He claims he is about to run out of fuel."

Chapter 4

Ratty's first sight of the Mother nearly caused him to fall a thousand meters into the scenery. He had twisted around to see how Scrob was doing, because the solitary flier chasing after them had to be Scrob. Having stolen, rented, or otherwise acquired another machine in Elaterin, he had been gaining slowly all morning, while Ratty and Joy cruised on relentlessly over the phantasmagorical landscape of Pock's World. Unable to talk to his kidnapper, Ratty had been packing his portable recorder with incredible visual memories of geysers, old lava beds, ripening fields, jungle, and rugged terrain like nothing he had ever seen before. Cliffs were steeper in low gravity, waterfalls slower, the trees higher and more widely crowned. If all else failed, the show would have to be *Last Views of a Lost World* by Ratty Turnsole.

Since dawn he had assumed that the oddly flat light was just sunlight through a haze. He should have guessed the truth when the flyers crossed a wide expanse of water, apparently a channel between two large lakes or seas—large enough that both of them stretched away over the curvature of the world. A stupendous wave, a wall of foam about a hundred meters high, was sweeping through this gap. He had even guessed that it must be a tidal bore, but he had not looked around to see what might be raising such a tide. Then he turned to check on Scrob and almost fell off his flyer. There was no sun. It was Javel that lit up the world. The Mother was a vast brightness in the sky, a disk of curlicue red and white cloud bands, a world terrifyingly huge. It was a substitute sun, its light bright enough to feel warm on his face. After Ratty recovered his balance, he was able to reconcile what he was seeing with what Brother Andre had said. The sun was still below the horizon and might not rise for days. Then, presumably, the weather would get even hotter.

Scrob caught up at last, greeting Ratty with a gesture that he had not met before but whose meaning he could guess. He responded with the Ayne equivalent, wondering if it would cost him teeth when the opportunity arose.

The opportunity came quite soon after that. Joy put her flyer into a shallow dive, taking Ratty's with it. Scrob followed. Her objective was a village on the shore of an irregular lake, one that looked small enough not to come raging ashore at high tide. As she had at Elaterin, she avoided the settlement itself, and landed instead on a grassy knoll a short distance away.

She dismounted, hauled off her goggles, and turned to grin at her prisoner.

"Sorry. I couldn't resist it! I mean no harm."

Ratty smiled back. "No offense. I'll follow you anywhere, lady. Where are you taking me?"

"To meet Monody."

"That's the big peach? She who must be obeyed?"

Scrob's flyer landed beside them. "Idiot!" he yelled, but he was speaking to Joy. "What would you have done if a mirbane had attacked when I wasn't there?"

"Given it Ratty of course."

Scrob leered. "Hey! Good idea!"

"Fine by me," Ratty said. "But my knights-errant's union insists I charge at least one kiss a day for being standby human sacrifice." (Had Brother Andre's accusations of human sacrifice been based on fact or just prejudice?)

Scrob bristled. "You shut your filthy mouth, off-worlder! Do you know who you're speaking to?"

"Somebody-important's daughter, but she's so lovely I don't care who she is. I know her mother has terrible taste in gorillas."

"Scum! You want me to beat some manners into this tourist, my lady?"

"That will do, both of two!" Joy said, obviously enjoying the rivalry. "Scrob, go and refuel. And requisition something to eat. No! Better still, leave our two flyers here and tell them I'm on my way and want lunch."

Her guard looked doubtful. "Is that wise?"

She stamped her foot on the grass. "Do as you're told!"

Scrob shrugged his beefy shoulders and sent his flyer howl-
ing into the air, leaving Ratty alone on the hillside with Joy. She
attempted a haughty expression.

"It was very improper of you to propose kissing!"

Ratty never refused such blatant offers. A good kiss required a tight hug and two tongues. Chest-to-chest contact
made a kiss even better. This was a very good kiss indeed. The
taste of her mouth was sheer paradise. It was not an easy kiss
to end.

Joy had flushed almost as red as a normal Pocosin, staring
at him in disbelief. "You dare!"

Had she not realized she was issuing a challenge, or had
she truly not believed he would accept it?

"You didn't exactly struggle. Sit down and tell me what I
did wrong." He let himself fall backward straight-legged,
braking his landing with outstretched arms. It was easy in the
lower gravity. He left his legs straight and patted the grass
beside him. "Here."

Biting her lip as if to stop a smile, Joy accepted his challenge in turn and sat down elbow-to-elbow. He put his arm
around her. She went rigid for a moment, then relaxed when
she realized he was not about to do more.

"You could get beheaded for this, you know?"

"I charge more than one kiss for beheadings. Now, who are
you really?"

"Monody."

He hesitated, then said cautiously, "You said you were taking me to meet Monody."

"I am. I was on my way to visit Wisdom when I heard
about the off-worlders at Elaterin." Grin again. "I not supposed to meddle in real business yet, just ceremonial stuff, but
the chance was irresistible. I know she'll want to meet you,
and she doesn't get about much any more."

Ratty felt synapses ticking over. "How many of you are
there, Monody?"

"Four: Wisdom, Duty, Love, and Joy."

"Incarnations of the Mother?"

She nodded. He inspected her red and white curls. He
looked up at enormous, cloud-swirled Javel. "That's why you
wear your hair like that?"

"No." She made an effort to appear serious. "I'd better begin your education, Friend Ratty, because I really wouldn't
like to see your beautiful head chopped off."

"You could keep it on your dressing table and kiss it as often as you liked."

She sniggered. "You are incredible! Listen! Many centuries ago—roughly ten thousand years standard— the link from Malacostraca was completed and the first settlers began coming through. For a long time life was very hard here. They had to take massive tonic to combat the bad air and the poisons, and most of them died young. The geneticists kept working on the problems, of course, modifying the germ plasm, using *in vitro* fertilization to maximize genetic diversity." She looked to see how he was reacting to her recitation.

"This is true of all frontier worlds."

"Yes. And they brought in fertilized ova from the older worlds. That's standard practice, too, to widen the gene base. The first improvement they devised was the red pigment that keeps Pocosins from dying of skin cancer before they're twenty. But one of the imported ova rejected the treatment. It developed into a female infant with unchanged skin color. She seemed healthy otherwise, so she was fostered out and grew up into a remarkable young woman."

He studied her smirk, almost nose to nose. "An incredibly beautiful one."

"I didn't mean that!" She colored and looked away. "No other man would *dare* say things like that to me."

That explained a lot. At her age she should have learned how to deal with sweet talk from boys on the make. It was wonderful to see the pleasure his ham-fisted flattery was giving her, but now her reaction was starting to interest his hormones, and he had no intention of letting this encounter get out of hand. Human sacrifice or not, raping a juvenile high priestess was likely to be a capital offense. "Why not? It's true."

"Where was I?"

"You had just grown up."

"Yes. Monody—she was the first—was born with this hair of mine, part red, part white."

"Mosaicism."

"What?"

"It's called 'mosaicism,'" he said, just to prove that he could play the jargon game too. "Women have two X chromosomes and men have only one, so any gene on an X chromosome has to function adequately without a matching partner. Otherwise women would get too much of whatever proteins it produces, or else men would not get enough. Early in its development a fetus suppresses one X, but it isn't consistent in the one it suppresses, so half your cells use the X you got from your father and half the one you got from your mother."

He was quoting a cog-doc he'd done some years ago, but he thought he'd got it right.

Joy smirked and patted her curls. "I had no father. Do you find that freakish?"

"Far from it. It excites me. It makes me wonder naughty things."

"You *mustn't* say things like that! Scrob will flatten you, and Bedel would back him up. Monody truly was remarkable. There are lots of wonderful stories about her. I won't ask you to believe those, 'cause I know off-worlders don't accept her miracles. But when she was grown up, about my age, the settlers suddenly began dying off even faster, and the doctors could find no reason. Monody organized a pilgrimage to Quassia. That's the city of the Old Ones—not Tourist Quassia, but Real Quassia. There she was granted a vision of the Querent. You don't have to believe it, but when she came back down from Quassia, she spoke of her revelation and announced that all those who prayed to the Mother of Worlds would be cured of the unknown disease."

"And it worked?"

"Oh, yes. Within a fortnight it was obvious that none of her followers were dying but others still were. Everybody lined up to join the Church of the Mother, and Monody was high priestess.

"One part of her revelation I must tell you, though. She announced that she would bring forth a daughter to be her successor and after the right number of days she did bear a daughter. Some people scoffed, but the geneticists tested mother and child and showed that they were identical."

The geneticists in question would have been followers, of course. "Parthenogenetic birth is not uncommon," Ratty said. "It doesn't occur naturally among humans, but other species use it. Men are an expensive luxury."

That brought back her dimples. "But a nice one!"

"So ever since then, the high priestesses have followed her example?"

"Not quite. The first Monody's quickening was a gift from the Mother, but when her daughter was grown, Monody told her to go and make love to a man."

"Ah. Someone like Scrob?"

"Any man." From the way she was watching for his reaction again, he could tell that something big was coming. "The man doesn't father the child. See, our oocytes do not undergo meiosis. That's when an ovum cell discards half its chromosomes, you know. A sperm does much the same, then sex brings the two halves together and makes a whole, a zygote." She certainly knew her technical bafflegab. "Ours is a special form of parthenogenesis called pseudogamy. It's rare, but it does occur in other species. Our ovulation is triggered by the presence of seminal fluid in the uterus. Then my ovaries will release an ovum identical to the ovum that formed me and the ovum that formed my mother and so on, back through every Monody."

"Seminal fluid, mm?" Ratty could never recall hearing that mentioned on a first date. So the central dogma was a virgin priestess ever renewed. More likely her bizarre hair coloring was just a dominant gene passed on in orthodox fashion. In that case, what did they do with the male babies?

Joy sighed. "Now you see why I need someone like Scrob? It's time I made my choice. Monody keeps nagging me, all of them, especially my mother! She's Love and anxious to be Duty. I don't know... Scrob's nice enough. He's willing, too!"

"I don't doubt he is!" Ratty's imagination was already in overdrive.

"It's an honor to be the Child Giver," she protested. "He gets to wear the cape all his life and be a gownsman, even an important one if he has any talent. Mother's Giver, Bedel, is already Duty's chief advisor on science matters. Givers have special privileges, like a right of appeal directly to Duty herself. Scrob could live off that alone all his days!"

Oh, she was lovely, and if she were just two years older, or if he didn't have a conscience... but he did, damn it! "You want my opinion, as an outsider?"

"No! Yes."

"I think you're being treated very badly." She obviously did not realize that she was terrified, but she was, and justifiably so. "If you wanted Scrob it would have happened by now. Send Scrob away. There's no shortage of boys, with muscles or without. Tell them you need more time. One day something will just go *click!* and you'll know. It never needs words, Joy, it just happens."

She sighed. "Scrob will be wondering what we're doing. We'd better go."

Her lips were in place to be kissed, so Ratty kissed them. Her arms went around him and he thought she was going to pull him down on the grass. She didn't—but it was he who ended the kiss.

She sighed. "A few more minutes and you'd have *clicked* like mad."

"I know. You're taking quite a risk, Joy. Men can start behaving irrationally when you tease them like this."

Walking back to the flyers, she said, "I wonder if Scrob can kiss like that?"

"Teach him. You do it very well."

"Stop that! And behave yourself when we get to the village, or they'll tear you to pieces."

Chapter 5

Hunches were usually the work of the devil. People who prophesied or thought they heard the Holy Spirit speaking to them were in grave danger of error. Nevertheless, Brother Andre had a strong hunch that whatever message young Braata was so anxious to deliver must be extremely important. He had seemed like a level-headed young man, not one to gamble his life.

While the airship retraced its route over the sea and the passengers studied the forward view screen, the two gowns-men had fallen silent, catching up on cognition, no doubt. When Oxindole suddenly started laughing, everyone looked at him in surprise.

"We have found your missing commissioner," he said. "Early this morning a youth wearing a red cape brought two flyers to Elaterin and demanded fuel in the name of the Mother. Of course they were happy to give it to him. Shortly after that he returned on foot in a seriously overheated condition and requisitioned the fastest flyer in the village."

Gownsman Skerry cackled and Andre nearly did. Suddenly he was awash in nostalgia, remembering a girl on a flyer.

Skerry said, "Joy?"

Joy or Love! It had been fifty years, and Andre had never met this current girl, but he knew her. Everyone else just looked puzzled, even young Solan.

"A moment," Oxindole said, eyes unfocussed. Then he chuckled again and told Skerry, "She left Ushabti at first light on her way home to Abietin. She had put a block on calls, but that has been overridden. Love reports that her errant daughter is currently cadging a meal off some unfortunate village named Fanfaronade and has admitted to having an uninvited guest along. Her immediate future looks somewhat clouded, her mother says."

"I'm sure it will be!" Andre agreed meaningfully, earning puzzled looks. "I recall a similar incident long ago. Friend Ratty is in no danger." No physical danger, although his immortal soul might be threatened.

"But a certain young priestess is!" Oxindole said. "Her mother was just the same at her age." As Duty's consort he was the equivalent of Joy's foster grandfather.

"Dad!" Solan shouted, pointing at the screen. "There's the flyer!"

⊸▸◌◦ ⟵ ⊰ — ⊱ ⟶ ◦◌◂⊸

The propellers slowed and stopped. The airship hung motionless, drifting between a steel-blue sea and a sky speckled with miniature clouds. The flyer climbed toward it. The floor hatch was located in the passenger cabin, and soon one of the crewmen came in carrying a roll of dowels and rope.

"You need us to get out of the way, Captain?" Oxindole asked.

"If one of you wouldn't mind? To preserve the trim."

Andre opened his mouth to volunteer, but Athena Fimble beat him to it.

"I must be close to your mass, Captain. And I am not at all sure that I want to watch." She headed forward, to where the other crewman was presumably handling the controls.

The captain opened the hatch, and a gale blew in.

Oxindole said, "We must all try not to fall out. Is this going to be easy or difficult?"

"It's tricky," the man admitted. "Very tricky. Can't land on water, so we'll have to do it this way, but the wash from the flyer blows the end of the ladder about, you see."

"You can't weight it with something?"

"Don't have anything suitable, Gownsman. Anything heavy enough might hit the flyer or the rider."

"Me!" Solan shouted. "Let me! I can do it."

His father said, "Shush!"

"No, Dad! I've seen it done on *Wild Adventure*. You need someone small. It's always the lightest. Naik did it in *Space Boy*."

Cog dramas, Andre decided, not real life. Everyone waited for the crewman to comment, but he didn't, and there was sudden tension.

"What's involved?" Skerry asked.

"It's not *really* dangerous," the man said, giving him a steady stare. "The real danger's to the rider, when he transfers to the ladder. He can slip, or the ladder can tangle in the wings.... The boy could help steady it, see. We'd tie the ladder to these cleats and tie the lad to the ladder, so he isn't going to fall in the sea or anything. He might get banged on the flyer, or swiped by the wings."

"In which case he breaks a few bones," Skerry said. "But it's in a good cause. You really dare try this, son?"

Solan nodded earnestly. "Yes, sir."

"Then I'm proud of you. Carry on, Captain."

The man trussed the boy to the ladder at waist and ankles. Now the flyer buzzed noisily a few meters below the hatch, but the rider was having trouble holding it there, and his goggled face peered up anxiously.

"He can't come any closer than that," the captain said. "The backwash gets him. All right, lad. Just slide out and we'll let you down gently."

Andre closed his eyes. *Holy Mother of God, whose Son taught us that a man could have no greater love than to give up his life for another, I beseech you to succor this boy who risks his for a man he has never met. Pray for him and cherish him for your Son's sake. Amen.*

Rung by rung the ladder clattered over the lip of the hatch, held back by the captain and Oxindole. Solan spun on the end, starting to swing as he drew close to his objective. A flyer's wings were resilient and not sharp, but they moved at great speed; they could maim—Andre had known a man who had lost an arm to a flyer. The rider freed one hand from the controls and caught the boy's leg, holding him clear of the wings' silvery mist. Man and boy transferred grips as Solan descended; he took hold of the handlebars and slid down past the machine's head. Braata grabbed the ladder and hauled himself up with his hands, seeking to find a foothold without kicking his rescuer. He had barely cleared the saddle when the flyer's motor coughed and died. In a sudden, awful silence, the machine fell away like a stone, leaving man and boy gyrating wildly.

Braata came scrambling upward, and willing hands helped him into the gondola. Moments later, Solan was hauled in and the hatch closed. Everyone was cheering. Skerry wept as he hugged his son.

Braata was still the terra cotta human pylon he had been on Pock's Station, but now his shorts were green plaid instead of black. His mop of brown hair was a hopeless tangle. He pulled off his goggles and was about to kneel to Brother Andre, but then he saw Oxindole and knelt to him instead.

"Rise," the gownsman said. "You have a lot of explaining to do, Friend Braata. That is your name? Did you turn off that motor, or did the flyer really run out of fuel right at the critical moment?"

"I am Braata, Gownsman, but that is my STARS name. The flyer was rocking, so it may not have been completely out of fuel, but it has been running on fumes for some time."

"Well you probably have Solan, here, to thank for your life, so you may do that first."

Without rising, Braata pivoted to face the boy and clasped both his hands. "I am evermore in your debt, Young Friend Solan. Every day of my life I will know I owe it to your courage. And no matter how long I live, I will never meet a braver man than you."

Reality had just taught the boy how it differed from fiction, and his normally ruddy cheeks were still a pale pink shade. He licked his lips. "I won't do it again," he said solemnly. Everyone laughed.

Except Andre. The child had not intended to be funny.

"You're shivering," his father said. "Come and sit by me. Oh, how proud your mother would have been!"

The captain went forward, Athena returned, and the airship started moving. Braata was on his feet, for there were no seats to spare. He looked longingly at Brother Andre.

"We can have a private chat later," Andre said, "and I will hear your confession, if that is what you want. But your explanation cannot be kept confidential. What is this urgent message you risked your life to deliver?"

"I have much to confess when the time comes, father." He turned back to Oxindole and knelt so that their eyes were more or less level. "Honored Gownsman, my registered name is Zyemindar. As Braata, I hold the rank of engineer second class in STARS. Following normal STARS procedure, in my private life I must conceal my connection with STARS. My family believes I am employed by the General Asteroid Mining Corporation."

"So you are giving up a lucrative career and probably breaking oaths by coming to tell Brother Andre something. What is this so—urgent message?"

"I came to tell him and his companions—and you, Gownsman—that their mission is a sham."

A great surge of hope snatched Andre's breath away. "You mean that there is no Diallelon Abomination? The pirate probe was a fake?"

But that would not explain the devastation on Braata's face.

"Alas, no, Brother. When I reported to my supervisor this morning, I was told to proceed to Nervine Landing and stand by for evacuation as soon as the current radiation storm abates. Or... "

"Or what, Lieutenant?" Oxindole asked.

The boy drew a deep breath. "Or three days from now, whichever comes sooner."

Skerry barked, "No!" and started to cough uncontrollably.

Others tried to speak, but Linn Lazuline was the loudest. "What's happening three days from now?"

"Four days," Zyemindar said. "You know about the probe. While I was aboard it, STARS set it on an impact trajectory. I didn't know, I swear! And there's nothing anyone can do about it now. I made sure of that, may Lord Jesus forgive me. Next Sixtrdy it will sterilize the world."

Chapter 6

Ratty had never witnessed anything quite like Joy's visit to the village, not even the multitude cheering the new pope in St. Peter's Square. Here there were only a few dozen people, but they had worship enough for thousands. They groveling in the dirt for her, they sang hymns on their knees to her, and every face shone with love and devotion. The local gownsman—a plump fishwife with a rather grubby white cape—made a speech referring to Her Holiness's previous visit, 278 years ago, which had ever since been a source of pride in the community.

They had laid out enough food to feed a dozen priestesses, and they watched in delight as Joy sampled every dish, sitting in state in the village square. Boys rolled on the ground, punching and swearing, fighting over which of them would have the honor of washing and polishing the visitors' flyers.

Her Holiness's handsome young squire was accorded honors not far short of hers, but Scrob accepted the adulation with practiced grace. He listened carefully to complaints about taxes and harbor repairs and delays in providing medical services. The villagers were slightly disconcerted by her other companion, probably the first off-worlder they had ever seen, but even he was treated like royalty. Ratty would have needed a year to eat every dish that was offered to him, but he did the best he could. He asked about earthquakes and volcanoes and weather, recording everything. He noted that the buildings were made of wood and sat on skids.

Before leaving, Joy blessed every villager individually, from babe in arms to bedridden ancient. In her reply to the speeches, she promised nothing, certainly not miracles. She never claimed that she was the same woman who had trodden the same mud there so long ago. She did not deny it either. Nor did she claim to be the high priestess, because technically that was still Duty, her grandmother. Did the villagers understand those distinctions, or did they truly believe that this was the original Monody, immortal, young or old as she pleased to appear? Ratty was not crass enough to ask them, but while every inhabitant was intent on Her Holiness's speech, he did ask Scrob.

The gownsman shrugged. "They know and prefer not to know."

That pat little koan sounded like official doctrine from his training, but it was probably correct. Monody was eternal. A man might see her old in his youth and youthful in his old age. Why quibble? She was the Mother and appeared in whatever mode was necessary.

→×●←=□— ▷→●×←

Overhead Javel was waning to a crescent and the eastern sky was growing brighter. The flyers passed through a rain squall and were soaked. That was a minor nuisance, to be ignored. Later, though, they came to a thunderstorm athwart their path and Scrob grew angry, shouting and gesturing downward. Evidently he won the cognized argument, for soon the flyers swooped down to the shore of a misty pond in a woody glade.

Joy was pouting. "This is stupid!" she told Ratty. "We'll never get to Abietin if we have to wait this out."

Strong winds were rare on Pock's—air usually just went up and down—but a thunderstorm could be dangerous anywhere, and obviously Scrob did have some authority over Joy, for he ignored her anger, folding his meaty arms and looking stubborn.

"Go and see if the water's good for bathing," she told him sulkily. He dismounted and strolled off. "Your friends know where you are."

Ratty said, "Are you in trouble?"

She grinned. "Of course! I'm *supposed* to be in trouble. My job is to teach Mother patience. She'll scream and I'll scream back and nothing will happen. Wait until we get to Wisdom!

She'll tell me she was just the same at my age. She always says so, and she says Duty was worse, but Love was a goody-goody."

"You can't all be exactly the same. Clones never are."

"Not quite, no."

Massive rain drops were thumping down. Thunder rumbled. Ratty hated thunder. It reminded him of his parents' untimely end.

"Wisdom must have been quite a cutup," Joy said, watching Scrob and not Ratty. "She never appointed a consort. She had quite a few unofficial ones, Duty says, but none ever lasted long."

"Consort is not the same as child giver?" They kept sliding back to this subject.

"Not usually. Oxindole is both; he's Duty's giver and consort and chief advisor. Bedel is Love's consort but wasn't her giver." Joy pulled a face. "If I don't want Scrob in my bed even once, you think I could stand him for a lifetime?"

"That's up to you to decide. Not your mother. You."

She smiled. "I know, but thanks for the reassurance. Wisdom never told anyone who her giver was. Just a guy she met in a saloon, was all she would ever say. Which is stupid! Can you imagine what would happen if I walked into a saloon? He must have been a very unsuitable choice. Married, likely."

Thunder banged almost overhead and Ratty jumped. Scrob was up to his neck in the pool and beckoning.

Joy said, "Come on!" She dismounted and took off at a run. Ratty followed and they plunged in together without even breaking stride. Hot sulfur water was not much different from air on Pock's World.

⟶⟨ ⟩⟶

Abietin, the site of Monody's principal residence, stood in rugged, wooded country between two volcanoes, one of which was smoking and rumbling. The flyers passed low over a fair-sized city and came at last to the divine palace, very little of which was visible from the air.

They swooped down on a small park but, instead of landing, buzzed slowly along between trees many times larger than any Ratty had ever seen before, huge trunks soaring a hundred meters into the air before sending out branches. Furthermore, those branches seemed to intertwine, even merge, as if the trees were supporting one another. That might suggest that they connected underground also, so that the entire grove would be one enormous organism. Under this gigantic canopy, the palace buildings seemed like tiny wooden clothes chests arranged in curious patterns, but the way they loomed over people on the pathways showed that many were very large.

The flyers landed outside the first permanent building Ratty had seen since the blockhouse at Elaterin Landing, and perhaps the largest and strangest he had ever seen. It occupied a clearing in the forest, and its roof was suspended on cables from a flanking ring of a dozen or so gigantic trees to form an oversized, irregularly shaped tent of what seemed to be multi-colored glass. Ratty just hoped that, whatever it really was, it was not breakable by earthquakes. The huge edifice had no walls—in case of tremor, just run? Even on a dull day like this, the play of color was fascinating. In direct sunlight it must be a blizzard of rainbow.

Its floor was only slightly raised above ground level, a sheet of hexagonal black tiles, unfurnished and unbroken except for a lonely stone pillar in the center. Several people were coming and going across this overwhelming space, and it soon became clear that the focus of their interest was that gloomy-looking monolith. Joy and Scrob headed in its direction without a word. Ratty went along, busily recording.

"Is this a church?"

"It is *the* church! The temple of Quoad," Joy said.

The monolith at the sacred center was a phallic symbol if Ratty had ever seen one. Arrivals went to it and apparently kissed it, although it was far too large for even long Pocosin arms to surround. That seemed to be the whole of the ritual, for then they walked away.

"Quoad's a god?"

"The first martyr." Joy was scanning the mill of people and in a moment changed direction slightly to approach a man wearing a red cape. He was unusually tall, even by local standards, and he stood awaiting their arrival with his arms folded and jaw clenched. Joy muttered something secular under her breath.

Scrob laughed. "You're in trouble!"

"So are you!" Still she marched forward with her nose in the air. The gownsman did touch one knee to the mosaic to honor her, but when he stood up again his expression was not at all respectful.

"Live and die happy, Bedel!" Joy said brightly. "This is Friend Ratty Something. He was anxious to meet Wisdom, and since I was coming this way, I thought—"

"Silence! You are welcome, honored emissary," he told Ratty, "and I apologize deeply for this child's misbehavior."

Gownsman Bedel, Ratty recalled, was consort to High Priest-ess Love, so he was in effect Joy's stepfather. He was not only tall, he was well built and good-looking, and his manner impressed. But then, any Monody incarnation should be able to choose an alpha male to be bed-mate and confidant.

"No need to apologize, Gownsman. I have had one of the most interesting and enjoyable days of my life. I wouldn't have missed it for worlds."

Joy beamed until she saw Bedel still glowering. But then he turned his displeasure on Scrob, who wilted and hung his head.

"You did not exactly justify our trust in you, Companion! You are confined to your room until eclipse prayers—incommunicado. Meditate on adult responsibilities."

Scrob muttered, "Praise the Mother. The elders of Fanfaronade had petitions."

"File your report. If it is well done, that will be noted on your record."

"No!" Joy said. "I want his cape, Bedel."

The consort rolled his eyes heavenward. "But why, for her sake? What's he done?"

"He is just not acceptable." Joy had colored, but she looked convincingly determined.

Bedel sighed, ran an appraising glance over Ratty, then back to Joy: "Cannot this wait until tomorrow?"

"No. Scrob has to go."

"Joy, I have far too many things to worry about without having to find and train a companion for you every time you take a childish dislike to someone who is only trying to do his job. You may find yourself stuck here at Abietin for days, you realize?"

"I hate the sight of him! I've *told* you!"

"Oh, very well, child. Companion, you are relieved of duties. You have our thanks. All in all, you did very well, and you will receive the full compensation you were promised. In fact I will double it, in recognition of the impossible job you were given, herding this wayward brat. You lasted longer than any of your predecessors. File your report and go with the Mother's blessing."

Scrob grabbed the red cape on his shoulder and tore it away, ripping the cloth and sending the jeweled pin rattling across the floor. As he strode off to pay his respects to the central pillar, he was still glaring murder over his shoulder at Ratty, who thought it wisest not to comment.

"Joy," said the gownsman, "you go to your room and stay there until your mother sends for you. I have told the Brain to allow you no cognizing at all." Bedel turned again to Ratty. "Let me show you to your quarters, Friend Ratty. Emeritus Wisdom will receive you shortly. I have grave tidings to report."

"What sort of bad tidings?"

"As bad as they can get. STARS did not wait for your report."

Chapter 7

Athena found herself babysitting.

"Does it mean we're all going to die?" Solan whispered.

The two gownsmen were cognizing, no doubt advising many other people of Braata's dire news. Braata, or Zyemindar, had gone off with Brother Andre to the galley, where the motors made enough noise that voices would not be overheard. Linn and Millie Backet were studying the scenery. Athena had finished up next to Solan.

Outside the landscape was a rugged plain of red-weathered lava with scattered patches of yellow sulfur and islands of dark green forest. Inside, a child who had shown heroic courage only an hour ago was now terrified, and with good reason.

"No, it doesn't," she said, keeping her voice low. "First of all, Solan, STARS is a shady, shifty organization. It has lied before and without doubt will lie again. I don't think Braata is lying to us. He's a brave and honest young man. He belongs to Brother Andre's church and wouldn't lie to a priest, which Brother Andre is. You wouldn't try to lie to Monody, would you? But I am not convinced that STARS has told Braata the truth. It may be hoping to deceive us by deceiving him. There are some odd things in his story.

"My job, the reason we came here from Ayne, is to find out if there really are cuckoos on Pock's World. I am a suspicious person, and I will look very hard at all the evidence. STARS may be lying about that, too." What other arguments could she find to comfort him? "I know that STARS has good reason to threaten this terrible thing. It must convince us that its story is true, or it will lose a big political battle."

Solan stared up at her with big, dark eyes. "What about the boy in Hederal?"

Athena's heart stopped beating. It started again reluctantly. "What boy in Hederal?"

"The one you're on your way to see. He's not human, Dad says."

"Where did they find him?"

"They caught him a week ago. I don't know where exactly."

With a mouth suddenly desert-dry, she said, "We shall look at him very hard and make sure he is not a STARS fake, too."

"But if he is, then you'll let STARS destroy the world?"

"I'll fight them all the way, I promise."

On the opposite side of the cabin, Skerry had another coughing fit. His hands were shaking worse than ever. The man was desperately ill. *Your mother would have been proud of you,* he had said. How long since she died?

Brother Andre returned, looking grim. Braata followed him in. Solan started to rise, and Athena put a hand on his shoulder.

"Friend Braata will never take your seat!"

"Of course not!" Braata smiled and sat on the floor, long legs crossed.

"Honored friends," Oxindole said. "The situation seems to be even worse than we thought. Skerry?"

"I have been checking on the pirate probe," Skerry said hoarsely. "I contacted the observatories at Gadroon and Voussoir, which have no ties with STARS, so far as we know. They have confirmed that there has been a change in the pirate's orbital elements, and while they cannot be certain yet—not without more observations—they agree that it will impact Pock's on Sixterdy or at least come perilously close."

He paused, and Linn prompted: "But?"

The gownsman was staring at his child. "The machines can find no reason for the change, no natural reason. They even allowed for the effects of the radiation storm and the increased drag from Javel's atmosphere. In other words, they confirm that STARS has deliberately altered the pirate's orbit. I think that answers the question of whether it will be a direct hit or a near miss. I don't suppose STARS has missed once in thirty... thousand... years."

Skerry was close to weeping as he pronounced this death sentence. He held out his hands to his son, and Solan went across to his embrace, stepping over Braata's knees. They hugged.

"I have cognized Her Holiness, of course," Oxindole said. "And between us we conferred with leaders of some major governments. Others are being informed. Nothing much can be done until we determine the exact orbital elements, but if imminent disaster is confirmed, then Her Holiness will have to decide whether to reveal it to the population."

"Can there be any doubt of her choice?" Brother Andre said. "The Monody I knew would not have kept the world in ignorance. She is Wisdom now, but can her daughter be so unlike her?"

"I never try to second-guess any of them!" The gownsman spoke sharply and then smiled. "But you are probably right. People have a right to know their fate, she will say. And I very much doubt that we could keep the secret. All attempts to contact STARS have met with failure. However it has issued a statement accusing Engineer Braata of murder and grand larceny and demanding that he be apprehended and turned over to it for trial."

"I never murdered anybody!" the youngster said hotly. "I knocked out a guard, but he was breathing when I left—his lip was bleeding, so I turned him face down to be sure he wouldn't choke. I did steal the flyer, and I damaged a lock."

In her time Athena had watched a thousand liars testify. She did not think this boy was another. Yesterday he had been brash and cocky; now he was chastened and haunted. Nothing trivial had changed him.

Oxindole said, "Why don't you start at the beginning again and go through it one more time, just in case we've missed something?"

"As you wish, Gownsman." Braata paused to collect his thoughts. At least two of his listeners were recording. "I am registered as Zyemindar 4,756. I was born in, and am a citizen of, Calade. I am Zyemindar to my family, who believe I am an explosives specialist employed by a minor mining company, which is why I must often visit asteroids—Pock's formed too far from its star to collect a decent complement of metals, as you know, but fortunately Javel drags in fragments from the inner parts of the system. Professionally I am STARS Engineer Sec-

ond Class Braata. Eleven days ago, I was assigned to
Operation Check Point, the expedition to intercept the pirate
probe. It was a dicey trip because we would be cutting our fuel
limits very fine. Check Point was commanded by Friend
Chessel, whose true name I do not know. I believe she is a
project manager in Research.

"We matched orbits with the probe and were able to study
its exterior during our approach. Full-spectrum readings
showed clear evidence of erosion by the galactic medium, and
the external fittings were compatible with those of an interstellar probe. We located an access lock that seemed to be in good
shape, and I made the first entry." He grinned at Solan, whose
eyes were wide. "That is one of the honors of being the bomb
man! I found no booby-traps. I reactivated the lighting and
cooling systems. Heat could have been a serious problem—
probes are cooled by circulating huge amounts of water
through them, and if that system is turned off after a long trip,
the water may overheat in places, causing the probe to explode—but the living quarters were barely above normal temperature, in line with estimates from other data that we had
missed the invaders by no more than twelve days."

"That would have been an interesting encounter!" Millie
said brightly.

Zyemindar-Braata smiled politely. "But a brief one, because
our little bus was only a can, and the probe's projector could
have shattered it. I then summoned the others, but I had used
up almost half of our available time.

"Wandering through an abandoned probe was a creepy
experience. We could *smell* that there had been people there
recently. There were dirty dishes in the mess, food spoiling in
the freezers. Even the hydroponics had been drained, which
never happens." He shivered. "We went looking for the entangler first, naturally, and established that entanglement had
been broken. Now *we* cannot reestablish a string once it has
been broken, not without starting from scratch and sending
one end of the link in a probe. We *think* it will always be impossible, but there is always a faint suspicion that one day
someone will find a way, so Captain Chessel told me to set up
my charges and put a four-day delay on them. Of course I left
a babysitter."

"Perhaps you would clarify that term to calm the fears of
an ignorant cleric?" Andre asked drily.

"Sorry, Brother. Just a monitor that stops transmitting when the charges detonate, so we know they have gone off. I concealed it as well as I could."

"Thank you. And they did go off?"

"Yes, Brother. And later the captain called me to the Wong-Hui projector—that's the main engine. She told me to mine that, also, with the same four-day delay. This I did." Braata stared miserably at his feet. "The time is up by now."

"You did not question that long time lag?" Skerry whispered hoarsely.

"No, Gownsman. The probe's orbit was unstable, passing so close to Javel that it was sure to break up soon. But a domesticated asteroid is a valuable property, so I assumed that STARS planned to refurbish it and reuse it at some later time. I assumed that Chessel had reset the projector to stabilize the orbit. She would have had to program in one or more course corrections at the right points in its orbit, so a delay of several days seemed quite reasonable. I had no authority to supervise her actions, Gownsman! I didn't know she was aiming it at the world. I suspect she did not know, either. She was just obeying orders."

"We believe you, Engineer," Millie said. "Or at least I do. But why destroy expensive equipment like that? Why not just leave it harmlessly circling Javel?"

"Because a probe is never harmless, Friend Millie, any more than a loaded gun is harmless. It *looked* innocent enough, but that girlie is huge! There must be a hundred kilometers of tunnels in the mother. We had no time to search for hidden control panels, no time to make certain that there was no hidden delay equipment still operable. There could even have been crew hiding away somewhere. I thought I was disabling the drive so that the neither the cuckoos nor anyone else could ever hold the probe over us as a threat."

Oxindole said, "There is no doubt that the projector started up as directed and the orbit was adjusted?"

"None," Skerry muttered. "The chances of hitting Pock's by chance are infinitesimal. It was deliberate."

"And there is no hope of restarting the motors again?"

Braata looked up at him like a man in a permanent nightmare. "I have always been proud of my competence, Gownsman. In my work you have to be good, and I am good. I did a fine job on that projector, an excellent job. I set it to shatter into the equipment into a billion pieces without cracking the asteroid in its hot and weakened condition. I did not know I was destroying my home world." He shook his head. "And in case you're wondering whether anyone else on the team tampered with my work after I turned my back, I can tell you that I was the last one out, with two minutes to spare, right at the limit of our return fuel supply. That probe is ballistic now."

Oxindole nodded. "I don't think any jury would convict you if the facts are as you say, but you may be in much danger from lynch mobs if the story gets out. Likewise, you have to be kept out of STARS's clutches. That's why Monody has subpoenaed you to appear before her, which means no one can arrest you in the meantime. If I release you on your own recognizance, will you give me your parole?"

"I so swear."

"Then you will proceed to Abietin and wait for her there. Monody is in Dugite at the moment, but I am sure she will cut her visitation short and head home shortly." Oxindole sighed— wearied and worried both. He peered out the window behind him. "There's old Bubinga huffing and puffing and burning down forests, so we are not far from Hederal now. The Church keeps a chapter house there, honored friends. You will notice that the sun is just rising, so we shall have no more darkness for half a fortnight, except during eclipses. I suggest you pretend it is a sunset, not a sunrise, and rest for half a day. By then we should have more information on the pirate's trajectory, and we will ac-company you to inspect the hominin."

"This is true, then?" Athena said. "You actually caught one of them?"

The big man started. "Didn't I tell you? I am deeply sorry! I believe it was news of Friend Braata's plight that caused it to slip my mind. When we identified the pirate probe, Friend Skerry, here, suggested that the invasion, if that is what it was, would necessarily work to a long-term plan. He pointed out that adolescents are lighter to transport and have a greater ability to adapt to a new environment than adults. So we put a watch on schools and universities, and caught one trying to enlist in Hederal College."

"What are you going to do with him?"

The gownsman shrugged. "I prefer to call the thing 'it.' We've been questioning it and examining its physiology and genotype. I was assuming we'd simply put it to death as a dangerous animal, but if we're all going die in a few days, Monody may let it live long enough to watch the fireworks."

Chapter 8

Ratty felt as if he had spent an entire day traveling from Elaterin to Abietin, yet the sky was growing brighter, not dimmer. His quarters were luxurious enough for a king and big enough to stable a team of darii. Even the medic was larger than any he had seen outside a hospital, although that might be just a comment on the rigors of the Pocosin environment. It clucked and buzzed at him, spouted out a vile-tasting potion, and warned him to take better care of his skin. *Right, turn off the rain.* He shunned the bathtub, changed into fresh shorts, visor, and sandals, combed his hair. Enervated by the constant steamy heat, he cast a longing look at the great bed. Someone tapped on the door.

Bedel had explained the symbols. A cloth draped over one shoulder indicated a servant of the theocracy that effectively governed the world. White meant priestess, brown a palace attendant, blue a guard, green a high official, red a personal companion to one of the incarnations, and the rest didn't matter for now. The two boys who wheeled in the trolley wore browns with thin beige stripes, and they brought delicious odors with them. Ratty's mouth began to water harder than the climate.

The taller boy raised the first cover. "This is scrob, honored guest. This is pickled lapsable. And this—"

A woman entered by the open door. The boys dropped to their knees at the sight of her red cape. It had thin blue stripes, whereas Bedel's had been solid red.

"Emeritus Wisdom will receive you in the Rotunda now, Friend Ratty."

He sighed. "Just leave it, lads. I'll eat when I get back."
The boys were dismayed. "But it will get cold, honored
guest."

"Oh, we usually eat our food cold on Ayne," he lied. "Lead
the way, Companion."

⸺⸺⸺

Rain was again dribbling through the forest canopy so high
above, but Pocosins ignored weather. Her Holiness was waiting in a conical pit, like an amphitheater designed to hold several hundred people. From its center, where a circular pool
steamed and bubbled, it rose in a dozen or so benches of black
stone. Ratty paused at the top to record the scene, admiring the
clever use of color even under a gray sky and the high-arched
trees—the pool itself bright turquoise, brilliant cushions scattered at random on the lower levels, and the old woman sitting
alone near the water, draped in white. The place was old, with
many of its stones cracked and heaved, but if you didn't mind
rain, if both your skin and your clothes shed water, then it was
a reasonable enough locale for a private chat. He set off down
one of the two stairways spiraling inward like the arms of a galaxy.

Wisdom, oldest of the incarnations, was shrouded from chin
to wrists and ankles, but even that failed to hide her extreme
scrawniness. Her face was drawn into deep furrows, the trade-
mark variegated hair had lost its bloom and body, floating
thinly above her scalp. She must be old even by Ayne standards,
and Pocosins were not known for longevity. She nodded a cool
welcome when Ratty touched one knee to the ground as Bedel
had instructed him earlier.

"Be seated, honored emissary. No, this side. This ear hears
better." She studied him for a moment with eyes nested in
wrinkles, eyes that spoke of weariness and suffering. "I apologize for the way my errant great-granddaughter abducted you
today. It was shameful."

"I loved every minute of it, Your Holiness." Surprisingly, he
could discern traces of Joy's beauty still lingering in the rav-
ished face. This was Joy's destiny, three generations from now—
unless STARS stole it from her.

"Call me Wisdom," the crone said sharply. "I'm done with
all that holiness business. Before we get down to serious matters, tell me about this cleric you brought with you between the
stars. He claims to know me?"

So Ratty sat in the sulfurous steam and hot rain and re-counted much of *The Saint of Annatto*. The old biddy listened intently, but at the end she nodded as if amused.

"Yes, Jame was a saint even in my day, and just as impossible to deal with as any saint is. Well, I will see him again, even if I have to drag my rotting carcass out of here one last time, and I swore I never would. But Bedel thinks they will gather here. Most problems come to Abietin eventually." She smiled, keeping her papery lips together to hide her teeth. "We die of cancer at forty-four, young man. That's forty-four in our years, you work it out in yours." About eighty, he thought. "I know the day I will die, within a couple of fortnights either way, and my last ambition was to see the next Joy, so I could hand over my duties to my daughter, such as they are. And now STARS is about to cheat me of that! And cheat Joy out of three-quarters of her life! Well, what do you say?"

"I find it incredible," Ratty said. "Even if there has been an infection from Malacostraca, common decency insists that you be given time to hunt down the cuckoos."

"Monsters!" She sighed. "And STARS is worse. What do they save us from by killing us all? Spiders! That engineer who ratted won't live long. I knew a STARS man once. He said he was a professional spaceball player. He was so good in bed I offered him a long-term contract and he confessed he had an unbreakable commitment elsewhere. Impudence! He died soon after that. I'm sure it was because he'd told me." She sighed and muttered, "I knew a lot of strong young men, more than my share, all dead now."

Assuming he was not supposed to have heard that, Ratty said, "I have no idea what to do. Time must be very short. Even STARS may not be able to change the probe's trajectory now."

"You just hope they're keeping your shuttle seat open, boy. They'll have to guard the landings from mobs. Thousands trampled. No matter!" Wisdom dismissed the end of the world with a wave of a twisted hand. "I can't help. My wisdom doesn't extend to this, so Duty will have to decide on her own what to do without it. Small loss!"

"What *can* she do?"

"Pray."

"Ah. Of course."

Rain was roaring on the leafy canopy far above, spraying down like a shower. No climate, only weather.

The old woman pouted at Ratty's evident disbelief. "If we have only a few days left, the Mother would expect us to make the most of them. Joy has not been told, so don't spoil her happiness yet."

"I have already promised Gownsman Bedel that I will not." Ratty hoped he was done with babysitting the youngest Monody, but saying so might not be tactful.

Wrinkles writhed around her mouth to form a smile, and the pain-dulled eyes even managed a twinkle. "We are not just an odd family, Friend Ratty. We are a unique family."

"Yes, Your Holiness."

"Our standards are not everyone's"

No, they weren't.

"So you promise not to be offended if my great-granddaughter decides to treat you as stud of the week?"

Not as offended as I am by a crone pimping her great-granddaughter to a total stranger. "That would be a great honor, but not appropriate, surely? I'm not a Pocosin, nor a member of your faith."

"Why do those things matter?" she snapped. "Variety adds spice. You're male, aren't you? You've got a working prod, haven't you?"

Suddenly... Surely not? Wisdom, Joy had said, had never named her giver. Brother Andre's tour on Pock's had been unusually short, and Ratty had picked up faint rumors of a scandal... No, that was ridiculous.

"I'll be leaving in a few days."

"While Joy will be dying with the rest of us here. I suppose that will solve my problem."

"Um, what problem?"

"I told you!" the old woman snapped. "If she doesn't pick out a giver soon, I won't see her daughter!" She scowled. "When Joy is born, Joy becomes Love, Love Duty, Duty Wisdom, and I get to be Memory, for a little while." Had she forgotten about STARS and its dread purpose? Or was that just too horrible to consider? "Oh, begone, boy. I'm tired. They're coming to put me to bed."

Ratty rose and touched his knee down again. "It has been a great honor to speak with you, Holiness."

"No it wasn't." She dismissed him with a wave. As he started up the stairs, she called after him, "Be kind."

⊷⊷◦⊷ ⊷⊹ — ⊱ ⊹⊶◦⊶

Mouth watering again, he hurried back to his room. The first thing he saw when he walked in was Joy, sitting cross-legged on the bed, chewing. She wore her usual bare minimum and a grin even bigger than usual.

"Hurry up and eat!" she said. "I want to show you something."

"I thought you'd been confined to quarters?"

"I don't pay any attention to that. Hurry! We don't have much time."

He went to the trolley. Before he could decide what he wanted to try first, she was at his side, practically leaning on him.

"Take two slices of that and a piece of that and spread it with that fish jam there; roll it up and you can eat it as we go. Put two of those in your pocket." Then she reached around his neck and he realized she was pinning a red cloth on him.

Alarmed, he pulled away. "Wait a minute! What are you planning?"

"I can't leave the palace without an attendant. You saw what this did for Scrob, didn't you? Mm, it matches your nipples."

"Yours are bigger and prettier."

"Stop flirting! It's disrespectful. And do hurry! It may be foggy up there." She adjusted the cape on his left shoulder and began fastening a weighty holster around his waist. This was getting much too intimate and ridiculous.

"Darling priestess, don't I need a license to carry this thing?"

"Oh, it isn't loaded, but the rule is you have to be armed. Let's go."

He drew the gun, confirmed that it was fully charged, and buttoned it back in the holster. Whatever this hellion had in mind could not be seduction, not when the biggest bed in the galaxy was standing right behind her. He needed food and sleep....

She had only four days to live. So what did it matter? What did anything matter on Pock's World now?

"Ready, then," he said. "Lead on, Holy One. I hear and obey. Your smallest whim is an irresistible command."

"That is much better! Keep that up and you may even outlast Scrob."

He bowed her out the door. "How long was that?"

"I dunno. Two fortnights? I'm sure Mother wasn't serious about him. She was picking the worst blockheads she could find just to make me make my own choice. I ordered a two-seater."

As he followed her out into the rain, a flyer zoomed in overhead, buzzing ferociously down to settle on the grass. The boy riding it dismounted and knelt to Joy, who dismissed him with a blessing that made his face light up. The machine was identical to the flyers Ratty had seen earlier, only bigger, but he wondered if it was truly meant for two people. Joy opened a locker and brought out a set of goggles, which she handed to Ratty. She put in a package that she did not explain. He had to sit directly behind her, so she was between his knees, and he would have nothing to hang on to except her.

"Devious little minx, aren't you?" he said in her ear.

"What's a minx?" she asked, busily checking the settings on the boards. She touched a lens and the flyer began to vibrate in a deep bass register that sent shivers racing up his backbone from his crotch to his scalp.

He looked at the five-meter wingspan and the gigantic forest. "What happens if you hit a tree trunk on the way out?"

"I don't know. You want me to try it and see? Hang on, here we go!"

The flyer roared and bounced into the air; Ratty's arms closed around her automatically.

She said, "Wow!"

"Is that a comment on my hugging or your flying?"

The flyer shot forward. "I didn't know these were so peppy!"

Ratty howled. "You mean you've never driven one before?" He should have seduced her when he had a bed handy. Too late now. Forest giants whistled by on either hand.

They left the forest park and soared higher into the mist and drizzle, but Joy kept the ground in sight. The landscape was rugged, all rocks and jungle and waterfalls, steadily rising.

"What happens if you run into a cliff?"

"The flyer probably won't let me. This lens turns red if there's anything ahead. I think it's this one. No, that's the fuel gauge. We're going to see the ruins."

"The Old Ones' ruins?"

"The Querent city. There's not much to see. The tourists are shown some junk on the other side of town, but we're going to Real Quassia, where Monody was given her revelation. They're very old."

Joy was shouting ahead, into the blowing mist, so he had to lean over her shoulder to hear. It was very intimate contact. If she had planned it, as he suspected, then her mother's strategy had worked and Joy had picked out her target. His fans on Ayne would forgive many things, but not statutory rape.

"How can you know how old the ruins are?"

"That's easy. Half of them are buried in old lava and we can date the minerals. Nothing survives in the jungle except stone, and even that weathers. Nothing survives on Pock's for long. Mountains crumble and sink. This world turns over its surface every million years or so. Everything gets buried in lava sooner or later, or just collapses into the ground when the volcanoes have sucked out the magma below."

A cliff loomed out of the fog on their right. A waterfall roared somewhere close, audible even over the noise of the flyer itself.

"We don't have oceans or mountains ranges, just scenery," Joy shouted, zooming around a rock pillar. As long as she kept lecturing, Ratty had to keep his chin on her shoulder.

"Do you have any idea where you're going?"

"Roughly."

Roughly could have been rougher, because a few moments later the flyer soared up into brilliant sunshine and there was a hillocky island straight ahead, a heap of black ridges and green gullies in a billowing sea of cloud. A few other peaks showed in the distance, all lit by the eerie light of a low sun— a real sun in a blue sky. Javel had disappeared.

"Mount Garookuh!" Joy crowed. "That's where we're going."

Several thunderstorms were heading there also, but the flyer arrived first. She set it down gently on a hummocky green space that would qualify as the main summit. It supported one notable spire and many green or black pillars and pyramids, even a few lonely trees. Everything seemed unreal in the low light, streaked with elongated shadows.

"Watch you don't break an ankle," Joy said, sliding down. "Mattress moss won't eat you, but it feels like it's trying to. And there can be rocks or tree trunks buried in it. There's a lot of lightning up here, so the trees get struck."

Lightning he could do without!

"Let's go look at that!" Holding his hand, she led him toward the nearest hillock. The ground cover was well named, billowing and bouncing underfoot like heaped air mattresses. They both stumbled repeatedly, sprawling into hot wet sponge.

It was only a few meters to their objective, but Ratty was gasping and puffing by the time they arrived. Joy found a patch of black rock on the side of the green heap and tugged more of the surrounding plant cover away.

"This is a Querent wall, see? If you look close, you can make out the stonework."

Well, maybe. The rock was weathered to powder, but with an effort he could see joins in it. He stared around the bizarre landscape, trying to make out a city among the humps and ridges. "Has this ever been excavated?"

"Not here." She leaned against the mossy wall, puffing as hard as he. "It's too holy. Tourist Quassia and some other places, yes. I told you—nothing but stone survives, and even that doesn't last."

Ratty looked around the bizarre mountain top. "Why would the Querent build anything up here?"

"They built all over Pock's, but all the low-lying sites have been buried in ash or lava long ago. This was their great holy place a million years ago, give or take."

"How do you know that?"

She smiled at the scenery. "They told Monody." She flashed a glance at Ratty to see how he had taken that. "They worshiped the Mother here, in their city of Quassia, although Garookuh was a lot higher in those days. The geologists say this part of Pock's is sinking and will probably turn into an ocean soon. A small ocean. Do you know we have boiling seas in some places?"

He put an arm around her.

"See that spire?" she said quickly. "That's Quoad."

"I thought he was the martyr? Did he get turned to stone?"

"No. That was where he died. It's the holiest of holies. The pillar back at the temple is a smaller copy of this one. You see how there's nothing growing on it? I would have taken the flyer closer, but Quoad stands right on the edge of the drop. It's almost sheer down into the caldera, even after all this time, and there can be nasty downdrafts so I didn't dare. The caldera's still active, once in a while spouting steam and hot mud. If I'd had more time I could have found the path, but I didn't. We can look for it afterward if you want, and then we can walk over to Quoad, but this is close enough for— There's ancient legends about Quoad, you know? The pillar Quoad. Querent legends. They said its roots are down in the center of the world and its hands reach up to the Mother and—"

"Stop!" he said softly, tightening his hold. "Joy, you're trembling! Stop worrying. I'm not going to do anything. You don't have to do anything. It's a wonderful place and I'm grateful to you for bringing me here. That's all. Nothing else is necessary."

She twisted around and buried her face in his neck. He hugged her tight—both arms now. Her hair was damp in his face. He liked the smell of it, exotic, unfamiliar. She was still shaking.

"You don't want to hear where the Querent went to?" she mumbled.

"I don't give a spit for the Querent. Did you ever come up here with Scrob?"

"*Scrob?* Of course not!"

"No, he wouldn't appreciate it," Ratty said, suspecting that he was just starting to appreciate it himself. "Why were you in such a hurry to get us here?"

"It's time," she whispered.

The poor kid was obsessed!

"It will be time when you want it to be time, and not a minute before. Don't pay any attention to what your mother says. Don't throw yourself at a decadent old off-worlder pervert like me just because he's not going to be around— I mean because he'll have to go home to Ayne very soon. You'll know when it's time and who—"

"It's time *now!*" She pushed him.

The moss rocked under his feet, and the two of them went down together and bounced. In the sudden release of tension they both burst out laughing. She tickled him and set them bouncing again. He rolled over and tickled her. She squealed and punched. They rolled and bounced and giggled like children.

But they were not children, and he had ended on top.

"Idiot!" he said. They were nose to nose. Eye to eye. His hand was cupping her left breast and she must be aware of his epically tumescent GM phallus red-hot between them.

Silent stare. She was waiting for him to make the next move.

Not to have kissed her then would have been a slap in the face.

One of *those* kisses... On a scale of one to five it scored about a forty-nine.

Eventually he pulled back, breathing hard, knowing that if he was going to stop at all he must stop now. His hand still insisted on fondling her breast. The light.. The sun was going out. Puzzled, he looked at the sky and then down at her smile. It was blissful.

"What?"

"Click!" she said, eyes bright as diamonds.

Huh? Oh, *Click!*

"You're certain?" he mumbled.

"Do it!"

He sucked on her right nipple. She gasped and clutched his head with both hands. He had never know a woman with skin so soft. There was no hurry. He was going to do this properly. He was going to calm her fears and then rouse her to such a frenzy of passion that all her life she would judge all lovemaking by this first time. He had all the time in the world.

The sun was going out.

Chapter 9

The chapter house at Hederal was many mansions, an array of wooden buildings on a hillside overlooking—so Athena was informed—a spectacular view of the town and river valley. Rain and fog hid that. She was assigned what her guide called a cabin, but it was as large as a house and luxuriously appointed. She changed, tied her hair in a ponytail out of the way, and stepped out into the downpour again, heading for a promised meal. Old Ayne had its faults, but at least a girl could get dry there once in a while.

Solan emerged from the next cabin, closing the door with care unusual in a boy his age. He waited for Athena.

"Hungry?" she asked.

He offered his wan little smile. "Starving. I have a black hole inside my tummy, Dad says." He fell into step beside her.

"You father isn't coming to dinner?"

"Maybe later, he says, but I think the medic drugged him. He's in a lot of pain now."

"He's very brave to keep working. Courage must run in your family." If Skerry was dying, what had prompted his son's reckless offer in the airship? Had he felt suicidal, or had he been trying to impress the father he was soon to lose?—*Watch! This is what I will be.*

"He says he'll last longer if he can keep working. It's funny," Solan added in a non-funny tone. "We thought he might last another few fortnights, and now both of us will die next Sixtrdy. At least we can go together."

Stop it, boy! "We must never give up hope," she said.

But often young eyes saw more clearly. Young minds were readier to accept the world as it was, instead of hiding it behind dreams. Chyle had been like that, and Solan knew there was no hope. STARS had seen the opportunity of diverting the probe to make an easy kill. It had planned geocide right from the start. General Sulcus had never said that the commissioners could vote on the sentence. Their job was to confirm the evidence, and it sounded as if the evidence was cut and dried. Tomorrow she would meet a non-human hominin, *Homo novus*.

⇒►❧⥾ — ⥿❧◈⇐

As they reached the main house, the rain stopped. A sliver of sun was showing over the horizon, lighting the base of the clouds.

Indoors, she was introduced to a newcomer, Cardinal Phare, a short, plumpish man with an irritating air of infallibility. He wore a red tunic above his red shorts, a red visor, and a jeweled pectoral cross. Either he had brought fresh garments for Brother Andre or the friar's robe had changed color to a darker brown. Clearly Gownsman Oxindole was displeased at the presence of another purveyor of Christianity on the Mother's world, for he soon pled pressure of work and excused himself. Only seven went in to dine: Athena, Millie Backet, the two clerics, Linn, Braata-Zyemindar, and Solan.

The food machines offered a dozen choices, none of which were familiar. Athena watched in amusement as Solan piled his plate even higher than Braata's. He had not been lying about his internal black hole. The boy looked puzzled when Cardinal Phare said grace.

"Old Ayne custom," Linn explained. "You give thanks before you eat. If you don't have anything to eat, you aren't allowed to complain."

"Because," Brother Andre said, "there may be reasons of which you are unaware."

"This blue stuff is delicious!" Backet remarked loudly.

"Don't ask," Linn warned.

Athena had no appetite. She could find nothing delicious in this funeral feast. The conversation took off after trivia, but Brother Andre soon brought it back to business.

"I have some questions for you, Braata. When exactly did you learn that the world would end on Sixtrdy?"

Braata looked miserable. "Just this morning, Brother, when I was told STARS would evacuate Pock's by Frivdy at the latest, and non-essential personnel would leave on Forsdy."

"Were you told who ordered this?"

Interesting question, Athena thought. Whose hands were bloody?

"I was told it was ordered by management," the STARS man said.

"And who is management?"

"I have no idea, Brother. I don't know if there is a planetary management or an overall sector board. I knew my supervisor and her supervisor. The rest were just people."

Lin's heavy voice rolled into the conversation. "Do you know *when* that decision was made?"

Braata shook his head.

"When did you mine the projector?"

"Five days ago."

Athena watched anger bubbling all around the table. That had been before Sulcus began recruiting them.

Linn said, "And from then on, the die was cast? Pock's World was doomed from that moment?"

"From the moment we left the probe," STARS's man said. "When we could see what had happened, when we found the abandoned food and so on, Chessel reported on tight band. She cognized me to ask whether I had brought delays that could be set for four days, and I assured her I had. I think that was when she was given the settings that aimed the probe at Pock's." He sighed and pushed away his plate almost untouched. "She may not have known what she was doing any more than I did. She would just upload the numbers she was given."

"You acted in good faith," Linn said. "And we must remember that STARS is doing its duty by its lights. Even the gownsmen admit that the cuckoo hominins have infiltrated Pock's World. Historically STARS has burned any planet in danger of being taken over by synthetics. We cannot deny the evidence if the Pocosins themselves accept it."

"You're on STARS's side now?" Athena said.

Lin's smile was as polished and bloodless as ever. "No. I hate the thought of the shock wave this will send through the sector economy. But that was never the question. We were all in denial. If I am indeed introduced to a cuckoo tomorrow, and am convinced that it, or he, is genuine, then I must admit that STARS has enough evidence to proceed to sterilization *according to its traditions*. Whether such an extreme and literal scorched-earth policy is morally justified or necessary nowadays is another matter. Strict quarantine could avoid economic catastrophe."

He was right, of course, damn him! Linn was always right and always had been. She knew that.

"Economic catastrophe'?" the friar said. "Friend Linn, our Lord taught us that it was very difficult for rich men to enter the Kingdom of Heaven. There is a theory that God gets bored with them eternally talking about money."

Linn smiled, unruffled. "You have found my money useful enough in the past, Brother."

"You give it away, which is good. I put it to work, which is my duty. We are now discussing more important things."

"Would it work?" Athena asked. "Is the probe big enough to wipe out a world?"

"Yes!" Surprisingly, the assertion came from Solan. "My dad says it is. Not most worlds, he says, but Pock's is only just livable at any time. A big strike would split the crust. Lava would pour out. The hot bits raining down would start forest fires all over the world. The carbo... gas..."

"Carbon dioxide," Braata prompted.

"Yes. It would go up until we'd all suffocate, Dad says. If we don't suffocate, we'll fry. The carbon stuff will hold in the sun's heat and the air will get hotter and hotter until the seas boil. The whole world will get boiled."

Braata nodded. "You're right, young friend. With a high-oxygen atmosphere, fire is always a problem. I remember doing this as a problem in class. We had to work out the minimum impact required for sterilization for each world in the sector. Pock's was by far the lowest, because of the high oxygen, because its crust is so thin and its internal heat flow so great, but mainly because you can use Javel's gravity to accelerate the missile. And the pirate is in a retrograde orbit, which doubles the impact. So there will be blast and crustal movement, but mostly terrible fires. After that the smoke and soot will block out the sun, and the temperature will plunge for several years. When the sky clears, the excess carbon and sulfur in the atmosphere will produce a massive greenhouse effect, raising the temperature high enough to boil water, and the resulting water vapor will trap even more heat. Nothing will survive."

Linn laughed, "You won't get to check your calculations, will you? You ratted. You won't be up there on the Pock's Station grandstand watching the forests burn and the seas boil. Sounds like you're going to miss a great show."

Braata was not intimidated, although he was pale for a Pocosin. "Brother Andre will confirm that it is better to burn to death than to burn for all eternity, and that is what STARS is going to do."

"The bright side," Millie said, "is that we are relieved of the awful responsibility of condemning a world to death. We just have to confirm that the evidence is genuine."

"People like you make me sick." Linn reached for the wine.

Athena held out her glass for a refill. She had just realized that she was murderously furious as she had rarely been in her entire life. She had been used! That was what hurt. No one had ever turned her to their purpose like this before. Chyle's death had made her rage, but only against the injustice of heaven. A few sleazy warts on the body politic had roused her temper, and once an unfaithful lover—once and only once. *But this...!*

"I won't wait for hellfire!" she snapped. "I want to make STARS burn now! I am still not convinced that it did not fake this whole thing just to block the Mongo Bill. The timing is too slick to be coincidence. The boy we will be shown in the morning may have been bred in some ghastly laboratory just in case a freak may someday be needed to bolster STARS's claim of indispensability. It may have a whole zoo of them tucked away on some minor planet somewhere.

"Even Linn questions the moral justification, and I don't need to question. I *know* it is wrong to destroy a world. So fifty hominins have invaded? Pock's has caught one already. We have his DNA and we have his face. At the very least, the authorities should have been given a year or two to track down the other forty-nine. The rest of you can waffle all you want. The report I file when I return will be a denunciation of STARS as a gang of mass murderers. I will not only throw my party's full support behind the Mongo Bill, I will urge President Carabin to go before the Sector Council and call for an all-out effort to wrest control of space travel away from these faceless monsters. STARS should be replaced by an organization answerable to the Sector Council. Whoever is destroying Pock's World should be put on trial for geocide."

After a moment's silence, Brother Andre said, "Your sentiments do you credit, Athena, but you should perhaps refrain from expressing them until you are safely home on Ayne."

"I call on the rest of you to be my witnesses!" Athena was a long way from being drunk, but she was at least as far from sober. "Even STARS cannot be brash enough to leave the entire commission here. If I do not return, you can make a martyr out of me. Or you can sell your silence to STARS for a lifetime of wealth. Your choice." She drained her glass. No matter what anyone did, that rock was going to slam home four days from now and burn up the world. And she had been used as a tool to give this ghastly geocide an aura of respectability. "Four days!" she said.

"Three now." The piping tone came from Solan. "See how the light is failing? Eclipse has begun. End of Toody, start of Thirdensdy. In bright week Javel blots out the sun during eclipses; in dark week, we see Pock's own shadow crossing Javel! So our days start at the same time all over the world. Yours don't, do they?" He was looking at Athena.

"No," she agreed. "On Ayne we take a long time to start a new day. But on Pock's World enlightenment can come very quickly."

Across the table, Linn smiled sourly at her metaphor. Solan looked puzzled.

"Totality lasts about two hours," said the archbishop, who had been feasting heartily during all this. "Time for Compline, Brother."

⊷⊱ ⊰ — ⊱ ⊰⊶

The paths were well lit, flashing silver in the rain. Athena walked back with Linn and Solan. They bade Solan goodnight at his door, and he went in quietly, carrying a plate of food he'd brought in case his father was awake.

"Skerry has terminal pancreatic cancer," Linn said as they continued. "Oxindole told me. It's into his lungs and everything else now. His wife died a fortnight ago of a brain tumor. Pock's is a tough world."

"Very."

"That was quite a speech you made. The opening of your presidential campaign, was it?"

"I told you I had decided not to run. I couldn't run for parking attendant now. I'll be forever tainted by the destruction of Pock's World."

Linn snorted. "Make that speech you made a while back and you'll ride a landslide. Carabin is in STARS's pocket, of course. Most politicians in the sector are, whether they know it or not. If you want to muzzle STARS, you will have to run. Your opponents will be *extremely* well funded. And you will have to win big—big to do any good."

Where were the brave words now? Had the noble purpose died so soon? She did not reply.

"But Senator Fimble is going to retire to Portolan and make a cute little baby for pretty boy-toy Proser. President Fimble, now—President Fimble would have been something."

They were almost at her door.

They walked in silence, reached it, stopped.

"Is the offer still open?" she asked.

"Certainly. Lifelong ambition, remember?" He had been waiting for the question, damn him!

"You want to come in, then?" she said. Decision made.

"No, let's go to mine."

They walked on. "Do you remember the first summer at college?" he said. "You were getting it off with Joe and Tiny."

"Joe, yes. Never Tiny; I was never stoned enough to need Tiny." She wished she were stoned now. This was going to be a cold-blooded commercial transaction.

Linn thumbed the door open and let her enter first. Lights came on.

"Lights brightest," he ordered. "Secure door, no callers. This way to the bedroom, darling. We went skinny dipping one night, a gang of us. One night in particular, I mean." He stopped her in the doorway. "Wait here a moment."

He walked across the room to the bed and turned. He was still wet and shiny from the rain, his curls sparkling. And he was still a hunk, just as he had been at sixteen. The humiliation would not be physical.

"I watched you come walking up out of the sea," he said. "You went straight to Tiny. Joe wasn't there, but others were. You were not stoned, and you did go to Tiny. Remember now?"

She nodded, feeling her face burning. This was going to be even worse than she had expected.

"Remember what you did when you got to him?"

She nodded.

"I swore then that one night you would come to me like that. And do what you did then." He dropped his shorts.

"Slowly," he said, as she started to undress. "Good. Now walk slowly. And smile. It doesn't count if you don't smile."

Thirdensdy

Ratty wakened unromantically when hot water ran up his nose. He spluttered and choked and wondered where in the world... And which world? He was bathing in wet moss with an entirely gorgeous naked girl who had demonstrated a natural knack for love-making as if she'd been doing it for ten thousand years. He had been deprived of tender caring love for a long time, ever since a one-nighter with Whosit-the-Busty, but Joy had made up for it in spades, doubled and redoubled—greatest lay in the universe already and just started her training! The air was almost chilly on his face and above him spread infinite starry space, not the familiar stars of Ayne, a hundred light years away. And the singing...

Singing? He sat up, which was not as easy as expected in the hot mush. Joy grumbled and made sleepy noises. On the horizon loomed the great dome of Javel in eclipse, black against the stars and yet not black. The Mother glowed with a metallic bluish light, a flickering, ever-changing glow racing hither and thither over the mightiest of worlds. Almost he could see shapes in those lights, faces calling him, writing flashing strange scripts.... How could he hear singing across the vacuum of space? This was a holy place. This was where the Mother spoke to mortals.

He floundered through the moss, staggering and flailing arms to keep his balance in the low gravity, going to see why the voices were calling him, wondering what they were saying. But the singing wasn't coming from the Mother, but from off to his left, from the tower that Joy had called Quoad, vastly larger than the one in the temple, a gargantuan phallic symbol if ever there was one. Oh Mighty Pillar of Andesite, hear my prayer... Quoad was inhabited, too. Bluish lights ever moving, drifting up the spire, floating down, dancing, writhing, waving, and it was they who were singing to him, calling him. Louder and sweeter soared the songs, odes to the Mother and Quoad. Mighty Quoad. Who was Quoad? Igneous extrusion, phallic symbol, pagan god of virility, did it matter? Dazed and ever-happier, Ratty kept stumbling, ever falling and yet soon moving again, not even remembering getting up, and the lights were brighter, closer, their song soaring to the heavens, to the Mother.

From this new angle, Quoad was crazily tilted out over the edge of the crater. A staircase, a set of crumbling steps, zig-zagged up the nearer face. The luminous souls were beckoning him to climb those steps and join them. They would guide him, help him climb, go home to the Mother, and that was Joy's too-human voice yelling, but raucous, too mortal. Angels' song was sweeter.

Wham! She cannoned into him and they splashed down to-gether. Water up his nose again. No! No! He struggled. She wrestled and clung, still shouting in his ear.

"What? Let me go, love. They want me. They're calling... let me go." He must go, yet he mustn't hurt her. She was slippery and persistent and amazingly strong, a hundred hands and legs, tree octopus. "Can't you hear?"

"No! There is no song!"

Yes there was. The song was building, growing desperate. He freed himself, struggled to his knees, and there was the Mother, almost sunk below the edge of the world, flickering and gleaming—and suddenly a speck of gold at the edge, brighter than stars, spreading into a line, widening, brightening, and some practical sanity muttered in his ear that this was sunlight refracted in the Javelian atmosphere. Brighter and brighter, curving around the edge of the disk until the sun itself peeked over and stabbed at his eyes.

Perforce he looked away. The angels had gone, the singing had ended.

"Gone!" he said. He was kneeling in a tangle of Joy, except that Joy was weeping and sobbing; also still digging her fingers into him like tiger claws. "Sorry, love," he muttered. "You were saying?" Then the two of them collapsed into the sponge, and he got his arms around her and comforted her.

"You're back? You're all right now?"

He nuzzled. "I was always... all... right." He closed their mouths around the kiss and it developed from there, for there was only one thing a naked man could do with a beautiful naked girl in a warm and totally intimate embrace like that.

⤖⬅⚐ — ⬔➤⬌

This time it was a peal of thunder that shocked him awake. Rain was splattering all around. He could see nothing through the fog. Lightning flashed close with a head-smashing peel of thunder, so close he thought he could smell it.

"Let's go!" Joy said.

He grabbed and pulled her flat again. "No! We're safest here, lying down. It's the trees that get struck, not the moss." *Roar!* "That's why it's evolved to hold water, I expect. It's so conductive it can't build up a local charge.

"But if the flyer gets hit?"

"We'll have to walk down."

"You're trembling!"

Trembling? He was shaking like a maraca in a rhumba.

Roar! said the storm again.

He told her how his parents had died. She comforted him, which was nice. But then she asked the embarrassing question he had been dreading.

"What were you doing when I caught you?"

He laughed awkwardly. "I saw the lights on Javel. Thunderstorms, of course. The whole planet must be a seething mass of thunderstorms. Aurora, too? Pretty! I wanted to find a better view."

"But you were heading for Quoad!" She was not convinced. "There's ruins all around here you could have climbed on. You had a better view of the Mother where we were."

"Oh? Didn't see that. You said there was a cliff on the other side? Downdraft... There's probably a big regional downdraft when the eclipse shadow arrives, yes? Do the clouds usually clear during eclipses?"

"Often, yes."

"That explains it. I mean explains it scientifically, no disrespect to your goddess. I'm sure she arranges her appearances that way. And the pillar is some different sort of rock, so it might have different conductivity or capacitance or something, and you have temperature differences and this soggy moss, so there's all kinds of induced currents, I expect. The lights on Quoad would be what's called St. Elmo's fire, a static discharge. And the sounds—"

Roar!

He flinched. She must think him a terrible coward.

"You saw lights on *Quoad*? *What* sounds? *What* lights?"

He pulled her down again. Obviously he had alarmed her. "Joy, I have to confess something. I have a dozen implants in the mess I call a brain. The external contacts won't work here, but I can still adjust my sleep patterns and tune out distractions when I need to concentrate on something—a few useful tricks like that. Something in there must have been resonating with the electrostatic fields. I heard... I heard a sort of warbling humming, like somebody singing without words."

"Holy Mother!" she whispered. "And you saw lights on Quoad?"

"You mean you didn't?"

"No. Darling, the thunder's stopped. Why don't we find the flyer and our clothes?"

"No hurry," he murmured, wondering if he might be good enough for another try.

"No. Let's go!"

Why was she so insistent all of a sudden? He struggled to his feet and helped her up. Where had they left their clothes?

They found their clothes. He turned his back on her while he dressed, wondering as always why nudity was sexy and undressing could be, but dressing never was. Shorts, sandals, and visor didn't take long, but Joy had just picked hers up and carried on toward the fliers, mother-naked. He bounded over the moss—running turned out to be easier than walking—and caught up with her just as she arrived.

She opened a locker and pulled out the bundle she had packed. She tossed it Ratty. "Dress me."

Shaken out, the garment was revealed as a white cotton gown.

"I like you better the way you are," he said.

"Don't be impudent! After what we just did, I have to wear that. Always. Except in bed," she added with a return to her childlike grin.

He slid the garment over her head. It was sleeveless but otherwise covered her to the ankles.

He knelt to her. "You are still the sexiest woman in the galaxy, Priestess."

She touched his head. "Mother bless you."

He rose and resisted the temptation to kiss her yet again. "Who was Quoad?"

"Quoad is the pillar." She straddled the flyer.

"But Quoad was a person, a martyr, you said."

"Quoad the martyr died on the pillar, so it was named after him. Hurry! Get on! I'm starving."

Chapter 2

By morning the sun was still low in the east, little changed from the previous night. Athena knew it was morning because of her hangover. It was not a wine hangover. It came from too much Linn, from too little sleep, and—above all—from nightmares about the coming holocaust.

The sky was cloudless and deep indigo, with the valley glowing like a green jewel of vineyards and orchards suspended on a blue ribbon of river. In three days it would be charred black.

The air car that came to fetch the commissioners was a reminder that Pock's world's rustic facade did hide some high technology; the fact that it was a military vehicle was a sad comment on human priorities. Their destination, Colonel Cassinoid Veterans Hospital, also belonged to the Hederalian army and was a predictably ugly collection of wooden modules lined up in ragged rows. Its watch towers and shock fences showed why it had been chosen to contain the alleged cuckoo.

The greeting party waiting at the edge of the pad comprised about a dozen civilians, several Hederalian army officers, and three armed patrolmen in STARS black. Back on Ayne such STARS anthropoids were a sore point. They ostensibly guarded shuttle landings, but twice in the last year some trigger-happy goons had burned people severely. The resulting uproar had sparked the Mongo Bill—and so, perhaps, started all of Pock's trouble.

The man who stepped forward to greet the visitors wore STARS black, too, but his visor carried only the company logo, not military insignia, and he was unarmed. He was big even for a Pocosin, a man of middle years with a massive belly, shaven scalp, and a head like a red granite boulder perched on a stack of pancakes. There was something atavistic about him, as if he ought to be wearing skins and carrying a club, or covered with body hair like the men of Saumur or Strigate. Perhaps he had been chosen for his ability to project sheer menace.

"My name is Glaum. I am Chairman of Pock's World STARS."

Millie had pushed herself forward as usual. "A pleasure, Friend Glaum, although it would have been more of a pleasure if you had made yourself available to us sooner. We have many questions to put to—"

"You're Backet," Glaum growled. "Senator Fimble, Brother Andre, Friend Lazuline, Gownsmen Oxindole and Skerry. Also Young Friend Solan, whom I congratulate on what he did yesterday, even if his courage was misplaced in aiding an escaped criminal. Friend Ratty, I understand, is liaising with the youth wing of the Mother's Church at Abietin, and the turncoat Braata is on his way there."

Having thus demonstrated a complete grasp of all the secrets, Glaum indicated a woman with a gesture that seemed to dismiss the rest of the company out of hand. "Doctor Eryngo, who heads up the investigation."

Eryngo was thin and graying, wrapped in a white lab coat. She looked as if she had not slept in several days and owed the universe an apology for her existence. Athena's cynical eye summed her up as a good choice for an outside expert, one who would cause STARS no trouble.

She bobbed her head to the group.

"STARS has provided us with some very old records on other cuckoo infestations—Soldier Ants, Ghouls, Zombies. Our team has not finished analyzing them, but we have established a close enough match to leave no doubt that the present specimen includes material from previous species. We have tentatively named this new variety a Changeling. Shall we now proceed inside and view the specimen?"

Millie had been silenced by Glaum's snub, and Athena found herself in the lead as the assembly proceeded to a nearby building.

"Doctor, when you say an updated variety...?"

"The match is not exact. The present specimen displays some unique features."

"It is not human?"

"Absolutely not!"

Two more STARS guards flanked the door. "Admit the visitors, Sergeant," Glaum said, "and the gownsmen. Keep the locals out."

In her present mood, Athena had suffered more than enough of this oversized ape. In Doctor Eryngo's place she would long since have exploded and ordered the boor out of her sight, but apparently he had managed to cow the entire Hederal army also, because she heard no whisper of objection from the military at her back.

"No, Friend Chairman!" She threw her full senatorial authority into that bark. "The prisoner is suspected of being synthetic, but STARS is not a disinterested party. The gownsmen may attend, but the rest of you will wait outside, please. We shall examine the prisoner with only Doctor Eryngo present, advising us on her conclusions."

Glaum smirked down at her as if she were a comical kitten. "Examine all you want, but the sergeant and I will watch. STARS is responsible for your safety, and this thing is dangerous."

There were more doors inside, more guards. The precautions seemed absurd by the time they reached the prisoner. His windowless room was half cell, half laboratory, and smelled unpleasantly of both. A waste bin held bloody swabs; machines buzzed and flickered; syringes and sample bottles lay scattered in disorder over a big white workbench. Two guards sat by the entrance, three men in white coats were clustered around a hologram. All were dismissed to make room for the newcomers.

The *specimen* lay spread out on an examination table in the center, clamped at wrists and ankles, wearing only cotton briefs. As if that were not enough restraint, the table was surrounded by the bluish glow of a shock fence. At first glance the figure was a pubescent Pocosin, a year or two older than Solan. It was scowling, making a brave effort to look brave while being utterly vulnerable to its enemies.

His enemies! Athena would not think of a boy as *it*. And she would not treat an animal like that. "Release him!" she snapped. "We came here to talk with him, not to remove his appendix."

"It has no appendix." Eryngo wore medical insignia on her white tunic, but she would earn no medals for bedside manner. She must have cognized a command, because the prisoner's manacles and anklets clicked open. "I'm leaving the containment field on. Be careful! It is dangerous and will attack without warning."

The boy sat up and swung his legs over the side of the table. He scowled at the newcomers.

He was repellently ugly. His head seemed almost pear shaped, too large above the eyes, tapering down to a small mouth and a tiny chin almost buried in an oversized heap of neck. All his proportions were wrong: shoulders narrow, torso stringy with ribs showing, limbs skinny and too short, hands and feet too long. His eyes were too big, although largely hidden by epicanthic folds, and his nose too flat. His hair was brown, but short and smooth, more like animal fur than human hair.

Ugly, yes, but not truly weird. Yet after a moment Athena wondered whether her imagination was just trying to see what it expected to see. He was human, if grotesque.

"Surely the field is enough defense?" Gownsman Oxindole protested.

"I'll knock his head off if he tries anything with me," Linn said.

Eryngo sighed. "I doubt that. Yesterday a lab technician got too close to the shock fence. The specimen reached one hand through and crushed his larynx with its fingers. He survived but needs extensive reconstruction."

The visitors all stepped back a pace. The youth made an obscene gesture.

"How can it reach through a shock fence?" Linn said. "That would fry every nerve in its arm."

"We don't know yet," Eryngo said. "It has such an astonishing resistance to pain that we think it can block off sections of its spinal column. It won't say. It won't tell us anything. It is resistant to veritaynine. It said nothing under a full adult dose. We went up to a quadruple dose, and that just put it into shock. We suspect it has that response under conscious control, too." She sighed again. "We tried using a brain scan while we interrogated it with pain as negative reinforcement, but frankly its brain structure is so bizarre that we can't be certain it still wasn't slipping lies past us."

"I'm sure I would, if I were in his place," Athena said. She brought one of the departed guards' chairs over to the shock fence, close enough to make her skin prickle. When she sat down, the prisoner was higher than she, which was good. She did not offer any hypocritical smiles. "What's your name?"

He pouted for a while to show he was not scared of her, but he did not speak.

"We call it Nine," the doctor said.

"Why Nine?" Millie demanded from a safer distance.

"One of my technicians named it. We needed a name so we could give it orders," she added weakly.

"They said seven was a lucky number," the boy said, in adult register. He seemed to speak Pocosin without an accent, although that was hard to tell through a translator.

"That's good!" Eryngo sounded enthusiastic for the first time. "It doesn't usually speak without enforcement."

"I'm not surprised," Athena said. "My name's Athena, not that you care. What's yours?"

"Umandral."

Eryngo made a noise indicating mild surprise.

"Umandral, we were brought here from Ayne as a commission to confirm STARS's claim that you are not human. Is that true?"

The boy drew back his lips to display his teeth.

"It has no canines," Eryngo explained.

"STARS claims that you came from Malacostraca?" Athena prompted.

Silence.

"How many of you came?"

Umandral ignored the question, staring sulkily at the bystanders. Millie and Skerry had found chairs; the rest were just gazing in fascinated horror at the non-boy.

"It won't answer that," Eryngo moaned. "Why don't I show you around it? Drop your shorts, Nine."

Scowl.

"Do I have to use the writhe again?"

"You will not use the writhe while we are here," Linn said emphatically. "Tell us what you've learned."

"Well, its esophagus is in front of its trachea. It can drink and breathe at the same time. You can probably see—put your head back, Nine. You could see if it would cooperate."

Incredulously, Athena said, "You mean he has one throat for speaking and another for eating?"

Eryngo looked relieved that some information was getting through. "Exactly. It can never choke on food, the way we can."

"Is that true, Umandral?"

The boy dropped his feet to the floor and stepped right up to the shock fence, certainly close enough to hurt a human, and near enough to make her nervous. She tried not to show that.

He opened his mouth at her and said, "Ahhhhh!"

Athena looked away quickly. "Thank you."

He stayed close to the barrier, like an animal peering through the bars of its cage. Or a youth showing how tough he was.

"I'll show you some images," Eryngo said. "If you'll just look at the holo..." A three-dimensional image of a naked boy floated in the lab, then the flesh peeled away, leaving only bones. "On cursory inspection it appears quite human, of course. The skull is larger than human and has an additional blood supply to the brain. Brain size is 1,822 milliliters, almost 500 above adult human mean. Note that it has no incipient wisdom teeth to impact."

Athena said. "Ayne took wisdom teeth out of the genome ages ago. Most worlds did."

Glaum said, "But the earliest cuckoos had them. Carry on, Doctor."

"And no canine teeth, either," Eryngo said. "Just incisors for cutting, plus the standard molars and pre-molars for grinding."

"What's wrong with canine teeth?" Millie demanded.

The boy said, "I don't have to tear my meat. Do you?"

Eryngo sniffed. "And a smaller dentition leaves more room in the skull for brain. Most of the cranial sinuses have been adapted to make a cooling system. Like earlier cuckoos, it has dispensed with many vestigial and redundant parts. Appendix, coccyx—and the little toe. Only four toes, as you can see." Her tone quickened. "But its germ plasm! The DNA is quite incredible and will need years of study. Almost forty per cent of Nine's genome is not terrestrial standard! We have identified some Malacostracan genes, both human constructs and nonhuman inserts, but at least fifteen percent is totally new. That's why we have named it *Homo chimericus*. Because most of the inserts seem to control brain function, we are fairly sure that they come from some non-human intelligent species!"

Millie muttered, "Oh, no!" while the other commissioners exchanged shocked glances.

Athena tried to imagine what Ratty Turnsole would make of that news and her mind reeled. The mere suggestion that the cuckoos might be sent by unknown intelligent aliens would cause a huge jump in sector paranoia.

Eryngo seemed to take silence as assent. "Chromosome Three, for example—"

"Means nothing to us," Athena said. "Gownsman Skerry, is your department up to date on this?"

Slouched on a chair in a corner, Skerry looked sicker than ever. Solan hovered anxiously nearby.

"Most of it. Tell them about its eyes."

"Ah! Its eyes!" The hologram morphed into an eyeball as big as a man's head, floating like a balloon. "Our eyes, original terrestrial mammalian eyes, are badly designed. The nerves from the rods and cones run on the *inside* of the retina before combining into the optic nerve and going out to the brain. Nine's are wired on the *outside*, see here? Nine will never suffer from detached retinas, and its vision is not obstructed by the nerves, so it has no blind spot. Even other cuckoos had not achieved that.

"And Nine's immune system is just amazing! According to STARS data, the earliest well recorded cuckoo devoted twice as many genes for its immune system as we do. Nine has at least twice as many again. We injected two cc's of cultured neritic fever virus from Disgavel, and in less than an hour its bloodstream was totally clear."

Athena squirmed. "It didn't make him sick?"

"Only briefly."

"It makes me sick!" Millie Backet said hotly.

"We'll be able to use some of this for human benefit," the doctor said. "And some of its adaptations to Pock's environment are definitely non-standard. I can't wait to see what we'll find when we start the invasive tests and dissection."

Athena felt ready to start some dissecting of her own. What was so terrible about having two throats? A very sensible modification. "Why don't you treat *him* as a human being?"

"Because it isn't!" Glaum said.

"An intelligent being then," Athena insisted. She smiled at Umandral as she would at a human boy. "You are intelligent, aren't you?"

"No," he said. "Or I wouldn't have let a troop of monkeys capture me."

"Human or not," Linn said, "Nine is evidence and will go back to Ayne with us."

Glaum laughed. "You won't want to do that! You still don't understand how dangerous it is."

"One adolescent boy? Even if he escaped, what could he do?

"That's what we're about to show you. Drop your pants, thing."

The alien showed his teeth again. "Make me, fat man!"

Glaum held out a hand to the sergeant. "Give me the writhe."

"Oh, stop it!" Athena said. The STARS chairman had refused the boy's challenge, and for the first time she realized that Nine could not possibly be human. If he were, the chairman would have snatched at an excuse to hit him. He was that sort of man, yet he was hiding behind the shock fence.

The cuckoo sneered. "Ask them how many of them it took to arrest me." He went back to the table and jumped up to sit there as before, leaning on his weedy arms.

"Six," Eryngo said, "adult men, armed with writhes. It killed one and injured three. When they brought it in, the specimen had a black eye, two loose teeth, some internal bleeding, and four cracked ribs. In two days all that damage had healed."

"He's a superman?" Millie squeaked.

"We're trying to tell you," Glaum barked. "It is not man at all. Explain, Doctor."

Eryngo hesitated. "But the agreement we signed—"

"I waive the terms in this case. STARS," he explained to the others, "has always held back some information about the cuckoos, mostly because it would cause panic. I ask you to keep this to yourself."

"I make no commitment," Andre said. "We shall include all relevant data in our reports."

Glaum shrugged his blubbered shoulders. "Then I will rely on your discretion. Cuckoos are hermaphrodite. We believe it can change sex at will, or with minimal medicinal assistance. The reason I wanted you to see this thing's crotch is that it has no external scrotum. Tell them, Doctor."

Eryngo's smile lit up her drab face. "As you all know," she said eagerly, "human sex chromosomes can be X or Y. Males have both an X and a Y. Females have two X's, although in their somatic cells one of them is suppressed into an inactive state called a Barr body. Each of Nine's cells has a Y and an X, *and also a Barr body!* That implies three chromosomes, YXX. In humans, that condition is the well-known aneuploidy that causes Klinefelter syndrome!"

She frowned at her audience's blank looks. "In Klinefelter syndrome the subject is male but is usually sterile and has other abnormalities. Starting with the Ghouls that infested Sweven, in the New Hope Sector, cuckoos have solved those problems. According to STARS's historical data, each individual suppresses one of the three genes in somatic cells, so that one-third of them are seeming females and two-thirds are seeming males. We shall need to catch a pseudo-female before we can work out how the procreation is managed between the two sexes, but it is likely that meiosis discards one chromosome in the pseudo-male partner and two in the pseudo-female, to leave three in the zygote."

"So they have sex," Linn said dryly. "You didn't bring any cuckoo girls along, sonny?"

Behind him, Skerry muttered, "They must have done. The DNA investigation of the probe was not designed to find such anomalies."

Umandral showed his incisors. "I'm going to use yours."

"I'm getting to that," the doctor said. "The pseudo-male penis can double as an ovipositor."

"Please put that in simple language," said Brother Andre, glowering, "although I am sure it will sound even worse."

"What it means," Glaum boomed, "is that if this *thing* is allowed to grow up, it will start impregnating *human* women, inserting fertilized *eggs* into them."

Nine smirked.

"That does appear to be correct." Eryngo nodded at the visitors' incredulity. "It has twinned genitalia, male and female. Human embryos have potential to develop both, you know— Müllerian ducts and Wölffian ducts—but genes on the Y chromosome cause the Wölffian ducts to grow into male sex organs and the Müllerian ducts to be absorbed. Without a Y chromosome the reverse happens, Wölffian ducts are absorbed, and Müllerian ducts become the female vagina and so on. This Changeling grew both. Let me show you."

The hologram became a floating, oversized pelvis. "Notice how wide his hips are? The females must need very wide birth canals to pass those heads, and this specimen may at times be female." The image began adding soft organs at her cognition. "*These* are Nine's internal testicles, so it could mate sexually with a pseudo-female, which would have a uterus. *These* organs are ovaries and contain ova, but they connect to the vas deferens. Apparently when this specimen matures—if it were allowed to mature, I mean—it would be able to insert its own fertilized ova into the uterus of a human female. We're not certain yet, but we think it could either accept sperm from another pseudo-male or self-fertilize the eggs. It's a form of parasitism."

"Great Mother preserve us!" Skerry said. "So it gets the best of both systems? It can reproduce sexually to avoid the perils of monoculture, but it can also reproduce itself asexually and parasitically!" He shuddered.

Eryngo said, "We assume that the pseudo-female can also reproduce either sexually or parthenogenetically, but we cannot be certain. It is the pseudo-males that are the immediate threat."

Glaum was sneering. "The last communication ever received from Jibba claimed that the Soldier Ant cuckoos could even impregnate *men*. The parasite can insert its ova into any body cavity, even a stab wound. The embryo behaves like a parasitic fluke, burrowing into tissue until it finds a home with a good blood supply, like the liver. The fetus can be carried to term unless surgically removed."

Millie Backet shrieked in horror. "But not born, surely?"

"Why not?" the doctor said. "All parasites use their hosts' bodies and take over their chemistry; many alter their hosts' behavior. When you catch a respiratory infection, the virus makes you cough so you will spread it. An infection spread in saliva will make its host more prone to bite. Some parasites drive their hosts to suicide or make them change sex. I would not be surprised if a wretch parasitized by one of these monsters did all he could to have his baby safely delivered."

"Now think about concentration camps," Glaum suggested. "And cages full of human brood stock. That's where Pock's World is heading if these monsters prevail. Do you still want to take this horror back to Ayne with you, Friend Linn? Suppose it escapes?"

"It is the work of Satan. Destroy it now." Brother Andre spoke quietly, but his words were colder than outer space.

Doctor Eryngo said, "We have a lot of tests to run yet. A fortnight or two, and then we'll sacrifice it and start dissecting."

No one mentioned that she had only days to live, and Athena was reminded that they must not be bamboozled by the cuckoo freak into forgetting that STARS was the more immediate danger. STARS had its own agenda.

"How do you explain his Pocosin coloring?" she asked.

Eryngo said, "That's a very easy chromosome splice, germline therapy. Can even be done on adults."

Aha! That was interesting. "So we do not know for certain that Umandral was pre-adapted to Pock's World in vitro? He could have been recruited less than a year ago and given genetic therapy?"

The doctor hesitated. "We have not catalogued all its adaptations yet. I need much more extensive DNA evidence before I could express an opinion."

"It knows the answer," Glaum said. "Were you born that color, thing?"

"Were you born that ugly, animal?"

"'Animal?'" Athena repeated sadly. "You think you're better, so you have to prove it by wiping us out?"

The boy turned his sneer on her. "Of course we are better. Infinitely better! You are the dregs of a billion years of evolutionary tinkering, survival of the least-bad. We are conscious design, the best possible. You will kill me, but I have a billion siblings to carry on the struggle. If you want a truce, we will sign a truce, and when the time is ripe we will ignore it, because we know that we are the future and you are the primitive animal stock from which we sprang. We cannot recognize you as equals. The idea is laughable."

"Our ancestors created yours," Athena said. "The creator must be greater than his creation."

"No! It is true that the human Diallelon was the first to seek to improve your botched genetics, but my ancestors took over the work and perfected it. We are a self-made species. We will bury you."

"You haven't yet," Glaum said. "STARS will burn Pock's World and you with it." The big man's brutal features and Nine's childish ones held matching hatred. The human race had fought its way to the top of the food chain long ago and would not accept the novelty of genuine competition.

"A few dozen less of us and six hundred million less of you? You wage war by wiping out your own side!" The cuckoo's threats were less frightening than his silent contempt had been. He looked like a boy and now he sounded like a boy, parroting what he had been taught. He was a child facing a horrible death.

The dangerous cuckoos are the nestlings.

Athena turned sadly to her companions. "Does anyone else have any questions to ask Umandral?" All heads shook. "You,

Solan? Would you like to stay and play with Umandral for a while?"

"*That?* That *thing?*" The detestation on Solan's face mirrored the alien's exactly. "It would eat me!"

The hatred was instinctive; hominins tolerated no rivals.

"You haven't answered my question, Nine," Glaum said. "I asked if you were born that color. Now that the commissioners have seen you, we can start serious interrogation. You can turn off some pain, but not all of it. If I shine the writhe in your eyes, for instance? Won't that be fun? And we want to know where your brothers went. You came here to Hederal, but you must have an idea where the rest were headed. So I'll make you a promise—as soon as we catch one to interrogate in your place, we'll put you out of your misery and the pain will end. That's a reasonable reward, isn't it?"

The youth said nothing, but his eyes were those of a cornered animal.

Before Athena could object, Linn intervened.

"You will not start any of that until the commissioners approve, Friend Glaum. We may have more questions to put to the prisoner later. He is not STARS's captive, anyway. Is torture permitted in Hederal, Colonel?"

Eryngo shot a worried look at Glaum, as if in search of instructions. "Torture of people is not," she said. "But Nine is not human."

"That doesn't matter," Linn announced. "He's sentient. We came a hundred light years to see this boy, and you will not maltreat him any more until we are finished with him. You may continue your investigations, but avoid pain, indignity, and unnecessary violence. We shall confer with all the major police and security forces on the planet about this threat. That will take at least a fortnight."

Even Millie Backet had enough sense not to mention that the world was going to end early Sixtrdy. Somebody had reacted, though. Athena was watching Nine, and Nine was studying faces. He had noticed that wrongness.

As she rose to leave, he suddenly said, "Athena?"

"Yes, Umandral?"

"I wasn't born this color." He studied her with big, dark eyes. "They spliced the Pocosin adaptations into us about eighty days ago, roughly."

"Thank you. And what planet were you born on?"

He smiled, and suddenly his top-heavy face looked appealingly babyish. "I don't know what you call it. It has three moons, one of them very small and retrograde."

"That's not Malacostraca," Skerry said.

"Of course not," Athena agreed. "As soon as the new genes took, the invasion force was dispatched by entanglement to the probe, right? A hop or maybe two. Just an hour or so altogether?"

Nine nodded warily.

"And the probe had been parked in distant orbit around Javel for years, maybe centuries. It just needed a minor course correction to bring it in when it was needed?"

"Of course," the boy said. "You are clever to work that out."

"No. I lied," Athena said sadly. "We know from analysis of its orbit that it arrived in the system within the last two or three fortnights. You are clever to have noticed that the rest of us are not entirely friendly with the STARS team. You saw a chance to drive a wedge of distrust between us, didn't you? Do you have any idea what his IQ is, Doctor?"

"He won't cooperate enough to be tested, of course. Based on his neuron density and firing rate, we estimate it as between 200 and 250."

Millie said, "Oh dear! That is very high!"

"It's higher than that," Umandral said indignantly.

Glaum looked over the off-worlders. "Well? Have you seen all you need here?"

"It seems so!" Millie had regained her self-importance. "If we need to summon you to appear before us again, Chairman Glaum, how do we get hold of you?"

Glaum said, "Write a note on a piece of paper and swallow it."

Solan and Umandral both laughed, and that uniquely human reaction made Athena feel even worse.

Chapter 3

Bright week had begun, so the sun would not set for seven days. Ratty went to bed in daylight and awakened in daylight. Joy's bed was large for one person, snug for two. He had no complaints about that. Fondling was a wonderful way to be awakened. "If you insist," he murmured. He rolled over and co-operated. Mattress moss was nice, but bed was better.

"That was wonderful," she said later.

"It was. The woman is very well named."

"She has a very good teacher."

"Of course she does, but he has never had a more reward-ing pupil." It was silly lovers' pillow talk, and it hurt horribly because he had given Bedel his word not to tell Joy about the end of the world. She was going to die. What he was doing was practically necrophilia.

"My pregnancy will be a matter of worldwide interest. Monody is reborn only once in a generation. Everyone will want to hear all about the giver she chose this time. Streets and chil-dren will be named after you. You will have to get used to hav-ing people grovel to you."

I don't have time. There is no time. "They always do."

"Oh, lover!" she told his collarbone, "I thought I knew what would happen, and I hoped it would be fun and we might do it again a few times, but now I can't leave you alone, can't keep my hands off you. Is this *love?*"

He squeezed her as tight as he dared without hurting. "It's infatuation. It can be the start of love. I feel it too. Enjoy it, because it's the most exciting experience life has to offer and it never lasts long enough." *And this time it will be brutally short.*

"When do you have to go home? Why can't you stay? You *will* come right back?"

"Let's discuss that after we've seen Bedel. Where are my friends? I'm supposed to be investigating a cuckoo infestation, not indulging my basest instincts in orgiastic decadence."

She punched him. "Don't be rude! This is much more important. Let's see... Mother's back. She wants to meet you. She sends her congratulations."

"You already told her?"

"Of course! I cognized everybody as soon as we were airborne last night. I even described your birthmark. The whole palace must know by now. The whole world will know by eclipse."

Just wonderful! "That's wonderful," he said.

"Mm... Duty will be here shortly, and Oxindole is on his way from Hederal with your friends. Brace yourself for a family gathering."

Even the most junior Monody incarnation had apartments fit for a queen, and Joy's bedroom opened onto a flowered courtyard containing a steaming natural hot pool. The sun was shining, the sky above the trees was blue. Ratty had just followed her into the water and settled neck-deep with a sigh of delight when another door flew open. Four girls came rushing out, squealing in great excitement. He yelped and folded up tight, while they lined up along the brink to admire the happy couple. They wore short pink capes on one shoulder and very little else; not one of them looked any older than Joy herself.

"Meet Giver Ratty, girls," she said brightly. "Isn't he gorgeous? Don't be shy, darling. They've seen men before. Find some clothes for him, Lakshmi. Red cape, of course. Otherwise dark blue, I think, and *snug*. Really snug!"

"I can't see how big he is!" said one, presumably Lakshmi. They all screamed with laughter.

"Stand up and show her!" Joy commanded.

She was serious. Reluctantly Ratty obeyed, sickly pale brown by local standards. All four priestesses at once began sniggering even harder. When Pocosin faces turned red, they turned *very* red.

Worse, Joy joined in. "His back's even worse!" she said. "Turn around and show them, dear!"

Only then did Ratty realize that his arms and chest, even his legs, were covered with a wickerwork of scratches. Most of those had come from Joy's struggle to keep him from reaching Quoad, but that was not the implication. He sat down again quickly. There was not one hickey on her, he was pleased to note. Pocosin skin was remarkable stuff.

"Yes, dark blue," Joy said, "and don't forget *tight*."

⊷❦⊷ ❧ — ❧ ⊷❦⊷

Pocosins slept indoors, Joy said, excepting the very poor. Eating was mostly an indoor activity, because rain spoiled the food. Anything else was done outside as often as in—except toward the end of dark week, when the weather might turn cool.

The family had gathered in the stepped conical pit he had seen the previous day. Wisdom was there again, shrouded like a corpse as before, with Bedel and a slightly older version of Joy in a matching white gown. Ratty and Joy descended the stairs hand in hand, and dipped their knees to her simultaneously.

Had he been given his choice at the start, Ratty might have chosen Love over Joy. She was undoubtedly older than he, but she had a full-bosomed ripeness that made her daughter seem leggy and brash. If Joy was Monody as youth, her mother epitomized her as lover. Her gaze as she inspected her wayward daughter's choice held a convincing sultriness, suggesting that Bedel might have his hands full at times. She was a woman in her prime, trained to command, experienced, and ready now, if the universe unfolded as it should, to take her place as Duty, the ruling incarnation. She came forward with hands outstretched.

"Blessings on you, honored ambassador and friend. Congratulations, both of you. By the Mother, child, did you have to *rape* him like that?"

"Don't be vulgar!" Joy shouted.

Love gave Ratty a warm hug. "You are indeed welcome, Ratty, and please believe that to be chosen by Monody is an honor any male on Pock's World would die for. I know Joy seems like a scatterbrain, but she looks out for her own interests, and we all have a good eye for men. Don't we, love?"

"Certainly." Bedel embraced Ratty more formally. "I knew this was going to happen the moment I set eyes on you, friend. I thought it would take her a day or two longer, but I knew you were doomed. Come and sit with us."

"Just think, Bedel!" Joy said waspishly. "You might have been hugging Scrob."

"Don't be absurd," her mother said. "I was testing your sense of humor. Sit here, Ratty dear. Besides, you must agree Scrob had nice arms. His mother's an astrophysicist, you know."

Food was on the way, Bedel said. And so were the other commissioners. Duty herself was just landing. Then his tone changed, and even through machine translation Ratty's trained ear detected an Official Release. Here came the family's considered judgment—

"We happily accept you into the family as Joy's child giver, Ratty, and you are welcome to enjoy the privileges of consort during your brief stay on Pock's, but the office of consort carries certain duties. You would have to swear an oath to the Mother, for example, and we recognize that you are not of our faith. You would be responsible for Joy's safety and would need weapons certification. I will appoint a couple of blue-capes to guard you both instead. Also, Joy is now of age..." He smiled. "As of today! From now on she will attend family conferences; an official consort is an advisor and has the right to express opinions even to Duty. Recognizing that this may conflict with your duties as commissioner, we suggest—"

Joy opened her mouth to explode.

Ratty squeezed the hand he was holding and said, "Just a moment, love!" They were treating Joy as a child. But if she were a child, what did that make him, after last night? He couldn't have that. "Your Holinesses, Gownsman Bedel, it is true that I cannot in good conscience swear an oath to your Goddess. I certainly swore no oath to STARS, if that is what worries you, and I put my responsibilities to Pock's World well ahead of my loyalty to Ayne at the moment. So here is an oath I can swear in good faith."

He clasped both of Joy's hands in his. "Your Holiness, I solemnly swear that I love you truly, and I will continue to love and serve you with all my heart and soul for as long as I am able and you permit. This oath takes precedence over all other oaths and commitments."

Joy *Oohed!* with delight and kissed his cheek. "That's lovely!"

Bedel did not appear to share her view. "I see the food is coming, but if you lovebirds would rather go off somewhere and read poetry, we will understand."

He should have been able to improvise better than that. Again Joy opened her mouth to protest, and again Ratty halted her. Love was a matter of trust, and he had had enough of this hypocrisy.

"As your advisor, Your Holiness, I advise you to stay right where you are."

Joy glanced quickly at him, then at the others. Her eyes narrowed as she studied her mother. "Are they hiding something from me, darling?" She was young and inexperienced, but she had the Monody brains.

"Here's the food," Bedel said, looking as if he would like to serve roasted Turnsole as hors d'oeuvre. Five pages laid five trays beside five people in a silence so frigid that it was a wonder the hot pool did not ice over. Then they went trotting back up the stairs.

Old Wisdom was the first to speak. "He's quite right. I wish he wasn't, but he is doing his duty as consort. She has the right to know." She looked more haggard than she had the previous day.

"*Know what?*" Joy yelled.

"Ratty's companions have been spreading evil rumors," Love said. "Fortunately there is no truth to them. Tell her, dear."

Looking straight at Joy, and certainly not at Ratty, Bedel said, "You know that STARS discovered an interstellar probe in orbit around Javel, three weeks ago. Like all such probes, it is a captured nickel-iron asteroid. STARS has now leaked a story that the probe will impact Pock's early on Sixtrdy, and the resulting explosion will cause planet-wide destruction and fire, followed by years of darkness and bitter cold. Some minor life forms may survive, but no human beings. STARS is claiming that it has arranged this in order to destroy the cuckoo invaders. Fortunately there is no truth to this story."

Inevitably, Joy's first reaction was disbelief. She tried a smile. She looked at her mother, then at Ratty. The dream face became shadowed by horror.

"Do you believe this?"

"Bedel himself told me the news yesterday," Ratty said. "He made me swear not to tell you. Were you lying to me, Consort? Is this some obscure Pocosin joke?"

"I was taken in myself at first. I am sorry to have deceived you."

Ratty interrogated people for a career. His VERIT45 implant was not working at the moment, because it relied on the Ayne

Brain's computational power, but he did not need it to know that Bedel was lying now. He had not been lying yesterday.

Joy probably agreed with that assessment, because her arm around Ratty was trembling.

He said, "I am happy to hear the good news, of course. Sterilizing an entire world always seems so *excessive*, doesn't it? So what has changed? Who exposed the STARS deception?"

"Monody did," said Love. "Duty. As she pointed out, it is inconceivable that the Mother will allow her children to be destroyed in this way. STARS is lying. Meanwhile we should eat." She turned to inspect the tray beside her.

"You mean your, er, mother... senior incarnation..."

"Duty."

"Monody as Duty has been granted a divine revelation on the subject?"

"Yes, she has. She will be here shortly." Love was more convinced than her consort, but neither of them was going to persuade Ratty now.

"What does Skerry say?" Joy demanded.

Ratty was too busy watching Bedel squirm to ask who Skerry was.

"Skerry has to rely on the data provided to him, dear."

Joy said, "I? Know? That? What? Does? He? Say?"

"We should not repeat vicious lies," Love said with her mouth full.

"Tell her," said Wisdom. "She's been to Quassia. She is not a child now."

"Oh, go on, then, tell her." Love bit into a purple fruit.

"According to Skerry," Bedel said, "the latest readings are for impact early on Sixtrdy, bull's-eye on the Hostie Caldera. There is no margin for doubt, he says."

"But the numbers may be faked," Love insisted. "STARS is bluffing or just wrong. It will not happen."

Love ate. Bedel tried to. Wisdom picked at a few things, but she probably never ate much. Joy did not touch her tray, so Ratty could not. He was ravenous, but if he took one nibble it would show that he was different. He was not under sentence of death; he was going home soon. His conscience kept whispering in his ear, asking him how sincere his oath had been. He had sworn to love and serve Joy as long as he could and she permitted—suppose she too had a divine revelation and forbade him to take his seat on that final shuttle? She wouldn't do that, would she?

She shouted, "Stop cognizing in the middle of a conversation!" She glared at her mother. "You know that's rude. Ask him yourself."

"Sorry," Love said. "Just habit. Ratty, what was it that you saw on Quoad?"

Oh, how Ratty wished he had not mentioned those! "Lights, pale blue mostly, standing on the stairs or moving up and down. Not unlike the flashes on Javel." He suspected that there was still a lot of cognizing going on, although Love was smiling as a mother should be smiling on her daughter's wedding day, not like a woman condemned to watch her world die. Bedel was silent and troubled.

"There are always lights on Javel's dark side," Love said. "Monody taught us that they were the souls of the Querent dancing for the Mother. Your explanation of aurora and electrical storms is popular among non-believers. But lights on Quoad are rare. Did they speak to you?"

"Yes." He noted her shocked reaction. "I could not understand the words, but I felt they were calling me to go to them. I was on my way there when Joy tackled me." Why had she? What would have happened if he had reached the base of the rock? "Is it a good omen or a bad one?"

"You must ask Duty that," Bedel said. "Here she comes now."

Two people were descending the stair. One was a Monody in a sleeveless white robe. Behind her, surprisingly, walked the skinny attendant who had greeted the team on their arrival at Pock's Station. Joy pulled free from Love and wiped her eyes. She went back to find comfort from Ratty, making him feel more guilty than ever.

The ruling High Priestess was the last link in the chain. She resembled Love much more than Wisdom, but her walk was more deliberate, her body thicker, her back a little bent, her face at once plumper and more drawn. Goddess as youth, mother, matriarch—and now as ruler. Each sported Monody's distinctive halo of red and white curls, fading in stages from Joy's flame to embers and ashes on her great-grandmother. The wheel of life rolled on; it was almost time for a new baby Joy, for Joy to become Love, Love Duty, Duty Wisdom, and for the crone to lay down her burdens. Probably Ratty was simply seeing what he knew should be there, but he sensed in Duty a woman who had served her Goddess long and well and was now eager to hand over the reins and retire to a less strenuous position as adviser. She greeted him with a smile and the family embrace. And a joke. "Joy, kitten, did you have to *rape* him like that?"

"He needed a lot of persuading, Holiness," Joy said. She did not smile.

"That's odd. He looks quite normal to me."

Braata had undergone changes since the last time Ratty saw him. He wore green and blue checked shorts instead of STARS black and Duty introduced him as Friend Zyemindar. He looked distinctly older, and uncomfortable in present company, but he was still defiantly flaunting his crucifix, so the others' coolness was understandable. A hint of his former good humor flashed when he congratulated Ratty on his red cape, but then he turned somber again as he folded his extreme lankiness to sit by himself, as far from everyone else as he decently could.

Duty stepped bodily into the pool and lay back to soak. She was monarch, and the rest waited for her to begin the conversation.

At last, "It's been a pig of a day already," she announced to the clouds, "and can only get worse. Zyemindar is a STARS employee. He started the rumors, but I am satisfied that he did so in good faith. He was used, even if he doesn't see that yet. How many of your faith are there in STARS, anyway, my son?"

Braata said, "I do not know, Holiness. Very few, I suspect."

"Exactly. Proves my point. Tell them what's going on now."

"Your Holinesses, Gownsman, Friend Ratty, there is no change, really. The world's astronomers have been netcognizing all night, and they spliced me in at Her Holiness's request. I provided the codes for the babysitter I installed, and they were able to confirm that the charges had blown, so the Wong-Hui projector is now rubble. The pirate will soon be obscured by Javel, but it will be tracked from some of the mining asteroids." He sighed. "The result seems certain. I am sorry."

"There could be a second projector hidden on board?" Bedel asked.

"No, sir. It must be at the center of gravity, or the probe starts spinning."

"Is there any chance," Wisdom asked in her croaky old voice, "that these charges you set off caused the pirate to break up?"

"None, Your Holiness. That is one tough nugget! It has withstood centuries of acceleration and deceleration, abrasion by the galactic gas and dust, and a few extremely close passes of Javel. You might as well try to kick over one of those trees. In any case, it would make no difference. The pieces would still hit us all at once. Indeed, that might be worse."

In the gloom-laden silence, Ratty became aware that Joy was weeping in his one-armed embrace. She had her face down, but he could feel the sobs racking her body. It was a logical reaction. He knew how terrified he would be if he was not guaranteed a seat on a STARS shuttle out. He wondered when the commissioners were due to leave, but he couldn't ask that in this company.

"I do not for a moment believe it." Duty rose and stepped out of the pool. She sat on the bench next to Bedel's tray and helped herself to a piece of fruit. "The cuckoo may be genuine, but that is no reason for STARS to sterilize the whole world. The Mother will not permit it to happen, but the threat alone will be a disaster. People are going to panic. I shall make an announcement shortly, and we shall hold a major invocation at Real Quassia late on Frivdy—we cannot possibly organize it any sooner, and any later will be too late. Even then, we shall have to skimp on preparations, but it will give the people something to look forward to."

To Ratty she seemed far more convincing than any of the others. Duty was a clever and competent woman, and she had found the only response possible. Heretical as it seemed for a professional reporter like him to think so, this was a case where people were better off not knowing. Denial was the best defense. He felt a strong urge to go over to Braata-Zyemindar and beat his brains out. STARS's plan would still be a secret if the turncoat had not exposed it.

Duty said, "I am curious about the messengers you saw on the pillar. We Monodys see them sometimes, but not often. It is extremely rare for anyone else to do so."

"If you will pardon my secular beliefs, Holiness, I do not find my experience so surprising. The mattress moss must be an excellent conductor, the pillar itself is probably an intrusion of dissimilar lithology within the country rock of the mountain, and the cliff provides updrafts and downdrafts. These things could easily produce the glow discharge known as St. Elmo's fire. I have an unusual number of implants in my head, so what is so strange if one or two of them detected a varying electrical potential and interpreted it as a signal?"

Duty's smile was as formal as his response had been. "And if you will pardon our beliefs, you had just participated in our most sacred ritual, the calling forth of a new incarnation in a series dating back a hundred centuries. So what would be so strange if the Mother wanted to tell you something?"

He shrugged. "With respect, I did not understand the language she chose."

"Would you be willing to make another try? I will be going to Real Quassia this evening to offer my personal prayers. I should be grateful if you would agree to accompany me."

Joy said, *"No!"*

Her mother snapped a furious, "Joy! You—"

She was cut off by Duty, whose voice was quieter but held more authority, a hundred centuries of authority. "Joy, you forget who you are. A generation from now, you will succeed to the throne I am soon to relinquish. You are Monody, and Monody is eternal. The Mother has promised. You carry your own successor in your womb already. It is possible that unpleasant things will happen on Sixtrdy, but the end of the world will not be one of them. Do you understand?"

Joy raised her tear-stained face. "I understand, Holiness, and ask you to forgive my childish doubts."

Duty smiled. "Of course we forgive you. We always have, haven't we? Now, Friend Ratty, will you come to Real Quassia with us this evening?"

Ratty said, "I am your granddaughter's consort, Holiness, even if only temporarily. If she grants permission, I shall be honored to come. I shall only witness, though. An unbeliever going through the motions of worship is hypocritical."

Monody nodded acceptance. "There we do agree, but you are welcome to witness and tell us if you see anything this time. Joy, I promise I will see he returns safely! Here come your fellow commissioners."

Chapter 4

Millie was first, of course, clutching her bag to her chest with both arms, scurrying down the spiral stairs at a dangerous pace. When she reached the pool level she hesitated, agog at the four incarnations.

"I am Monody, Director," Duty said, not rising. "Wisdom, Love, Joy and Love's consort Bedel. You know Friend Ratty, of course. Do please find a place to sit."

Even Backet could not face down ten thousand years of authority. She obeyed, still tongue-tied.

Duty regarded the next visitor with no greater warmth. "Welcome, Brother Andre! This is an unexpected reunion."

Ratty watched with professional nosiness as the cadaverous brown-robed friar came striding down. The bony smile was more formal than warm, but his nod to Duty was respectful enough to be almost a bow. "Very unexpected, and in tragic circumstances. The last time I saw you, Priestess, you were about one year old—less than a Pocosin year, more than an Ayne."

Ratty's mind flipped paradigms. The saint had spent less than one and a half Ayne years on Pock's, so whatever the scandal that had sent him home in disgrace, it had not been *that*.

Wrapping her wrinkles in a smile, Wisdom patted a scarlet cushion beside her. "Come and entertain me, ancient one. I promise you I will restrain my lustful impulses this time. I regret I can no longer hope to ensnare you in mortal sin."

Andre gave her one of his rare smiles as he obeyed. "I confess that I am enjoying the memories of your former attempts, though. "I have prayed for you nightly, all these long years."

"You still dream about me, then?"

Obviously they were old sparring partners, and Ratty guessed that a genuine friendship lurked beneath their banter. It was an unexpected facet of the saint of Annatto.

Ratty found it easier to imagine the present Wisdom as a voluptuous Love than matronly Duty as a toddler. She would have been a new mother when Andre met them, not much older than Joy was now. There would have been another Duty and another Wisdom behind them, of course, and perhaps even one more, Memory.

Ratty wondered if they kept score somewhere; was Joy recorded as Monody 567? Or 601? Or didn't they care?

Linn Lazuline came next, studying the group with interest. Athena, surprisingly, had acquired a stringy Pocosin boy as escort. She sat beside Ratty, but in all the flurry of introductions, no one explained to him who the boy was. The large red-caped man at the rear could only be Gownsman Oxindole, Duty's giver, consort, and senior advisor, and the smiles they exchanged were those of intimates. There was ample room for thirteen people on the innermost bench, and brown-caped pages swarmed around, laying out more cushions and whisking away the food trays. In the confusion, Joy slipped away to sit beside her mother, leaving Ratty between Braata and Athena.

"Bad news, I gather," he murmured.

Athena nodded grimly. "Very bad. It convinced us all. He calls himself Umandral and looks about thirteen Ayne years. Grotesquely ugly, but not so different that you think '*Alien!*' at a glance. Of course, that's the danger. No, he isn't human. Even we could see the discrepancies. His teeth, his throat... and a sense of great wrongness." She accepted a glass from a tray offered by a young brown-cape.

So did Ratty. Certain human hospitality rites were universal. "Worse than Solidagians? Jaspians give me the creeps, too."

"Much worse. Even Solan here could feel it. According to the medic, some of his DNA comes from an unknown intelligent alien species. I suspect she's pushing theory ahead of facts, but he does feel alien. He despises us, and I found myself reacting the same way to him."

"But the deed is done? What we decide doesn't matter? The probe is certain to come down on Sixtrdy, I'm told."

"Apparently." Athena sniffed her drink and then took a hefty swig of it. "The cuckoo we saw is a pseudo-male. As an adult it could breed either sexually, with its own pseudo-females, parthenogenetically, or by parasitizing human beings. That means that it would take only one of them to start a colony! A group would provide more genetic variability, but in theory just one would suffice." She shook her head. "I am close to believing now that STARS is justified in what it is doing."

Ratty trusted Athena's judgment more than any of the others', and her reversal was troubling. "Even without waiting for our report?"

"I asked Skerry about that."

"Skerry?"

"Gownsman, Secretary for Science. Solan's father. He says the probe just happened to be properly positioned. It needed only a slight course correction. If STARS had let that opportunity go by, it might have been a year or more before impact became feasible."

To sentence a world to death and delay the execution for a year would be extreme torture. "How does Friend Linn feel?" Linn was three cushions farther around the circle, ogling Joy.

"I think he's coming around too, but he won't say. Brother Andre denounced Umandral as an abomination and was ready to kill him on the spot. We go home tomorrow. A car will pick us up here at the palace."

"Tomorrow?" Ratty felt a stab of grief. To go home and leave Joy to her death? He wondered if he could negotiate a later departure.

"Her Holiness refuses to believe that the world will end."

Athena shrugged. "She has to say that, doesn't she? STARS may be lying, but I can't believe the Pocosin astronomers are, and they make their own observations."

Ratty looked across the pool at the woman he had slept with. Yes, he had enjoyed one-night stands before, but not with a... virgin, to use an overloaded word. To be a girl's first love, then say thanks but I've gotta run... He felt a deep and ancient instinct muttering that a man did not go away and leave his mate to die. A shallower one screamed that Joy was not his mate and never could be in the sense of bearing his children. She was not looking at him. Perhaps she felt betrayed and would demand his cape back, so she could return it to Scrob.

People passing silent cog messages in company could never refrain from glancing at one another, and there was a lot of that going on among the rest of the natives. Even Joy and Braata were doing it. Only Wisdom seemed excluded, intently whispering with Brother Andre. Reporting on dead friends, no doubt.

Duty sighed and somehow caught everyone's attention.

"Honored friends, we rarely meet off-worlders and would genuinely love to entertain so many distinguished guests. Alas, the terrible rumors are spreading, and we must prevent panic. I am due to make a statement shortly, and I will announce a major invocation for Frivdy evening. We all have urgent preparations to make, as you can guess. Our youngest incarnation, Joy, will stay and act as your hostess, and you are all welcome to remain at the palace until your departure tomorrow. If we can help your investigation in any way, Joy will be happy to organize it. Friend Ratty, she will see you have transportation to Real Quassia this evening. Now, if you will excuse us..."

Duty, Love, Bedel, and Oxindole rose and set off up the stairs, leaving the five fact-finders and the boy with Joy, Wisdom, and Braata.

Brother Andre was frowning at Ratty. "What is this about Quassia?"

"I promised to attend a prayer service there tonight."

The old man clenched his big jaw for a moment and looked at Wisdom, beside him.

She smiled at his anger. "He saw the Querent! The Mother wishes to speak to us through him."

"How did you acquire that red cape, young man?"

"That is a personal matter I prefer not to discuss."

Andre sighed and nodded as if his worst fears were realized. "Ritual fornication."

"I had a great time," Ratty said. "You should have tried it when you had the chance. Meanwhile stay out of my business."

"It is my business. You promoted me to sainthood, remember? I will pray for you, my son, and I warn you now: You may find yourself called to judgment much sooner than you expect if you return to Quassia this evening!" He glanced at Joy and then quickly looked away again, shuddering. "Did she tell you about Quoad? The real story? Or get Priestess Wisdom here to tell you how Gownsman Bombardon died. I had the story from his widow."

"Then why don't you tell me?"

"He went to fornicate at Real Quassia and did not return."

Ratty prided himself on never becoming emotionally involved in an interview. But this was not an interview, and his emotions were already deeply involved. The old man's meddling roused an astonishing rage in him.

"Oh, shut up! You prattle about love, but you don't know what it means. You call it a sin, and that just reveals your ignorance and jealousy." He reined in his temper, already ashamed of himself. "I love Joy and I trust her with my life. If she wants me to go back to Quassia and climb to the very top of that pillar, I will do so without a moment's hesitation. I will stand on my hands there if she asks me to."

"I know what love is, and I know what lust is, and they are not the same. They are opposites."

Wisdom remarked to Joy in a stage whisper for everyone to hear, "He approves of martyrs in his own church, you see, but not in others. It's a small-minded distinction."

Andre smiled at her affectionately. "But a valid one. I never could make you understand the difference between martyrdom and human sacrifice."

"And how do you feel about sterilizing a world?"

The old man's face hardened to rock. "What do you mean, *how do I feel?* I am appalled, of course, but the cuckoos are undoubtedly the work of Satan and must be stopped. I just wish STARS could find a better way."

Wisdom cackled. "But your god will permit it? You tried to tell me he is a god of love. He hurls down fire and brimstone, and he is a god of love?"

"It is STARS throwing down the fire and brimstone in this case. The Lord has reasons that we cannot understand, and sometimes he must let some suffer for the good of many. The defense of the rest of the galaxy may require this. Do not presume to judge the Lord."

"Well your god may permit it. Our goddess will not."

Andre sighed. "You are being deceived by the evil one. Cardinal Phare is sending an air car for me. How is Gownsman Skerry?"

Pause for cognition... Joy answered.

"Resting comfortably in his own bed. Solan, you can go and see him now if you want.

"Thanks, Joy!" The boy jumped up eagerly. He glanced shyly at Ratty and blushed. "Congratulations!"

"Thank you."

Andre rose more circumspectly. "We shall both call on Skerry. I expect the car will be here soon."

"Before you go," Athena said, "we never decided who should chair our mission. I nominate Friend Backet."

"I second that," Ratty said quickly. He appreciated that the Senator didn't want her name prominent on the report. He felt the same. She was also trying to calm the storm waves, and he approved of her peacemaking also.

Linn gave them both a cynical glance, guessing what they were thinking. "I'll third it."

Millie's face lit up like a fireworks display.

Andre's smile was more genuine. "I concur, but I will not necessarily sign with the majority. Motion carried."

Millie sighed joyfully at the prospect of the Backet Commission's place in history. "I thank you all for this very flattering appointment. I shall circulate a brief draft for your comments."

Andre took Wisdom's hand and kissed it. "I hope I shall get the chance to see you again, Priestess. I shall pray for you always."

She smiled without showing her teeth. "And I for you, Jame. Live and die happy."

"You will return, I hope?" Athena asked.

Andre nodded. "I hope so, too. Pagans are not the only ones who fear the end of the world. I will be at St. Michael's, hearing confessions, providing what comfort I can. Come, young friend."

Before he and Solan reached the steps, Braata was towering in their path.

"Father, may I come with you? Please?"

Andre frowned. "I don't see how it can matter now, but you gave your parole. Priestess?" He turned his head, not quite enough to look directly at Joy. "Can Friend Zyemindar be released on my recognizance?"

"Just a moment..." Joy pouted. "Gownsman Oxindole is not answering calls. I have left a message."

"I am sure he will agree," Andre told Braata. "As soon as he releases you, come to St. Michael's." He gave the younger man his blessing and set off up the stairs with Solan hurrying ahead of him.

Braata nodded respectfully to Joy. "I shall be in my room, Holiness." He ran up the stairs and disappeared. He, especially, must need time to meditate. His loyalties were more tangled than anyone's.

It was like a children's counting song, Ratty thought—and then there were six. Joy still did not look in his direction.

"No," Wisdom said, as if answering a cognized question aloud. "I shall go to the temple. I expect there will be many people there."

Joy took a deep breath and began playing hostess. "Friend Athena, Friend Millie, Friend Linn, what can I offer you? Refreshment? A tour of the palace grounds, since the weather is so clement?" Her voice was toneless, her face a lifeless mask.

"I should love to see some of the sights!" Millie said eagerly. "The ruins at Quassia?"

"Did I see horses as we came in?" Linn asked.

"We do have horses," Joy agreed. "I am informed that our lower gravity enhances their performance." She might have been reading from a guidebook.

"That sounds like fun," Athena agreed. "But it seems dreadful to consider *fun* when the world is about to end. Is there nothing we can do to help?"

"Just refrain from spreading alarm," the girl said. "It would be best if you do not comment on the probe or related matters. I am told that Gownsman Skerry is having reports prepared for you to consider and take home. And also he has requested samples of the physical evidence from the pirate probe. These are not ready yet. If there is anything else you wish, please do not hesitate to ask." Still Joy was showing no more emotion than a music box. "I have summoned guides who will assist you."

Heart aching, Ratty watched in silence as the three Ayne folk walked up the stairs. A group of brown-capes appeared at the top to wait for them and then conduct them away. White-caped priestesses came down the other staircase, four of them with a carrying chair. They took Wisdom away, leaving him alone with Joy.

He walked around the pool and pulled a cushion close to her. She was as rigid as a pillar of basalt, staring down at her hands.

He must not be the first to touch. "I gave Bedel my word I would not tell you. That was before I knew how you were planning to honor me."

She nodded, bit her lip, still said nothing.

He tried again. "I meant what I told the friar about Quassia.
I trust you absolutely. I love you. He's a crabby old fanatic."

"Joy died."

"What?"

"When the present Wisdom was Love, her baby died. Some
childhood infection. We're not immortal. It happens." Still she
did not look at him.

Ratty tried to work out the rest, spare her having to say it.
"You mean what we did last night, the seminal catalyst thing,
it only works once? Even if you go back to Real Quassia someday with another man, it's just one ovulation per customer, once
per incarnation?"

She nodded.

"Unless?" he prompted. "Did Bombardon jump, or was he
thrown?"

"The wind blew him off."

And it had worked. Women had no conscious control over
their ovulation, but that did not mean that there was no men-
tal factor involved. If the bereaved Love-who-was-now-Wis-
dom had believed that her lover must make such a sacrifice to
let her bear another child, then it might well have been necessary.

"So that's why you were worried when I headed for Quoad's
pillar last night? That's all there is to this human sacrifice
thing?"

She hesitated, then said, "Can you really do handstands?"

"In this gravity? Easy!" He removed his red cloak and sandals. He dropped his hands to the edge of the pool and swung
his legs up. There was nothing to it. She pushed, of course, and
he toppled. He fell slowly in the low gravity, but the water he
displaced was lighter, too, so he created a tsunami that soaked
the innermost bench. By the time he surfaced, spluttering, Joy
was in there with him and they embraced.

"Why?" she demanded when they broke off the kiss and just
hugged hungrily. "Why is the goddess so cruel? Why do I only
get one day to love you?"

Here was his test already. "I have sworn to obey you. You
can forbid me to board the shuttle."

"You would obey me?"

He thought about it, then nodded. "Yes, I would."

"But if I gave you that order," she wailed, "that would prove
I didn't love you. And because I do love you, I couldn't give you
that order!"

He said it before he saw where it would lead him: "You
mean you don't believe that your goddess will save the world,
as Duty says?"

She gasped. "You mean you do believe?"

"Oh, I believe gods are powerful." He just didn't believe
they were sentient.

"You will stay with me, here on Pock's World? You love me
that much?"

He had an erection like the Quoad pillar.

"I will stay with you forever if you want me, my darling. I'll
be your gownsman or floor scrubber or anything you want.
Let's find a handy bed. No, forget the bed. Hot water's fine.
Hold on tight." He unfastened his shorts.

Chapter 5

Millie was met at the top of the stairs by an imposing, ma-tronly priestess who gave her name as Desipient. She wore a white top above a bare midriff and calf-length shorts, plus a one-shoulder cape of white with thin brown stripes. It wouldn't have passed in a church on Ayne, but this was Pock's, and travel made one tolerant of odd customs. With her silver-streaked hair in a simple cut, she was a more reason-able example of what a female cleric should look like than some of the freaks Millie had seen on Disgavel and Overgang.

"You wish to do some sight-seeing, Director?"

"If that is possible. My mission has completed its work, and we go home tomorrow. The secretary general has told me many times about the famous Querent ruins. She saw them on her state visit three years ago."

"That is certainly possible, but those clouds are about to rain on us. Perhaps you would like to see your quarters first?"

Millie allowed herself to be tempted into inspecting the rooms assigned to her, and yes, a bath and a change of clothes would be very welcome. Possibly something like Desipient herself was wearing?

Then shopping. The palace had a gift shop for visitors, and Desipient insisted that anything she fancied would be comple-mentary. It would all vanish in a few days, of course, but Millie did not say so. She picked out a few small gifts for her nieces and nephew, materials that could pass through the en-tangler.

After all preliminaries had been taken care of, most pleasantly, it was mid-afternoon, or so she was told. The sun that had risen two days ago had still not reached the zenith. The rain had ended for now. She left her bag in her room, taking only her visual recorder, which was a poor substitute for being able to store one's memories directly in the Ayne Brain, but a necessary one when visiting worlds whose systems were not compatible with Ayne systems. She could view the mechanical records when she got home and download them to her friends' visual cortexes that way. They would hardly know the difference.

She was alarmed to find herself in front of four insectile fliers like the one Friend Braata had crashed into Draff Water the previous day. Even if it did feel like a week ago, so much had happened since. The machines were worryingly small, like toys standing on the grass. Beside them stood two big men, both wearing the blue capes of palace guards, with multimode weapons hanging at their hips.

"Sergeant Gestant," Desipient said of the older, "and Patrolman Flisk."

Sergeant Gestant was impressive, solid and imperturbable, balding, monolithic. Millie approved less of Flisk, who was taller and leaner, with a restless air, like a hungry feline. His thick black hair was as shiny as a helmet. She did not like the way he stared at her.

"Guards?" she said. "Is there danger?"

Desipient laughed. "None, I am sure, honored Director. People are upset at the terrible rumors, you know. They may resent any off-worlder today, so it seemed wise to bring an escort. Please do not concern yourself. This may be a wonderful opportunity. Quassia is normally packed with tourists, but most of them are now at the space ports, lined up for DNA clearance before departure, so we should not see many people there. I think the Brain will let me speak to you through your translator during our flight. The sergeant will control the flyer for you."

The flight went smoothly. Millie felt like a bird, soaring up over the palace and the town. She saw three volcanoes and lost count of the number of lakes and little rivers. Pock's was all scenery, as Brother Andre said. What a pity it was going to be destroyed so soon! Desipient kept up an informative, educational commentary.

This was going to be a wonderful wind-up to the finest trip of her life! Such wonderful memories she would have to share with her sisters and their families, and her coworkers. The whole sector would read the Backet Report. It would mean a promotion, of course, and a substantial raise. She would be able to buy that shore cottage she had her eye on, and to commute to work by boat on fine days.

They spent some time at some famous hot springs, whose name Millie missed but could retrieve later. The natural terraces were very decorative. And then the celebrated grove of caongo trees, the tallest in the Ayne sector and perhaps the entire galaxy.

And then Quassia!

As Desipient had predicted, there was no one else at the ruins. There was not a great deal to see, either—mostly ferny hummocks and tumbledown stone walls—but Millie was determined to see all of what there was. She and Desipient walked over the entire site for hours with their guards stalking along behind like great cats, rarely saying a word. Desipient was knowledgeable, explaining the curious pentagonal plan of the best-preserved buildings, showing how the scale of the staircases indicated a very tall race, perhaps three meters, the astronomical layout of the dolmens around the Great Plaza, and how the two wells drilled through solid volcanic rock were evidence of a higher technology that had otherwise all rusted away. It was all extremely educational.

The best for last, of course. Desipient led her up a long staircase—a human-sized timber one, built for visitors—to the summit of a knoll, the highest part of the entire site. Up there stood the infamous Altar, just like its pictures, a single slab of rock, about head-high and twice that across, badly weathered but originally pentagonal, with the remains of what looked like a spout. Millie worked her recorder lavishly.

"And they used this for sacrifices, didn't they?"

"We think so," Desipient said. "But the important thing is that this is not a native rock. It is a metamorphic gneiss that occurs nowhere on Pock's and never in meteors, indeed nowhere in the Javelian system. It masses thousands of tons, and moving it through interstellar space is far beyond anything we can imagine."

Millie aimed her recorder at the spout. "What is there up there, on top?"

"Very little to see. It is so weathered."

"Even if it was used for sacrifice, that doesn't mean that the Querent were sacrificing each other, does it?"

"No, although Pock's had no large native fauna. A little refreshment, Director?"

To Millie's surprise, Sergeant Gestant was laying out bottles and beakers and plates on one of the many picnic tables. "Where in the world did he get those?"

"The flyers have lockers. So you are going home tomorrow?"

Millie sat down, realizing that she was thirsty and quite peckish. The view from up here was really very fine. She took more pictures. The sun had not visibly moved, but Javel was a thin crescent across the sky, and she knew enough astronomy now to know that eclipse could not be far off. The day was almost gone. Back to the grind tomorrow.

"Yes, STARS will be sending a car for us. Tonight I must prepare a short statement of my mission's findings, and I do believe that all the members will sign it." As chair, she could put her signature first. The secretary general had not expected a unanimous report and it would be a considerable feather in Millie's hat if she could obtain one, certainly a commendation in her file. She had always known that she lacked a great creative spark, but she took pride in being *thorough* and *effective*, and this mission would confirm her reputation as an achiever of results.

The guards joined the women at the table. While Patrolman Flisk poured scarlet wine into silver beakers, Desipient waved tongs over a plate of greenish lumps.

"Have you tried talion yet, Director? It is our greatest delicacy."

Millie was fairly sure that talion was what Brother Andre had called rotted tree octopus, but one could not visit a world without trying its greatest delicacy.

"I don't believe I have. Oh, that is plenty!"

"You will love it. And what will your report say, or is that a secret?"

"I shall stay with the facts and avoid controversy." Talion tasted exactly as one would expect rotted tree octopus to taste, only worse. Millie took a drink. "Just that we are satisfied that an alien species of the cuckoo type has infected Pock's World. That they are a danger to the entire sector and STARS was, I mean *is*, justified in taking drastic... *stern* measures to contain it." She gulped down another slimy lump. "Regrettable though the results may be," she added tactfully. Repressing a shudder, she reached for her beaker. Her companions were eating something else.

"Monody insists that the world will not end, that we have nothing to fear," Desipient said.

"Well, she has to say something like that, doesn't she? Can't have panic! It was a STARS engineer who let out the secret prematurely."

The ground trembled. Millie almost dropped her wine. "Oh!" She had spilled some on her tunic, a great bloodstain over her bosom.

"No need for alarm," Desipient said. "It will come out in the wash."

If it ever got there. There was little point to doing laundry on Pock's now.

Surprisingly, Patrolman Flisk spoke up. It was the first time she had heard his voice. "Pock's shakes all the time, although the Mother protects this area. It is because of her special care that the Querent ruins have stood for so long."

"It is astonishing, isn't it!" Millie agreed. "To think that when the Querent were building this place, our ancestors were chipping pebbles and trying to discover fire!" She laughed. "Ratty Turnsole would say, 'Yes, but now we own the galaxy, and where are they?' Oh, no more for me, please!" Too late. More of the disgusting, glistening green stuff had appeared on her plate.

Flisk stretched a brawny arm across the table to refill her beaker. "Sometimes she sends us signs."

He had a very deep voice, a preacher's voice. He also had the staring, shiny eyes of a fanatic to go with it. Now Millie knew why he had made her uncomfortable, right from the beginning. She had met his type before. It was compromise, not zeal, that made worlds go round.

She laughed. "You mean the tremor? Well, I agree that Javel's gravity field stresses the crust. But you'll never persuade me that Javel is a goddess signaling." If he hoped to convert her to planet-worship, he had a disappointment coming.

"It is hard for you to understand," Flisk agreed, still staring.

"But I am impressed by Quassia. I agree it has an extremely *spiritual* quality. And I am very lucky to have seen it today when there is nobody else here!" She raised her beaker in a toast. "To the Querent, wherever they are! And to everybody else, wherever they are going."

Sergeant Gestant slapped both hands down on the table. "They are home with their families, their wives and children. And that is where I should be. Even if the rumors are false, people are worried."

Millie gasped with embarrassment. "But they are true! I mean, if you wish to go—"

"Obviously we do not need two guards," Desipient said. "Flisk will see us safely home."

"Of course!" Millie said. "Thank you very much for your help, Sergeant." Why could the foolish man not have asked sooner?

Gestant rose and strode off to the stairway.

Desipient said, "There is nobody here. I have always wanted to see the Altar."

"I thought that was the Altar." Millie pointed to the great slab towering over the picnic ground.

"That is the Altar stone. The actual altar is on the top, where you can't see it. Nobody is allowed to see it, and tourists are never even told about it."

Millie said, "Oo! Did the secretary general see it when she was here?"

"I am certain she did not." The priestess glanced around. "Could we manage it, do you think, Flisk?"

The big man jumped up. "Easy! I, too, have always wanted to say a prayer at such a holy place."

"We must be quick." Desipient said, glancing up at the sky, where the glare of the sun was close to the needle-thin crescent of Javel.

They were quick. Flisk hefted a timber picnic table single-handed and carried it over the Altar Stone. Even in low gravity that was an impressive feat. All three of them climbed up on it, and then he lifted Desipient right over his head so she could scramble onto the Altar Stone. She helped Millie when he lifted her, and then up came Flisk himself, who must have made a standing jump.

After all that, the top of the Altar Stone was a disappointment. It was badly weathered and corroded, and tourists had scratched graffiti all over it, despite what the priestess had said.

"Over here," Desipient said. "This hole leads to the spout you saw. And look at the engraving."

Millie said, "Oo!" again, for at once she made out the shadowy image of a bipedal figure carved into the rock, arms and legs spread-eagled. Where the head should have been was the hole. "But they must have been giants!"

"Indeed they must," Flisk said. He lay down and spread his limbs. Big as he was, he came nowhere near fitting the mold. "But obviously the Querents sacrificed Querents to the Mother."

"They chopped off their heads?" Millie stepped back in revulsion. All those poor people! Well, not real human people, but sentients. How terrified they must have been, and what wicked, senseless, useless deaths!

"Oh, no. The heads would have plugged the drain." He sprang up again.

"Wait," said the priestess. "I am sure Friend Millie would like a picture of you down there. Better still! Let me take your recorder, Millie. It has near-infinite sensitivity, doesn't it? Here comes eclipse. You lie down there, and I will record it for you to show your friends."

What a revolting idea!

"No, thank you! I couldn't possibly!"

Darkness swirled over the world. Overhead the stars appeared, outlining the great disk of Javel, glowing with mysterious lights.

"I insist." Flisk's great hands reached for her.

Millie screamed and struggled, but she was helpless against the giant. He forced her down with her head over the hole. *Yuck!* Obviously the graffiti louts had been using this unique cultural relic as a urinal. She had drunk enough to feel slightly nauseous already, and the odious stench—

"Ow!"

An incredibly heavy knee on her back crushed all the air out of her lungs. She flapped her arms and struggled to find enough breath to protest.

"No, no! Please! Please! I have done nothing to deserve this. It's not my fault that Pock's World will burn."

"But you may suffice to prevent it!" he said. "Think of that. Now lie still! Spread your legs and arms... Right. Holy Mother, eternal refuge, receive this unworthy offering and spare your children."

Strong fingers gripped her hair and yanked her head back. Cold steel like fire at her throat...

Forsdy

Athena Fimble had always been a better rider than Linn Lazuline, and she enjoyed proving it yet again. Abietin horses were incredible beasts, twenty hands high, colored gold and copper, breathtakingly fast and nimble. They were normally controlled by cognition, but a few had been trained to respond to rein and knee commands for the sake of visitors. The sheer exuberance of a long, hard ride in sub-standard gravity had helped to work off some of her dark mood.

Whatever one thought of holy Monody's geotheism and peculiar means of reproduction, her hospitality could not be faulted. Athena's quarters were more luxurious than her own rooms back in Portolan, including a private hot pool and three young priestess attendants displaying a dazzling array of clothing for her selection. She chose a gown in some dark material of variable color that flickered in a myriad stars. It had a long, formal train but was topless, a style she would never dare even look at back home, but appropriate for a shameless hussy involved in bedroom fund-raising with Linn Lazuline. Her visor, too, was studded with gems. By the time she was dressed and groomed, it was almost eclipse time, the start of her last day on Pock's World.

"You are invited to dine with Her Holiness," the senior priestess said, "after the eclipse service. You may attend that, also, if you wish. Many visitors find the singing impressive."

Athena did not hesitate. Abietin's choir was famous throughout the sector and regularly toured the worlds. Linn soon arrived to escort her, looking even more knock-'em-down hunky than usual in a silver dhoti with matching visor and sandals. She was well aware that their agreement had one more night to run, and the smoky look he gave her as he offered his arm confirmed that he had not forgotten either. They set off after their guide through the dappled sunshine of the titans' forest.

"This is getting like the old children's rhyme," Linn said. "Now we are two. Brother Andre is saving souls wholesale at St. Mick's, and the well-named Ratty has gone to offer his all at Real Quassia. Oh, I do hope the goddess accepts him. No one could call Turnsole a *human* sacrifice, after all."

"Stop that! You are not to make rude remarks about Turnsole! He's one of the divine family hereabouts. Hold your tongue until we're safely on the shuttle and on our way. And Millie?"

"Millie, I am told, is still sightseeing the sites. Or sighting the seaside, possibly? Seeing the sidelines? She will probably view the entire planet before embarkation time, if she has to travel at supersonic speed to do it."

"Are you tipsy?"

"A little." He dropped his voice and bent close. "Athena, they're all going to *die* just two days from now. Yet they're still smiling and passing the soap and pouring drinks. It's indecent!"

She had noticed the same thing. "It's faith. Monody says it won't happen, so it won't."

"A whole world refusing to face the truth? That's horrible!"

"It's human, Linn. People ignore bad news whenever they can. Isn't there any chance, any chance at all, that they're right and it will miss?"

"Not a hope. I am certain STARS hasn't missed a shot in twenty-eight thousand years." After a moment he muttered, "Frankly, I wish I hadn't come here."

Christians often got worked up about the end of the world, but the largest sect in the world was in official denial. She wondered what was happening in the mosques and churches and synagogues, and at the shuttle landing grounds.

The Abietin temple resembled a gigantic tent of multicolored glass. Sunlight streaming down through tree foliage made the lights dance, sending a billion flecks of color racing over the crowd like midges. There was a fair-sized crowd there already, constantly milling, for it seemed that each newcomer had to proceed to the central monolith and then move outward again to make way for others. The singing had already begun, although the choir was invisible and as fine as any Athena had ever heard. The contrapuntal singing baffled her translator, and the solos were banal paeans of praise to the Mother. She removed her earplug to concentrate on the music, which was what mattered; the music was splendid.

The edge went off the day as the sun slid into eclipse. Totality brought a few moments of utter darkness until eyes adjusted enough to reveal the incredible disk of Javel behind the treetops, its eternally flickering lights turned to polychrome flames by the canopy. A faint glow atop the rocky pulpit brightened and then resolved into Monody, clad in a shimmering white gown. The apparition was certainly not old Wisdom, but it could have been any of the others, most likely Duty herself, pre-recorded or projected by hologram from Quassia. Athena heard her words through her translator, but the natives would be cognizing them.

She cut straight to the heart of the problem: "My children, strange and evil rumors are being spread." She conceded that a small asteroid was due to fall at the start of Sixtrdy, but that was by no means to be feared. Meteors fell all the time, and as usual the target area was being evacuated. The Mother would not desert her children; love her, trust her, go in peace. Short, definite, and effective—Athena could sense the congregation's worry draining away. She saw many tears of relief.

It was not her job to shout out that this was all a lie and they must perish.

⟶⟶◄ ◄ — ► ►⟶⟶

The dining room was small and intimate, with its walls and ceiling merged in a masterpiece of wood carving, a tangled grove of plants, animals, and even curiously playful little people. No doors or windows were in evidence. Attendants glided silently in and out through gaps in the latticework and the light came from no visible source.

Four low couches stood around a circular table, whose center slowly rotated, so that the guests could choose from the many dishes on offer. The diners were required to recline on one elbow to eat, and there were indeed four people present: Athena, Linn, Braata, and Monody—in this case Joy. She wore the usual white gown and seemed childishly happy to be playing hostess. She inquired about their ride, and how they had enjoyed the choir, and so on.

"The service was extremely moving," Athena said hastily. She did not like the way Linn was gulping his wine and worried that he might make some sarcastic remark about denial. Linn Lazuline would never make a fool of himself, but he might lose control of his cruel streak and expose other people's follies. "And was that you preaching?"

"It was me! My first official act!"

"Not second?" Linn murmured audibly, but he raised his goblet and proclaimed, "A salute to the newly fledged priestess! Duty herself could not have done it better."

Joy beamed at the praise. "And next week I am to tour Ryotwary!"

"Where or what is Ryotwary?"

Ryotwary was a school, it seemed, and Joy was eager to talk about it, and the events being planned. The doubts that had troubled her that morning had melted away.

That was certainly not true of Braata. Still flaunting his gold crucifix, he picked at his food and offered nothing to the conversation.

"You a prisoner here?" Linn inquired jovially.

The engineer smiled cynically. "Apparently. Seems they don't want me running around spreading alarm and 'false rumors.'"

"He is here for his own protection," Joy snapped. "He revealed STARS secrets, and Wisdom believes that STARS may try to hurt him. He started all the stupid panic with his lies about the end of the world. There have been almost a hundred people killed already. And fires! It was criminally irresponsible. The families of the dead are another group that may try to settle scores with him. He is safe here, though."

Braata said, "It is a pleasant enough place to die, but I would like to say farewell to my family first."

"You still can. You have three-quarters of a lifetime ahead of you. You may spend a lot of it in jail, of course." Pouting, Joy reached for a drink.

"Where did Director Backet go?" Athena asked.

"Quassia. She and a guide and a couple of guards. To view the eclipse. That's what tourists do."

"So they're with your, um, sisters? With Duty and Love and Ratty?"

Joy laughed. "No. They went to Real Quassia. Friend Millie was taken to Tourist Quassia. To a nonbeliever it's just as good. Better, because it has a lot more Querent stuff visible." Pause for cognition. "They left there ten minutes ago, heading for Orchid Valley. We track the fliers." She grinned. "Priestess Desipient is skilled at escorting off-worlders around. Lots of useless info and no humor."

"They were made for each other!" Linn declared, raising his glass in another toast. Everyone smiled. More denial.

One more night, Athena thought, one more night of prostitution to raise funds by raising Linn Lazuline. Tomorrow, Frivdy, she would go home to start planning her campaign for the nomination, and ultimately the downfall of STARS. But Pock's World would be long dead by then.

"You are quite sure you won't stay on a few days longer?" Joy inquired, all dewy innocence.

"Quite sure, thank you," Linn said. "I did ask Friend Glaum if I might stay on at Pock's Station to watch the impact. He did not sound encouraging."

"He does not want you to find out that nothing happened," Joy said. "Consort Oxindole is helping coordinate the cuckoo roundup. He expects to have almost all of them within three or four fortnights."

Linn smiled. "And they will all be put to death?"

She nodded uncertainly.

"How, exactly? Vivisection, chemical euthanasia, or public beheading? Or will you sacrifice them to the Mother?"

Athena wished she could kick him under the table, but that was not possible when reclining on a couch.

"We do *not* sacrifice people to our goddess! You shouldn't listen to the lies that scraggy old priest keeps spouting. The only offerings she accepts are acts of charity to help other people."

Joy was trying to imitate Duty's tone of authority, but she was no match for Linn Lazuline. They looked close to the same age, but he must be three times as old as she was and had wielded enormous power since long before she was born. He was also close to drunk.

"So what happened to Gownsman Bombardon that Wisdom would not discuss?"

"I have no idea. I never heard his name until this morning."

"I have." Linn smiled like a contented carnivore. "A Joy died. Love could not conceive again. She tried at least seven men, one after the other. She took them up to Quassia, kept them around the house, tried 'em drunk and tried 'em sober. Finally she picked on Bombardon. He was married, but she was getting desperate. She dragged him up to Quassia for a romantic eclipse. Bombardon threw himself off the pillar, into the crater—apparently after the sweaty stuff, not before, because it worked. Out popped your grandma, in due course. Granted that this is not the usual climax to a fertility rite, do you still insist that your goddess never accepts human sacrifices? Will you give me your sacred oath on that, Monody?"

Joy stared back like cornered prey. "I knew the story, I just didn't know his name. His death was an accident."

"I am waiting for your oath, Monody."

"The Mother will sometimes accept voluntary sacrifices," Joy admitted, "in desperate situations."

Athena tried not to remember that Ratty Turnsole had gone to Quassia with Duty and Love. Not for a fertility rite this time, but the situation was certainly desperate. She couldn't see Ratty sacrificing more than his loose change to anyone or anything.

"You fail to understand," Joy said, with a pathetic effort at dignity, "the distinction between sacrifices and offerings. Brother Andre ought to know the difference. Monody was very clear about it."

"But sometimes her followers get a little muddled?" Linn persisted. "Let's talk about the infamous Altar Stone, then, the one the tourists buzz around. Three years ago—Pocosin years—there was a boy by the name of Feaze who came to an untimely end, yes?"

Athena had had enough. "Linn, darling, you are sloshed and so am I. Will you see me safely back to my room, please?"

He scowled as if she had stopped him pulling the wings off something. Then he smirked. "Safe until you get there, anyway."

Athena made her farewells and they departed.

Eclipse had ended. The sun blazed again, although people were asleep and the forest trails deserted.

As they walked along, his heavy arm draped over her shoulders, she said, "You don't really think Ratty is in danger do you, at Quassia?"

"Regretfully, no."

"Where did you learn all that scandal about human sacrifice? Not from Brother Andre."

"Scandal? It's no scandal. It's true. I did my homework before I came here. Officially there's no such thing as human sacrifice, but there are ritual suicides, and sometimes some of the faithful get confused as to which is which. Probably there are breakaway cults. The Feaze boy had his throat cut on the

Altar, no explanation, no culprit ever arrested." He cupped a
hand around her breast. "Arouse me. Tell me how you are planning to earn your next two million."

"Kneecaps," Athena said. "Kneecaps can be very erog-
enous."

⸺⸺⸺

The night before, Linn Lazuline sober had been a wonderfully skilled lover. Drunk he was clumsy, rough, and selfish.
Twice he got up and went to the medic for stiffener. After his
fourth orgasm he fell into an exhausted slumber, snoring like
a pig. Athena was surprised, because this was a side of him she
had never observed before, even when they were children together. Was he feeling guilty because he had bought her? Could
he really be so depressed by the looming death of Pock's World?
Linn had his faults, but she didn't think murder was among
them.

Despite all the wine and all the sex, she was unable to sleep.
Partly that was because he had insisted on full daylight, and she
did not want to order the drapes to close now in case they
wakened him. Likewise, she could do nothing about the heat.
They were well into bright week now, and every day would be
hotter than the last.

But this was her last day here. In a few hours a shuttle would
lift her away from this cruelly doomed world. Very soon after
that, she would be back at Shadoof Landing, cognizing Proser
for the latest news. She would open her campaign the following day, with a cog-conference denouncing STARS's geocide.
Yes, she would say, she was satisfied that there had been cuckoos on Pock's. She had seen the evidence. Yes, they were a
danger, but modern surveillance methods would have rounded
them up smartly. DNA testing would keep the world quarantined with no need to slaughter two-thirds of a billion innocent
people. STARS must be tamed, gelded, and its fangs drawn,
before it murdered any more worlds.

STARS would fight back, of course, and in thirty millennia
it had never lost a battle. She must make plans to counter its
lies. More than lies—she must prepare defenses against all
kinds of dirty tricks, even raw violence. People as rich as those
behind STARS could bribe nearly anyone to do nearly anything,
and they need never soil their own fingers. They must spend
mind-boggling trillions every year just keeping out of the public
eye. Never once had the Ayne Senate managed to force STARS
personnel to testify at a hearing. She did not know one single

STARS employee by name, other than young Braata, and that had not been his real name.

And the odious Glaum, of course, but she suspected he had been a stand-in, a bit player, not one of the True Stock. They never revealed themselves. He was a boor, and *They*... What sort of people must *They* be? Surely *They* would belong to the Beautiful People, the sector elite, the top families. They would be physically perfect, mentally brilliant, rich by birth, sons and daughters of STARS employees, because wealth and power on that scale were always handed down in families.

Much like that man in her bed right now, with his thick sweaty leg pressed against hers.

She remembered what she had said two days ago: *On Pock's World enlightenment can come very quickly.*

Why had she taken so long to see the obvious truth? Linn was rich as rich could be; his family had owned a piece of everything since time began. Linn might even be the head honcho of the whole swarm, because STARS's CEO for the Ayne Sector would almost certainly live on Ayne, the commercial and political hub. And Linn Lazuline could twist anything to serve his own purposes, even the death of a planet. If Linn was STARS, he had known about the pirate probe that very night at Portolan, when he had propositioned her. He would probably have been disappointed if she had accepted right away. This deception would have been much more fun. He had staged it for his own amusement.

But now he was seeing the victims with his own eyes and wishing he had not come, hence the drinking and the frenzied copulation.

He had been the loudest STARS critic on the commission ever since he turned up on Ayne 3, spouting explanations of why he had not been ferried up with the rest of them. Even tonight, he had let slip a few revelations about Monody's faith that were certainly not available in the Ayne Brain. Athena's research before she left home had failed to turn up that story about the boy called Feaze only three years ago. Linn's research had accessed some other source.

Then there was one. She had no evidence, but her suspicions were dangerous. Somehow she must keep her knowledge a secret until she was safely home. Until she collected her ill-gotten twenty million? Why not? When you owned a piece of the galaxy, what was twenty million? Linn could give her that much out of one pocket and her opponents two hundred million out of another. It would amuse him to organize the puppet show. As head of Lazuline, Inc. he could complain loudly about STARS's tariffs, while as CEO of STARS he threatened to hold whole planets to ransom.

Suppose she told her suspicions to the Monody clique? Suppose she slipped away now and informed Oxindole or Bedel or Duty herself? Would STARS blast the planet when its own leader was held hostage? Likely it would. He was no prince of the blood, just an officer on a corporate board; he could be replaced. His death on Pock's might be seen as fitting punishment for incompetence. Impact might truly be inevitable, as he had been insisting.

One thing was certain: if she went public with her suspicions and they were true, then STARS would never let her leave Pock's World. She could not hope to prevent the tragedy, only avenge it, and to do that she must return to Ayne and fight on her own turf.

Chapter 2

Ratty was breakfasting alone on a terrace beside a gently steaming pool. Ravenously hungry, he was gobbling like a New Winish swamp dragon. It was a fine morning, almost too hot already, although the grass was wet and shining like diamonds. The sun was higher than yesterday; Javel had already set.

Athena Fimble came strolling out to join him. She took a chair and they exchanged greetings. She was wearing a bra, although yesterday she had gone topless like the natives. Her eyes were red as if she had not slept enough, and there were a couple of conspicuous hickeys on her neck. A page came running out, and she told him to bring the same as Friend Ratty had, only one third as much.

"No Joy this morning?" she asked.

There had been so much Joy that he'd thought for a while he would have to order some booster from the medic in their room. Fortunately he'd risen to the occasion just in time. "She's been called to a family conference. Riots are breaking out all over."

Athena nodded pensively.

He wondered who'd done the hickeys. Linn Lazuline, probably. Athena Fimble would not go for one-night stands with strangers.

She said, "How was the service last night? Obviously nobody offered your beating heart as a sacrifice to the Mother."

"Most people accuse me of not having one. No," he admitted, "it was really very moving, apart from the rain. The music was superb. Not a large congregation, but about a hundred reporters, so there were probably many millions cognizing. Tomorrow night will be the big show. Impact is due shortly after the start of eclipse. That's the holy hour. You think STARS arranged that deliberately?"

He nibbled another of the brown things. Very tasty, but probably better not to ask what they were.

"I would put nothing past the bastards," Athena said. "On the other hand, Pock's has two hours of eclipse every day, so it could be just coincidence." She thanked the waiter who brought her food. As the boy left, her eyes wandered as eyes often do when their owner is about to reveal a confidence. "Something you should know..."

"I'm listening."

"Who runs STARS?"

"You think I wouldn't shout it from the rooftops if I knew?"

"What have you heard?"

He shrugged and swallowed. "Ayne sector is one unit, with its headquarters on Ayne. It denies having any contact with other sectors, but who believes anything STARS says? Who the high panjandra are—search me."

"Describe them."

What was she getting at? He racked his brain up a couple of watts. "Rich, of course. Secretive, but with a good cover so that... *Gawdamity!*"

She nodded.

"Linn Lazuline?" Ratty whispered, aware of his heart sinking stone-wise. "You got any evidence?"

Again she nodded. "Very slight, but last night he let slip something about a human sacrifice here a few years ago, a boy called Feaze. That fact isn't in the Ayne Brain."

"It makes sense!" Oh, yes, it made sense. Why had he never joined those few obvious dots? "It even explains why STARS is so dedicated to destroying cuckoos. Remember your hearings on monopolies a few years ago? Gravy, Inc. especially?"

Athena nodded, frowning. "We uncovered precisely nothing. We couldn't find out who owned Gravy or why none of its competitors ever thrived. There were too many suspicious deaths, both in the past and even during the hearings. I called off the investigation before any more people got slaughtered."

"Well, guess who owns a big part of Gravy?" Ratty said, and chuckled at her shocked expression. "Yes, Lazuline the Vulture. I found out enough to be sure, but I couldn't nail down evidence to prove it. Now, listen. Gravy's gravity shaft was the last big tech breakthrough, thirty or forty years ago. A tiny research company suddenly filed a heap of critical patents and ballooned into a huge industrial giant in no time, sector-wide. Where they got their initial financing was never explained and many of the reputed inventive geniuses died young. With me so far?"

She nodded, biting her lip.

"Let's suppose, just for the sake of argument, that STARS, Inc. has its equivalents in Canaster Sector and Avens Sector and so on. All over the human bubble, no doubt. And also suppose that they keep in touch secretly. They may use private entanglement links or just radio beams—they have all the time in the galaxy, after all."

"You mean they trade news of technical breakthroughs!" Athena Fimble was a smart lady. "I've often wondered if there are secret leaks between sectors. Gravy, Inc. wasn't the only one, you know. Brain implants followed much the same pattern, a few centuries ago. A whole technology appeared like magic, sprang up fully armed."

"A wonderful racket," Ratty said. "But it depends on keeping the sectors isolated. That's why the cuckoos must never be allowed to spread and tell tales. That's why STARS can't afford to give Pock's World time to hunt down the invaders—because of what the invaders might tell them."

"When I get home," she said, "I'm going to call for hearings on the geocide of Pock's World. It's a sector crime, but there are Ayne citizens involved. I'll subpoena Sulcus Immit, if he can be found, and Linn Lazuline. And I'll call for him to be interrogated under brain scan."

Ratty whistled. "Good luck."

"Meanwhile, keep that under your hat." She hesitated. "This may be bad news for you, friend. I thought I'd warn you."

Obviously. If Linn Lazuline had enough influence with STARS to slam the shuttle door in Ratty Turnsole's face, then Ratty Turnsole wasn't going to be going anywhere. How the sleazy scum bucket would enjoy that! Yet the news did not feel like quite the utter disaster it should. He muttered thanks as he tried to work out just what crazy notion was twirling inside his head now. He knew the sensation of a flash of brilliance trying to hatch. Give it a little while....

"I think I'll tell Oxindole what we suspect," Athena said. "If the Pocosins have Linn locked up here and there is any way at all to prevent that impact, then maybe STARS will relent."

"I doubt if STARS can or would. Look out."

Lazuline himself was striding toward them, big and virile, leering. "What a wonderful day! I wonder where the nearest good beach is?"

By the time Linn had pulled up a chair, Ratty was satisfied that his companions had indeed been sleeping together, as he had suspected yesterday. But no more! The emotional cinders of a recently exploded affair were unmistakable. Smiles were faked, greetings flimsy, and no doubt the hickeys had been deliberate.

"I doubt if you'll find any surf on Pock's World, Friend Linn," he said. "The odd tidal wave is all. Don't let me talk you out of trying those."

"Depends when the shuttle will leave. Is whatever you're eating approved for human consumption too?"

Linn gave his order. Then he and Athena made small talk while Ratty admired in silence. They were real pros, both of them. The world was about to end, they were probably not an hour past a raging quarrel, and yet they could talk calmly and politely about nothing at all.

When was the shuttle due to leave? What time was it now, anyway? He had no functional implant to answer his questions.

Father Andre was the next to arrive, looking haggard, as if he had not slept at all. "I am told that the shuttle has been delayed. No new deadline was supplied. Those look good. Bring me half a dozen swallet, please," he told the boy.

Athena said, "They are delicious. They must be sinful, they taste so good."

"Gluttony is a sin, sister, but nothing in the Good Book prohibits the enjoyment of good food in moderation."

Ratty eyed some storm clouds building beyond the temple grove and decided that they probably weren't heading in his direction. "How are things at St Mike's?" he asked.

"Much as you would expect."

"Forgive me, Brother. That was an extremely stupid question."

Mollified, Andre said, "Obviously you survived your visit to Quassia. Did you witness any angels this time?"

"None. But the singing was wonderful. Love and Duty prayed. Javel was mostly hidden by clouds, and it rained a lot. It was interesting, but not very."

"Not as much fun as your previous visit?" Linn said.

"Nothing could ever match that," Ratty said.

The mood was brittle.

Athene put it into words. "We are the survivors. We did not choose this. We did not condemn everyone else to die. Why do we feel guilty?"

The question was obviously aimed at Andre. He said, "Because the presence of death makes us appreciate life, just as sickness makes us appreciate good health."

"Or," Linn said, "the absence of Friend Millie Backet makes us appreciate the good things of this world. Where is our beloved, interstellar celebrity leader? Anyone know?"

"Sleeping off a surfeit of sightseeing, I expect," Athena suggested. "Or preparing the report."

"With her name at the top?"

"Of course."

But Millie's absence was strange. If anyone was certain not to miss the shuttle, it was Backet.

The next arrivals were First Minister Oxindole, accompanied by a Monody. For a moment Ratty thought she was Duty, then he recognized Joy—he had never seen her looking glum before. He jumped up to find a chair for her and give her a kiss. It must be at least thirty minutes since they parted, after all.

The gownsman took a seat also, but he pulled it back a couple of meters so that he was not part of the group. He waived away the pages.

"Bad news?" Linn inquired.

"More and more bad news. I deeply regret to inform you that your comrade, Millie Backet, has been brutally murdered."

For a moment the only reaction came from Brother Andre, who bent his head in silent prayer. Ratty expected Linn to come out with some abrasive comment, and he was not disappointed.

"Trust Millie! Granted that the Sector Council is a gaggle of galactic nonentities, you would think it could have found someone with a few brains to represent it on a matter as important as this."

"You mean that Millie wasn't a genius like the rest of us are?" Ratty said. "Perhaps not, but she was sincere; she took her duties seriously and would have worked hard on that report. I don't think you should sneer at stupid people, Friend—I use the word ceremonially of course—Lazuline. You need stupid people to buy all the shit you sell, just as Athena needs their votes and Brother Andre and I need them to believe what we tell them."

For a moment there was silence.

Father Andre looked up and smiled. "There is hope for you yet, Friend Ratty."

"I'm getting religion, Brother." That wasn't all he was getting, either.

"We sent her off with a priestess we believed to be totally reliable," Oxindole said. "And two guards. Tracking the fliers, we know that they visited a few of the usual attractions and then went to Tourist Quassia. For once it was deserted, because of the crisis. The sergeant left them there. He claims he could see no danger and he wanted to comfort his family. I think he knew very well what was going to happen. He has been placed under arrest."

"What did happen?" Linn demanded, showing his teeth.

"They threw her down on the Altar Stone and cut her throat."

"Like the boy Feaze?"

The gownsman sighed. "Yes. And others. But may I say right now, especially to Brother Andre, that this barbarism has nothing to do with our faith. Your church claims to be the original Christian church, and you are not responsible for every crackpot cult that has split off during the centuries. That Quassia may have been holy to the Querent, a million years ago, but to us it is a place for milking tourists, nothing more."

"I understand," Andre said. "I was cursed and spat at few times last night. STARS brought us here, and they blame STARS."

Oxindole nodded and said, "Thank you," softly. "And more bad news. Another solar flare has recharged the Javelian magnetosphere. In other words, the radiation storm has failed to dissipate. Your departure has been postponed until tomorrow."

"And if space is still hot tomorrow?" Ratty inquired.

"Then you will need therapy when you return to Ayne. As it is, you will be issued prophylactic anti-rad tonic prior to take-off. Gownsman Sperry assured me last night that you need fear nothing worse than a few days' nausea and perhaps some temporary hair loss." He pulled a wan smile and stood up. "Meanwhile, the palace is at your disposal. I can no longer spare Joy to be your hostess, I'm afraid. She is officially of age now, and we need her for more pressing duties."

"A moment, Gownsman," Athena said. "How is Gownsman Sperry today?"

The big man frowned, as if the question were intrusive. "Still dying. Why do you ask?"

"I am concerned about his son, Solan. His mother is dead, I understand. Has he any other family?"

"I believe not. Monody will see him placed in a good home."

"I have nothing to do today, and I'm sure you all have your hands full. With your permission, I'll make sure he isn't left alone to mope."

Oxindole nodded. "That would be very generous of you, Senator."

So now it was Ratty's turn. He had grasped that brilliant idea that had been flitting around his cerebellum. Releasing Joy's hand, he jumped to his feet. "Another moment, Gownsman. I have a request. I wish to be inducted into your church so that I may be eligible for permanent appointment as consort to the incarnation presently known as Joy."

Joy screamed shrilly and threw herself on him.

Which was a pity, because he missed Linn Lazuline's reaction. Had Ratty's suicidal announcement managed to spoil his day?

Linn said, "You must have fucked all your brains away."

"Well!" Oxindole said. "That is a surprise. Joy can accept your vows, Friend Ratty, and I certainly won't try to stop her appointing you to the position you crave. You'd better come with us, then, because we have much to do."

He had done it! He was still shaking, still trying to detach Joy, who was embracing him like a tree octopus on a monkey puzzle. Even he found it hard to believe that Ratty Turnsole had thrown away his life for love, or even for the pleasure of balking Linn Lazuline of the pleasure of murdering him personally.

Chapter 3

Huffle was not the most luminescent object in the galaxy. One of his brothers told him once that he would not rank an M in a stellar catalogue. When Huffle found out what that meant, he injured his brother severely. Another time a cousin said what a pity that the extra intelligence genes his parents had paid for had been spliced in backward. Huffle had understood enough of that crack right away to hurt his cousin even more—his physical genes worked only too well.

On the brighter side, at nine Pocosin years old he stood well over two and a half meters tall and was broad in proportion. He began to win adult wrestling matches. At ten he took the world belt, and the Hederalian Army was happy to enlist him. His family was even happier.

Now Private Huffle was on dawn watch with Sergeant Terest, guarding the Thing. He liked Sarge Terest because he did not want to talk all the time about stupid things Huffle did not understand. He mostly just sat and cognized, which was fine with Huffle, who liked to cognize, too. Porn mostly, but sometimes sport. He had a voice implant and a one-to-see-with, but that one didn't work right, only black and white. The doctors said they couldn't fix that to let him cognize in color the way most people did. But girls in black-and-white were still girls, even if blood didn't look as good.

Guarding the Thing was fun. It looked like a boy, until you looked real hard. It lived inside a shock fence in a cell full of medical stuff that Huffle mustn't touch. There was a table inside the shock fence, too, but the Thing slept on a mattress on the floor below. That was where the fun came in. Huffle would wait until the Thing was asleep and then writhe it. It would waken with a scream of pain. Huffle would laugh and wait until it went to sleep again. Then jolt it again.

Terest said it was all right to do this, as long as he held the writhe down low where the cameras wouldn't see him doing it. The Thing wasn't even human, he said, so it had no rights, no lawyers or nothing. And Huffle must keep the writhe on a low setting, because he would be in trouble if he damaged it. Huffle usually just kept the writhe set on 2, which was standard and hurt plenty. Often the jolt made the Thing bang itself on the table leg, which was even more fun, but its own doing, so the cuts and bruises were not Huffle's fault.

Now the Thing had gone back to sleep, and it was time to jolt it again. Terest was lost in whatever he was watching—probably porn, from the bulge in his shorts. Huffle twisted around so the camera wouldn't see him slide the writhe out of its holster. He fired, but the Thing didn't move.

"That's funny. Sarge, what's wrong with the Thing?"

Terest said, "Huh?" and then, "What'ch mean?"

"I just writhed it, and it didn't move. See?" He writhed it again.

"What'ch set on?"

Huffle peered at his writhe to make sure. "Standard."

"Try 4."

Four was one above Agony and one below Convulsions. That ought to be fun! He'd never jolted anyone that hard before. Huffle let the Thing have it. It twitched some and rolled off the mattress, but that was all. No scream.

"It's alive, anyway. I'll try closer." Huffle got up and walked over until the shock fence was making his hair stand on end and he could look down at the Thing.

Its eyes were open, staring up at him. It shot a hand through the fence and grabbed his ankle. That was impossible. No one could stand the pain of a shock fence. The Thing looked like it was hurting bad, chewing blood out of its lip, but it kept hold of his ankle. He was going to call out to Sarge to come and see what the Thing was doing, and then...

Something funny happened. In his head.

His thumb pushed the setting on his writhe up higher, up past the seal, which meant alarms would go off at HQ. Funny, that, because he hadn't told his thumb to move at all. The setting went all the way to 7, which was Brain Dead and a division

inquiry. His hand turned to aim the writhe across the room at
the camera. He wondered why it was doing that. His finger
pulled the trigger and the camera exploded in a spray of green
sparks. Hey! Pretty! Then his wrist adjusted the aim.

Terest said, "What'ch doing, you crazy—" and collapsed in
a heap as Huffle's finger moved again, all on its own.

Now the writhe pointed itself at a control panel on the wall.
Pretty blue and red sparks! The tingling of the shock fence
didn't stop, though. The control for that was outside in the
corridor.

Suddenly the Thing yanked Huffle's foot out from under
him. He'd been thrown a time or time in his wrestling career,
but not onto concrete. He hit the floor hard, sending the writhe
skittering away, far out of reach. The impact hurt, but not like
the hurt of having his legs in the shock fence. He screamed and
went on screaming.

He didn't have to put up with that from a runt like the
Thing—he massed three or four times what it did. He kicked
with his free boot to smash its chest in. Except that the Thing
caught hold of that ankle also and blocked the kick.

It was smiling, saying things he couldn't hear over his own
screams. It let him squirm and struggle for a little while, all his
muscles jerking in violent spasms, bouncing him up and down
on the concrete. Then it pulled him farther in, so the fence got
his gonads. He had thought he was hurting bad before that happened.

When Private Huffle passed out, the prisoner hauled him far
enough inside the fence so that the charge went into his head.
And that was that.

Chapter 4

The first attempt on Ratty Turnsole's life had come just before his twentieth birthday. There had been others since, but for those he had been prepared. He easily convinced the palace guard that he knew all he would ever need know about weapons and martial arts. He was issued a writhe.

Joy admitted him to the Church of the Mother.

Bedel swore him in as her consort.

"And try these," he added, handing over a small bag. "One at a time, mind! One of them ought to connect your implants to the private network."

"Now what, Your Holiness?" Ratty said, adjusting his elbow-length cape. Adjusting his mind to all this was going to take a lot longer. He was nuts.

Joy was still bouncing up and down with happiness. "Undra! And hurry. We're going to be late."

"Duty left Car One for you," Bedel said. "You'll make it."

They ran hand-in-hand.

"What's Undra?"

"Undra's where the World Council meets. Monody presides."

Car One would have seated eight in comfort. Apart from Monody and her new consort, it held only two blue-caped guards, Omass and Kropotkin. They were solid and steady-eyed; Ratty decided he could safely leave security matters to them, because they wouldn't listen to him anyway.

Joy insisted that he sit beside her, of course. The guards spaced themselves around the circle to balance the craft's trim, and it took off like a shuttle, eyeballs in. Scenery started hurtling past below them. Car One could outrun anything on Pock's World, Joy said trustingly. Ratty didn't mention that he owned two or three that were faster.

He picked through the disks in the bag, clipping each in turn to his visor headband. The fifth one connected. Joy was there in his mind.

—Oh, good! Now we can chat. Have you noticed Kropotkin's muscles?

Yes, but I still prefer your tits.

—Stop that!

You started it. He put the bag away. *Now tell me about Undra.*

Pock's World had many governments; he had forgotten that. Leaders or deputy leaders from the Theriac Emperor on down to independent mayors were meeting to discuss the crisis—and this stripling girl was going to chair their deliberations? But she was Monody, and she would be in contact with Duty and Oxindole through the private network. Hard work for her, it would be a grinding bore for her consort.

Love and Duty were already elsewhere, trying to calm riots and demonstrations. Even old Wisdom had roused herself to help, cognizing with senior priestesses around the world. This seemed like a waste of valuable pleasure time when everyone was going to die in less than two days, but Ratty must pretend to believe, just as almost everyone must be pretending to believe. He doubted very much that Duty herself believed her own edict.

Meanwhile to relax in a luxurious air car with his arm around the most beautiful girl in the world was a precious way to spend his final hours. A line of three volcanoes went by on the left, one of them smoking. Joy was in idling mode, lazily feeding him pictures of her favorite beaches and jungles. She was a bird fancier, and Pock's had zillions of brightly colored birds. Once in a while she would cognize images of Ratty in copulatory mode, and he would retaliate with memories of her thrashing and moaning in orgasm.

Love?

—Yes, love?

Can you cog Wisdom?

—Of course.

I'm a very nosy person.... I'd love to know what happened between her and Brother Andre fifty years ago. That's about thirty of your years. His church sent him home in disgrace, you know.

For a few moments there was silence. Then Joy started to snigger.

Tell me!

—She says he was trying to convert her. She wanted to audition him as a full time stud. Neither of them succeeded.

No. But?

—But they were caught skinny dipping in the hot pool.

Ratty's efforts not to explode in laughter were almost successful, but a sort of snorting noise did escape through his nose, loud enough to make Omass and Kropotkin look at him askance. The story was not something he would have included in *The Saint of Annatto!* But saints were allowed a few juvenile peccadilloes, even skinny dipping.

Suddenly Oxindole was there in his mind. Evidently the private network did not use file pictures, for he was seated at a meeting with many other people, and he looked as close to frantic as he was ever likely to look.

—Omass? How soon could you get Her Holiness to Hederal?

Omass appeared. *—Twenty minutes, Consort.*

—Joy, there's a major riot surrounding the hospital where they're holding the cuckoo. We want you to go by there and see if you can calm them. People have been killed already, so you're not to take any risks. Understand that, Omass? If just the sight of Car One doesn't work, then you'll probably have to give up and let it happen. And look out for gunfire!

Faces flashed as Joy and the guard acknowledged. The car banked steeply.

"Never a dull moment," Joy said aloud. "What can you show us on this, captain?"

Omass took a moment to answer. "There's file records of the commissioners' meeting with the cuckoo on Toody."

"Good!" Joy said, settling back in the crook of Ratty's arm. "I've been meaning to cog those."

⇒⊶⊷ — ⊶⊷⇐

Hederal was a fair-sized city, even by Ayne standards, but the volcano spouting red fire in the distance was typically Pocosin. The ugly compound of buildings called Colonel Cassinoid Veterans Hospital stood in irregular rows, as if jangled by earthquakes. Around it raged a mob that Ratty's practiced eye estimated at ten or twelve thousand. In some places people were dangerously close to the shock fence perimeter, liable to be seriously hurt if a crowd surge pushed forward. Hovering several hundred meters overhead, Ratty could receive the cognized warnings from the watchtowers and see the flicker of firearms as the mob responded. A couple of buildings were blazing already.

"Too dangerous!" Kropotkin growled. "We can't take Her Holiness down near that, Cap'n."

Privately, Ratty could not have agreed more. In his view, they should just let the mob have that pear-faced juvenile freak with the bizarre plumbing. Nine, or Umandral, might think of himself as the wave of the future and brag of a billion siblings, but he looked too much like a beetle. Stamp on him! He wasn't worth risking real people's lives. How did one persuade the Hederalian army to back off?

He could tell that Joy wasn't thinking that way. This was her first big chance. She was excited by the challenge and the images of the alien and the way he was being treated had outraged her. "Can you project me from here, Omass?"

Pause. Then the guard said hesitantly, "A little lower we could."

"They've noticed me," she said. "See all the faces looking up? Take us down and I'll speak to them."

To Ratty's horror, the two guards looked to him for approval. Damn!

"Well, if you're going to cognize them, my love, then I'm the expert. You sit on this side, with that mountain in the background. I'll sit over here." The width of the car put them a little farther apart than he liked for interviewing, but it would do. "Can you raise any file pictures of that cuckoo, Captain?"

—*No! Wait!* Oxindole appeared.

Ratty snapped aloud, "Go away we're busy!" and cut him out. "A still shot of the kid sitting on that table? For god's—I mean goddess's—sake, don't have any mouthing off about ovipositors or being infinitely better or impregnating men." An image formed in his mind, the freak sitting on the table baring his teeth in what could be taken as a smile. "That's perfect!"

He sat down beside Omass. "Give me that, so I can splice it in. Now take us down slowly. Kropotkin, you keep watch for trouble, I mean shooting, and if there's any nonsense, whisk us out of there at ten gees. Joy, love, relax; you're too tense. Keep your eyes on me. I'll do the cognizing. I'll signal like this when I'm going to put you on, and like this when I'm going to show the cuckoo, and like this when it's taken off again. We'll only hold him there a moment." Definitely, the less the mob saw of Umandral the better.

"Okay, Captain, take us down."

He sat back and smiled reassuringly across at Joy, although it took every atom of his training and experience not to show how terrified he felt. "You got your words ready? Speak aloud, just to me."

She nodded.

"And remember you are talking to your lover. You love them all, even the smelly ones."

Omass muttered, 'Try now."

Ratty gave her the signal.

"I am Monody," she said. "You are the goddess's children, and what you are doing is wrong." She paused and Ratty was just about to ask a question when she went on. "Innocent people are being hurt and killed. That is evil, my friends. It is wrong. It is true that there is a visitor from another world inside the hospital, but he is no threat to you. He came in peace. He is only a child. Would you like to see him?"

Ratty raised a hand in readiness.

"His name is Umandral. Here he is. "

The boy appeared, smiling.

Fade back to Joy.

"That is Umandral," she said, with a smile. "Does he look dangerous? Does he frighten you? He is our first visitor from the Canaster Sector in hundreds of years, and he deserves a better welcome than a riot. Go in peace and be about your business. I am on my way to Undra, and I came here to pick up Umandral and take him to meet with the World Council. He is an ambassador with an important message to deliver to us."

Gaddomit! Where did she get that from?

"Live and die happy."

CUT!

Joy sat back and said, "Ooof! How did I do?"

Ratty managed not to scream. "Wonderful, but why did you add that last bit?"

She smiled nervously. "I couldn't think of another way to finish. And if we just go away, the mob will come back and get him, won't they?"

She had a point there, but the guards were looking mutinous.

"Take us down, please," Ratty said. "Land on a roof, drop me, and then go back up high and wait. If anything goes wrong, carry on to Undra without me."

The car resumed its descent. Omass's face twitched as if he were cognizing.

"Building 17," he said.

"Copy 17," Kropotkin muttered.

Omass swore under his breath. "Your Holiness, the thing...
the alien... they're saying it killed two guards in the night.
They have it confined still, but it's murderously dangerous."

Joy looked aghast. She had told the world she was going
to deliver an ambassador. How would he look in a strait-
jacket?

"Keep going," Ratty snapped. "I'll go in there, and I'll bring
somebody out with me, understand? Then the crowd will dis-
perse. Joy, you'd better explain to your mother or Oxindole."

"Shut up, Ratty. I've got the whole family fighting inside
my head."

That was not really a bad thing. Ratty had just realized that
he was not a proper Pocosin color yet. Some trigger-happy
maniac in the crowd might decide he was another alien and
pick him off when he landed. And if he came back out with
someone, the same reasoning applied even more. Building 17
was near the center of the complex, a long way from the perimeter fence, but an easy shot for even a fairly stupid gun.

And now the car was rocking in its own backwash, with
Building 17 right below it. Even before it touched down,
Kropotkin, if he was the current driver, ordered the door open.
Ratty jumped out, ignoring Joy's efforts to hug him. He strode
across to the entrance, blinking in the wind of the car's ascent
as it rushed upward to safety.

There was Joy in his mind. —*Darling, are you all right?*

*I haven't had time to be anything else yet. Watch but don't in-
terrupt.*

The safe light was on over the shaft, so he stepped in and
dropped two floors, to ground level. Half a dozen men in military garb were waiting there, glaring at him. A scrawny
woman in a white coat he recognized as Doctor Eryngo. Their
manner softened slightly when they saw his cape.

"Consort Ratty," he said. "What's the situation, doctor?"

He was answered by one of the gun boys, with a major's
leaves on his suspenders. "It killed two of my men in the night.
It's still within the shock fence, but it may be armed. We
have—"

"*May* be? Don't you know?"

"It burned out the surveillance equipment. It couldn't get
at the shock fence controls, though. We drilled some holes in

the door and hit it with two dormeiscene darts. That's enough to fell a mirbane."

"Lead me there and keep talking. What happened?"

The officer strode off. Ratty kept pace, although the goon was half a meter taller.

"Nothing! Not a flacking thing! We tried again with double the dose. Still nothing. Now it's hiding behind the table, so we're drilling a hole in the outside wall. This time I'm going to burn holes through its head."

Eryngo, trotting along behind them, made whimpering noises.

Ratty remembered the end of the commissioners' visit, when Solan and Umandral had laughed together. By all the gods, that thing was sentient! Joy was right to want to rescue it.

"No, you're not. Not until I say so. Why did it, he I mean, attack your men?"

"Who knows?"

He must not lose his temper. "You had him under surveillance, didn't you?"

"They were writhing it," the big man admitted angrily.

"That's torture. Would you stand for that if you didn't have to?"

This time there was no answer. They had reached a bend in the corridor, which was being guarded by four men with guns. Ratty had seen this area in the playback of the commissioners' visit. He wanted to go in there less than he had ever wanted anything.

"Does he have implants?"

"It did have," Eryngo said. "But we couldn't tell what they did, because we don't know how its brain is put together. So we burned them out with a gamma ray laser."

No solution there, then.

"The room on the left?" Ratty removed his writhe and holster and handed them to the major. "What's the code for the shock fence?"

"I forbid you to—"

"And I will have you busted to latrine cleaner. And excommunicated. Answer!"

"OAK 479."

"Right. Get back out of the way, all of you! I don't trust your trigger fingers. Move! Right back, out of sight."

All this amazing authority came from the red towel draped over his left shoulder. With cold lizards wriggling in his belly, he walked along to the door. It had holes in it, and there was sawdust on the floor. His mouth was too dry and his bladder too full. He punched the code into the control on the wall; the light turned green.

He knocked and opened the door a crack. "I'm not armed. Is it safe for me to come in?"

After a moment a boyish voice said, "Just look out for those thugs behind you."

Ratty went in with his hands up and kicked the door shut behind him. The room stank like a cesspit, probably because the body at his feet had been leaking fluids. He had been a very large man but now his brain had boiled out through his eye sockets, he was very dead. There was another body at the far end of the room. Ratty went over and bent to have a closer look.

"Vegetated," said the boy.

Ratty turned to look at him. He had propped the table on one side and was crouching behind it, down on hands and knees on his mattress. He seemed too young and pathetic to be a remorseless killer.

"How do you feel after all that shit they pumped into you?"

He shrugged. "They've done worse. I'm coming out of it."

"You're Umandral. I'm Ratty Turnsole."

"I know. Seen you on a cog-doc. Thought you were Ayne-based."

"Made a career change. Now I'm consort to a Monody incarnation."

"Lucky you." Warily, not exposing any more of himself than he had to, the boy squirmed around so that he was sitting cross-legged. Ugly as sin, yes, but sentient, human.

"Yes." Ratty gestured vaguely at the corpses. "Why did you kill them?"

"They pissed me off."

"I want to get you out of here, but murders make it harder. Monody is overhead in an air car." Had that been a trace of a nod? "And you cognized her message, right?"

The boy nodded again.

"So your implants are still working?"

Pause, then another nod. "Some."

"They must be as indestructible as you are." A world of supermen would devise super-technology, of course. "So you know there's a lynch mob after you?"

"Yes. They're smarter than you are."

"You sure know how to plead your case. Young Friend Umandral, I'd like to take you out of here and see you treated as a person, not a lab rat, but how can I trust you?"

The boy pouted. "How can I trust you?"

"Because I'm your only hope. That head gun goon says he's going to kill you, orders or not. Here!"

Ratty snatched up the writhe lying beside the wall and lobbed it to the alien. He threw it faster than he normally would and it went higher because he forgot to allow for the gravity. No matter—a skinny arm shot up and caught it. Then Umandral shifted his grasp to the handle and put his finger on the trigger. He looked thoughtfully at Ratty.

Who shrugged and showed his empty hands. Now his bladder *really* felt like it was going to explode.

The boy smiled. "Thanks." He tossed the writhe away.

"My pleasure." For not being vegetated. "I must have your word that you won't break any more laws while you're in my custody. No more killings? You won't try to kidnap Monody or do anything nasty like that? Because I'm climbing a pole for you, lad, and if you misbehave, then I'll be slush."

Suddenly the boy moved, inhumanly fast. One moment he was cross-legged on the mattress, and the next he had gone past Ratty and was standing in a corner out of sight of the door. Ratty jumped, hopelessly late to have done anything, even if had been armed.

"I promise," Umandral said quietly. "I'll need some clothes." He had only a cotton strip around his crotch, not enough even by Pocosin standards.

Ratty pulled a face and took another look at the smaller corpse. He was not truly dead, and his sphincters had not relaxed. He was big, but not like the other one.

"This will be baggy on you. Let's try." Ratty stripped the body and handed shorts and boots to the alien. Then he went over to the door, opened it slowly and put an arm out first, to show his skin color, then his head. The major and another man were standing at the end of the corridor with guns aimed.

"Put those pissy things down!" he yelled. "Umandral and I are coming out. We're going to go up to the roof and fly away, understand?"

"You have no authority!"

Oxindole, if you're kibitzing, I need some backup now.

—You've got it. Hold on a moment.

The major snapped to attention, swung down his weapon to aim at the floor. His eyes widened, his face turned brilliant scarlet. "Yes, sir! No, sir! Of course, Minister! You are free to go, Consort." He spoke as if the words hurt. "The prisoner is released into your custody."

Ratty said, "That's better. Now clear all your men out of here. Nobody between us and the roof."

Monody's face appeared, but not Joy, probably Duty. —*Very smoothly done, Consort! We haven't decided whether to give you a medal or cut your head off.*

When will you make that decision, Holiness?

She smiled. —*After we see what happens at Undra.*

Chapter 5

As the shaft elevated them up to the roof, Ratty said, "It is customary to touch one knee to the ground when being presented to Her Holiness. Do you have religious or egalitarian misgivings about this?"

The boy said, "Nothing serious. I don't believe in her stupid goddess, though."

"I don't either, but I'm too polite to say so."

"I'm too smart to lie about it."

"You would lie if you were getting what I'm getting."

Umandral grinned at him. The start of trust?

They emerged on the roof. A faint rushing sound resolved itself into cheering from the crowd.

"People are weird," Ratty said. "They are making you welcome. Wave."

Umandral snorted with adolescent contempt, but he waved. His oversized pelvis gave him an awkward, rocking gait. Glamorous he could never be, not by human standards.

Kropotkin was standing at the door of the car, glowering nervously at the alien. Inside, Omass had his writhe already drawn, his finger on the trigger.

Ratty paused before entering. "Listen, both of you. Young Friend Umandral is superhuman. He is fast enough to run rings around both of you, and he can tune out pain so that a writhe wouldn't stop him. Put the damned things away. You can't do any good against him." If the world was watching this through his implants, he hoped someone was censoring the proceedings. "Your Holiness, may I present Young Friend Umandral of Canaster Sector?"

The boy stepped in and dipped as expected. Then he sat down, stretched out reedy legs, folded even thinner arms, and kept his face expressionless. He kept flipping back and forth between terrifying monster and surly kid.

"You are welcome to Pock's World," Joy said graciously, although Ratty could see her nervousness.

"I am glad to hear it, Priestess. After all the shit they've been giving me, I was starting to wonder."

Joy sniggered. Ratty deliberately laughed aloud. He went to sit beside her. The door slammed shut, and Car One whined straight up into the shy.

"I can arrange for you to say a few words to the World Council if you wish," Joy said eagerly. After a sensational start to her first public duty, she must be plotting even greater triumphs.

No, no, no! Worse and worse.

"I would love that," Umandral said solemnly.

"But what will you say?" Ratty asked.

"Nothing but the truth."

"That's what I'm afraid of. Like how you're planning to wipe out the human race on Pock's?"

"Yes."

Joy gasped. "There are six hundred million of us and only a... how many of you?"

"He won't answer that."

"Billions," Umandral said, "depending how many planets you include. Forty-eight still at large on Pock's world. That makes the odds heavily in our favor."

The two guards growled. Joy was nonplused.

Ratty said, "You seem to tell the truth all the time, even when it is not to your own advantage. Are you capable of lying?"

The boy shrugged. "I can, but I hate to. It is virtually impossible to deceive us, so telling lies is bad policy. The Children soon learn not to."

"'The Children'?"

"We are the Children of the Future. You are the Past. Of course, if Pock's World is sterilized by an impact, we shall die with you. The prospect is harder on us, because of our wider knowledge and more effective imaginations. We can analyze all the ways it may kill us—the initial searing fireball, the flash deaths farther away, the shock wave that can kill folk without leaving a mark or roll them in a debris wave until they are shredded, the rain of fire all over the world as the ejecta fall, the days of choking darkness when the air is full of smoke and soot and the sun never shines, the killing wintertime that will follow, and then, after that, when the skies clear, the greenhouse effects that roasts the entire—"

"And which one exit would you choose?" Ratty asked acidly.

"The last, because the earlier effects would be so interesting to watch." Umandral sounded sincere. The strangest thing about him was that Ratty had to take him seriously, as he never would a human boy of that age. He sensed the presence of a mind already superior to his.

"So is the world going to end tomorrow?"

"A few minutes after tomorrow was what I overheard."

"It will end?"

Umandral nodded solemnly. "It seems so. What did STARS do to our ship?"

"According to a turncoat STARS employee—who may, of course, be a plant, lying to us poor dumb humans—they destroyed the computers and the entangler equipment so that no one could leave or board after they left, and they programmed the probe itself to impact Pock's World. They also set delayed charges to disable the Wong-Hui projector to prevent anyone changing the new trajectory later. Independent observers predict impact, as you say, for a few minutes into eclipse on Sixtrdy."

"If what you have just told me is true, then Pock's World is doomed."

"One of my senior incarnations," Joy declared, "has been assured by our Goddess that the impact will not occur."

The boy shrugged again. "Wishful thinking is self-deception, the most stupid of all forms of lying. Denial is one of the greatest weaknesses you humans have, so it has been eliminated from our genome. We can accept reality without anxiety. Of course, her lies will never be proved against her in this case, will they?"

Joy pouted. The guards glared.

Unfortunately, Ratty agreed with the punk. It was thirty hours or so to Armageddon. "And how do you feel about this?"

Umandral gave him an exasperated look, as if the question was too stupid to bother with. "Sad, of course. But we all die, and it will be a better death than what Eryngo and her scats were planning for me. Before being captured, I could look forward to a much longer and richer life than any of you could.

Mostly I am regretful that we cannot complete our mission to upgrade this world."

Joy said, "Some lies are told for good purposes. If the human population of Pock's World believed that it must die on Sixtrdy, there would be panic and suffering. Is not a lie to the contrary a kindness?"

"The Children would neither consider it so nor find it necessary."

"The Goddess's children would. We shall arrive at Undra shortly and I am told that the leaders assembled are anxious to see you. If we let you address them, will you promise not to say anything to make them unhappy?"

Ratty opened his mouth to protest and saw a gownsman he did not know, wearing a cape of green with white polka dots.

—*Please stay out of this, Consort. We shall see that you are in control.* The image smiled wryly and disappeared.

In control? As far as Ratty was concerned, Joy was in nobody's control, never had been, and never would be. And Umandral was worse.

"If you will promise not to return me to prison," the cuckoo said. "I know nothing about the probe's current trajectory except what you have told me, so I promise not to foretell it. I would speak honestly about our plans for mutually beneficial cooperation between humans and the Children."

Joy beamed. "Then we shall all listen! Consort Ratty will ask you some questions, won't you darling?"

Both Omass and Kropotkin looked at Ratty disbelievingly. They thought she was crazy, and so did he. The Children's program to improve Pock's World would almost certainly begin by removing the present inhabitants or using them as brood stock. If the probe's impact did not kill all the human beings tomorrow, then the Children soon would.

⊷⊶⊷ ⊷⊶⊷

Grandiose buildings were rare on Pock's World, because it tended to shrug them off. The World Council met in a former volcanic vent, a natural amphitheater with steep rocky walls and a grassy floor. Thirty-one governments were represented, each having sent a delegation of three or four persons, and each group sat apart under its own transparent umbrella. A steady drizzle was falling, and clouds hid both the sun and Javel.

"Acoustics?" Ratty said incredulously in the robing room where Monody was preparing to make her entry. "You use voices? At the close of the thirtieth millennium?"

"It's traditional, darling." Joy eyed her hair in a mirror as an attendant primped it. "The council's been meeting here since long before cognition was invented. And everyone can chat with their friends during the speeches. Are you boys ready?"

Ratty looked at the cuckoo. "I am."

The cuckoo said, "So am I." Someone had found him clothes to fit.

Ugly runt! On impulse Ratty asked, "How old are you, sonny?"

Umandral took no offence. "In round numbers, 425.1 million standard seconds. That's about 15.121 of my home years. In Pock's years, 7.56. On Ayne 13.456, or 13 years, 7 long-fortnights, and 12 days."

"How did you work all that out?"

"In my head."

"That's what I was afraid of." Ratty hoped the brat had used an implant, but he probably hadn't.

⟶⇥⟵ ⧉ — ⧉ ⟶⇤⟵

Worrying about what might be about to happen, Ratty escorted Monody as she made her entrance through a tunnel, emerging on a balcony-rostrum while a choir sang a hymn to the Mother. Almost all the delegates knelt to her, even the Theriac Emperor in his gold robes. A few dissenters merely bowed.

She recited a prayer, then bade them all be seated, her voice reverberating strangely across the arena. Every delegation would include at least one reporter, so the world would be watching this meeting of the council as it had not watched any such assembly in centuries.

Joy retired to her throne, and from there she presented new Consort Ratty. What he was about to do was very much what he had done for a living on Ayne, but a live audience would be disconcerting. Joy had warned him that he would be applauded; he was not prepared for a deafening standing ovation, the whole crater echoing with cheers. He did not flatter himself that he was good enough to have earned that acclaim.

He raised a hand for silence and introduced the visitor, Young Friend Umandral. The cuckoo waddled forward to join him, and Pock's World had its first view of the alien.

Now, would the cuckoo stick to the agreed script? Somewhere a control was programmed to cut him off, but neither humans nor human machinery did well when trying to outguess this gawky-looking kid.

"Will you tell us exactly where you come from?"

"The name of my world would mean nothing to you. It is roughly eighty-three light years away, in the Canaster Sector." His double throat produced an unpleasantly harsh overtone.

"And why did you come?"

"Out of goodwill. Because we can offer much technology that your world sadly needs. We can show you how to double your life spans, abolish poverty, raise your children's intelligence, and adapt your genome to the world so that you won't suffer from cancer and allergies and won't need tonic."

So far, so good. Why had he and his friends landed in secret?

Because STARS, Inc. had historically blocked all attempts at communication between the sectors.

Why would STARS do that?

Because STARS, Inc. controlled the flow of technology in order to profit from it.

He looked such a wimpy dork, and yet he had killed three men with his bare hands and injured others. He must have handled that giant soldier like a rag doll. What would an adult be capable of?

Here came the big questions.

"Now, when you left your probe to descend to Pock's World, you left it in a safe and stable orbit around Javel, right?"

"We did."

"So you do not believe these rumors that it is aimed to impact Pock's World tomorrow and kill us all?"

He had refused to consent to a simple negative. Ratty himself, he had argued, had told him that independent observers confirmed the impact trajectory. He had conceded, though, that this was third-hand hearsay. So the agreed compromise answer, hammered out in the air car, was, "To the best of my knowledge that is simply not true."

What Umandral said was, "Certainly I believe that."

But only Ratty heard him. Over the loudspeakers, Umandral's voice said, "To the best of my knowledge that is simply not true." The mike went dead, so there could be no retraction.

During the riotous cheering that followed, as the two of them were walking back to their seats below the throne, Ratty said, "You went back on your word to me, you snotty little shit."

The boy looked at him pityingly. "It made no difference. I had detected the two-hundred-millisecond delay, of course, so I knew you would have some sort of intervention ready. I was quite impressed by the way your primitive technology made the switch."

"You lied to me, earlier, when you promised to stick to the script!"

"I did warn you that I find lying distasteful. I told the truth knowing that you would block it. The deceit is yours, not mine."

"So you haven't cut all sense of ethics out of your genome? But isn't breaking your solemn word worse than just lying?"

"In most circumstances, yes. I would never break my word to any of the Children. You I just can't see as an equal."

"Mutual," Ratty assured him. "So we can never rely on you to honor an agreement?"

"Only when it is in our interests to do so. That's true for your species also."

Arguing with Umandral was unsatisfying.

⋯⊷⊰ — ⊱⊶⋯

No matter—the brief interview had been a planet-shattering success. Governments of a world had assembled to debate the end of that world, and the alien had put their minds at rest. The impact story was all vicious nonsense, and the Goddess's assurance could be believed. Members of the entire sacred family and their senior staff kept popping in and out of Ratty's mind, thanking him, congratulating him, and begging him to forgive doubts that they had never previously mentioned.

He thanked them all politely, but what he really wanted to do was go home to the palace at Abietin and climb into bed with Joy and a magnum of champagne.

Chapter 6

Athena had found Solan huddled in a corner of his father's sickroom, which was a comfortable and engaging place, expertly furnished and opening out on a rocky grotto with flowers and water. Skerry himself was lost in a coma or a very deep sleep, monitored by a medic machine and unresponsive. A priesthood that had survived ten thousand years could hardly be expected to deal with the end of the world as a routine matter, and the boy had evidently been forgotten in the current turmoil.

"Your dad doesn't need you right now," she said. "Why don't you and I go riding?"

Gloom. "I don't know how."

"I can teach you."

His eyes went bright. He looked at his dying father.

"He won't mind. We won't be long."

She took Solan to the stable and even there found a curious shortage of people. If the palace staff were heading home to be with their families, that seemed like a disappointing lack of faith in their high priestess's assurances.

The few attendants around did not interfere as she saddled up the mare she had ridden the previous day. She put the boy on the saddle and led the horse around for a while, then mounted behind Solan and let him experience a walk and a canter. Falling off was much less fearsome in low gravity—not that Solan had any lack of courage—and when she suggested that they find a pony for him, she won his heart. Within an hour she had taught him the basics and had to restrain him from attempting aerobatics.

Eventually she dragged him away so that both they and the horses might eat lunch. Skerry was still unconscious, and she could read enough on the unfamiliar medic's data panels to know that the prognosis was hopeless. Fortunately the lad did not understand that output; he was raring to get back to the pony. He wanted to try jumping, galloping, and a full-sized horse, preferably one of the twenty-hand stallions. She let him have another hour or so in the saddle, but by then she was weary and sore, and suggested that they go swimming instead. Then boating.

He was much better company than Linn Lazuline.

When Javel and the sun were close enough for her to declare evening, she took Solan back again to check on his father. A nurse was in attendance now, clearly relieved to see him. She adjusted the bedside equipment, and the patient roused enough to recognize his son. He probably understood little of the boy's excited chatter, but he knew enough to say goodbye.

"I suggest," Athena said, "that Solan come and stay with me for a week or two. Until the crisis is resolved, I mean."

Skerry seemed to understand that also, for he nodded and muttered thanks. Father and son were not naturally demonstrative, but Athena was, and she could not let them part like that.

"Why don't you give your dad a kiss?" she suggested.

Solan understood then. He paled and did as she bade him.

"Time to go," the nurse said, and Skerry's smile faded back into his final sleep.

As they went out the door, Solan took Athena's hand. The guests' terrace was deserted, Ratty and Linn and Brother Andre all being busy elsewhere. She chose a comfortable love seat and sat the boy beside her.

"Everything has a purpose," she said. "And tears are to wash away sorrows. If you want to cry your eyes out, no one will think less of you for it."

He thought about it. "I'm not ready for that," he decided. "Probably tonight. That was how it was when Mom died." His emotions had been tempered to adult strength already.

"Would you like something to eat, then?"

"No thank you, Friend Athena. Tell me about Ayne."

"It's a bigger world than this one. You'll weigh more there, so you'll have to grow more muscles, but we have tonic that will help. My house is called Portolan. I'm going there tomorrow morning. I have a very big house, with horses and boating and fishing." And no one to leave it to when she died. "There are quite a few children of your age running around."

"What if the probe hits Pock's World, Friend Athena?"

"You won't be here."

"And if it doesn't?"

"Then I'll bring you back to your family."

"Got no family."

"Then it will be your choice. You can come back here or stay on Ayne with me, whichever you like."

Solan stared down at his knees for a while. Finally he said, "Thank you. How many horses?"

Frivdy

Joy tickled him, and skillfully, too. He rolled over and grabbed her hand. Then her other hand. He kept forgetting she was ambidextrous.

"It's morning," she said, which meant that this was the day the shuttle would leave, so he must cuddle her tight and assure her that he wasn't going to leave her.

So he did that.

"No," she told his collarbone. "You must go. I know you don't really believe that the probe won't hit, so you must go. You can come back later, when it doesn't."

"You mean you couldn't live with the guilt if I stayed here and died?"

"Yes."

"But you would be dead too, so you wouldn't have any guilt to live with."

Then Joy, the ebullient, irrepressible Joy, began to weep, which wasn't part of the game he had thought they were playing, and something he had never known her do before.

"You could come with me," he suggested. "Millie Backet won't be taking her seat in the shuttle."

"Don't be stupid."

"Just a quick trip to Ayne to visit my family."

"I didn't know you had family!"

"Eight boys, seven girls."

She wept even harder.

"I don't understand this," he said. "Do you believe, *really* believe, that the probe will miss?"

"Of course I do." —*sniff*.

"That Pock's World will survive?"

"Of course it will." —*snivel*.

"Then I'll be here with you for as long as I live." Even if the probe missed, his life expectancy would be a lot shorter on Pock's than on Ayne. Was he a fool or was he a fool? "So what are you crying for?"

"Duty!" —*sniffle* —*snuffle*

"*Duty?*" he repeated. Then he understood. "Oh, Duty! That's why she's so sure? In desperate circumstances, the Mother will accept sacrifices?"

"Of course. Tonight."

"Why Duty? Why not old Wisdom? She's got nothing left to lose."

"No, has to be Duty."

So he held her and let her weep.

⋙⋘ — ⋙⋘

Joy's eyes were still pink when Ratty escorted her out to the guests' terrace in search of breakfast. The medic, informed that he had decided to remain on Pock's World permanently, had issued him half a liter of the vilest muck he could imagine, probably straight from the sewers of a major city. After that, breakfast held no appeal. Metabolic adaption was never easy, and Pock's World had the most extreme environment ever colonized. He was in for a miserable few weeks if he lived; by nightfall the probe's impact might seem like a welcome release.

The weather was close to perfect, cloudless sky and a soft breeze. Athena was there already, accompanied by young Solan. That would be a promising story lead if Ratty were still in the reporter business.

—*Skerry died last night*, Joy cognized.

Glances were exchanged, and Athena's was a warning not to comment, so nobody did. Solan was concentrating on a plate of something that Ratty preferred not to look at, because it wasn't quite dead. The boy stopped eating when he noticed the next arrival—Umandral, Child of the Future. Two armed guards followed the cuckoo out of the palace but remained by the door to watch. Were they there to keep him from running away or to defend him from xenophobic Pocosins?

Solan stared at him in horror as he approached.

"You met him on Toody," Ratty remarked.

"I could never forget *that*," the boy said.

Ratty shared his distaste but said politely, "Good morning, Ambassador Umandral."

The youth smiled as if humoring him. "Greetings to you, Liberator Ratty."

Pages were taking orders. Ratty confined his to coffee, most revered of all terrestrial friends, a shrub that thrived exquisitely in Pock's hot climate and volcanic soil.

"The STARS air car is on its way," Joy announced. "Your companions have been warned to hurry."

"Do you know what the radiation level is?" Athena asked.

Joy passed the question, then spoke the reply. "High acceptable, but variable." Pause. "They don't expect to fry you."

The next arrival was ex-STARS engineer Braata. He bowed to Joy, nodded politely to everyone else, and took a seat outside the group.

Then came the godlike Linn Lazuline, good-humored as ever. He greeted everyone jovially, even Braata.

Pages and waiters still bustled around, and Ratty did not notice the next arrival until he was looming over the diners— Brother Andre, looking even more exhausted than he had the previous day. *Skinny dipping?* Ratty struggled to keep a straight face.

The papal legate declined a seat and inspected the congregation with disapproval.

"I assume that the Backet Commission is about to depart from Pock's World?"

"Very shortly," Joy said. "I apologize on behalf of my senior incarnations for the fact that they are unable to see you on your way, Friend Andre. They are either occupied elsewhere or resting. I hope that my—"

"You are more than adequate," the friar said with the fatherly smile that so rarely illuminated his craggy features. "As the senior in years, may I ask the surviving members of the mission what they have concluded and how they will report? Ratty, you are recording this, I assume?"

"I am." Ratty had to shout over the painful whine of an air car, a noise he had not heard near the palace before.

"Very well. We are all satisfied that there are cuckoos. You already know my own opinions: you cannot compromise with the Devil, and STARS did make the right decision when it arranged to sterilize Pock's World. So I vote Aye. Senator Fimble? Your vote, please?"

"I disagree," Athena said. "Yes, the cuckoos exist and may very well be dangerous. I believe that the authorities should have been given time to round them up. Further—"

"Excuse an interruption, Friend Athena," Umandral said in his unpleasant squawk. "But you should know that I was chosen to be the one captured. My name was drawn, and I accepted the assignment. There is no chance at all that any human 'authority' could round us up faster than we could increase our numbers." He showed his little teeth in a smile.

"You gave yourself up, in effect?" The friar looked surprised, an admission of fallibility that Ratty had never seen on his face in all the cognition his team had assembled for *The Saint of Annatto*. "Knowing that you might be tortured and probably put to death?"

"I was certain I would be."

"Then why did you agree?"

This time the youth was openly contemptuous. "I don't think we have time to discuss faith and duty, priest. Your mind is already made up."

"Friend Umandral," Ratty said, "is dedicated to telling the truth under any circumstances, except when he doesn't want to."

"When lies serve my purpose better, you mean."

"When lies serve his purpose better."

The air car mercifully fell silent, having landed on flowerbeds a hundred meters away.

"To conclude," Athena said, "I believe that the proposed destruction of Pock's World is deliberate geocide, unjustified and inhuman."

"Very human," the cuckoo murmured.

"Extended quarantine would have been practical, and the correct option."

"One aye and one nay." The friar turned to Ratty.

"Another nay. Quarantine was the correct response, and STARS is committing geocide. I would add that I have spoken at length with Umandral, and I believe that his people have much to teach us. I can't see why the two races could not cooperate."

"You are wrong," Brother Andre said. "One aye and two nays. "Friend Linn?"

The self-proclaimed local STARS boss, Chairman Glaum, was on his way from the air car, coming in a straight line, regardless of flowerbeds.

Linn looked to Umandral. "You can parasitize adult humans of either sex?"

The cuckoo smiled, showing his undersized teeth. "My own sexual apparatus is not yet sufficiently mature, but in a year or so, yes. I will be capable of inserting a zygote directly into a uterus by rape, or implanting a parasitoid fluke into a male by either anal rape or subcutaneous implant—I mean surgically or via a stab wound. The parasitoid would seek out his pancreas, which is an organ with a good blood supply and redundant functional capacity, and there it would develop until it came to term. At that point the human incubator will voluntarily cut himself open to release my child."

There was a moment's silence before Linn spoke again.

"I find your apparent honesty disconcerting, but I cannot find any hidden deception in it. Turnsole, you said on our way here that my vote would only carry conviction if I voted against my own business interests. I must do so now. I believe STARS made the correct decision."

Ratty shrugged. Obviously, if Linn Lazuline *was* STARS, then his own interests were quite different from what they appeared to be. That alone might explain why he had put himself on the commission. He was polishing the other side of the same coin, that was all.

"So we are tied," the old man said sadly. "Two Ayes, two Nays. I congratulate Friend Linn on his perception and disinterest. But the cuckoos are the work of the Devil, and the sterilization of Pock's World, while infinitely regrettable, is justified to preserve the human race, God's children, made in his own image."

"Easy to say when you have a ticket out," Athena snapped.

"No. It can only be said at all if you don't. Are you planning to take that boy home with you, in Millie Backet's place?"

"I am. He agrees and the Church of the Mother approved."

"But has STARS?" Andre wheeled to face the oversized Glaum in his black shorts and visor, who had now arrived. "Are our seats on the shuttle transferrable, Friend Glaum?"

"No. We are hard pressed to find enough spaces for all our own people."

"My family, for instance?" Braata jumped to his feet, surprising everyone. He strode forward. "I can see you abandoning me, although you have never given me a hearing or a trial, but you are punishing my parents and brothers for my alleged sins."

Glaum ignored him.

"I give my seat to Solan," Ratty said. "I am staying with Joy."

"You can vacate your place but not assign it to someone else." The big man folded his arms to indicate immovability. His face bore a natural sneer.

"I, too, wish to assign my place to someone else," Andre said. "So it seems that a mission of five will be returning only two survivors, who will report that STARS refused to transport three children, three refugees, to save them from the holocaust STARS plans to inflict on Pock's world. Athena, Linn, you will put this news to good use back on Ayne?"

"Indeed we shall," Linn said. "All religions will join in, Athena can raise the state, and I will muster industry. Their deaths will not be in vain."

Glaum shrugged, indifferent. "It is time to go. I will not keep the shuttle waiting even one minute. Get in the car, Friend Linn, Friend Athena... and take the brat if you want, since he is here. Nobody else. We leave in thirty seconds, ready or not." He turned on his heel and marched off.

Ratty jumped up and handed his recorder to Athena. "See that Jake at my office gets this, will you? And good luck."

They were all moving now, hurrying after Glaum, clasping hands and making farewells as they went.

"What's your reason for staying, Brother?" Athena asked.

"Because I voted for cauterization, of course," the old man said. "I cannot sentence the people of Pock's World to martyrdom and not remain to share that burden. Ratty is staying, too, but I beg you, don't let the other hacks like him declare me a saint! Now go with God."

Everyone but the travelers stopped at a safe distance from the car and watched Linn, Athena, and the boy scramble aboard. Then the door dropped, the motor began to whine, and clouds of dust roiled up.

Joy enveloped Ratty in a wild embrace.

Braata went over to the friar and knelt to receive the blessing of the Saint of Annatto.

Back at the terrace, Umandral was still eating breakfast.

Chapter 2

"How are you?" Joy asked as they went back indoors. She was regarding him with concern.

"Have felt better," Ratty admitted. The immigrant's tonic was giving him hot flashes, double vision, and waves of nausea.

"Can you stand yet another family gathering?"

"Of course." The side effects might not seem so bad there. If that failed, he could always ask to be flogged with barbed wire. "What's the agenda?"

"Tonight."

Oh, yes, the non-end of the world. Plan a party? Count me a no-show.

He had not yet learned his way around the family quarters, which were enormous. The room to which Joy led him was probably Duty's grand audience chamber, for it held a chair much like a throne. Two smaller chairs flanked it, and directly in front was what he at first took to be a circular red-and-white rug on a black marble floor. Closer inspection showed that it was a hologram of Javel at the full, seemingly floating below glass. There were stars in the darkness behind it, and he guessed that it must be a projection from a Lagrangian satellite. He had never heard of a religion putting its prime deity underfoot before, but he noticed that as Joy was careful to go around the image and not step on it. She led him to a pair of chairs on the right of the disk.

He had barely sunk down and leaned his aching head back when Love and Bedel entered, so he had to rise and bob. They sat on the chairs opposite. In a few moments Duty herself entered, with Oxindole and Wisdom. Duty took the throne and they went on either side of her. Ratty had seen the Monody family being informal, so this meeting was more than just a chat. He assumed that it was being recorded and possibly broadcast.

"First," Oxindole said, "we welcome Consort Ratty to the family and congratulate him on his faith and courage. We assure him that they are not misplaced. Secondly, we must attend to a painful but traditional task. The last time this ceremony was held was back in 28,928, or 532 Pocosin years ago, almost a thousand standard.

"I confess that corundum worms got into our data vaults a few centuries back, and the records are not as good as we should like, but we do know that Joy makes the first appeal."

Joy took a deep breath and recited: "Grandmother, our Holy Mother strictly forbids suicide, and what you are planning is most certainly that."

Duty smiled fondly at her. "No, dearest Joy. You sound just like that tiresome priest from Ayne. I promise you that I have no intention of jumping. I shall merely ask the Mother to spare her children and take my life instead. Three times I shall ask. If she refuses my third appeal, then I shall come back down."

"Bah! You know how the wind howls up there, Grandmother! No Duty has ever come back down."

"And the Mother has never refused a request we have made from there. No, the danger is real, and Duty's duty is clear." For a woman discussing her own imminent death, the old lady was amazingly calm, smiling and showing no resentment.

Then her daughter, Love, took up the baton.

"It falls to me to show that what you propose is blasphemous. Although the Mother will intervene with mercy and lift intolerable burdens, even for Monody she will never break the laws she has set to bind the universe. To ask her to quicken a corpse or move the world from its ordained orbit would be desecration of your office and our faith. I call Friend Zyemindar, formerly Engineer Braata."

Ratty's double vision seemed to be getting worse. He watched two Braata-like men walk in from the door. Two names, two men? Or a two-headed giraffe? When they reached the edge of the Javel hologram, they stopped and bowed toward the throne. A good Christian must not kneel to pagan priestesses.

Bedel, not Love, asked the questions.

"When you disabled the alien probe, how did you gain entry?"

Evidently Braata—and despite Ratty's blinding headache there was probably only one of him—had been coached in what he would be asked.

"Via the shuttle dock, Consort. A probe of that type usually has many ports, proving access to different areas of its surface, but often their entrances are welded shut by the abrasion of interstellar dust. The shuttle docks are at the stern, sheltered in a minor crater, and we knew they must have been used quite—"

"And you had no trouble gaining access?"

"The hatch was locked, of course. We were in a hurry, so I blew it with a shaped charge."

"And were not yourself blown away into space by the internal atmosphere escaping?"

"No, Gownsman. All shafts have many successive safety doors to prevent leakage. Always some are left closed, some open, so you close the first open one you come to and open the first closed one after that, and you have set up a substitute airlock to preserve the internal atmosphere. When I opened my faceplate it made my ears pop."

"Did you evacuate the probe's atmosphere when you left?"

"No, Excellency. Our mission was, first, to make sure that the probe was not still manned, or capable of being re-crewed through the entangler; secondly to make sure that it could not be used as a missile. That was why we demolished the projector. Our third task was to make the probe safe for future reuse. We turned the hydroponics back on and restarted the climate controls. Shipping a new atmosphere up to it would be an enormous project."

"So the probe may still be inhabited?"

"It certainly includes living bacteria, because food was rotting and everywhere stank horribly. I suppose in theory there could be hominins hiding in there somewhere."

"Then it is possible that the probe can still be steered away from its projected impact?"

"No, Consort. Our orders were to make sure that it could not be steered. I mined the control centers, the power plant, and the Wong-Hui projector. All those charges later blew. That is a dead rock."

"How about attitude jets?"

For a moment Braata looked blank. "Oh, your pardon. No, there are none. A rock like that is far too massive to turn with jets. It is steered by turning the projector, and even that may take a week to alter its attitude significantly."

"So there can be no doubt that it will impact Pock's World?"

"I cannot answer that from observation, Consort. I can only testify that I am aware of no way to change its course within the next few hours. A few days' work by a space tug might achieve something, and it could be refitted in a few years, but hours? Never."

"Thank you. Now I understand that the probe practically skims the top of Javel's cloud cover at periapsis?"

"I know it goes very close. If it were not a nickel-iron monolith, tidal forces would have broken up it apart by now."

"And there has been extensive solar flare activity in the last few days. Cannot this cause a planetary atmosphere to swell and increase drag?"

"Again I can speak only to theory, not from observation. Yes, the tenuous uppermost reaches of the atmosphere may rise and increase drag, but that effect at periapsis would tend to change the orbit at its outer limit, apoapsis. In fact Pock's World is much closer to the probe's periapsis. The probe passed periapsis a couple of days ago, moving at maximum velocity."

And now it was almost here. Braata did not say that, but the thought was inescapable. Ratty glanced down at the hologram as if he might see the monster on its way. He quickly added vertigo to his list of complaints. He would have to go and lie down soon.

Bedel glanced at Oxindole as if to ask if he had any questions for the witness, but it was Duty who spoke.

"Engineer Braata, you are fortunate that we do not shoot messengers on Pock's World, for the news you bring us is dire." Her smile robbed her words of sting. "Nevertheless, we thank you for it. It was kind of you to come and advise us. My blessings may not mean much to you, but you have them anyway. Live and die happy."

Braata hesitated, then made a slightly lopsided bow, as if one knee was trying to bend. He turned and departed, feet tapping.

"I call Gownsman Trover," Bedel said.

Gownsman Trover turned out to be a buxom woman sporting a green cape like the one Skerry had worn. She admitted to being director of the Voissoir observatory.

"Tell us," Bedel said, "when you last observed the pirate probe."

"About an hour ago, Consort, using radar."

"And?"

"It was slowed slightly by its passage around Javel, about two seconds more than predicted. We recalculated ground zero then as being about fifty kilometers west of Hostie Caldera. Today's measurements indicate no change in that prediction."

Bedel sighed. "So in your opinion Pock's World is doomed. Do any of your colleagues disagree?"

"Yes, it is doomed, and I know of no qualified person who disagrees." Trover looked and sounded close to tears.

Duty blessed and dismissed her.

"There is my case, Mother," Love said. "Clearly the Goddess has decided to gather all her children to her and end this world. She may be defending us from the cuckoos, or she may have other reasons that she has not revealed to us. Whatever they are, we have no choice but to accept them. To ask her to deflect that missile now would be futile and presumptuous."

Duty shook her head. "And not to ask would show a sad lack of faith." She turned lovingly to her own mother, slumped in the chair beside her. "Now you, Wisdom, dear?"

The old woman sighed as if she found the proceedings absurd. "So Joy tells you it's wicked and Love tells you it's useless. What am I supposed to tell you?"

Oxindole said, "We're not sure, Holiness. This is where the records are spotty."

Duty laughed and patted her mother's withered hand. "What do you want to tell me?"

"What I've said from the start. You'll either die trying or you'll die with the rest of us ten minutes later. You've got nothing much to lose and a world to save. Of course you'll do it."

No doubt Duty said something memorable then, but at that moment Ratty Turnsole passed out and slid to the floor.

Chapter 3

The air car would have held eight, but there was no one there except Glaum, Linn, Solan, and Athena herself. She did not speak to Glaum the boor, being more inclined to wring that plinth he called a neck, and she was finding it hard to be courteous to Linn Lazuline now.

As far as she had been able to work out, STARS's branch on Pock's World must have learned of the cuckoos two or three days before her political conference at Portolan. A messenger would have come post-haste to Ayne to report to head office. It might have taken a couple of days to organize a meeting of the STARS board, either face-to-face or by cog-com, but the decision to sterilize must have been made quickly. The orders were sent, and the Braata mission dispatched to redirect the probe. Only then had STARS gone public. But Linn had known what was going to happen when he came to proposition her at Portolan.

On the first day of the Backet Commission's venture, Ratty had called the sterilization solution overkill, but it made sense now. It was not the cuckoos themselves that STARS feared, at least not as an immediate threat. But if Umandral and his companions ever convinced the Pocosins that there were worlds out there with higher technology, which STARS was censoring for its own purposes, then the ancient monopoly would be in jeopardy. It wasn't the cuckoos who must not be allowed to escape from Pock's, it was what they knew.

So the decision had been made, and the fact-finding farce proposed as a public relations gesture. Likely Lynn had organized that himself. Delegates from both the Sector Council and the Catholic Church were obvious choices, and they had selected their own representatives, Millie and Brother Andre. Whoever they were, their votes were fairly easy to predict, one aye and one nay. But Linn had used the junket to manipulate his youthful dream girl into bed at last and the gadfly Ratty Turnsole into a deathtrap. It all made revolting sense now.

Athena knew how she was going to get even, but revenge depended on a safe trip home to Ayne, and if Linn stood as high in the STARS hierarchy as she suspected, that depended on his goodwill. Mum was the word, for now. She watched the fabulous Pocosin scenery rush by below and had Solan tell her whatever he could about it.

The two men remained mainly silent also—Glaum no doubt cognizing, and Linn showing as much interest as Athena in viewing a world that he and his accomplices had already condemned to death. Just as Nervine Landing came in sight, he suddenly spoke.

"Friend Glaum, is Pock's Station in danger from the impact?"

The big man shrugged. "No immediate danger. Its view of the rising fireball will be spectacular, but its orbit will carry it well to the north of ground zero on its first pass. Three orbits later it will directly overfly the crater, but by then there will be no danger. In the long term it needs supplies of food and so on from the surface, but that is all. STARS will leave a few observers on the station and evacuate them later to Pyrus 1."

"I repeat that I should like to view the impact," Linn said. "Worlds do not die every day."

Glaum's smiles were always contemptuous. "You are not the first to ask, but STARS has refused all such requests."

Linn sighed. "The path to Heaven is paved with broken dreams."

It was an innocent enough remark. It sounded sufficiently like some obscure quotation for its lack of relevance to pass without comment, but something about the way it was said... And the way Glaum glanced at Athena before he answered...

"I suspect there have been a couple of exceptions. Large donations to favorite charities or research programs may have been involved."

"My foundation is always looking for worthy causes to support."

And Glaum nodded.

"That's the most active volcano in the world just now," Solan remarked, pointing a weedy finger.

Linn went back to staring out the window.

So did Athena. On the face of it, Linn had just been asked for a bribe and had agreed to discuss the amount. But his remark about the path to Heaven could have been a code, and in that case the hints of bribery were mere camouflage; Linn had revealed his STARS rank to Glaum and issued orders. Or perhaps they both belonged to some secret neo-Masonic-type fraternity. Either way, she was convinced that Linn was now in charge.

Nervine Station came in sight—a bleak, dark lava flow studded with five blockhouses. Those were marked off by shock fences, uninhabited islands in an ocean of people. The STARS forces were having trouble keeping the crowds under control: she saw puffs of happy gas and flickers of writhes in use. Air cars buzzed around like feasting mosquitoes.

"Busy place," Linn said.

"Panic," Glaum remarked. "Everyone wants into the ark. No one boards a shuttle until their DNA has been checked. Shuttles are breaking down from lack of maintenance. We've had one near-crash already."

"But we are guests of STARS," Athena said. "You will see that we receive priority?"

Glaum's eyes flickered momentarily in Linn's direction. "Of course," he said.

The path to the Heaven was still open, no matter how it was paved.

Even with Chairman Glaum's weight behind them, they had hours to wait at Nervine. The waiting room was packed, mainly with off-worlders and only a sprinkling of Pocosins. Linn disappeared. In the stress and confusion, Solan's hard-tested nerves finally cracked, and he sobbed his heart out in Athena's arms.

After that, the ride up in the shuttle was a relief, and a great adventure for the boy. Alas, Pock's station was even more crowded than the Nervine blockhouse, with people being shuttled in faster than the entangler could transmit them onward to Pyrus. There was no food or water left, the air was foul.

Exactly how an entangler worked was outside both Athena's expertise and—until now—her field of interest. Her knowledge was confined to the popular understanding that the travelers' bodies were destructively mapped, the information was transmitted by entanglement link, and the atoms that were ripped away in the process became feedstock for the reconstruction of arrivals. This raised the interesting question of what would happen if everyone were leaving and no one returning. Would the Pocosin entangler fill up with human soup and be forced to shut down? Would the Pyrus 1 entangler run out of raw material? These were not matters she wanted to think about, let alone discuss with anyone who might know.

Tired and hungry, they at last approached the door to the entangler: six ahead, five ahead, four...

She jumped when Linn appeared beside her, but he was smiling, not gloating. "I wish you bon voyage and happy memories."

So she was not to be held against her will, and her sense of relief told her how worried she had been about that.

"You are staying to watch the fireworks?"

"It will be a once-in-a-lifetime experience."

"Once in six hundred million lifetimes. I find the idea morbid and repugnant."

He looked down thoughtfully at Solan and seemed to decide to ignore him. "Live and die happy, as they say on Pock's."

"I shall launch my campaign tomorrow."

Linn nodded. "I shall watch it with interest."

Solan went through the door first. Athena followed.

◦─◦◦◦─◦◦─ ◦◦◦─◦◦◦─

Their replicas were reunited in Pyrus 1. Solan complained about the gravity. But the crowd was not as oppressive and food was available. There were even places to sit. He went to study the wall view screen for a while, then came back and flopped down on the floor at her feet.

"Are we nearly there yet?" he asked wearily.

" 'Fraid not. Climatal 2 is next, then Ayne 3. From there we take a shuttle down to Shadoof Landing. And from there we get an air car to my house."

"I didn't know it would be so long."

"In all, it's about a hundred light years."

"How long in just hours?"

"I don't know."

Long enough, perhaps, that by the time he arrived at Portolan every person he had ever known would be dead or dying. Or would be dead in a century, relativity-ly speaking. She changed the subject.

"On Ayne we all have at least two names. You'll need another. I'm Athena Fimble, so you can call yourself Solan Fimble if you like. My partner is Proser Ryepeck, so you could be Solan Ryepeck. Or Solan Pocosin. Or Solan Skerry, or Solan Skerryson. Think about it and decide."

"Skerryson!" Solan said at once.

⁓⁓⁓⁓ ⁓⁓ ⁓⁓⁓⁓

The crowd of refugees dispersed across the sector. At Climatal 2, the wait was mercifully brief.

At Ayne 3 they walked right through.

"This is the end?" Solan said as they settled in the shuttle.

"Not quite. We come down at Shadoof Landing. And from there we take a car to Portolan. You can sleep in the car if you want."

He frowned in the solemn way he had, which she had already come to love. "But I shan't want to sleep if I'm flying over a whole new world."

"I didn't say you had to sleep."

"Good."

⁓⁓⁓⁓ ⁓⁓ ⁓⁓⁓⁓

At Shadoof the gravity shaft elevated them to the roof. The sun felt right. The air smelled right. It was wonderful to be home. More than wonderful—heavenly! She turned to the ranks of rental cars. But here, wonder of wonders, was Proser, running to greet her. He hugged her, kissed her, swung her around like an adolescent showing off his strength. There were certain to be reporters to capture that indignity, but she didn't care.

"We heard the news," he said. "Refugees coming through. Pock's is no more? I've been sitting here for a whole day, running up a fortune in parking." He looked down. "I don't know you!"

"This is Solan Skerryson. Solan, this is Proser Ryepeck."

"Greetings, Young Friend Solan."

Solan bowed. "Live and die happy, Friend Proser." He spoke in Pocosin, but Athena was still wearing her translator and interpreted.

Proser raised eyebrows at the greeting and peered around. "Where are the others?"

A crowd of reporters had already gathered, staring.

Her hair was a mess. She raised her voice to speech-making mode.

"Linn Lazuline stayed behind to watch the death throes of Pock's World from the safety of Pock's Station. Millie Backet,

I regret to report, was murdered by religious fanatics in the panic. Both Ratty Turnsole and Brother Andre elected to remain on Pock's World, although they knew it was going to be cauterized. For different reasons... Is one of you named Jake, an associate of Ratty's? He sent this for you.

"Now, please!" She held up a hand before the mob could start rapid fire questioning. "I am very tired. Tomorrow at Portolan I will be happy to deliver a full report. I will also have a personal announcement to make. And you are all welcome to come early and enjoy our hospitality before the meeting: food, drink, swimming, boating. Anyone who asks a question now will not be admitted."

They laughed.

"The car's away over there," Proser said. "You look tired, Young Friend Solan. Would you like me to carry you?"

"I'm pretty heavy in this gravity."

"But I'm pretty strong." Proser scooped him up.

Chapter 4

"The medic's showing beta waves. He's coming around."

"At last!"

Ratty forced his lids half open. He was in bed, a bed. Two Joys were peering down at him. He tried to speak. Nothing happened. Someone wet his lips with a sponge. He couldn't focus the two Joys into one. The other must be Love, or perhaps Duty.

"Wha' happened?"

"You had a bad reaction, darling. Tell him, Bedel."

Bedel's voice came from somewhere nearby. "One of your implants contains dysprosium. It reacted with the tonic you got. We nearly lost you."

Just like old Ratty, Ratty thought, always early for the party. Have to wait for the others now. He didn't say anything.

"There's still just time," Bedel said. "At least one shuttle is still waiting to load at Nervine Landing. We can't get hold of anyone at STARS, but we think Car One will be allowed through. We can get you up to Pock's Station before impact."

No! He thought about it. Nothing in the galaxy would be worth getting out of bed for at the moment. "No," he said. "Said I'd stay. I'll stay."

Bedel loomed over him. "Listen, Ratty. Even without that reaction, your life expectancy on Pock's isn't much more than twenty years, at best. If you can't tolerate adaption tonic, you won't last five."

"Standard or Pocosin?"

"Pocosin years."

"Well, then. No. Not going."

"But why, man? Pock's will kill you. Fungus and cancer and—"

"Love Joy. Promised Joy." He was definitely waking up. "Joy there?"

"Darling? You mustn't—"

"Must. Now send them all away and come into bed."

She sniggered and lay on the cover to cuddle him. "I don't think you're well enough for that yet, dear."

"You may be super... surp... *superised*. Don' wan' you go without me."

"Go away, all of you," Joy said. "He's staying, and I love him madly. So go away."

⊶❖—❖⊷

Eight people went to Quassia in Car One: three Monody incarnations, two consorts, one cuckoo, and his two guards. Duty understandably wanted to pass her last hours together with Oxindole, her giver and her consort for two generations, so they were making their own way there. The sky was blue and cloudless, with no sign of climate in any direction. With bright week drawing to a close, the sun hung low in the west and Javel was rising below it, a thin crescent behind the hills. Sunlight cast long shadows over the landscape.

Ratty sat with his arm around Joy, her head on his shoulder. He had failed to surprise her in his sickbed, but just cuddling was a fitting way to say goodbye. There was little conversation in Car One. He exchanged intimate little images with Joy through the adapter on his headband.

"Why did you choose to die?" Umandral demanded once, aloud. He could eavesdrop on Pocosin implants to some extent, but he had not yet admitted being able to cognize to them. He was addressing Ratty.

"A reason called love," Ratty said. "I expect you've cut it out of your genome as an illogical redundancy."

The cuckoo shook his oversized head. "No. We understand love. And duty. And joy, too."

"Then why did *you* choose to die?"

"I hoped I might negotiate, but you were all too scared of me."

"Talking of scared," Ratty said. "Why did you spout all that stuff about parasitism when Linn was leaving?"

Umandral spread his hands in an ancient human gesture of resignation. "It's all in medical reports."

Love said, "Friend Umandral, you claimed to be ambassador to the Pocosins?"

The cuckoo nodded. Ratty had no idea why the Monody family kept the alien so close to them. Perhaps Duty was afraid that the secular governments would steal him or fight over him.

"You do seem rather young for such a responsibility."

"I am smarter than any adult human. What do you want to negotiate?"

She managed to smile at his insolence, although not very convincingly. "Well, for starters, would it be possible to add a more senior member of your group to your delegation?"

"I expect so. In return, will you warrant safe conduct for both of us, guaranteeing that we shall both be unmolested and free to depart at the conclusion of the discussions? And that those discussions will not last longer than two hours unless both sides agree? And that they will be cognized so that the rest of the world can watch?"

Bedel was grinning, and in a moment the others joined in, even Wisdom.

Love herself made an effort to keep a straight face. "You do not beat around bushes, Ambassador. Roughly, and without prejudice, what topics would you want to see on the agenda?"

"Citizenship for all of us Children, with all the rights that human citizens have. In return we would obey your laws and reproduce only with our own kind and in the manners permitted and possible to humans. I should mention that we regard criminality as a major malfunction and will accept capital punishment for any misdemeanor by one of our kind. We would provide a list of more than one hundred technical innovations, and means to introduce them without damaging your economy or social structure."

Love nodded. "On the understanding that Monody does not rule the world and can use her influence only to persuade secular governments and other faiths, I accept that agenda and guarantee the safe conducts."

Umandral closed his eyes for a moment, then opened them. "Deputy Mission Leader Ignitor also accepts the terms and will call on you at Abietin at your convenience."

Even Love started to smile, until reality threw a cold shadow over the conversation. Her face darkened. "Tell your

Ignitor that noon on Sevundy will be convenient. And he is to ask for Duty."

"She," Umandral corrected. "Ignitor is currently female. Your present Duty will have to provide the miracle, of course."

An icy silence fell. Impact was due twelve minutes into Sixtrdy. Nowhere on Pock's World would Javel rise on Sevundy.

Now Mount Garookuh was visible straight ahead, a low, irregular ruin of a mountain cloaked in greenery. The tallest spike at the highest summit must be Quoad. The sky was peppered with more air cars than Ratty had ever seen before. He glanced at the western sky, where Javel grew ever closer to the sun. Little more than an hour to go, he estimated. No matter what sacrifice Duty offered to her goddess, he expected no miracle. Even if there were, he would gain only five Pocosin years.

Chapter 5

The Monody family stood on a rock platform at the base of the Quoad spire, the four incarnations and three consorts. Facing them stood the assembled choir, and in back of them, it seemed, half the population of Pock's World. Quoad's shadow lay across the crowd like the hand of a traditional clock. Earlier, Ratty had managed to catch a glimpse of the crater, which was now behind him, and he had seen more tens of thousands gathered on the hills that formed the far rim.

Somewhere in that western sky, invisible to mortal eyes, the pirate probe was hurtling towards its destiny, and his.

—*The sun's disk has contacted Javel*, said a voice in his head.

—*Eclipse has begun. Thirty-one minutes to totality.*

Joy's grip on his hand tightened. Ratty glanced around. Duty had disappeared. The prayers had been said. The choir sang on.

The air had been absolutely still when they arrived, an ominous sign to the true believers. Now the wind was rising, robes and cloaks starting to flap. Even in Pock's sultry atmosphere, a wind could feel cold, especially on top of a mountain. He moved to Joy's windward side to shelter her in his lee. He was surprised to see her smiling through tears, but of course a wind was good news for the faithful. Duty must fall, not jump.

Joy and the others had turned their backs on the congregation and were staring up at the great spire, so he did the same. Already the senior priestess was climbing the ragged staircase that zigzagged up the near side.

—*Twenty minutes to totality.*

The steps were in shadow, but he knew how broken and rotted they were. Even in daylight and even for a youngster, that would be no easy climb. For a grandmother and soon-to-be great-grandmother to attempt such a feat in this rapidly gathering gloom was close to insanity. She was almost invisible, a white smudge, but he could still make out her robe flapping.

He shivered and staggered slightly at a more violent blast. Duty believed that the fate of the world hung on her efforts. What happened if she blew off before she reached the summit? He dared not break the spell by asking. Probably that would count as a loss. Obviously—if anything in religion could be obvious to a skeptical eye—the sacrifice would have to be made at the top of the column. Close didn't count. You had to put the ball through the hoop, the priestess on the top of that grotesque, gargantuan phallic symbol.

Halfway now.

Joy's grip on his hand was almost painful.

Two-thirds. The wind was blustering ever stronger, approaching gale force. Clouds were moving in, rain starting.

—*Ten minutes to totality.*

Duty fell. She slid or rolled down two or three meters before she stopped. The crowd cried out, a mighty protest in the night, instantly snatched away by the ravening wind.

For a while she just lay there. Dead or wounded or just dazed?

—*Five minutes to totality.*

Duty was upright again, crawling up the cliff, ever so slowly. Even if she were down on hands and knees, Ratty could not imagine why the wind did not hurl her off. At that rate she wasn't going to make it in time.

The choir tried to sing again. Soon it gave up, unable to compete with the wind. The sun was a mere speck of light, dangerous to look at. Ratty glanced eastward. The hills in that direction were vanishing even as he watched. The shadow of the giant planet came rushing westward over the landscape.

—*One minute to totality. Twelve minutes to impact.*

Then he was cognizing a view of Duty. Some reporter was watching her through a night scope, probably from an air car. She was not even on hands and knees now, but right down on her belly, dragging herself centimeter by centimeter up a nearly vertical slope. Her white robes were ripped and muddy. When she turned her head, he could see dirt and blood on one side of her face. Her goddess was testing her hard.

—*Totality. Sixtrdy has begun. Just over eleven minutes to impact.*

The world was dark. Much of the sky was clouded now, but in all the gaps the stars came out, millions of them. Behind the great dark Quoad pillar stood silhouetted against the disk of Javel came into view, lit by thunderstorms, crowned by aurora.

But he could still cognize Duty, and it looked as if she had almost given up the struggle. One hand clawed weakly at the rock, but she lacked the strength to move herself. For the first time in his adult life, Ratty Turnsole felt ashamed of his former profession. What right had he or anyone else to intrude like this on that old woman's suffering, her desperate struggle to die where she chose? She was doomed. She could never make her way safely down now. She had so far to go and only a few minutes left.

—*Ten minutes to impact.*

Joy had buried her face on his chest, sobbing. He suspected he was weeping, too, and yet he could not bring himself to reject the cognition. But his eyes were seeing other things. He could hear more than the wind and the massed sobbing of the crowd. There was singing. There were lights on Quoad.

"Look!" he shouted. "They've come. The souls of the Querent!"

Bedel and Oxindole together were saying what and where and what could he see. But the Monodies could see. Joy and Love and Wisdom all cried out in wonder as blue lights danced over Quoad. Ratty could see, and he thought he heard Umandral exclaim something in an alien tongue.

He was seeing double now, a real—seemingly real— view of the pillar and the ghostly Querent, and an internal cognition of the wounded or dying Duty. She had given up or passed out. The lights flickered and danced around her, and she was not responding. Ratty's head was filled with singing. St. Elmo's fire and his implants, or the souls of the Querent sent back by the Goddess to save her world? Who cared? It ought to be the start of a miracle, but Duty was not responding.

The Querents were all over the pillar now, many almost at the base. Singing. Calling. Urgent. If they were just an electrical discharge, as sanity told him, then Duty was in grave danger of being struck by lightning and fried like his parents.

Being fried might be a better way to die than being blasted by a meteorite. What was he doing just standing there like a ghoul, gloating over this tragedy and doing nothing? Duty was old and hurt. He was young and had muscles bred for much higher gravity. He had only minutes of life left to lose, and the lights were calling him. If the Querent visions meant anything at all, however improbable a miracle must seem to a lifelong skeptic, they were calling on him to *help*.

Joy cried out in dismay as he released her hand, vaulted over the fence—and was almost blown flat by a vicious gust. He regained his balance and bounded up the slope of rocks and moss that formed the base of the pillar. Then the Querent were all about him.

—Five minutes to impact.

He reached the steps and started scrambling up them on hands and feet.

He saw Love in his head, superimposed on all the other images there. "Well done! Oh, well done, Ratty! The Mother's blessing on you." And Joy, cheering and weeping at the same time.

Duty still prone, unable to do anything now but hold on. The hurricane wind was the problem. His Ayne muscles would be the solution, if there was one. Sharp fragments cut his hands but he paid no heed. He could see violet light streaming from him now, hear it buzzing, and he wondered how he looked to the planetary audience, because that was probably real St. Elmo's fire, visible even to sane people.

That was raw electricity. He was in grave danger of being frizzled like his parents. He stumbled at the thought and hastily put it out of his mind.

—Three minutes to impact.

Lungs busting in the awful air, he came to where Duty sprawled on the rocks, a fluttering bundle. She was conscious and knew him. The gale snatched away the words when she tried to speak.

He cogged her: *I'll carry you. Can you hang on?*

—Yes, yes! My ankle...

Wasting no time in trying to be gentle, he hauled her up to her knees and dragged her over his shoulder in a position most undignified for a high priestess. Now he must get to his feet and battle the wind head on.

—Two minutes to impact. That man assisting Monody is believed to be the Ayne commissioner and cog-doc celebrity, Ratty Turnsole, whose appointment as giver she announced yesterday at Umbral.

Duty was no lightweight, even on Pock's, and the two of them together doubled wind resistance. He rarely managed more than two or three steps before he had to drop to a crouch to avoid being blown clean off the stairs. The Querent whirled around him, their song a paean of triumph and joy. Back and forth the staircase wound across the higher side of the pillar; zigs were bad but zags worse.

—*One minute to impact.*

Then the wind hurled him flat, so he struck his face on a rock and cried out in pain. But the hurricane must mean that this was the top. There was nothing ahead but darkness. Duty was back in his head, a file image of her as the Mother incarnate, calm and regal with her two-tone hair in perfect order.

—*My thanks and blessings on you, Ratty Turnsole. Live and die happy. Now help me up, please.*

Even that was a struggle, but he staggered to his knees again and half-lifted, half-supported her as she raised herself to stand there momentarily, balancing on one foot, a tattered and be-draggled scarecrow raising her arms in supplication. At once the Goddess accepted her sacrifice. A wild gust lifted her from the rock and swept her away, far out over the crater. For a moment the cognition followed her down, dropping slowly in Pocosin gravity, turning over and over, then dwindling more swiftly, vanishing into the depths.

The wind caught Ratty too, and nearly tipped him over the brink. Head, shoulders, and half his chest went before his hands found purchase. The whole world was in his head together: Joy, Love, Wisdom, Bedel, Oxindole, Querents, the assembled multitude cheering and singing and weeping. No matter whether a miracle followed or not, the old woman had won her battle, had gone to her Goddess. Courage was the one virtue that all times and places applauded.

Was assisting suicide a crime on Pock's?

—*Eight.* Eight what? Seconds? The crowd fell silent. Even the wind seemed to fade away, its work completed.

—*Six.* Ratty squirmed back from the terrifying edge. The lights had gone. The Querent had returned whence they came.

—*Five.* The faces vanished from his mind, all except Joy's. They blew kisses to each other. They kissed. This might be fare-well. Or they might linger and die horribly later.

—*Four.* He had never known seconds to go so fast.

—*Three.* There would have to be a miracle, wouldn't there? After Duty's feat of faith and courage? Brother Andre and his like would be praying, also.

—*Two.* The impact wouldn't be the end. Quassia was too far from Ground Zero for the crowds to get a quick death. But the shock wave might topple Quoad and send its occupant hurtling down into the crater.

—*One.* There would be a fireball. Then a meteor storm, causing widespread fires. But then the secondary effects of—

—*Impact,* said the reporter.

—*Minus One,* he added uncertainly. Nothing. Absolutely nothing!

—*Minus two!*

Ratty stared at Joy, her eyes wild with hope.

—*Minus three!*

No fireball.

It worked!

Screams of triumph and gladness swept over Quassia. People cheered. They embraced. They danced. The world was saved. The Goddess had granted Monody another miracle.

Then the sky exploded brighter than the sun, lighting the world like noon. The clouds boiled away. A disk of fire blazed above the western horizon—white, gold, orange, then red fading to black. Night rushed back.

Even the wind seemed to have stopped breathing. Ratty wondered if he had been struck blind, but no—just dazzled. His vision was coming back. The starry sky, Joy's horrified face. Bedel... Love who was now Duty...

Joy said —*What happened? Are we dead or not?*

The sky lit up again as whole galaxies of stars began to fall.

Sixtrdy

Portolan had always been a wonderful tool for manipulating the media. Athena was ending her involvement in the Backet Mission in the way it had begun—with a party at Portolan. She was also planning to launch her election campaign. Every senior reporter on Ayne had turned up, more than fifty of them. They had been wined, dined, and recreated, and now they were slumped on comfortable chairs in a cabana on the beach, struggling to remain alert, critical, properly cynical, and reasonably objective.

Ratty's recordings of the Backet Mission had been pouring out of his office in a torrent. Almost every inhabitant of Ayne must have caught at least some of them by now. Now Athena was releasing some her own, especially Solan's courage in helping to rescue Braata from the flyer.

In the past twenty-four hours, Solan had become amphibious, because salt water compensated for gravity. At the moment he was a kilometer or so along the beach, riding a miniature donkey she had bought for him to use until his body adapted. A fall-off-able horse, he called it. Proser was keeping an eye on him. Proser was efficient at anything, and he and Solan had hit it off.

Braata's rescue complete, she waited for questions. Not many reporters were as sharp as Ratty Turnsole had been, but a few came close. Like Wiln Wassaider, for example, a fat man who had a big enough reputation to claim a front row seat.

"That was the boy you had with you yesterday, Senator."

"It was. Solan Skerryson. His mother passed away a few weeks ago, and his father, the man you just saw with the green cape, died the day before we left. Solan had no other family. Now, of course, he has no friends either and would be dead like all the rest, had I not brought him home with me. Proser and I plan to adopt him."

"Is he to be poster boy for your campaign then?"

The dumber ones woke up. Athena laughed.

"You are getting ahead of me, Wiln. In a sense, yes. But I hope he can be left out personally. You cannot interview him because he is too young to have implants, and he speaks only Pocosin. He must be almost the last person left in the galaxy who speaks Pocosin. But I may involve him in a peripheral way. If you want to turn to discussing politics, I am ready to declare my candidacy for the office of president."

No one objected.

"Very well. You all saw President Carabin's statement on the Pock's World geocide. He expressed deep sorrow." She paused. Not an eye was blinking. "Well, I express bloody fury! I am outraged, appalled! STARS has just pulled off another monstrous crime to add to the grisly toll with which it has soiled human history. Jibba, Malacostraca, and now Pock's—and these are only in or near our own sector. We know of a dozen others, all the way back to Earth Sector itself. I accuse Juleth Carabin of being STARS's lackey, of being in STARS's pocket. I seek election as his replacement. My platform is that Ayne and all other sector worlds must disband STARS, prosecute its leaders for murder on an astronomical scale, and take control of all space-faring activity."

They were still with her. She pressed on.

"STARS will fight back, of course. It will fund my opponents with billions from its secret hoards. I expect all the usual dirty tricks that the Carabin clique had used in the past, raised to the tenth power. STARS will buy support from cog-drama stars, religious leaders, business figures. It will threaten violence. I will fight back! I will appeal over their heads to ordinary voters and their sense of justice and moral right. STARS, Inc. must be stopped!"

Ratty's former helper, the one called Jake, raised a hand, and she let him speak.

"We haven't released all the records you brought back yet, senator." He paused until the angry murmurs died down. "They will be shared with all of you before we publish them," he said. "Right at the end, the alien made some drastic and frightening claims."

This was going to be the worst of her problems. The opposition would use Umandral's last speech to terrify the electorate with visions of men impregnated with baby cuckoos.

"You look like a healthy and strong young man, Jake," she said. "You could rape most women, couldn't you? If you wanted to?"

He smiled, seeing where her argument was going. "Probably."

"Have you ever raped a woman? Do you plan to?"

"I haven't and never will."

"Umandral is a boy, but he is incredibly strong. When he was in jail, one of the guards deliberately tortured him with a writhe, for his own amusement. You don't do that to people, either, do you, Jake? The guard was the Pock's World heavyweight martial arts champion and weighed three times what Umandral does, but Umandral killed him with his bare hands. That doesn't mean he does things like that without provocation, any more than you go around raping women! And do remember that he is only a boy and he was enjoying shocking us. Don't let the opposition frighten you with bogeymen."

Several voices spoke up and she chose to answer one that asked, "What opposition?"

"To start with, I believe I have identified the leader of STARS in this sector. I cannot prove his guilt yet, but I believe he can be unmasked." She paused again, for this would be the most dramatic moment in her speech. "One of the members of the Backet Mission has yet to return. The moment he sets foot on Ayne, he will be subpoenaed as a material witness in a civil suit I am bringing against STARS, Inc. on behalf of two-thirds of a billion people whose right to life it has violated. Because the law requires a personal involvement, however slight, I have signed the complaint on behalf of the boy Solan Skerryson, currently in my care. The witness I seek, of course, is industrialist and financier Linn Lazuline."

They all tried to speak at once. She chose Wiln.

"You are confident that Friend Lazuline will return?"

For the first time in her political career, Senator Fimble said, "Huh?" like an idiot.

He bunched his fat jowls in a smirk. "Word came in just an hour ago from Climatal 2 that the entanglement link between Pock's Station and Pyrus 1 was broken at the expected time of impact. You said that Lazuline remained behind to watch the disaster. You told us then that you considered his interest 'ghoulish.'"

"You saw..." She floundered. "The man named Glaum, who claimed to be STARS CEO on Pock's World—you saw him assure Lazuline that the station would be a safe vantage point from which to watch the impact."

"Perhaps it was. But already some experts are suggesting that the fireball from the impact broke the line-of-sight contact between the Pock's and Pyrus systems. Ionized gas will do that. Maybe STARS miscalculated?"

Athena certainly had. Had Proser not been distracted by Solan, he would have caught that news flash and alerted her so she would not have made such a fool of herself. Her presidential ambitions might have fallen flat on their face coming out of the gate. Without an entanglement link, Linn would never be coming home, and without witnesses to the destruction of Pock's, her lawsuit could not proceed. STARS would win again.

Without an entanglement link there would be no way of learning what had happened on Pock's World, not for centuries and probably never, for who would spend the trillions needed to send a probe to a murdered world?

Sevundy

Ratty Turnsole was just starting to appreciate the astonishing extent of Monody's realm of Abietin. Its hundred or so hectares contained lakes, rivers, geysers, and the sunny side of a volcano. Within it nestled innumerable buildings, from temples and palaces down to quaint little villages for the staff, almost all of which blended into a pleasing and uniform design. Monody had succeeded herself for ten thousand years, and, although she had paid tribute to changing fashions to some extent, her personal taste had always prevailed.

A few exceptions proved this rule, and one of them was the stupendous triumphal archway known as the Great West Gate. A gift from some devout but long-dead secular ruler, the Gate was a fantastic edifice of spires and pillars of gilt and mother-of-pearl in an ancient style known to its critics as *Baroquemost*. Even had the arch included a gate that could be shut, it would have served no practical purpose, because the boundary wall dividing town and palace was only a meter or so high. As Duty—the new Duty—herself admitted, it was a planetary landmark too hallowed to demolish and too earthquake resistant to do the decent thing and just fall down.

For formal conferences and audiences, attendees were required to enter Monody's realm by the Great West Gate. They would disembark from their cars in the large city plaza outside. Under the arch they would be formally greeted; inside the grounds they would be sent on their way in another air car to wherever the ceremony was to be held. That was tradition.

Protocol also required that senior dignitaries be welcomed to the palace by a Monody consort, an honor usually delegated to the most junior of those fortunate men.

That explained why Ratty Turnsole was wasting that fine Sevundy morning in a dull little cubicle at the base of the GWG. His chair was comfortable enough, he had an antique view screen to show him who was arriving, and his implants would advise him of names and proper forms of address. The new High Priestess had summoned the leaders of all the minor religions of Pock's World to meet the Children's ambassador, Ignitor. The result might be a stupendous dustup. On the other hand, the timing was promising. The previous Duty's achievement in saving the world from destruction had given the Church of the Mother so much standing that other faiths were certain to keep their heads down for quite a while. Some of them might even be driven out of business.

It was a steaming hot day at the end of bright week, with the sun close to the western hills. Javel loomed huge in the east.

Ratty would have been thoroughly bored had his companion in this nonsense not been Young Friend Umandral. Duty had sent him along as well, officially to identify Ambassador Ignitor and unofficially so that each arriving delegate could have a prior look at this weird artificial creature. Ratty had been eager for a private chat with the cuckoo ever since that peculiar miracle. He had questions to ask.

Finding a chance to ask them was the problem. The delegates came thick and fast, and most of them wanted to tarry and question the alien. The Vajray na Lama wanted to know whether he was a higher or lower incarnation than a human— Umandral's response had been predictable but fairly tactful. The President of the Church of Latest Saints wanted to discuss the cuckoo's rank in the hierarchy of angels. With the help of a gang of aides, Ratty did his best to chivvy the holy visitors along. About fifteen minutes before the ambassador herself was due, there came a gap.

How many more?

—*Only one, Consort. The representative of one of the Christian sects, Cardinal-Archbishop Phare.*

He might sulk and not come. Ratty hustled Umandral into the hosts' cubicle on the grounds of needing to wet a dry throat. He poured them each a glass of water, wondering whether his companion would need two, one for each throat.

He sank into the comfortable chair, quaffed half his own glass, and then went straight to the point.

"I have something to ask you about yesterday's miracle."

"Me?" The kid perched on a stool and tried to look innocent. "You should question your parthenogenetic bedmate about miracles, not me."

"There have been two voluntary martyrdoms in this affair. I speak as a lifelong cynic and skeptic. Duty let herself be blown off a rock. You, according to you, allowed yourself to be captured by security forces who would certainly treat you as a laboratory specimen, to be tested to destruction. Both of you demonstrated astonishing faith in something."

"This is true." Umandral looked amused. He sipped water, his thick neck showed no adolescent lump moving as he swallowed. "But don't tell your Joy, or Love, or whatever her name is now. She might try to enroll me in her cult."

"I doubt that. Let's go back to Malacostraca, then."

"Malacostraca?"

"Yes, Malacostraca. Its star is in the Canaster Sector, but it used to have contact with the Ayne Sector through Pock's. When it was infected by a brand of cuckoos called the Zombies, STARS sterilized the planet, or said it did. The stories differ, and STARS never explained. Pock's was accepted as belonging to the Ayne Sector after that. Don't play dumb. You're too smart to do it believably."

And hopefully young enough to be flattered.

"It isn't easy," Umandral agreed, nodding his oversized head. "Your standards of stupidity are low. The truth is that STARS tried to sterilize it. Malacostraca had four orbital stations, and STARS dropped them all, almost simultaneously. But Malacostraca is a much tougher world than Pock's. The impacts did tremendous damage, both to the inhabitants and to the environment. The planet hasn't recovered yet and won't for another thousand years, but there is still life there, and civilization. A comfy billion or so people."

"Humans or Zombies?"

The cuckoo smiled. "Children. Not exactly like me, because they are adapted to Malacostraca and I to Pock's. They're not like you at all."

So that was the fate in store for Pock's was it?

"That brings me back to—" Ratty said, "Oh damn! Here comes the opposition." He was looking at the screen. His implant hadn't reacted yet. He jumped up and strode out with the cuckoo at his heels. Aides and heralds came hurrying out a door opposite.

A barefoot old man in a long brown robe was striding into the archway. He had not been invited. Ratty waived back an aide and advanced to greet the friar himself.

"This is an unexpected pleasure, Brother Andre! We expected Cardinal Phare."

The old man looked weary and dusty in the heat. He bared long yellow fangs. "I am the papal legate in this matter. It is my duty to lead this conference out of error and enlighten the delegates so they will reject the seductive words of that devil spawn." He grimaced past Ratty's shoulder.

"Well, you are welcome in the cardinal's place. Isn't he, Deputy Ambassador?"

"I suppose so," Umandral said. "A couple of questions arise, though. Where were you while the rest of us were at Real Quassia, Brother? May I call you 'Brother'?"

"No. You are no brother of mine. I was assisting at Mass in St. Michael's Cathedral."

"At Quassia the people were praying for deliverance from the probe. What exactly were you praying for?"

Oh, very sneaky! Ratty wondered if the kid might even be as smart as he claimed.

Brother Andre could see the traps on all sides of that question. He hesitated.

"Did you beg your God to destroy the world to get rid of me?" Umandral asked. "If you did, He refused. Did you ask Him to save it? If so, your prayers were answered and you should ask for equal credit with the Church of the Mother. I doubt that your request will be granted."

"We prayed that God's will be done on Pock's World. He chose to grant us life so that we could do our duty, which is to hunt down and destroy you and all your like."

"So you still retain free will and the right to choose your destiny. On what basis—"

"That's enough!" Ratty said. "Leave discussion to the conference. My aide over there has a car ready for you, Brother."

"The rule of my order requires me to travel on foot."

Ratty was tempted, and Duty would probably bless him if he gave in. But he didn't. "It is at least ten kilometers to the meeting place. You will be late, perhaps even miss the whole event."

Andre pouted but agreed to accept a ride and strode off with an aide.

"That's the lot," Ratty said. *How long until the Ambassador arrives?*

—More than ten minutes and less than eleven.

"Come, Young Friend. Let us finish our discussion about miracles." Ratty ushered the cuckoo back into the cubicle.

He sank into his chair again. "A few hours before impact, radar showed the probe bang on target to impact Pock's, close to Hostie Caldera, wherever that is. But it missed. It was a few seconds late, I am told, and a few seconds at that velocity is a long way. As it came down, the Station intervened. It hit the Station instead, and the impact vaporized both of them."

Had Athena made it safely home? There would have been chaos up there at the end. He would never know. He could only hope that she had not been trapped in Pock's Station to be vaporized. Lynn Lazuline, now... No, the gods were never kind enough to vaporize scum like him.

"I don't understand why the debris didn't destroy the world anyway, but—"

"That's easy," Umandral said, back on his stool. "If it had hit the ground, it would have plowed right through the crust and blasted out a crater hundreds of kilometers in diameter. An enormous chunk of Pock's World would have been blown into the air and come down as a rain of hot rock, some of it hours or days later."

"Yes, but—"

"And remember that the probe was in a retrograde orbit around Javel. Pock's orbit is direct, and of course the station's orbit around Pock's was also direct. Probe and station were of roughly equal size and mass. They impacted in a head-on collision. There was some flash damage directly below the impact, as you know, but the mass of rock involved was tiny compared to what would have been disturbed by the expected impact. The expanding gas ball depressed the atmosphere, causing an immense shock wave, but even that was catastrophic only locally. The small part of the debris that fell in solid form was no coarser than dust, and the grains burned up as that meteor shower we saw." The kid loved to lecture.

"So my question is, how did the probe get delayed? A multi-million-ton boulder takes a lot of delaying."

Umandral shrugged his little shoulders and spread his big hands. "How should I know?" he asked mockingly.

"Then I will ask you this. I reviewed the records of the spectators when the flash came, when the meteor storm lit up the sky. Most people were aghast and terrified, thinking that this was the end of the world. A few, the well-informed, were jubilant, because they already guessed that the danger was over."

"And?"

"And you had tears in your eyes."

Umandral scowled, as if caught out in a weakness.

"I believe," Ratty said, "that there was a third martyr."

"I don't understand."

"Yes you do. Talk about water, then."

"Water?"

"Space probes need a large supply of water—for their cooling systems, their hydroponics, the needs of their crews." Ratty had watched a zillion cog-dramas involving space probes and researched probes for some of his own cog-docs. "I realize that your probe was only crewed for a short time. In all the centuries it traveled through interstellar space, it was uninhabited. But it would have needed a large crew before that, when it was being tunneled and equipped, and you admitted that there were at least forty-eight of you living in it near the end. So that rock was made to carry a lot of water.

"I cognized Braata's original report in the airship and was surprised when he said he found the climate control system turned off. Normally it would be left on—not to prevent the probe freezing solid, but to keep it from exploding as the heat from the hot leading surface spread through to the water reservoirs. And on Frivdy he confirmed that the probe, like others I know of, was built with many shafts accessing the surface. You wish to comment now?"

"No." The cuckoo was scowling.

It was like pulling teeth with eyebrow tweezers. "Who was the third martyr, Friend Umandral? Before you all loaded into the shuttles to descend to Pock's World, you held two lotteries, didn't you? You lost the second draw and accepted the job of hare, to alert the hounds that cuckoos had invaded. Who lost the first draw?"

Umandral sulked for a moment, then said, "You mean who *won* the first draw?"

"All right, who won the first draw?"

"Labba. She was my sister."

Now they were getting somewhere. "I'm truly sorry about your sister, and I understand that you must honor her heroism.

So you knew what happened to Malacostraca. You knew STARS would try to sterilize Pock's World. Your superiors set a trap for STARS, and STARS fell right in. You put the probe into a cleverly chosen orbit, an orbit where a very slight deflection would create an impact trajectory, but if STARS refused that bait, it would have to wait a long time for the orbits to line up again. One of you had to stay behind in the probe until that deflection had been made and the impact trajectory was established. Then she had to calculate exactly when to vent the volatiles, right?" Ratty wondered if Labba had used a clandestine computer or done the calculation in her head. It didn't matter.

—The Ambassador's car is approaching the gate, Consort.

Thank you.

"Labba opened the valves to flood the probe with hot water, and at the right moment, she blew open the final lock on whichever shaft or shafts happened to be pointing in the right direction. The pressure dropped to vacuum. The probe vented all that air and steam out into space, tons of it. And the impulse was just enough of a nudge to raise the probe a hair's-breadth in its orbit and save the world."

Umandral blinked a few times. "And Labba went out with it."

"I guessed she must have."

"You asked me whether we understood love."

"I said I was sorry."

"You're a sneaky devil, for a primitive!"

"Thank you," Ratty said, rising. "Time to go."

"You got one thing wrong, though. After Labba won the first draw, I was excused from joining in the second one. I insisted, and I won that one."

Ratty stared hard at him and decided he was probably telling the truth.

"Bully for you. Why?"

"I wanted to be worthy of her."

"I couldn't have done that."

"You? You nearly killed yourself helping that woman on the pillar."

"I had only a few minutes to live."

"You could have gone home to Ayne and chose not to. I make that four martyrs, Friend Turnsole."

Ratty laughed awkwardly. Wagering one's life to get laid was not in the same league as saving a world, as Duty had done, or even saving one's mission, like the two cuckoos. "I didn't think Linn Lazuline would let me go home."

"You didn't ask him."

As they went out the door, Ratty said, "So? You're saying we're both either heroes or damned fools, you and I. So what happens now? You demand citizenship, else you start carrying out all those threats you threw at the Ayne mission in Hederal? Ovipositors? Impregnating the natives with parasitoid cuckoos? You colonize us? In five hundred years Pock's will be like Malacostraca is now, inhabited by Children of the Future and the humans will be all gone?"

The alien shrugged. "That option is still available to us. It has worked on other worlds, but we'd rather not do it that way. You don't understand yet? Even you, Sneaky One? Of course your mate is effectively sterile, and you won't ever have offspring of your own. And Brother Andre is celibate."

"What has our saintly friar got to do with it?"

"Nothing. That's the point. But if you were going to be a true father, and your children could be genetically modified before birth to be twice as smart, how would you decide? To leave them burdened with genetic diseases and the innate human design faults—bad backs, hernias, myopia—or to have the sort of superior design the Children can offer?"

The aides were lining up in the archway. An ungainly looking woman was emerging from the air car out in the plaza.

"Bribery!" Ratty said. "Just as Brother Andre predicted."

"Yes," Umandral said, "he knows, but he doesn't understand. We bribe you into letting us live. And we abide by the treaty. But the Pocosins won't be able to resist our offers any more than the humans of Malacostraca did. They're all still there, or their descendants are. But they are Children of the Future now, like us. The humans have gone. Do you mourn *Homo erectus*, Friend Ratty?"

Ratty laughed. "No."

"Does Brother Andre?"

"Probably." Nobody would choose to have kids as ugly as this insectile freak. But few parents-to-be would resist a genetic nip here and a tuck there. In a couple of generations the "Children look" would be high fashion, and everyone would choose it for their offspring.

Ratty sighed. "Do these gifts of yours include the ability to remove a brain implant?"

Umandral glanced at him appraisingly. "I expect so. It would be easy in our brains, which are far more complex than yours but much better organized and more accessible for implants. Even for you, though, we could run a nanotube down in between the neurons and vacuum out unwanted matter one molecule at a time."

So even one of the Monody incarnations could be bribed, with her lover's life. Who could refuse?

"Sounds like fun. And what's in it for you, Child Umandral? You personally? You left your world and embarked on a dangerous interstellar adventure. You let yourself be caught and tortured and threatened with death. What's your motive?"

"Love," the alien said loftily. "To bring hope to all you poor defective humans. We're just like the saintly Brother Andre."

The ambassador was entering the archway, but Ratty continued to study the boy.

"No. I told you I'm a cynic. What you want to do is father a world. One way or another, your children will inherit Pock's. You may procreate them, or implant them, or just contribute germ plasm to fertility labs, but Umandral will be a founding father of nations."

The cuckoo chuckled. "And founding mother. That's more work."

"So you were offered a chance to go forth and multiply. Isn't that a rather primitive motive for a superhuman species?"

"No. It's the defining characteristic of life. We win, but you don't lose anything—except your delusions of superiority. You're wasting your time, trying to argue with me, Turnsole."

"I suppose I am," Ratty said. He turned to bow to Ambassador Ignitor.

Our titles are available at major book stores
and local independent resellers who support
Science Fiction and Fantasy readers like you.

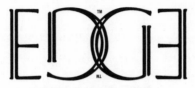

EDGE Science Fiction
and Fantasy Publishing

Tesseract Books

www.edgewebsite.com

Our titles are available at major book stores and local independent resellers who support Science Fiction and Fantasy readers like you.

Alphanauts by J. Brian Clarke (tp) - ISBN: 978-1-894063-14-2
Apparition Trail, The by Lisa Smedman (tp) - ISBN: 978-1-894063-22-7
As Fate Decrees by Denysé Bridger (tp) - ISBN: 978-1-894063-41-8
Avim's Oath (Part Six of the Okal Rel Saga) by Lynda Williams (pb)
- ISBN: 978-1-894063-35-7

Black Chalice, The by Marie Jakober (hb) - ISBN: 978-1-894063-00-7
Blue Apes by Phyllis Gotlieb (pb) - ISBN: 978-1-895836-13-4
Blue Apes by Phyllis Gotlieb (hb) - ISBN: 978-1-895836-14-1

Children of Atwar, The by Heather Spears (pb) - ISBN: 978-0-88878-335-6
Cinco de Mayo by Michael J. Martineck (pb) - ISBN: 978-1-894063-39-5
Cinkarion - The Heart of Fire (Part Two of The Chronicles of the Karionin)
by J. A. Cullum - (tp) - ISBN: 978-1-894063-21-0
Clan of the Dung-Sniffers by Lee Danielle Hubbard (pb) - ISBN: 978-1-894063-05-0
Claus Effect, The by David Nickle & Karl Schroeder (pb) - ISBN: 978-1-895836-34-9
Claus Effect, The by David Nickle & Karl Schroeder (hb) - ISBN: 978-1-895836-35-6
Courtesan Prince, The (Part One of the Okal Rel Saga) by Lynda Williams (tp)
- ISBN: 978-1-894063-28-9

Dark Earth Dreams by Candas Dorsey & Roger Deegan (comes with a CD)
- ISBN: 978-1-895836-05-9
Darkness of the God (Children of the Panther Part Two)
by Amber Hayward (tp) - ISBN: 978-1-894063-44-9
Distant Signals by Andrew Weiner (tp) - ISBN: 978-0-88878-284-7
Dreams of an Unseen Planet by Teresa Plowright (tp) - ISBN: 978-0-88878-282-3
Dreams of the Sea (Part 1 of Tyranaël) by Élisabeth Vonarburg (tp)
- ISBN: 978-1-895836-96-7
Dreams of the Sea (Part 1 of Tyranaël) by Élisabeth Vonarburg (hb)
- ISBN: 978-1-895836-98-1
Druids by Barbara Galler-Smith and Josh Langston (tp)
- ISBN: 978-1-894063-29-6

Eclipse by K. A. Bedford (tp) - ISBN: 978-1-894063-30-2
Even The Stones by Marie Jakober (tp) - ISBN: 978-1-894063-18-0
Evolve: Vampire Stories of the New Undead edited by Nancy Kilpatrick (tp)
- ISBN: 978-1-894063-33-3

Far Arena (Part Five of the Okal Rel Saga) by Lynda Williams (tp)
- ISBN: 978-1-894063-45-6
Fires of the Kindred by Robin Skelton (tp) - ISBN: 978-0-88878-271-7
Forbidden Cargo by Rebecca Rowe (tp) - ISBN: 978-1-894063-16-6

Game of Perfection, A (Part 2 of Tyranaël) by Élisabeth Vonarburg (tp)
- ISBN: 978-1-894063-32-6
Gaslight Grimoire: Fantastic Tales of Sherlock Holmes
   edited by Jeff Campbell & Charles Prepolec (pb)
- ISBN: 978-1-8964063-17-3
Gaslight Grotesque: Nightmare Tales of Sherlock Holmes
   edited by Jeff Campbell & Charles Prepolec (pb)
- ISBN: 978-1-8964063-31-9
Green Music by Ursula Pflug (tp) - ISBN: 978-1-895836-75-2
Green Music by Ursula Pflug (hb) - ISBN: 978-1-895836-77-6

Healer, The (Children of the Panther Part One) by Amber Hayward (tp)
- ISBN: 978-1-895836-89-9
Healer, The (Children of the Panther Part One) by Amber Hayward (hb)
- ISBN: 978-1-895836-91-2
Hell Can Wait by Theodore Judson (tp) - ISBN: 978-1-978-1-894063-23-4
Hounds of Ash and other tales of Fool Wolf, The by Greg Keyes (pb)
- ISBN: 978-1-894063-09-8
Hydrogen Steel by K. A. Bedford (tp) - ISBN: 978-1-894063-20-3

i-ROBOT Poetry by Jason Christie (tp) - ISBN: 978-1-894063-24-1
Immortal Quest by Alexandra MacKenzie (pb) - ISBN: 978-1-894063-46-3

Jackal Bird by Michael Barley (pb) - ISBN: 978-1-895836-07-3
Jackal Bird by Michael Barley (hb) - ISBN: 978-1-895836-11-0
JEMMA7729 by Phoebe Wray (tp) - ISBN: 978-1-894063-40-1

Keaen by Till Noever (tp) - ISBN: 978-1-894063-08-1
Keeper's Child by Leslie Davis (tp) - ISBN: 978-1-894063-01-2

Land/Space edited by Candas Jane Dorsey and Judy McCrosky (tp)
- ISBN: 978-1-895836-90-5
Land/Space edited by Candas Jane Dorsey and Judy McCrosky (hb)
- ISBN: 978-1-895836-92-9
Lyskarion: The Song of the Wind (Part One of The Chronicles of the Karionin)
   by J.A. Cullum (tp) - ISBN: 978-1-894063-02-9

Machine Sex and other stories by Candas Jane Dorsey (tp)
- ISBN: 978-0-88878-278-6
Maërlande Chronicles, The by Élisabeth Vonarburg (pb)
- ISBN: 978-0-88878-294-6
Moonfall by Heather Spears (pb) - ISBN: 978-0-88878-306-6

Of Wind and Sand by Sylvie Bérard (translated by Sheryl Curtis) (pb)
- ISBN: 978-1-894063-19-7
On Spec: The First Five Years edited by On Spec (pb)
- ISBN: 978-1-895836-08-0
On Spec: The First Five Years edited by On Spec (hb)
- ISBN: 978-1-895836-12-7
Orbital Burn by K. A. Bedford (tp) - ISBN: 978-1-894063-10-4
Orbital Burn by K. A. Bedford (hb) - ISBN: 978-1-894063-12-8

Pallahaxi Tide by Michael Coney (pb) - ISBN: 978-0-88878-293-9
Passion Play by Sean Stewart (pb) - ISBN: 978-0-88878-314-1
Petrified World (Determine Your Destiny #1) by Piotr Brynczka (pb)
   - ISBN: 978-1-894063-11-1
Plague Saint by Rita Donovan, The (tp) - ISBN: 978-1-895836-28-8
Plague Saint by Rita Donovan, The (hb) - ISBN: 978-1-895836-29-5
Pock's World by Dave Duncan (tp) - ISBN: 978-1-894063-47-0
Pretenders (Part Three of the Okal Rel Saga) by Lynda Williams (pb)
   - ISBN: 978-1-894063-13-5

Reluctant Voyagers by Élisabeth Vonarburg (pb) - ISBN: 978-1-895836-09-7
Reluctant Voyagers by Élisabeth Vonarburg (hb) - ISBN: 978-1-895836-15-8
Resisting Adonis by Timothy J. Anderson (tp) - ISBN: 978-1-895836-84-4
Resisting Adonis by Timothy J. Anderson (hb) - ISBN: 978-1-895836-83-7
Righteous Anger (Part Two of the Okal Rel Saga) by Lynda Williams (tp)
   - ISBN: 897-1-894063-38-8

Silent City, The by Élisabeth Vonarburg (tp) - ISBN: 978-1-894063-07-4
Slow Engines of Time, The by Élisabeth Vonarburg (tp)
   - ISBN: 978-1-895836-30-1
Slow Engines of Time, The by Élisabeth Vonarburg (hb)
   - ISBN: 978-1-895836-31-8
Stealing Magic by Tanya Huff (tp) - ISBN: 978-1-894063-34-0
Strange Attractors by Tom Henighan (pb) - ISBN: 978-0-88878-312-7

Taming, The by Heather Spears (pb) - ISBN: 978-1-895836-23-3
Taming, The by Heather Spears (hb) - ISBN: 978-1-895836-24-0
Ten Monkeys, Ten Minutes by Peter Watts (tp) - ISBN: 978-1-895836-74-5
Ten Monkeys, Ten Minutes by Peter Watts (hb) - ISBN: 978-1-895836-76-9
Tesseracts 1 edited by Judith Merril (pb) - ISBN: 978-0-88878-279-3
Tesseracts 2 edited by Phyllis Gotlieb & Douglas Barbour (pb)
   - ISBN: 978-0-88878-270-0
Tesseracts 3 edited by Candas Jane Dorsey & Gerry Truscott (pb)
   - ISBN: 978-0-88878-290-8
Tesseracts 4 edited by Lorna Toolis & Michael Skeet (pb)
   - ISBN: 978-0-88878-322-6
Tesseracts 5 edited by Robert Runté & Yves Maynard (pb)
   - ISBN: 978-1-895836-25-7
Tesseracts 5 edited by Robert Runté & Yves Maynard (hb)
   - ISBN: 978-1-895836-26-4
Tesseracts 6 edited by Robert J. Sawyer & Carolyn Clink (pb)
   - ISBN: 978-1-895836-32-5
Tesseracts 6 edited by Robert J. Sawyer & Carolyn Clink (hb)
   - ISBN: 978-1-895836-33-2
Tesseracts 7 edited by Paula Johanson & Jean-Louis Trudel (tp)
   - ISBN: 978-1-895836-58-5
Tesseracts 7 edited by Paula Johanson & Jean-Louis Trudel (hb)
   - ISBN: 978-1-895836-59-2
Tesseracts 8 edited by John Clute & Candas Jane Dorsey (tp)
   - ISBN: 978-1-895836-61-5
Tesseracts 8 edited by John Clute & Candas Jane Dorsey (hb)
   - ISBN: 978-1-895836-62-2

Tesseracts Nine edited by Nalo Hopkinson and Geoff Ryman (tp)
- ISBN: 978-1-894063-26-5

Tesseracts Ten: A Celebration of New Canadian Specuative Fiction
edited by Robert Charles Wilson and Edo van Belkom (tp)
- ISBN: 978-1-894063-36-4

Tesseracts Eleven: Amazing Canadian Speulative Fiction
edited by Cory Doctorow and Holly Phillips (tp)
- ISBN: 978-1-894063-03-6

Tesseracts Twelve: New Novellas of Canadian Fantastic Fiction
edited by Claude Lalumière (pb)
- ISBN: 978-1-894063-15-9

Tesseracts Thirteen: Chilling Tales from the Great White North
edited by Nancy Kilpatrick and David Morrell (tp)
- ISBN: 978-1-894063-25-8

Tesseracts 14: Strange Canadian Stories
edited by John Robert Colombo and Brett Alexander Savory (tp)
- ISBN: 978-1-894063-37-1

Tesseracts Q edited by Élisabeth Vonarburg & Jane Brierley (pb)
- ISBN: 978-1-895836-21-9

Tesseracts Q edited by Élisabeth Vonarburg & Jane Brierley (hb)
- ISBN: 978-1-895836-22-6

Throne Price by Lynda Williams and Alison Sinclair (tp)
- ISBN: 978-1-894063-06-7

Time Machines Repaired Whie-U-Wait by K. A. Bedford (tp)
- ISBN: 978-1-894063-42-5

Bonus Section

A *sneak peek* at
Michael J. Martineck's
next novel...

Cinco de Mayo

Michael J. Martineck

EDGE SCIENCE FICTION AND FANTASY PUBLISHING

AN IMPRINT OF HADES PUBLICATIONS, INC.

CALGARY

CHAPTER 1

ALISTAIR

Alistair Bache slammed his hands to his head, magazine flopping to his lap. Instant hangover? Stroke? Was he having a stroke? Valerie sprang up in bed, pressing the sides of her own head. Alistair thought he had woken her, but she squinted like the lights were too bright and that didn't make any sense. Nothing made any sense but pain.

And Lucy's crying. And Rebecca's crying.

The pain vanished. No residual—more of an afterglow. He was awake and feeling good, much to his surprise. Before the pain, he'd been too tired to turn a page.

Valerie was out of bed, running to the girls. He followed, confused. The girls never got sick at the same time. Simultaneous nightmares? The same moment as him? And the flash of a headache?

Lucy was four, Rebecca only two. They slept in the same pink room, in matching beds separated by a gulf of fluff and plastic. Valerie scooped up the smaller one and plopped next to the other before Alistair got there. They'd stopped crying. Both rubbed their heads and stared with glistening eyes at dark nothing.

"OK," Valerie whispered. "Everything's OK."

"My head hurt," Lucy said.

Valerie looked up at her husband.

"Head hurt," Rebecca echoed her sister, as she frequently did for no other reason than to play copycat. Alistair knew this was different.

"My head hurt," he said.

"Mine, too." Valerie hugged her girls tightly.

Alistair sniffed the air. He looked around. What could give everyone a headache at exactly the same time? What made a headache that left just as fast as it came? Gas leak? Carbon monoxide? Ludicrous. He'd never heard of anything like this. They didn't live in Bhopal.

On instinct, Alistair looked outside. They'd been in the house for five years, long enough to know all the squeaks and creaks and rhythms of their environment. It was an orderly neighborhood. That blonde lady walked her collie in the morning. That Sydney Greenstreet-like guy walked his daschund at night, defying blizzards, floods, locust, or anything. By 9:00 PM the suburb was dim, down to streetlights and landscape lights and the occasional blue TV haze from a bedroom window. Except tonight. Bulbs lit windows in every house.

"Looks like the whole neighborhood is up," Alistair said. The house lights gave him the creeps.

Protect. Defend. Circle the wagons. He wanted everyone under the covers, in the big bed, regardless of the fact that this made no rational sense.

"What's going on?" Valerie focused on him like she expected an answer. He always had one. He was adept at making them up when he didn't know the truth. Sometimes his answers were comical, sometimes insightful, on rare occasion correct. He knew what Valerie wanted. An outlandish lie was fine, as long as it soothed.

"Chemical cloud." Alistair put lots of certainty in his voice. "It must have drifted through the area. Came and went. Let's see if there's anything on the news. Come on everybody." He picked up Lucy; Valerie took Rebecca.

"*Muß ich zum Arzt gehen?*" Rebecca asked.

They stopped and stared at Rebecca's little rose mouth. Was that German? Alistair didn't know. He didn't speak German. None of them did, which of course, included two-year-old Rebecca.

CHAPTER 2

SUSAN

Susan Grove did not want anyone to know what she was doing. She sat, legs tucked under her, wrapped in a blanket, with two magazine-sized journals barely balanced on her lap. She was not ashamed of her ritual. Lots of people did it. She just chose not to tell anyone what she did every weeknight at 10:00 PM.

She pointed the Tivo remote and brought up that day's broadcast of Oprah. She hoped it was a good one. The journals were just in case it wasn't. She'd still watch it, but read at the same time.

Susan had no intellectual condescension for Oprah. She did not feel the show was beneath her in any way. Quite the contrary. While Susan knew, without overstatement, all that was currently known about the topography and neuroplasticity of the human prefrontal cortex, Oprah seemed to know about everything else. Oprah knew all Susan did not and was willing to share it.

The reason Susan never mentioned Oprah to any of her colleagues was stereotypical, in the sense that doing so would settle her into a stereotype. Susan did not want to be pigeonholed as another African American woman eating whatever Oprah ate, reading whatever Oprah read, and, most of all, following her spirit. She did not want to be 'one of them.' Susan had enough problems shedding unearned labels—she did not need another one.

She did need to know more about Oprah. Every show gave her a tiny glimpse into her success, not just in her nasty profession, but across her life. Susan was very good at grafting lots of little glimpses into a large, coherent picture. There really was no other way to see the human brain. Oprah's or anyone else's.

Extrapolating the big from the small was not always a gift. When it came to neurology, the skill proved useful enough to make her one of the most influential practitioners in the field. When it came to that guy from the pool that always gave her a hefty smile, it was a curse. Sometimes a smile—to paraphrase Sigmund Freud—was just a smile. It was not an overture to dinner, day trips, and a loving, respectful marriage that would warm her into old age. Oprah didn't make mountains out of cleft chins. Susan admired that trait and wanted to make it one of her own.

That had yet to happened. She never talked to the guy by the pool. She saw 70 reasons not to with every glance.

At 40, Susan had reached an age compelling her to attend a spinning class every other day, without question, and to eat more blueberries. The antioxidant data was not definitive, at least to her standards, but the downside was innocuous. She did not hate blueberries. She did not hate anything.

Except the pain in her head. Sudden, acute, severe, diffuse. No history of migraines. Intracranial bleeding was possible and terrible. She had to get to the phone. *What was a phone?* Oh my God, what was a phone? She was deteriorating rapidly. She told herself not to jump up. She begged herself not to scream. She could not help but cup her hands around her head. This was not how she was going to die. Not now, not tonight—alone on this couch watching Oprah.

The pain passed, like someone had wiped her mind clean. She felt...sparkly. She let herself sit up, dropping the journals to the floor. She was alive. She felt more alive than before the pain, as if her dopamine levels had abruptly doubled. That was an abrupt conclusion. There was 5-HT, and elevated norepinephrine levels could account for her lack of concentration. Guessing was not her nature.

She was not in her nature. She was in the bellybutton of the world.

CHAPTER 3

CINDY

Cindy hated Thursdays. She didn't care much for any of day of the week, but Thursdays were the worst. She didn't hate them like broccoli or subtitles—she hated each Thursday like an enemy. A serial killer or child snatcher or drug-dealing cop. She felt it first on Wednesdays as a shadow in the back of her head—a big, black cloud coming from the west. On Thursday mornings it was more of a twisting in the gut. As the day went on, the twisting got tighter and tighter. On Thursdays she nibbled lunch, skipped dinner, and by nightfall found herself unable to sit or stand. She had to walk around her three-room house, straightening, fluffing, folding.

She tried to look extra cute on Thursdays. Brad liked her jeans, with the black and white striped top that made her plum-sized boobs look more like peaches. She was not a natural blonde, but he'd never learn that. She had plenty of time to color each hair individually. She thickened each individual eyelash and carefully covered any spot redder than the rest of her face.

Cindy had learned not to overdo the make-up or the cleaning. It had to be just right. Invisible. What she really worked at was making everything look like it was no work at all. The unnoticed was safe. That's why fawns have spots in the spring or rabbits grow white for winter. The unseen goes free.

Brad slapped Cindy for the first time around their three-month anniversary. Cindy had turned 24 the night before. She'd had way too many Coors Lights and spent the day on the couch, drinking Squirt. Brad got home, kicked a pile of mail, grabbed her fucking disgusting sweatshirt and slapped her across the face. The honeymoon was officially over.

She had been too stunned to cry. He plowed into the bedroom and she didn't see him awake until the next night. Then he took her out to dinner, apologized, and she wrote it off. Everyone slips once in a while, right? The following Thursday she made damn sure there was no pile of mail on the floor by the door.

A month later he slapped her because the house was so fucking neat. He couldn't get comfortable. He was afraid to sit down in his own goddamn house. What did she do all day? If she had enough time to pick up every speck of dust in the living room, she didn't have enough to do.

Cindy had been a waitress when they met. Brad made her quit when they started dating. She didn't need to shake her ass for tips, he'd provide. After getting hit for cleaning too well, she thought maybe she did have a lot of time on her hands. Maybe she could pick up a shift. That earned her two more slaps. One for wanting to show off her stuff for a bunch of drunks, the other for insulting his ability to provide for his woman.

By month five she thought about leaving. The married Brad was so different from the dating Brad. As different as a bunny and a snake. She couldn't stand him touching her. A soft pet reminded her of the sting. If he came near her, she tensed up like she was going to snap. She never told him her thoughts, but he must have sensed something. He sweetened, smiling like the old Brad. Dark, strong, and shy. She remembered the things she liked in him: the jokes, the attention, the devotion.

He hit her again. Why was she all dolled up? Who was she trying to snag? Some guy in the neighborhood? That lineman who worked nights? While he worked his ass off, she whored around?

She knew when a hit was coming, as it started with his breath. Beer breath so thick you could practically see it, a golden spray of nastiness.

It was back to mom's after that. Mom was not too pleased. Her boyfriend was over and three was not what she, at least, had in mind. At breakfast, Cindy got the lecture about making things work, keeping your man happy, and how her mother didn't raise no quitters.

Cindy got hit for going to sleep before Brad got home. She went to her friend Lorna's for three days. Cindy got hit for burning Salisbury steaks. Back to Lorna's.

Brad said he'd change after that. Adjusting to married life, a new job, having things different in his house, that had been tough. He was tough, though. He'd fix things.

His house, Cindy kept repeating in her head. Every morning, she'd do something around his house. Not *their* house. Like she was a guest who wouldn't go home. This marriage wasn't going to work out. Brad could be wonderful, but only in sprints. He couldn't run the long race.

Cindy had $120 hidden in an envelope in a shoebox in her closet. That would get her to about the end of the street. Mom's was out; there was no Dad's. She had friends, half of whom were Brad's. Some of those guys wouldn't open the door if she was pounding, some of them would only if their wives weren't home. She had Lorna. She'd been leaning pretty hard on her lately. Brad knew all about that hideaway. Brad would beat on Lorna even more easily than he beat on her.

Brad sold her Ford Escort. She couldn't believe it. Sold it out from under her. How could he do that? Didn't she need to sign something? He said she didn't need a car and they needed the money. He never said how much he got for it. She started to cry and he raised his hand.

When Cindy was little there was this game called Payday. It was an old, worn board game at her grandparent's house. She and her cousins played it before the boring Sunday dinners. Landing on the 'payday' spot was the best. That was the day you got your money. You got closer to winning. Now, Brad had twisted that feature of life like he twisted her stomach. Paydays, when Brad went out right after work and got shit-faced and angry at nothing and came home swinging. Thursdays.

Cindy hated payday.

Limited Edition Available

If you collect limited editions of books, you need to check out the special "COFFIN" edition of *EVOLVE: Vampire Stories of the New Undead*.

Protected in a magnetically sealed miniature pine coffin; packaged in an open ended black bag; identified by a unique wax seal; and certified as an original; is a hardcover copy of *EVOLVE: Vampire Stories of the New Undead*.

Each of these "COFFIN" editions is identified by unique number: on the lid, the box and the book. Each book is signed by all of the authors, the cover artist, the editor and the publisher.

Only 50 copies of this limited edition are available. You must order your copy directly from the publisher. Limited to one copy per customer. We expect the COFFIN edition to sell out quickly. Act fast to avoid disappointment.

Limited "COFFIN" edition — $230.00 US plus shipping and taxes.

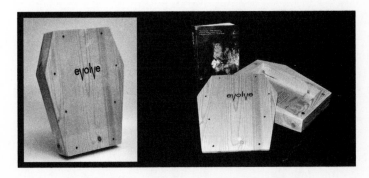

"If you're into vampires at all, this is a collection of stories you'll love." — Lisa C.